I .... She is the author ot ten novels, including *The Vintner's Luck* (longlisted for the Orange Prize 1999) and *The Dreamhunter Duet*, which Stephanie Meyer called 'like nothing else I've ever read.' Elizabeth was made an Arts Foundation Laureate in 2000 and an Officer of the New Zealand Order of Merit in 2002. She lives in Wellington with her husband, son, and three cats. Visit the author at www.elizabethknox.com

WAKE

ELIZABETH KNOX

corsair

First published by Victoria University Press, Victoria University of Wellington,
PO Box 600, Wellington

First published in Great Britain in 2015 by Corsair, an imprint of Little, Brown Book Group

1 3 5 7 9 10 8 6 4 2

ISBN: 978-1-47211-753-3 (trade paperback)
ISBN: 978-1-47211-792-2 (ebook)

Typeset in Bembo by TW Typesetting, Plymouth, Devon
Printed and bound in Great Britain by CPI Group (UK) Ltd, Croydon, CR0 4YY

Papers used by Little, Brown are from well-managed forests
and other responsible sources.

Corsair
An imprint of
Little, Brown Book Group
100 Victoria Embankment
London EC4Y 0DY

An Hachette UK Company
www.hachette.co.uk

www.littlebrown.co.uk

PART ONE

Later, when people talked about the fourteen, they called them survivors. It wasn't strictly true. All but one arrived after the deadly moment. They came alone or in pairs, some with their heads up and their eyes on the smoke.

Constable Theresa Grey had spent the morning helping break some bad news to a woman in Motueka about her teenaged daughter. It had been Theresa's job to hold the woman's hand, which she did, leaning forward, knee to knee, for over an hour. Then the woman's brother arrived, and the detectives thanked Theresa for her support, and sent her off.

As she drove, her grip on the steering wheel gradually erased the ghostly sensation of that stricken woman's hands. She began to feel better, to come alive to the drive and the sunny weather.

Then she got a call from the dispatcher at Nelson Central police station. 'We've a mayday from a helicopter flying out of Kahukura Spa,' said the dispatcher. 'Four on board. I'll give the spa a call and get back to you.'

Theresa pulled out, and accelerated. She passed a milk tanker and a Holden Captiva and glided back into her lane. She hit her siren and—because she was looking for it—spotted the smudge of smoke while still on the straight before the cutting that crossed the bluff west of Kahukura Bay. Theresa reached the cutting, and the smudge vanished behind the frothy white screen of apple blossom along the ridge of Cotley's orchard.

She picked up her radio again and tried to raise the community constable in Kahukura. Then she tried the dispatcher. No one responded.

Theresa was a young police officer, but she had initiative. She figured that if a helicopter got into trouble shortly after leaving the spa, it might try to put down in the clearing around Stanislaw's Reserve—300 hectares of old-growth forest enclosed in a state-of-the-art predator-proof fence. Sixteen of the world's 140 remaining kakapo nested in Stanislaw's Reserve—the rest were on an offshore island in the far south. Theresa's friend, Belle Greenbrook, was a ranger at the reserve, and rangers carried radios.

Theresa got lucky; Belle answered right away. 'Belle? We've a helicopter down. I'm at the turn to Cotley's Road and I can see smoke. I'm pretty sure it's coming from the field above the spa. Over.'

Belle said that she was by the east gate, with her chainsaw, clearing a fallen branch from the fence. She reckoned that, if she cut up over the ridge and ran to the main gate where she'd left her quad bike, she could be at the wreck in twenty minutes.

Theresa dropped the radio and put both hands on the wheel to take the long horseshoe bend. She was aiming for the bypass, which would take her straight to Kahukura Spa. The spa's driveway would offer the quickest route to the crashed helicopter.

But when she reached the bypass, Theresa saw fire in the far perspective of Kahukura's main road. She ignored the turnoff and floored the gas. Houses, hedges, churches all poured past her windows while she peered into the seething knot of oily, orange flame.

A woman ran out into the street in front of the car. Theresa braked, and her seatbelt clutched her so forcefully that she was grateful for the padding of her stab-proof vest.

The woman didn't swerve, or cringe, as the car bore

down on her, slid to a halt, and was overtaken by a drift of smoke from its own tyres. She didn't seem to see the car. She wasn't screaming, or crying, only fleeing. She was naked from the waist up, and her arms were marked by red notches.

Theresa jumped out and raced after the woman. She caught hold of her. The woman's skin was cold with shock, and slippery with blood. The V-shaped wounds on her shoulders and upper arms were as much bruised as bloody, and identical, as if inflicted by the same weapon. It looked like they'd been made with one of those can piercers from a standard bottle opener.

Theresa looked about for an assailant, but the only people in view were a couple in the driveway of a house back down the road. They were locked in a passionate kiss, holding each other's heads. It wasn't an open-air, mid-morning kiss, and Theresa felt faintly embarrassed. In a moment she'd have to go interrupt them to ask if they'd seen anything. But first she must look after the injured woman.

The woman let Theresa lead her back to the patrol car. Theresa popped her trunk, grabbed a bagged rescue blanket, and used her teeth to tear the bag open. 'It's okay,' she said, 'I've got you. You'll be fine.'

A dog ran from a property down the road, stopped beside the lip-locked couple, and barked at them. Then it flattened its ears and backed away, trembling.

Theresa wrapped the woman, and ducked her head to meet her eyes. 'You're safe now.'

There was a sharp concussion of an explosion in the fire up the road. Theresa flinched, but the woman didn't react at all. She just stared at Theresa, apparently intent. Only she wasn't meeting Theresa's eyes. Her gaze seemed to focus on the air millimetres from Theresa's skin, as if caught on the tip of each hair—the hair lifting all over Theresa's body.

Theresa became aware then of sounds below the roar of

the fire, and the skirling alarms of trapped and wounded cars. Unaccountable, frightening noises were coming from behind her, on both sides of the street. She heard a hissing, as if someone were busy spraying weeds, followed by a deep flutter, like a wind-baffled bonfire. There were thumps, smashes, a squealing noise, and the sound of someone gasping for breath. But there were no screams, no cries for help.

Theresa glanced again at the couple. Their heads were still pressed together, grinding and working. Theresa saw that their cheeks and necks were smeared and dark.

In the house nearest Theresa a scuffle broke out. Two men tumbled from an open screen door and commenced belting each other, neither of them making any attempt to block the other's blows.

Theresa told the injured woman to stay where she was. Then she went to the secure box in her car, punched in the code, and removed her pistol. She clipped its holster to her belt. Never before in her professional life had Theresa had to get out her gun.

She hurried into the yard, and tried to grapple the brawling men apart, using her hands and her baton. It wasn't clear which of the two was the aggressor, but one was taking a real beating, and was bleeding from both ears. He continued to fight, fearlessly and insensitively.

Theresa yelled at them to stop. She tried to haul the stronger man away. His arms were as hard as wood, his body solid, hot, clenched all over and slick with blood—far too much to have come from just his own injuries. Theresa's hands slithered off him. She lost her balance, and came down hard on one knee.

Once she was down, both men turned on her. Without exchanging a look, they simultaneously ceased hitting each other and began pummelling Theresa instead.

She scrambled away, dropped her baton, and drew her gun. She pointed it, swinging the barrel back and forth between them. 'That's enough! Don't come any closer!'

But they didn't even glance at the gun. They looked through her, as if she were an obstacle they meant to trample over to get at something promising that lay beyond her, something more worthy of their pitched savagery.

Theresa risked a backward glance. The injured woman was standing right behind her. She had followed Theresa, trailing the rescue blanket like a queenly mantle.

Theresa gasped. 'Jesus!' She scrambled to her feet and lunged at the woman, meaning to haul her off, throw her in the patrol car, and flee. That's what Theresa was thinking: she had to pull back somewhere safe and call for help. *Lots* of help.

But she only managed a few steps before one of the men barged her. Theresa sprawled on the grass, and the men began to kick her. She pushed the injured woman away from her, and flipped over onto her back. Her boots connected with someone's legs, and the kicking stopped. Theresa raised her head and held the gun out before her again. From the corner of her eye she saw the empty rescue blanket floating away over the lawn, bundling up the sunlight. The weaker of the two men was in flight, pushing his way through a hedge. But the other had got hold of the injured woman. And they were both giggling—sly, silly giggles. Then the man began to shake the injured woman, violently.

Theresa clambered up. She shouted, 'Stop that or I *will* shoot you!' She issued her warning. She followed her training. But no one had ever told her about the blank bit of human hesitation, of unwillingness, that appeared before her then. A gap between procedure familiar to her, and procedure she hadn't yet had to follow. She had to act to save the woman. But the idea of hurting the man filled her with a terrible queasiness. It was as if she were about to shoot *herself.*

Theresa stepped towards the man. Again she shouted her warning.

The shaking continued, and the injured woman's sweat-soaked hair bounced around her smirking face. Theresa tried one-handed to snatch her free, but the man kept moving like a machine, his limbs greasy and as inexorable as pistons.

In the pause where Theresa ran out of bearable options, she glanced once more at the other man, who was crawling away across the neighbours' lawn. He was on his hands and knees. But he wasn't walking on his palms. Instead his wrists were bent inward, and he was moving forward pressing the backs of his hands to the grass.

Theresa stopped shouting. Her breath left her in a grunt. Her arms sagged. Her body was in shock, but a small voice in her mind made itself heard. It said, '*Who does that?*' Behind her shock a deeply rational and analytical part of her was trying to make her attend to something more important than simply what she should do next. It was telling her that she was in lethal danger, and that her own death wouldn't be the worst of it. And of course she sought confirmation for her feeling. She glanced at the kissing couple.

They weren't kissing. Their lips and noses were in red strings and tatters, and still they kept pushing mouth to mouth, their bared teeth biting.

Theresa's arms came up. She stepped forward, jabbed her gun against the man's shoulder, and pulled the trigger.

He staggered back, but he didn't release the injured woman. Instead he used his good arm to grapple her closer, opened his mouth and sank his teeth into her scalp, like someone taking a big bite of an apple.

Theresa leapt at him. She pressed the muzzle of her pistol to his temple, and pulled the trigger.

He was at her feet, his head served on a bed of his own brains. The woman rolled free.

Theresa holstered her gun. She thought, 'He didn't look at me. He didn't even see me coming.' She picked up the woman, who immediately began to struggle.

'It's all right,' Theresa said. She half-carried the woman to her car, and laid her on the back seat. She leaned on the woman while fumbling at the buttons of the radio. But there was only empty static as she cycled through the frequencies looking for people she knew must be there—Kahukura's community constable, the dispatcher in Nelson, other emergency services.

The only open channel was to Belle. 'Tre? What's happening?' Belle said, then, 'There are fires on Haven Road. Over.' She sounded desperate.

'Where is everyone?' Theresa said.

The woman stopped thrashing and began to claw at her own face. Theresa had to drop the radio to catch her hands.

For the next minute Theresa fought to keep the woman still. She spoke to her softly. The woman was making vacant, inarticulate sounds. Blood glistened in the join of her lips. She was gnawing her own tongue.

Theresa cast about for something to slip between her teeth. A sunglasses case might do. She popped the glove box, found the case, and, holding the woman tightly with one arm, she tried to slip the soft plastic between her chomping jaws.

In a nearby house a window shattered. An old man slumped through it, skewering his throat on the shards left in the frame. He moved only feebly while his blood unfolded like a concertinaed red banner down the weatherboard wall.

Theresa reached for her radio again. She held it to her lips and depressed the talk button, but she couldn't speak. It was as if she were taking a sip of static—putting a pump bottle to her lips and tasting only air. She had ducked down below the level of her car windows. The only people she could see were those near her—the man she'd shot, and that one across the way, still gasping on his hook of glass, and the couple, head to head, slow-dancing on their patch of blood-soaked grass. No one else. Nothing new was happening in

Theresa's ambit, but she was still desperate for things to stop, to pause. She wanted to find *herself* and figure out what she should do—what she could do.

Theresa dropped her radio and concentrated on the woman. She held the sunglasses case in place, pressing down her tongue. She kept up her quiet reassurances, staring into the woman's eyes. Those eyes were mad and spiteful; the woman's nostrils vibrated with fury. Then, all at once, her eyes flicked sideways, and froze. She stopped struggling. Her face went stark, her body stiff.

Theresa pulled her straight, and began CPR. The woman's mouth was clamped shut, so Theresa breathed into her nose. But the woman seemed to be holding her breath. Her lungs were full, her chest taut. Theresa shouted, 'Please!'

The woman's chest suddenly collapsed, and she went limp.

Theresa pumped at her sternum. She breathed into her bloody mouth. But nothing worked. The woman was gone. Theresa gathered her, held her tight, and looked over her bowed head, out the car windows, and through its open door. Looking didn't help. She wasn't able to check for danger. Everything was melting. For long minutes everything was melting.

Theresa was startled back into the moment by an explosion. She flung herself off the body and out of her car. She took off, striding away along the centre line, leaving her car with its doors open and lights flashing. She scanned the road for danger as she went. She felt like a nervy animal, rather than an upholder of public order.

There was a garage on fire in one property, and through the open front door of the house Theresa saw a heavy shadow swinging in the hallway. She paused, paralysed not by fear, but by the conflict between that and her sense of duty.

As Theresa hesitated, a cavalcade of runners emerged from a cross street ahead of her. The younger, fitter ones at the front, others trailing. But however spread out the runners were, they were going the same approximate pace, flat out, the group as cohesive as a school of fish. Some were barefoot. One was in pyjamas and a dressing gown. Two bringing up the rear were dragging objects that bumped and bounced along in their wake. One man had a small dog on a lead—no longer alive. The other had a child. He was hauling the child along by his ankle. The boy's other leg was doubled back under him, his hip dislocated.

Theresa surged forward, gun pointed. She yelled a challenge—a wordless, simian roar.

But then a letterbox lunged at her. She sidestepped, and the box fell as far as it was able to, still attached to its pole, and followed by the body of the man who'd head-butted it out of its concrete footing, the man who had rammed his head into it as far as it could go. The man fell to his knees, hunched over the fallen box as if it were downed prey. He braced his shoulders and continued to push. The sides of the letterbox creaked and bulged, the man's ears doubled over, and—that resistance overcome—his whole head plunged into the distorted box, passage lubricated by blood.

Theresa saw that the man was wearing a postie's bright red and yellow uniform, and mail harness, though he'd lost his mail sacks.

He was a postie. A postie posting himself head first into a letterbox.

Theresa's face went numb. Her ears stopped working. And the two men who'd peeled off the rampaging group were nearly on her by the time she noticed them.

She raised her gun, but wasn't able to bring it level before the first man reached her. She didn't remember pulling the trigger, but the gun went off. She didn't hear the shot, only felt its kick. The bullet went into the attacker's leg and smashed his thigh bone. She didn't hear that either, but glimpsed powder burns, parted flesh, wet bone.

The man's momentum carried him along the road, head over heels. Both he and the recoil knocked Theresa off-balance, and, because of that, the second attacker overshot his mark. He swiped at her in passing, then slowed and doubled back. The maimed man was struggling up, dragging his smashed leg.

Theresa regained her balance and bolted. She'd spotted an avenue of escape, a high boundary fence—one of those double-thickness ones with a flat top. She saw how close to the eaves of its house it came. Theresa scaled the fence, planted her heavy soled boots on its top, and sprinted along it. She made the leap from the fence to the roof, and her free hand caught hold of the ventilation pipe of a toilet cistern. She grappled with her other hand, the gun scoring the coating on the steel roof tiles. Showers of volcanic grit fell past her as she swung a knee up onto the roof. The PVC guttering shattered.

Theresa clambered up to the spine of the roof, straddled it, and pointed her gun back the way she'd come.

Her pursuers had lost interest. They didn't even linger looking up at her, like dogs that have treed a cat. They just departed, one at the same breakneck pace, though not in pursuit of his group. The other dragged himself across the road to join the postie, who had finally torn the letterbox from its stand and, blinded by it, had blundered into a front garden rockery. The maimed man took the postie's hand. He did it gently, and for a moment Theresa thought he might lead the postie out of the shrubs, and onto more even ground. But instead the man brought the postie's hand to his mouth, as if about to kiss it gallantly. He pressed the postie's fingers to his lips, then commenced to savage them.

Theresa's spread her knees and dropped her head, shaken by a bout of retching. Everything went black. She was going to tumble off the roof. She clapped her free hand onto the ridge, and her fingernails prised more grit from the tiles. She put her gun down and planted her foot on top of it. Then she held on for dear life, fighting her own plummeting blood pressure. She tried to slow her breathing. 'I'm hyperventilating,' she thought. Then she made herself say it out loud. She might not be a police officer armoured with procedure anymore, but she was still a human being, with language.

There were no cries for help. That was the thing. Theresa had seen injuries, aggression, atrocities, self-mutilation, but had heard nothing from any of the victims or perpetrators. Nothing articulate or expressive. No matter how hard she strained her ears, Theresa couldn't hear anything human.

After a while she gingerly lifted her head. From her vantage point she could see over the rooftops of the houses on Beach Road. She couldn't see the beach, but further out was a trawler, coming into the bay, trailing a wedding veil of hungry gulls. It was such an everyday sight. Theresa stared at it for a time, resting her mind. Then she scanned the settlement: the billows of smoke, seemingly solidifying in the windless air; her patrol car in the fringe of the haze, lights flashing red, white, and blue. She peered hard at every corpse, checking for signs of life—not because she hoped to help anyone, but only to see whether they still presented any danger.

The postie was on his knees now, so tranquil that he seemed to be at prayer, his hands an offering to the maimed man and his voracity. The dragged child had been abandoned at the end of a trail of gore. And the running people had run on.

A block ahead, just before the road rose and forked for the bypass, Theresa caught sight of a man walking down the centreline. He was carrying a woman in his arms. There was something about the way he was moving, something less absorbed than the people Theresa had seen so far. He had a contradictory look of effort and aimlessness that seemed somehow normal. The others had been energetic and zealous—they'd moved as if they had places to be and urgent things to do.

Theresa stayed still and watched the man come. Once he was close she saw that he was a rangy fellow with thick silver hair and reddened, bright blue eyes. The woman in his arms was bonelessly limp.

Theresa called out to him. 'Hey!'

He spotted her, then glanced at the patrol car. He had been looking for her. He'd come to find the emergency services.

Theresa called out, 'Don't move. I'll be right down.'

He crouched and laid the woman on the ground.

Theresa slithered down the gritty roof, hung off its edge for a moment and dropped onto the lawn. She strode towards the man and he got up quickly, holding out his hands in a gesture of fearful supplication.

She went briskly past him and waded in among the rocks and flowering shrubs. She went right up to the man feasting on the postie's fingers, and shot him in the head. Only after she'd shot him did she say to him, '*Stop that.*' Then, ignoring his victim, she went back to the couple on the road.

Theresa hunkered down and put her fingers on the woman's neck. The woman's skin was cool already. She turned to the man. 'What's your name, Sir? Mine is Theresa—Constable Grey.'

'Curtis Haines. This is my wife, Adele.'

'Are you injured, Mr Haines?'

The man shook his head. He sat down on the road, and pulled his wife towards him so that her head lay in his lap. 'A woman back there in the antiques shop—she's dead too.' He stopped speaking and his throat worked.

Theresa knew she should ask for details. She was scared of the bleak, faraway look on his face—but she'd have to write all this up eventually.

This brief moment of forward planning came to an abrupt end, punctuated by a clang, as the postie collapsed, and his metal-encased head impacted with a rock.

'Mr Haines, I'm sorry,' Theresa said, 'but right now I'm reluctant to hear what you have to say.'

He nodded. He understood.

She unhooked her radio from her vest and put it down on the road to fiddle with its dials.

Curtis Haines said, 'You have a black eye and a cut on your cheek. You need first-aid.'

'Maybe later,' Theresa said, as though he'd offered to buy her a drink.

'That would be easier if you'd use both hands.'

Theresa's hand had been clenched for so long that blood had set like mortar between each finger. She laid the pistol down, giving it a little shake to loosen it. With two hands free she was better able to manage her radio. She reached Belle.

'Oh, thank God,' said Belle. 'No one survived the helicopter crash. Where are you?' There was a forgetful hesitation, then, 'Over?'

'Belle, I want you go back into the reserve and lock the gate. Keep out of sight. I'll be up to get you as soon as I can. Over.'

'Tre,' said Belle, 'what's going on?'

'I don't know.'

'So—you haven't got things under control?'

Theresa looked at Curtis Haines. He just stared back, his hands wandering over his wife's silky grey bob.

Theresa tried to pull herself together. In her best, steely, police officer voice, she said, 'Just do what I say, Belle. Over and out.'

A truck horn sounded somewhere to the west.

'I should probably check that out,' Theresa said to Curtis. Then she routinely attempted once more to raise anyone else. There was nobody. She clipped her radio back onto her vest, got up, and stooped to gather Adele Haines's legs in her arms. Curtis took Adele's shoulders and together they lifted her.

'Shall we use your car?' Curtis said.

Theresa didn't want to retrace her steps. For a moment she was lost in blank indecision. She only came back when Curtis spoke. He told her that his car was the Volvo up the road, opposite the hairdresser. 'If that's better,' he said, and she heard the kindness and concern in his tone.

They set out, and he led the way.

Curtis Haines and his wife Adele hadn't planned to stop in Kahukura, but when they got to the turn for the bypass Curtis spotted an antiques and collectibles shop. Adele was looking at the hairdresser on the other side of the road—*Curl up and Dye*. She laughed and pointed. Curtis smiled, then waited for his wife to notice that he was pulling over, and why. He waited for her face to light up. He loved watching her face light up.

Adele saw the shop. 'Thank you, darling.' She flipped her sun visor down, refreshed her lipstick, and got out of the car.

Curtis changed the CD. He reclined his seat and closed his eyes. He drifted off for a few minutes. It couldn't have been long, because the CD was only on track two: 'How High the Moon'.

What woke Curtis was a police car. It blasted past, sirens going. It went about half a kilometre down the road, then screeched to a stop. Its brake lights flashed and flickered. Its siren gave a few further whoops, as though in protest, then cut out.

There was something threatening in the silence beyond the car's sealed windows. Curtis turned off the stereo and let his window down. After a minute he heard, from somewhere up ahead, a woman shouting, her voice hysterical. Surely not the police officer. Whoever it was sounded as if they were trying to shout the world back into its proper order.

Curtis looked over at the antiques shop and saw that a strange woman had hold of his wife. The woman was younger than Adele, but nevertheless wore spectacles on a chain, as some elderly women do. The spectacles were balanced in the woman's spray-sculpted hair, their chain flapping against her cheeks as she was wrenched back and forth by Adele, who was struggling to free herself. Adele clawed at the woman's arms, while the woman held Adele's jaw open and dropped things into her mouth.

Curtis didn't know how he got out of the car. Later he remembered the dimpled brass of the shop's door handle in his grip and the cheery sound of the bell above the door. As it was, he simply found himself at his wife's side.

It was coins that the woman was posting between Adele's lips—lumpy coins, not perfectly round. Old coins, of blackened silver and greened copper.

Curtis grabbed the woman and shoved her away. He heard the money fall and roll about on the wooden floor.

Adele didn't make a sound.

The woman staggered back, then regained her balance and looked about. Her eyes were so wide that Curtis could see the strained pink fibres connecting her eyeballs to her eyelids.

There was a fireplace in the shop—not one that worked, for it was filled with a brass coal scuttle crowded with dried hydrangeas. There was a fire-set on its hearth, and Curtis was worried that the woman would go for the poker. He looked about for a weapon of his own, then saw that Adele was on the floor, struggling, her face blue. She was choking.

Curtis hauled Adele upright. He put his knuckles in under her sternum and pressed hard with his other hand. He pushed. She heaved limply in his arms.

Nothing. Nothing. Nothing.

Curtis pumped and relaxed, pumped and relaxed. He shouted his wife's name. He tried to use her name to tear at time itself, the seconds that kept passing.

He didn't even look at the mad woman. He had forgotten her. He wasn't waiting for the poker to fall, to injure him— he'd forgotten that too. He lowered his wife to the floor and sank down, holding her, rocking her, calling her name. Finally he got up and looked about for a phone. There was one on the wall behind the counter. Curtis ran to it, snatched at the receiver and punched in the emergency number before hearing that the phone was dead. He tried several times, then remembered that Adele had her mobile in the pocket of her jacket. He hurried back around the counter and bent over his wife, searching her pockets. But Adele's phone had no signal.

The woman was still in the room. She stood, motionless, in front of the hearth. When Curtis looked up from the phone's display and met her gaze she raised her brows and nodded at him in an approving manner, as if congratulating him on his distress.

Curtis picked up Adele and staggered to the door. Then the woman was beside him. He shrank from her, but she only wanted to open the door for him. Its brass bell chimed. Curtis plunged out into the street. He looked back in time to see the woman collapse. She gave a sigh, then folded and diminished, as if someone had let the air out of her.

Curtis peered up the road at the blue and red lights of the police car. He clutched Adele to him, and headed towards it.

At first he hurried, as if there was something that could be done. Then—because he was a year shy of sixty, and had problems with his right hip—he had to stop and rest for a while. He cradled his wife and stroked her hair. The sun had warmed it, but the skin on her forehead was cool. 'Darling,' he said softly.

In the road ahead the air was oily with the heat of fires, and full of flakes of soot.

Holly and her mother had spent the weekend at a family reunion. On the Sunday Holly's brothers had taken her aside to remark that Kate looked low, and to ask: was that rest home Holly had found really the best arrangement?

Of course it had been Holly who'd had to do everything: find Kate a place, persuade her to move, help her sort her possessions, sell her house.

The rest home Holly found was Mary Whitaker in Kahukura. There were better equipped homes, and better ventilated ones. There were places with fully carpeted floors and larger rooms. These were all more expensive, and closer to Nelson. But Mary Whitaker had grounds with mature rhododendron bushes and magnolia trees. It had daffodils, jonquils, and narcissi sprouting on its damp lawns. It had a veranda around three sides, and a 180° view of Kahukura Bay. Holly had totally zoned out when she first saw the view. The rest home manager had been telling her things about Kahukura—a quiet, tight-knit community—but Holly only stared out to sea, where two separate rainfalls were coming down from livid patches in a wholly grey sky. Thick pillars of shadow—rain, faraway, but still dynamic. She'd thought, '*I'd* come here to die.'

Holly wasn't keen to tackle her mother about her living situation—which she could do very little to ameliorate, anyway. She doubted that her mother's subdued mood was depression, but she'd promised her brothers she'd ask. Holly thought it would turn out that it was only a displeased silence, that Kate had a grievance, which Holly would hear about in due course.

It was an hour yet till lunch was served at Mary Whitaker. There was time to take a small detour along the winding gravel road that climbed around the boundary of Cotley's Orchard and led to a new subdivision, with roads and streetlights, and a billboard with a map of the sections for sale.

Holly drove up to the subdivision. She parked, and they got out to study the billboard and see which sections had sold and which were still to go.

It was a sunny spring day. The trees of the arboretum behind Kahukura Spa were coming into leaf, brilliant green below the sombre bush of Stanislaw's Reserve.

'Not a power pole in sight,' said Holly, admiring the view.

'Over this side the power cables are all underground,' Kate said. 'There used to be pylons crossing what is now the reserve. They moved them, and buried the workings when they had all the machinery up here to dig the trench for the predator-proof fence.'

'You're getting to be quite the local.'

'Well, Holly, it seems people go on chattering about property values and improvements even when they've one foot in the grave.'

They watched a helicopter take off from the spa, a sizeable red and white machine.

'I hate that noisy thing.' Kate frowned at the helicopter, which, without warning—without any sign of engine trouble—suddenly swooped at the hillside before it, and flew straight into the ground. Its props splintered. The helicopter momentarily disappeared inside a bloom of bright, black-edged fire.

Kate grabbed Holly's arm. She sagged, and Holly caught her. For the next minute Holly was busy, manhandling her mother to the car, leaning her up against it while she opened the door.

Once she was seated Kate groped for her daughter's handbag. She produced Holly's phone and passed it to her. 'Never mind me,' she said. 'I'll be fine presently.'

26

Holly punched triple 1. The phone didn't ring. She looked at its display. *No signal.*

Holly got in the car and started it. 'We should go and make sure help is on its way.' She turned to watch where she was backing. There was only the groomed hillside behind her. Then, without any warning, that view—new lawn and fluorescent pink boundary pegs—snapped closed, like the virtual camera shutter on her smartphone. There was a dark pause, then Holly became aware of her mother's hoarse shouting, and that she was being shaken.

Kate had one hand on the handbrake. 'You fainted, Holly. And, honestly, I thought I would too. The car stalled and rolled forward. We were nearly over the edge.'

Holly checked her phone again. 'We have to go somewhere where we can get a signal.'

Kate gestured at the spa, the town. 'Plenty of people will have seen the crash. You shouldn't move till you're quite sure you've recovered.'

They heard another loud impact down in the settlement. A truck blasted through the intersection by the supermarket with the twisted remnant of a motorbike beneath its front wheels. The sparks from the crushed bike were as bright as those from a welding torch. Then the bike's petrol tank exploded. The truck continued on regardless, surfing on flame, and leaving long flaming tyre tracks. The tangle of vehicles finally came to a halt at the next intersection, where they burned.

Holly and her mother stared at the fire. They waited to see people rushing to help—shopkeepers with fire extinguishers. To see what you would normally expect to see.

There was a thin thread of siren. It came closer, then was shut off. They glimpsed flashing red and blue lights in the smoke at the intersection.

Holly and her mother waited to see more help arrive.

Long minutes went by. Tens of minutes. During that time they heard gunfire. But no more police cars, or fire appliances, or ambulances appeared.

Then Holly saw a quad bike moving slowly around the wrecked helicopter, bumbling through thick grass.

She looked back at the intersection in time to see a woman with a stroller walk, apparently calm and deliberate, towards the flames. The woman stopped at the edge of a puddle of burning petrol, and stood for a time in a considering way. Suddenly she began pushing the stroller in and out of it, back and forth, as mothers do to soothe a crying child. The stroller caught fire.

Holly screamed. Her mother was screaming. They clutched one another, and Holly buried her face against her mother's bony shoulder.

Belle stopped well back from the wreck. She sat astride her bike, shielding her eyes with her hands and squinting into the flames. She couldn't tell what was blistered metal and what charred flesh. She could smell both every time gusts pushed the smoke her way.

She drove slowly around it, checking to see whether anyone had been thrown clear. But the bodies were all in the helicopter, and there was nothing to be done.

The fire had scorched and shrivelled a patch of meadow; but the grass was damp so it wouldn't spread. Belle peered through the fumes at the spa, at its rear walls with their pebbled-glass bathroom windows and steel fire escapes. Where was everyone? Her feeling that there should be something happening that wasn't was almost as disturbing as her feeling that something was happening that shouldn't be.

Belle told herself that she was mistaken about how long she'd been waiting. Time was dilating, the way it did during a car accident. Any minute now there'd be people all over.

Belle so clearly imagined the arrival of ambulances and fire trucks that she began anticipating TV vans as well. News reports started up in her head. *First on the scene was Department of Conservation ranger Belle Greenbrook. . . .* A helicopter crash was bound to make the national news. If she was interviewed, rather than say what she'd been doing when Theresa called, Belle decided to mention Boomer, whom she'd been following around for most of the morning. Yes, she'd take a little moment to talk about her favourite endangered flightless parrot, and the dustbowl he was preparing to give the right round tones to his courtship song.

Belle unclipped her radio, and pressed the call button. 'Tre?' And then, 'Over.' She let the button up; and listened to static. She'd been able to hear the siren as she was coming through the reserve, but she couldn't now.

Belle moved away from the screen of smoke. She looked down at the bay and at once saw more smoke rising from the town. There were vehicles on fire at the intersection of Haven Road and Grove Street. She heard glass breaking, and dogs barking—maybe every animal in town. And they weren't just barking; some were howling in pain and terror. The roaring flames of the wreck had masked the clamour of canine hysteria and grief.

Then Belle heard women screaming. The screams were coming from a car parked at the new subdivision. Belle waved, but no one showed themselves. She looked around for the cause of the screaming, and saw what the women had seen.

It was almost over by that time, so it took her a moment to work out that the flame-wrapped upright shape was a human being, still alive, and that there was something in front of it in the fire—

—Belle staggered to her bike and hit her horn. Then her legs gave way and she dropped with a thump into the damp grass, and lay there, incapable, only trying with her mind, not her hands, to tear the sight away from her eyes, the sight of the burning child. It was blinding her.

The screams had stopped, but the car didn't respond to Belle's signal. Instead, from out on the water, came a dense, deep blast from a foghorn.

Bub Lanagan was headed in to Kahukura. He had a few snapper for his friend George, who ran the Smokehouse Café. George always kept an eye out for the *Champion*, and would send someone down to collect Bub's catch. After that Bub was going to head over to Ruby Bay and see if he could sell whatever George couldn't use to folks in campervans parked along the beach. The school holidays had just finished, so most of those people would be tourists. He'd have to clean the fish for them. Then he'd use one of the rest-area barbecues to cook his own snapper. He'd crack a beer, then catch the tide into his mooring at Mapua, and call it a day. Bub knew he could just get by like this for as long as it took. Eventually he'd figure out what he should do. Or rather—eventually he'd be able to bring himself to hire someone to help him with the nets; or give up the *Champion*, and his father's fishing quota. In the meantime he had this: he had the catch of the day.

It had been five months since Bub's father had died. He still often caught himself checking behind him so that he wouldn't step on his dad's foot or accidentally nudge him into the scuppers or even overboard. Bub's dad had been a little fellow, five foot eight. Bub was six foot three. The *Champion* wasn't a very big boat, and Bub had always had to watch his step around his dad.

Bub cut the engines and coasted in towards the pier. With less noise the gulls suddenly seemed very loud. Bub looked up at them and said, 'We come crying hither.' He wondered what poet that was. Shakespeare, probably—Bub's mum had been a high school teacher, and very big on Shakespeare.

Then the gulls fell silent. Abruptly. Utterly. They left the boat, setting their wings at an angle and sliding away forward, skimming the water. The sea before the *Champion*'s bow filled with shadows and silver as a thick school of fish sped ahead of her into the shallow water. Bub looked astern, his eyes scanning the sea for whatever had scared the fish. Dolphins perhaps. But the sea behind the boat was empty, and as innocent as milk.

Bub grabbed his gaff, and made his way lightly along the gunwale to the bow. He picked up the mooring line and waited for the trawler to drift closer to the pier.

It was then that he noticed thick smoke billowing up near Stanislaw's Reserve. The short stretch of commercial properties in the centre of Kahukura obscured his view of the fire itself. It must be quite big. He'd have noticed it earlier if he hadn't been so busy watching the strange behaviour of the fish.

Actually, now that he was thinking about it, nothing in Kahukura looked quite right. Or—the only thing that looked normal was a guy with a sailboard who had come skimming around Matarau Point about the same time that Bub had brought the *Champion* into the bay. The sailboarder was now on the beach near the boat ramp. He was zipping his board into its bag.

Bub cast his line around a hawser and used the gaff to pull his boat into the pier. He made it fast. Then he took a more careful look around. His eyes were drawn to the roof of the old bank, and a huddle of people. They looked like a rugby scrum. Their arms were draped over one another's shoulders, their heads bowed together. As Bub watched, the people suddenly bounced up out of their huddle, high-fived, then all ran directly off the edge of the roof—every one of them, without pause.

Bub flinched. His eyes immediately sought the only normal thing they could find—that sailboarder, who Bub saw was now tussling with two men in blood-soaked clothing.

Bub bellowed. It was a sound of shock, and a challenge.

The sailboarder heard him and broke away. He clapped his hand to his neck and fled, flat out, towards the pier.

Bub jumped onto the pier to loosen the mooring line. He cast off, and ran to the wheelhouse to start his engine. It caught and roared into life. Bub yelled, 'Hurry!' at the sailboarder, who staggered, then collected himself and sped up.

He pelted onto the pier, pursued by the bloodied men. Bub let out the throttle a little and nudged the boat close. The sailboarder jumped onto the *Champion*'s bow and sprawled, catching himself on the guard rail. He used both hands, and his neck began to let loose small rhythmic spurts of blood.

Bub threw the engine into reverse and opened the throttle right out. The boat chugged back, her flat stern making a wall in the water before it. The bloodied men were nearing the end of the pier. Bub shouted to get the sailboarder's attention, then tossed him the gaff. The sailboarder caught it, but slipped on his own blood and went down on all fours. The bloodied men jumped. One went into the water. The other caught on to the *Champion*'s gunwale.

The sailboarder swung the gaff and began to poke at the man, while Bub roared, 'Smash him!'

The bloodied, smirking man began to clamber on board. But the sailboarder had a last adrenaline-fuelled burst of energy and stabbed the man in the face with the blunt end of the gaff, breaking his nose and tearing his cheek open.

But the man simply ignored his injuries. He swung one foot on board. The sailboarder dropped the gaff and began trying to prise the man's hands free of the rail. The man responded by sinking his already blood-smeared teeth into one of the sailboarder's wrists.

Bub rushed out of the wheelhouse and ran forward. For the next minute he tried to wrench the man's jaw open. He pushed his thumbs into the man's eye sockets, feeling gristly resistance, then wet give. The man would not open his jaws. Finally Bub got his hands around the attacker's neck and squeezed. He waited for the man to let go—of his bite, of his grip on the guard rail. He waited for sane self-preservation, for a sign of pain or weakness, for the reassertion of what Bub knew very well about the world, even the frenzied world of battle—for Bub Lanagan had once been a soldier. But what Bub expected to happen kept refusing to and, finally, after he'd throttled the man to death he still had to extract the man's teeth from the sailboarder's mangled wrist; one tooth, having penetrated bone, remained in the arm after the attacker's face—its pulpy eye sockets wreathed by broken blood vessels—had slipped beneath the waters of the bay.

The sailboarder had collapsed. The deck was wet with blood. Bub knew he must get up. He must break open his first-aid kit and do what he could for the man. He must stand up and steer the boat, which was still chugging steadily backwards towards the mouth of the bay. He must get on the radio and find out *what the fuck* was going on.

But before Bub was able to muster the strength to get up, the *Champion* became sluggish, and then her engine died. For a moment she coasted on across water as flat as that in a bird bath, in air that seemed weirdly airless, like the pressurised air in the cabin of a plane. Then Bub felt something comb through his frame. He felt warm, and numb, and his bones turned to wax. He sprawled, and the last thing he saw was that strangely subdued water slipping by, only a few feet from his eyes.

When Bub came to he found the sailboarder lying against

him, as if for warmth. Bub put out a gentle, exploratory hand and touched the man's head. The man's ginger dreadlocks were as thirsty as a sea sponge. Blood welled up under Bub's fingers.

Bub asked the man, 'What happened?' He waited for an answer, and for a moment he pretended that the sailboarder was still alive, that he'd managed to save him.

Bub lay on his back, shivering, and staring at his hands. He touched his head. It felt fine, no tender spots. He didn't know why he'd passed out.

He sat up and scanned the town. There were several limp bodies floating in the water near the boat ramp.

Bub decided to head around the coast and find help. He went back to the cabin, started the *Champion*'s engine again, brought the boat about, and put her full ahead, aiming for the open water. He tried not to look at the body in the bow. He'd not go up there again unless he absolutely had to. That bit of his boat was a crime scene.

The *Champion* charged forward, then her engines suddenly gave out and, once again, something combed through Bub's body removing all his fear, then all his feelings, then all his strength. His legs buckled, his grip of the wheel loosened, and he crumpled to the deck.

Bub had no idea how long he was unconscious. He came to, as he had the first time, feeling perfectly fit and well. It wasn't like being knocked out, as he'd been once when he was a teenager and had run his motorcycle into a stray cow on a dark country road. Nor was it like climbing out of the grey, chemical pit of a general anaesthetic, or waking from a drunken stupor. He simply came awake. The rising tide had carried the *Champion* back towards the shore, and out of the influence of—of *whatever it was*.

Bub decided not to repeat the experiment. He wasn't going to risk letting the tide carry him right out into that.

From landward there sounded a sharp blast of a horn.

Bub scrambled to the wheelhouse to answer it. He spotted the woman in the meadow behind the spa. She was on her knees next to a quad bike, near the first fire. Bub lifted his arm and waved to her. She waved back.

A few minutes later the *Champion*'s radio made some throat-clearing crackles. Bub snatched it up. He tried not to yell. '*Champion* here. This is Bub Lanagan. Is this the police? Over.'

'Constable Grey, from Richmond. Are you okay, Mr Lanagan? Over.'

Bub told the cop that someone had been killed. Murdered. Then he remembered what he'd done himself, and for a moment was too perplexed to speak.

'Mr Lanagan?'

'There are crazy people,' Bub went on, then gave a rushed, breathless account of everything abnormal he could see. Eventually he made himself stop, which was a mistake, since he hadn't got to the *thing*.

'Mr Lanagan,' said the constable. 'Do you think you could go for help? I'm at the bypass turnoff and heading west on Highway 60. There'll be help in Motueka. But you should take your boat around Matarau Point and see why no one has come from the Nelson end.'

Bub listened to the constable's very reasonable request. He stared at the dead sailboarder and whispered, 'What can I tell her?' Then, he told her that he was going in to check on his friend George.

The cop's voice was tremulous, squeezed, wavering in volume. She once again advised Bub to stay out on the water. She said the streets were very dangerous. She talked about possible contaminants.

Bub glanced at the horizon, and saw only the horizon, to the north out to sea a line where one blue met another, and east, Pepin Island, at the end of the long arm of the Richmond Range. There was no water traffic in sight.

Bub's radio coughed. 'Mr Lanagan?'

'I'm here. Can we hook up? Over.'

She screamed at him. *'Are you listening to me at all?'*

'Look,' said Bub, and was pleased to hear resolve in his own voice. 'I'm going to do a quick scout for my mate, George. After that I'm heading over to try to do something about the fire near the petrol station. When I've seen to that I'll come and find you. Over and out.'

She was still protesting when he signed off.

The Smokehouse Café had eleven bodies in its dining area. Bub found his friend George doubled over the deep fryer, his head and arms immersed in boiling fat.

Bub shoved the fire doors open and threw himself out into the parking lot. He doubled over, retching, then sagged, and sat down on the ground. He stayed there for a time, till the wind shifted and a gust of hot, metallic smoke wafted over him.

He got up and went back into the restaurant. He turned off the deep fryer, let the range hood run for a minute, then switched it off too. When he left the kitchen the fat was still singing its elastic song.

Bub knew there was something else he'd meant to do. He leaned against a wheelie bin, breathing in through his mouth and out through his nostrils until he'd pumped the stink of fat out of the immediate air around his face. Then it came back to him—what he should at least *try* to do.

He set off across the carpark and came out on Haven Road, a short distance from the intersection filled with the now blackened wreck of the burning truck. Though the awnings of a pub near the corner had burned away, the building itself hadn't caught. But the pub's collection of folding tables and chairs were on fire, and the fire had communicated itself to the potted box trees on either side of the entrance to the neighbouring real estate agents, and from those had progressed to the wheelchair ramp at the front of the pharmacy. Beyond that, the fringed yellow canvas awning of the local craft gallery was newly ablaze, and the breeze now and then chopped off rags of flame, which drifted across the wide road and fortunately faded before they touched the high shelter of the service station forecourt.

Bub stood for a moment, steeling himself, shielding his watering eyes and watching the progress of the fire. Then he made his creeping way around the burning truck. He averted his eyes from the sight of the charred frame of a baby stroller, and broke into a jog. He hurried into the service station—looked at the blood and bodies near the counter only long enough to check for movement. There was no movement.

Bub found the fire extinguishers next to the smoke alarms and first-aid kits and tow ropes. He took as many as he could carry. He left the service station and dropped the cans onto the road. They rolled into the gutter behind him. Bub peered at the one he held, trying to make sense of its instructions for use. His eyes jittered; wouldn't move from word to word. There were diagrams, but they didn't look like the extinguisher.

George's head had looked like a potato roasted in its jacket.

'Fucking pull yourself together!' Bub yelled. He found the trigger guard and flipped it.

Someone came up behind him.

Bub whirled, raised the can, and pressed the trigger. The spray seemed to form a momentary halo around the man's head, the cloud of particles billowing backwards as if the spray had hit a pane of glass. Then it drifted down to settle on the man's neck and shoulders. It shone, fizzing white, on his black clothes and black skin. The man's eyes were black too, and their whites creamy. He looked wary, but not alarmed. He kept his eyes on Bub as he squatted and groped for another of the cans. He located one and straightened slowly, still keeping his eyes on Bub. It was Bub who looked away, down at the man's hands. The guy activated the extinguisher by touch alone, and stepped past Bub to aim at the awning. The extinguisher released a stream of foam. Bub joined the man. They worked on the awning, exhausted their cans, and fetched more. They put out the ramp, the burning tables and chairs. When they got to the truck, the man went one way around it while Bub went the other. The truck's tyres and upholstery were still alight. Bub put them out, and finished by smothering the fire under the truck's gaping hood. When he stepped away from the wreck, the intersection was filled with a hissing quiet. Bub looked for the man. He made a circuit of the wreck. He found the last exhausted extinguisher set neatly upright on the kerb at the base of a power pole. But the man had vanished.

Before Bub went in search of the police officer he wrapped his jacket around his fist, broke the window of a parked car, popped its boot, and armed himself with a jack handle. Then he set off along Haven Road towards the patch of blue light in the smoke.

The patrol car had a body in its back seat. Bub switched off the car's lights and continued westward. He saw no one alive. After a time he stopped checking for signs of life, stopped *looking*, because he wasn't ready to digest what he was seeing.

Bub reached the end of the settlement and slogged up into the cutting. There he found the road partly blocked by an abandoned tanker and a Holden Captiva. He also found Constable Grey, and an older man.

The man was sitting on the open hatch of a Volvo station wagon, cradling an injured woman who was lying in the car. The young police officer was talking to someone on her radio. She was speaking slowly, her voice low and dull. She had a split lip, a black eye, and there were bloody grazes on her chin and hands. 'I tried it twice,' she was saying. 'Both times Mr Haines had to haul me out by my leg.'

When Bub appeared carrying his jack handle, Constable Grey pointed her gun at him. Bub raised his hands and explained that he was the skipper of the trawler. 'We spoke,' he said, like someone reminding someone else of an appointment in a more ordinary world.

The person on the radio had heard the flurry and was in a panic. Her shouts were distorted into a series of squawks and pops. Constable Grey handed the radio to the older man, saying, 'Please try to calm her.' Then she gave Bub her full attention. 'Why didn't you set off out to sea to look for help?'

Bub held up a hand to stop her. 'Because there's some kind of engine-stopping, sleep-making *thing* strung across the mouth of the bay, like a shark net.'

For a second Constable Grey just looked at him blankly, and then her knees folded. She sat down hard on the tarseal. She wiped her eyes with her right forearm, smearing tears which cleared the blood from her auburn eyebrows and made a pale band across her lightly freckled cheekbones.

The older man said to Bub, 'We hoped it was only local.' He kept patting the woman as if blessing her over and over. Bub saw that the woman was dead and beginning to grow livid.

It began to rain. Bub put up the hood of his parka. He studied the two distraught people. 'Okay,' he said. 'I'll feel safer when I'm back on my boat. You should join me. We'll leave your car at the jetty.' He extended a hand to the constable. She took it and let him help her to her feet. Bub put an arm around the older man's waist and got him up too, then carefully tucked some stray locks of the dead woman's swishy grey bob back against her head so they wouldn't get caught in the Volvo's hatch when he closed it. He looked at the man for approval. The man nodded. Bub fastened the hatch, then took the guy's arm and settled him in the back seat.

They left the empty Captiva and milk tanker and drove back into Kahukura.

Dan Hale was maybe only half a minute behind the police car when he reached the advisory speed sign before the downhill horseshoe bend. The Captiva and its two occupants had only just passed around the bend ahead of him. Dan shifted gears and pressed his brake pedal, and a tyre on the trailer blew. In his left wing mirror he saw a black spray of shredded rubber leaping in an arc behind the truck. The trailer wobbled and yawed. Dan briefly felt the torque on his cab as the trailer begin to tip—then the tanker hit the side of the cutting and brushed along it, raising dust and rubble. Dan pulled away from the bank, and felt a jerk in his steering wheel as the brakes in the trailer bit before those in the truck. The trailer stayed in line, and the mass of the milk tanker gradually slid to a stop.

For a minute or so Dan sat, his head down on the steering wheel, listening to the hydraulics hiss. When he did raise his head he saw a man in black clothes, with a face almost equally dark, picking his way through the scrub at the edge of the road. The man was carrying something small but heavy, and mysteriously iridescent, like a titanium-coated paperweight. He stepped onto the tarseal and met Dan's eyes. They regarded each other through the insect-splashed windscreen. The way the man was looking at Dan made him think that the iridescent thing might be a weapon. The look wasn't murderous, but the man seemed to be weighing something up. *Yes or no*—said his look—*life or death*.

Dan broke eye contact to rummage through the rubbish in the pocket of the driver's door for his steel-barrelled flashlight. But once he had the flashlight in hand, Dan saw that the guy was further off, in the orchard, rising out of a crouch and dusting his palms together. Then he walked away through the apple trees. Dan had the odd impression that the guy had gone around the *back* of his truck, rather than crossing in front of it. For some reason he'd done that, then had stopped in the orchard to push his paperweight thing into the soil before continuing on his way.

Dan waited till the man was out of sight before starting his engine and trying to reverse the truck back onto the road. And he found that things that were possible a moment before weren't any more. Not that he believed it, not till the kid turned up and showed him what the problem was.

Oscar Bryce spent the morning of his school-free 'teacher training day' shooting people, or setting them on fire, or freezing them solid then smashing them to pieces. The people weren't *technically* zombies, but rather Splicers, horribly altered citizens of a failed experimental utopia, infesting a city under the sea.

Since his last upgrade Oscar had been having fun waiting for the Splicers to walk into puddles of water, whereupon he'd hit them with a plasmid, his blue electricity, and they'd fry. Then, when he was in a bridge between buildings, something punctured the glass. The bridge filled with gushing green transparency, and he couldn't make it to the nearest airlock before it sealed him in to drown.

Oscar decided to take a break. He saved his game and went out for a bike ride to clear his head. He put his earbuds in, selected *Homebrew*, and biked over to the shoreline reserve. When he reached the stile with its 'no bicycles' sign he lifted his bike over it and went on. He knew the walking track would be empty. Earlier or later it would be full of women in calf-length trackpants exercising their dogs. But, late morning, he'd probably be able to pedal the whole distance without encountering anyone.

Oscar swooped into dips and skidded around corners, his tyres crunching on crushed shells. Sometimes he came dangerously close to the bluff, and at one close call he actually imagined his mother sitting alone in his room, on the edge of his empty bed. It was a morbid picture, and uncharacteristic of Oscar.

After his near miss Oscar decided to turn for home. He was going at a fair clip by the time he rode by the beach where he'd earlier seen a group of young men playing with a soccer ball, stripped to the waist in the spring sunshine. As he went past the Backpackers Hostel, Oscar saw the ball abandoned on the beach. Then he spotted two of the young men in the water. They weren't playing any more, or even swimming, only rolling limply back and forth in the low waves.

Oscar coasted to a standstill. He stared at the bodies and wondered what to do. Should he fish them out? He looked around for an adult, and shouted for help. He saw a lone sailboarder skimming in on the very last breath of wind, and a fishing boat chugging into the pier, pursued by gulls. Adults—but too far away. Then his eyes found someone else, a young man, in the backpackers' barbecue area, on his knees, bashing his head against the bricks.

Oscar stopped calling for help.

Another guy was lying face down while a girl pounded on him with both feet. That looked like a cartoon.

Oscar hesitated, balancing peril and blame. He shouldn't just *leave*, but he didn't understand what was happening. Plus he was shaking hard. He was a fifteen-year-old, six-foot-five, eighty-kilo *noodle*, and he probably should run away.

Oscar got back on his bike and rode towards home. But once he was on Beach Road he saw things he would later describe, without further elaboration, as 'crazy serial killer zombie stuff'.

He turned around and took the road out of town, pedalling as fast as he was able. He tried to phone his mum—but he couldn't seem to do that and ride at the same time. He was suddenly much clumsier than usual.

Oscar got onto Highway 60 and headed up the cutting, standing on his pedals and pumping as fast as he was able. There was a car pulled over in front of him. The two men in the car—a preppy guy and an Islander—were looking at him in a way that seemed pretty standard. He started making shooing motions at them, trying to tell them they should go back the way they'd come.

The driver's window slid open.

Oscar didn't pause. He actually couldn't make himself stop. 'Turn around!' he gasped as he went past.

Behind him one of the men shouted, 'Hang on a minute!'

Oscar heard the car door open and someone come sprinting after him. They caught up with him, and grabbed the back of his bike.

Oscar dropped his big feet onto the road and wilted, gasping.

'What's the matter?' said the Islander.

'Let me go.'

But the guy wouldn't release the bike, so Oscar left him holding it and kept running. He hauled off his helmet and tossed it behind him on the road. He'd warned them, but he didn't want to explain. He ran as much from that—having to explain—as from the crazy people.

After abandoning his bike, Oscar continued uphill at a steady jog till he came to a milk tanker. It looked as if it had run into the side of the cutting. There was a scattering of rubble around the rear tank, and a gouge behind the vehicle on the face of the bank. The truck was rocking and hopping. It would get so far, then its engine would lose all power— including brakes—and the cab would roll forward again and grind back into the bank.

The tanker driver looked busy, and irritated, and *sane*.

Oscar stopped by the passenger's window. He stooped, and clutched his knees to ease his stitch. He tried to catch his breath, then looked at the driver. 'Sup?'

'What does it look like?'

'People have gone crazy down there.' Oscar heard himself sounding like someone who expects to be disbelieved.

'Uh huh,' said the driver, not really listening. He depressed the accelerator again. 'I'm all clear on this side.' He jerked his head at the wing mirror by the bank. 'I should be able to reverse.' He sounded indignant. 'I only want to get safely back on the road and roll into Kahukura. I had a blowout. Could you take a look back there for me and see what the trouble is?'

This reasoned problem-solving was a sensible distraction for Oscar. It was a relief to put the crazies out of his mind and set himself the task of helping the tanker driver. The tanker itself was reassuring: massive, high off the ground, a possible fortress against crazy people.

Oscar set off alongside the silver tanks. After a while it felt as if he was trying to climb a much steeper slope. By the time he got to the end of the trailer, he'd begun to feel quite woozy. He stopped by the sign warning overtaking cars about the vehicle's length. Experimentally, he faced uphill and took a step. He was sure there was something *there*. Something he couldn't see.

He came to a moment later. The skin on his chin was smarting. He touched his face, and looked at the blood on his fingers.

'You fainted, kid.' The driver was cradling Oscar's head. His forehead was creased with worry.

'Um,' said Oscar, sheepish.

The man took off his sunglasses and looked sternly at him.

'There's something there,' Oscar said.

The man made to get up, and Oscar clutched his arm. 'No, don't try it. There really is something there.' He sat up and fished his phone out of his pocket. He had a message. 'R u OK?' It was from his mum, but had come nearly forty minutes ago.

Oscar started to shake again. His hands were clumsy, but he managed to find the three-minute video he'd made of his friend Hester eating a maraschino cherry and knotting its stem with her tongue. He had to prove the something to the driver. If he was right, that is, and his fainting wasn't the beginning of anything else—like losing his mind.

The truck driver had produced his own phone. 'This is still telling me there's no signal.'

'I'm not trying to make a call,' Oscar said. 'I'm going to show you the thing.' He scrambled up and went downhill a little to search along the side of the road for a stick. He spotted a dog-legged bit of eucalyptus, about a metre and a half long. He picked it up and returned to the driver. 'Look,' he said. 'This video is three minutes seven seconds, right?' He turned its volume right up so that he could hear his own and his friends' off-camera hectoring and encouragement— 'Don't swallow it, Hester!' 'Five bucks says she can't . . .'

Oscar placed the phone on the road and used the stick to push it ahead of him up the slope. He crawled slowly after it till the swarm of colour on the phone's screen, and the barracking voices, died away. Oscar then used the stick to scoop the phone back towards him. Its display lit up again. He repeated the experiment several times, then sat back and said to the truck driver, 'That's why your engine keeps stalling.'

'So it's like what?'

'I don't know what it is. It kind of draws energy away from things, I think.'

'Come on! If they had something like this, even *I'd* know about it.'

'Yes. But, I mean, they don't, do they?' Oscar was waiting hopefully for this adult to restore everything to the way it should be. To do something. To explain. But the driver just kept frowning at him, then after a moment went back to trying to figure out how to get his truck to the garage in Kahukura.

'No. No. Listen to me. Something weird and horrible is happening down there. People are trying to kill each other. People *have* killed each other.' Oscar shouted the last bit so loud he made his ears ring. Then he burst into tears.

When the police car went by, Jacob Falafa pulled in at the gate of Cotley's orchard. He'd been driving for hours after very little sleep and it was time for Warren to take a turn. But Warren didn't wake up when the car stopped, so Jacob took pity on his hangover and let him sleep a bit longer.

Eventually Warren gave an adenoidal snort, opened his eyes, and checked his watch. 'I hope Aunt Winnie won't think we expect lunch.' Warren's aunt Winnie Kreutzer ran a B&B in Kahukura. He couldn't really pass though without dropping in.

'We can say we had a late breakfast,' Jacob said. In fact they hadn't had any. They'd spent the weekend at the tangi of a former rugby teammate and had got away early. They'd picked their way on stockinged feet through the mattresses on the floor of the meeting house, stopping in the paepae to locate their dew-dampened shoes, and then left the marae before anyone else was up.

'Winnie will feed us, *sole*, but I'm warning you, plain toast and jam is against her principles.'

A cyclist appeared, coming from Kahukura, a tall bony kid standing on the pedals and pumping as fast as he was able. He saw them and made some urgent gestures. He seemed to be signalling them to go back the way they'd come.

Warren opened his window.

The boy went past, without pausing. 'Turn around!' he gasped.

Jacob jumped out of the car. He loped after the kid and grabbed the back of his bike.

The boy was sweating, quivering, and had the thousand-yard stare. Jacob was a nurse and knew it well. 'What's the matter?'

'Let me go.'

Jacob didn't release the bike, so the boy dropped it and jogged away up the cutting. He hauled off his helmet and tossed it behind him on the road.

Jacob regarded the spinning helmet, then turned around and peered at the sky over the trees. He saw the smoke.

'Get in, *sole*,' said Warren. 'Aunt Winnie will be able to tell us what's up.'

They never reached Warren's aunt. They got down onto the flat, then reduced speed sharply at the sight of the fire filling Kahukura's main street. They slowed to a crawl when they heard the cacophony of dogs. Then, when a melee of bodies erupted from a cross street and pelted across the road in front of the Captiva, they stopped altogether.

At first it looked as if the people were playing a very fierce game of Touch. But, when the melee came closer, Warren and Jacob saw the people weren't tagging, but *tearing* at each other.

Warren made a turn, bumping up over the curb. They fled, weaving around obstacles that had appeared after they'd passed through that stretch of road—an overturned car, an injured dog, and the man with a spade who'd injured it. The man chopped at the Captiva as it slowed to go around the dog, and his steel blade shrieked against the panel of the passenger's door.

As they drove, Jacob was trying to dial the emergency number, first on his phone, then Warren's when his wouldn't work. Warren kept turning to him, shouting, 'Come on for fuck's sake!' while Jacob yelled back that the network was down and, 'Watch where you're fucking going!' Their car was all over the road, and nearly off it several times, when Warren swerved sharply not just from obstacles, but at the sight of impossible horrors in ordinary front yards.

They were speeding when they came to the truck in the cutting. It blasted its horn. Jacob had a moment to recognise the boy in the truck's cab. Both the boy and the truck driver were giving him the double-arm danger wave.

Warren hit the brakes. He made to pull in behind the truck. But when the Captiva neared the end of the trailer, its engine stalled.

Jacob's view of the road collapsed into a point of light.

The next thing he knew his head was lolling on his suddenly boneless neck, and something heavy was lying across his legs. He tried to move whatever it was, and grabbed a handful of hair. He was poked and jostled. There was a ratcheting noise—the handbrake—then a thud. The car had come to a stop. Jacob was positive it was going backwards before it did.

He looked down and found the big, bony boy stretched out across his lap. The boy's legs were dangling out the open door, and the rubberised toes of his sneakers were smoking. He was holding the handbrake.

'What the fuck?' said Jacob.

'Sorry,' said the boy. He tried to get up without putting his hands on Jacob and only foundered about and elbowed him in the stomach. 'Sorry,' he said again, and wriggled backwards out of the car.

They were in front of the tanker again. Its driver was standing beside Warren's open door. He was nursing his wrist and grimacing in pain. 'I had to grab the wheel and steer you arse-end into the bank because I couldn't reach the handbrake,' he said. 'Oscar was about to lose his legs.'

'I blacked out,' Warren said.

'Yeah,' said the kid. He pointed back up the cutting. 'There's something there. It knocks out people. And engines.' His eyes were bright with excitement.

'We're not properly off the road,' Warren said. 'Whoever comes around the corner next is going to plough right into us.'

The boy had a soft, still-roundish face. But he also had a deep manly voice, and was very tall. He hunched his shoulders a little and went on. 'I don't think the—thing— is semi-permeable, or that anyone is coming in from the other side. I mean, Dan has been here for nearly an hour, and during that time there's been no traffic at all from that direction, and only me from this. Me, then you guys.'

'So, do you know what is going on—?' Jacob paused, waiting for Oscar to supply his name.

'Oscar. And this is Dan.'

'Jacob,' said Jacob. 'And this is Warren.'

Then Dan and Warren shook hands. It seemed the thing to do.

'I don't know anything,' said Oscar. 'But I'm pretending I'm in a game environment. I'm trying to think how things work in this environment, rather than how they're normally supposed to work.'

Warren said, 'Have you checked to see whether this thing extends beyond the edge of the road?'

'No!' Oscar flushed with hope. 'But you'll hit the bluff above the sea before you've gone very far that way. And how are you going to be able to tell whether the—thing—is there or not without passing out?'

'We could do what you did with your phone. Go real slow and hold it out in front of us, lit up, or playing a tune,' Dan said.

'I wouldn't trust arm's-length,' Oscar said. 'I started feeling strange about two metres out from where I fainted.'

Dan held up one finger. *Just a minute.* He hurried to the truck's cab and boosted himself up. He rummaged around in the lock-up behind the seats. After a moment he came back with a roll of masking tape—and his big flashlight. 'Won't this do just as well?'

'Yes,' said Oscar. 'If we tape it to my stick, facing the end you're holding so you can see *the instant* the light goes out.'

Oscar and Dan sat on the road and went to work fastening the flashlight to the branch. Jacob watched, bemused and admiring.

When they were done, Dan tested it by edging up to the back of the tanker. The flashlight was just past the trailer when its bulb flickered and went out. Dan stepped back, and it lit up again.

'Okay.' Warren hitched his belt. 'Jacob, perhaps you should wait here with Oscar till we come back. Then we can all set out together the other way.'

'Sure,' said Jacob.

When Dan and Warren had passed out of sight, Oscar began to pace back and forth on the roadside, flinging his feet down carelessly so that he sometimes slithered in the gravel. He asked Jacob if he thought they were in real trouble.

'Real?'

'*Bad* trouble,' Oscar said. 'I got a text from my mum and I haven't been able to answer it. She'll be all worried and stuff.'

Jacob concealed his shaking hands in his pockets. The thought of Oscar's mum waiting for an answer filled him with terrible anxiety. All he could do to alleviate the anxiety was make a promise: 'I'll look after you, okay?'

Dan and Warren eventually returned, having discovered that the field extended all the way to the sea. Dan locked the cab of his truck and the four of them set out through the orchard. They went slowly, taking turns with the stick and flashlight. They walked in a wavering line, veering back towards Kahukura whenever the bulb went out. The sight of that light, quenched then revived, was so harmless after the spectacle of people clawing at one another's bodies that it was almost impossible to believe there was any danger. Still, they played it safe, prodding at the empty air as though it were a sleeping tiger.

By late afternoon, they had made it only as far as the bush-filled gully below the new subdivision. Jacob spotted a car parked up there, with two people in it. He called to them, and a slim, grey-haired woman got out. Jacob mimed driving around the road to join them. She raised both hands and set them as if flat on the air above the car. She was showing them where the *thing* was. Jacob signalled for her to try climbing down. He shouted something about safety in numbers. But by that time an old lady had stepped out of the car too, and they all realised that the job of getting her down the slope should not be undertaken so late in the day.

It began to rain, and the two women took shelter in their car. The four retraced their steps back to the road.

Lily Kaye was running beside the inlet to the east of Kahukura. Late on a weekday morning the road was quiet. So quiet that she'd just seen an M-class Mercedes do a leisurely U-turn across both lanes.

When the survivors were first identified and spoken about, people would always single out Lily, who was already a celebrity. She was twenty-eight, and for the past several years hadn't placed any lower than fourth in the world in her sport, ultra marathons. Sometimes she was fourth, and laboured over the finish line in the muted shame of *almost*. There were always cameras, and the news services of her country—usually mildly congratulatory, mildly consoling. And she'd have to say that, yes, she did feel she'd given it her best but this time the competition was simply in better form. They'd ask her about her knee. She'd exonerate her knee, and, along with her knee, her doctor, her trainer, her physiotherapist. Other times she'd come first. She'd cross the line in a storm of light.

Lily reached the top of the cutting over the base of Matarau Point. She saw a long sweep of clean, pale sand, smoothed by the retreating tide. She saw Kahukura's waterfront reserve, its cobblestone track, and flourishing plantings of flaxes. She saw the long concrete pier with white-painted piles, and, to complete the picture, one fishing boat on its way in.

Lily shortened her stride. She would slow down, and then warm down. She'd do her stretches on the beach, and then have a protein shake and a bit of fruit salad at the Smokehouse Café. She'd call her fiancé and ask him to come and get her.

Lily was doing everything properly, and minding her knee, when she spotted something ahead of her blocking the road, a senseless, tangled mass.

What appeared to have happened was this: the old people had all tried to climb the fence, a stretch of chain-link along the top of the steepest bank of the cutting. They had clambered over one another, piling up in a pyramid against the fence until it hauled stakes and slid down the bank to the road, where it lay collapsed, a fishing net full of gasping fish. Many of the tangled bodies were in robes and pyjamas, and one woman wore an elegant bed jacket with swan's-down trim. Above the filmy flounces the woman's face was smeared with blood from a raw rip in her scalp.

It was impossible to say how many there were. They were bent at odd angles, most were bloodied, and some were clearly already dead. None were moaning or crying out, but they were making a sound.

Lily approached, her hands out before her, as if just by reaching she'd divine what to do. She tried to make sense of the sound.

'Ma ma ma ma,' was what the old people were saying. A

man with a broken tooth piercing his lip moved his mouth to utter that single syllable, musing and melodious, like a baby in its cot singing to itself on waking.

Lily shucked off her hydration pack and pulled her phone from its pocket. It showed no bars. Lily moved it about, as though a signal were an invisible butterfly she hoped to net.

One of the old men began to choke. Blood dribbled down his chin. Lily swooped on him, grappled him upright, but couldn't free him from the pile. His left arm flopped, as multi-jointed as one of those bamboo snake toys. It was broken in many places. Lily released him and backed off. She stood wringing her hands.

Lily had always considered herself tough. She wasn't a crier; tears were a waste of moisture. At the end of a race, whether she lost or won the first thing she'd do once she was away from the crowds was fill a bath with water and ice and sit in it for thirty minutes, to suppress the inflammation. She'd grit her teeth and take pain on top of pain.

Was hardihood not the same as toughness?

Lily tore her eyes away from the old people and looked at Kahukura.

There was something on fire down there.

The American, William Minute, was a lawyer who had come to New Zealand to depose twenty plaintiffs in a class-action against a multinational chemical company. Most of the people William had to meet had been flown to Auckland by the Kiwi legal team. But two were unable to travel. One was in Murchison, nursing his sick wife; another was sick himself, and in a community hospital near Granity. William would have to go to them. And the Kiwis thought, since he'd come all this way, it would be nice to treat him—and themselves—to a weekend at Kahukura Spa.

Monday morning William said goodbye to his

colleagues, who were waiting for a helicopter to take them to Nelson Airport. William had rented a big Mercedes and was looking forward to his drive. However, once the sprawling, many-gabled spa was receding in his rear-view mirror, William thought that, actually, it was less that he was looking forward to the journey than glad to be going, to be parting company with his company. Treats and fringe benefits were, these days, in shorter supply. And William liked mud baths, massages and manicures as much as the next guy. Or maybe a little more than the next guy. He'd enjoyed the spa's appetising whole food, and the clean smell of the narrow belt of old exotic trees behind his room. He'd liked the crystalline blue, heated outdoor swimming pool. However, he hadn't liked the concentrated period of having to be nice to people. The spa was a nice place. New Zealand was a nice place. He was having a nice time.

Now he was looking forward to being alone, to washing off the company of others, as he'd washed off the spa's soothing body balms.

The spa was behind him now, its sweeping drive and grand gateway. It looked romantic. It looked like that place in Calistoga where Robert Louis Stevenson had gone to nurse his lungs. (William had stayed there once, and had spent his stay daydreaming about the nineteenth century. He liked to think he'd have flourished back then—in a time with fewer rules, and without people always looking over your shoulder.)

He turned onto Bypass Road and drove southeast to go west. He'd been told that the road west was a dead end, that after a distance it came up against some national park. It was weird to be in a country that lacked roads in the obvious places.

Six minutes later William was out of the settlement, through the cutting that crossed the base of Matarau Point. He was well on his way.

Then he got a kind of itch. A moment later he could

see what he'd forgotten. He knew that his phone charger was still plugged in by his room's writing desk. Before he'd jumped in the shower he'd unplugged his phone, checked his messages, and put his phone in his jacket pocket. But he couldn't remember bundling up the charger and stowing it in his bag.

William pulled over, popped the hatch, and got out to check his bag. No charger.

He slammed the hatch and stood for a time staring at the road ahead, which grew straight and ran on, cutting across a tidal inlet. There were cars moving away from him along that road, and the sun shining on their windows seemed to form lines of code.

William scowled and shook his head. 'Idiot,' he said to himself—about his fanciful thoughts and his forgetfulness. He got back in his car and checked both ways before turning. There was no traffic near him, only—far off—a slender female figure running. Even from a distance it was clear how good her gait was. She looked like she could go on forever.

William did a U-turn. He was impatient, so instead of just reversing his course, he took the first left to follow the line of the hills, for the spa was on the slope just back from the flat of the town. As it turned out, the road he'd hoped was a shortcut first failed to warn him with a No Exit sign, then came to a dead end.

William slowed to turn—and thought he heard a gunshot. He let his window down. The air that wafted in carried the scent of burning petrol, metal, and rubber. From a garden up the slope came the bright chiming of an alarmed thrush.

William kept his window open and began to creep slowly back down the hill. He found himself on a street with newer houses, big places with monolithic cladding and double-height entrance ways.

A figure was lying by a neatly trimmed box hedge.

William pulled in, got out, hurried to the man, and turned him over. The fork jammed in the man's eye socket sagged, then slid out. It landed with a clink beside William's Berluti boot. The man's right hand was gloved with blood—he must have tried for some time to remove the fork, before lapsing into unconsciousness. William could see no sign of the eye, and the pit of the socket looked deep and dug at. He opened the top of the man's robe and put his ear to his chest.

Silence.

William began compressions. After ten he paused and grasped the man's jaw so that he could blow into his mouth. He saw that the man's lips were bloody too. His lips, and his teeth. William hesitated, his face only inches from the smeared mouth, his gaze flicking from the teeth to the hollowed-out eye socket. He drew back, then got up, and stood looking down—momentarily mesmerised.

There was something about the quiet of the street—all the immediate streets—that didn't seem normal. It was the furtive silence of secret, solitary acts.

William put his hand in his pocket before he remembered that his phone was plugged into the car stereo. He went back to the Mercedes, swiped the lock on his phone and saw that it said 'No service'.

He'd have to leave the body in order to get help.

He decided to try the house opposite, since the nearest was probably the man's own, where there was either no one home, or the perpetrator was lying in wait with another fork.

There were sunflowers in pots by the front door. In another few weeks they would reach the trellis on the wall. For now their robust ugliness looked wrong in a pot. 'Triffids,' said William's droll inner voice, and he had a vague sense that it was telling him something important—while remaining above-it-all, as usual.

No one came to the door when he knocked. But while

56

he waited he thought he heard sounds from the rear of the house.

A path took him around to a back patio—where he saw blood, lots of it, in thick swipes, and drag marks, and puddles, and splatters.

His body slammed into a state of cold, heightened vigilance, and his inner voice buttoned its chilly lips.

There was blood in the swimming pool too, and two floating forms, an adult and a child. William ran to rescue the child. He pulled off his boots and jacket and dived into the reddened water. He seized the small body, waded to the edge of the pool, lay her on the non-slip tiles, got out himself, and began mouth-to-mouth. After several breaths the child revived, and promptly sank her little milk teeth into his lower lip.

William prised gently at her jaw until it opened. He freed his lacerated lip, spat, and wiped his mouth.

The girl seemed determined to get away. Before William was able to react, she had flipped over onto her stomach and slipped into the water—like some aquatic creature making its escape. William lunged, seized, and lifted her. He clasped her to him. 'I'll get your mom,' he told her. That must be what she was trying to do—rescue her mother.

William was worried he wouldn't be able to revive the woman. He didn't want the kid to witness any more than she had already (*all that blood*) so he lifted her over the pool fence and checked that its childproof gate was closed. He hunkered down and reached through the fence to cup her cheek. 'Just give me a minute,' he said. 'Be a good girl and stay there.'

She finally met his eye. William saw exultation in her gaze. It wasn't a childlike expression. Nor was it adult, or even *animal*. It was only alert, alive, and alien.

William snatched his hand back, then immediately began to tell himself off. The child was in shock. Or, possibly, she wasn't neurologically normal, and the deep oddness of her expression was only something he'd seen before in the faces of autistic children, that mix of emotional vagrancy and quizzical disbelief.

William jumped back into the water and pulled the drifting body of the woman towards him. He rolled her onto the tiles, vaulted out again, knelt beside her, and tilted her head to clear her airway.

When he put his mouth to hers he got a mouthful of chlorine-and blood-flavoured water. Her chest was stiff. Water bubbled out of her each time William depressed her ribs. It came from her mouth, and through his fingers, with more blood. She'd been stabbed.

There was a squeak from the fence. William looked up and saw the girl pushing her face between the bars, her eyes stretched as she tried to worm through, her mouth pulled wide and lipless.

'Don't do that,' William said—and the girl abruptly collapsed, her arms hanging. Her head was wedged so tightly between the bars that even her dead weight didn't drag her free. She lapsed into blank stillness and then—after a moment—stopped breathing.

William came back to life himself. He pulled her free from the fence and carried her into the house. He found a phone and dialled the emergency number—and had just enough presence of mind to remember the New Zealand one. He put the phone down to start compressions, counted five, blew into her mouth, then snatched up the receiver and put it to his ear.

The phone was dead.

Six, seven, eight, nine, ten. Another breath. Eleven, twelve, thirteen, fourteen. 'This child is dead,' William thought. Then, 'But how can I be sure this child is dead?'

He raised his head and shouted for help, and listened to the sizzling silence of the house and neighbourhood. He tried to make some sense of what was before him. Then he made himself lift his hands from the girl's body. For a moment he just sat on his heels, holding his hands above his head, surrendering.

A minute went by. William pressed an ear to the child's chest. He heard and felt nothing.

He fetched a throw rug from a couch in the living room and covered her body, but not her face. He tucked the rug up around her ears and smoothed back her wet hair. Then he turned his back on her and just sat for a time and let a tide of feelings—to which he had believed he'd taught himself immunity—flow into him, and flood his reason. He remembered his cousins, on the porch, lying in auras of bare boards where their pyjama-clad bodies had melted that night's light dusting of snow.

William remained motionless and slowly grappled his competent adult self back into him again. Once he'd stopped shaking he got up, found a drinking glass, filled it from the tap, and rinsed his mouth. He put the glass into the ice-maker in the refrigerator door and filled it with crushed ice.

Then he went to retrieve his jacket and boots—and arm himself.

In the garage he found a long-handled axe. He left the property with the axe and the ice-filled glass. He got into his car, locked its doors and spent the next few minutes treating his lip by swilling the crushed ice in his mouth. While he did this he kept checking his mirrors, and out the windscreen. But nothing appeared, no one threatened.

William started his engine and drove back the way he'd come. He went by quiet streets and saw only two people. The first was a man in a upstairs window, rubbing his face and hands against the glass and smearing it with blood. William slowed to watch this performance, but didn't stop to investigate.

He did stop when he saw the young woman leaning against

an imposing brick gatepost. She was wearing a short-sleeved white jacket over a long-sleeved T-shirt. There was a long bloody streak on the shirt and splashes on her fawn pants and white trainers. Her whole outfit was some kind of uniform. She was a nurse, or an orderly. The arched ironwork sign above the gate said Mary Whitaker Rest Home.

William let his window down. 'Hey,' he called.

She looked up, pushed off the gatepost and came towards him.

'That's close enough,' he warned. His wounded lip made his words sound mushy.

She stopped, and stared at him with a gloomy, hangdog look.

William felt around behind him for the axe, picked it up, and climbed out of the car. He didn't once take his eyes off her, and he kept the axe concealed behind his legs.

'Sam,' whispered the young woman. Then, 'Help.'

For a moment it sounded to William as if she was invoking some *Sam* and appealing to this Sam for help. It didn't sound like an introduction, followed by an appeal to him. Still, William introduced himself and asked, 'Are you hurt, Sam?'

Her eyes were dark—green or grey, William couldn't tell which, but it was an unusual colour, and they were beautiful. Beautiful hazy eyes, in a beautiful, secretive, timid face.

'It's bandaged already,' said Sam, touching the patch of blood on her shirt.

William took a step closer. Sam smelled of smoke, and burned bacon, and cheap perfume. He got so close he imagined he could feel heat coming off her body, and that she was warm like she'd just woken up. Her eyes were dark grey; the green was only a reflection of the spring growth on the oak above her head.

He took hold of her chin. 'Sam, is there anyone alive up there in the rest home?'

'No,' Sam said. Then she frowned, reproachful. 'You

shouldn't take advantage of someone just because they're slow.' It sounded like something she'd been taught to say.

'I'm just checking on you. Starting with your injury.' William lifted her shirt and camisole and looked at the bandage. 'You look drugged. And I don't know that this isn't drugs. Or—say—ergot poisoning, from fermented artisan bread.' William quoted Kahukura Spa's exhaustively descriptive menu. But he wasn't really thinking about the spa's bread, he was remembering a film, *The Devils*, in which the inhabitants of an abbey were driven mad by ergot poisoning, so that the abbess and nuns first *saw* demons, then seemed to turn into them. He was only making knowledgeable, explanatory noises to soothe Sam, but really, now that he'd mentioned it, ergot poisoning wasn't a bad call.

'You'd better come with me,' he said.

'Yes.' Sam sounded fervent and grateful.

William tossed his axe into the back seat, got in the car, and leaned over to open the passenger door. Sam hurried to join him. She climbed in and put on her seatbelt.

William put his foot down and they sped away, out of the quiet streets to the bypass, then on towards Matarau Point.

'I won't be able to leave Kahukura for very long,' Sam said.

'You just said that everyone at the rest home was dead.'

Sam disregarded this. 'I never go away overnight.'

A minute later the Mercedes screeched to a halt in front of a tangle of chain-link and a tumbled mess of bodies. William froze at the wheel, staring wide-eyed through the windscreen.

But Sam jumped out of the car and went straight to them, moving from person to person, touching them tenderly and calling their names, sometimes formally, 'Mrs Harbin! Mr Young!', sometimes informally, 'Lorna! Audrey! Jim!' But she couldn't rouse any of them, and eventually she gave up, clapped her hands over her face and began to weep.

William watched as a young woman with a blond ponytail floated swiftly down the road and threw her arms around Sam. He recognised the runner from earlier in the day. He touched the axe on his back seat, but didn't take hold of it. Empty-handed, he got out of his car.

The runner said her name was Lily Kaye. She said she'd been there for over an hour. No one had come. 'Not from Kahukura till you. And not from Nelson.' She gestured at the tangle of bodies in the chain-link. 'I wasn't able to leave them. They were alive.' She began to cry. 'They kept trying to hurt each other. And there was one woman who I think was trying to tell me something.'

Lily and Sam were sobbing now in concert. William was wishing one of them would stop and supply him with more information. He really must try to be patient. His own fear was making him pitiless—and paltry.

Lily said, 'She was wearing face powder. Makeup is a sign of self-respect, right? So how does a clean, well-groomed old lady end up like that?' Lily peered intently into William's face, her expression desperate. 'None of them came back to themselves. They kept dying, one by one. And about an hour after I found them, the few surviving simultaneously heaved in a breath, and held it. Then the air went out of them, and they died. It was horrible. And so *strange*.'

William thought of the girl he'd tried to save; how she had just *stopped*. 'Look. It's possible no one has come because the settlement is locked in some kind of quarantine.'

'I thought of that. Of nerve gas.' Lily let go of Sam, who went back to the tangled bodies and began straightening clothes and wiping faces.

William said, 'I'm going to walk out. Whoever stops me, even if they can't help, might be able to explain.' He clasped Lily's arm, 'I won't be long. Look after Sam.'

Lily seemed glad to be given something to do.

William strode off, purposeful, around the last bend

before the crest of the cutting.

He got out of sight of the women and almost within sight of the road he'd meant to take. The air was fresher. It had all the expected smells, of the sea, flax bushes, and the cold water perfume of native forest. But there was something else as well, something astringent and clean.

And then, the next thing William knew he was soaked through and shivering hard. His bones ached with cold. Someone behind him was saying, 'You'll have to drive; I never learned how.'

Light flickered, then the world came up around him the way water does when you jump into it. He *had* jumped into a swimming pool. He'd been damp, but was now drenched. There was very little light. Someone beside him said, 'I suppose you have to run the engine to make the heater work. How does this fancy car start? I haven't driven one before.'

William began to shiver, big convulsive shudders. Then whoever it was beside him found the headlights. A wet road appeared, rain in black air, and a tangled mass of bodies lying on a length of chain-link fence.

William collected himself enough to show Lily how to start the Mercedes engine, and the heater. She turned the car and drove slowly back towards Kahukura.

William asked what had happened. His voice was hoarse, as if he'd spent the last few hours shouting his head off.

Lily showed him a rip in the elbow of her top. She had a graze; stripped epidermis pinpricked by exposed capillaries, glazed with a clear lacquer of lymph. She said, 'When you'd been gone for nearly an hour we went to find you. We came around the bend and you were lying in the middle of the road. I rushed to rescue you. Sam was close behind me. She said "something's wrong" and "stop" and "it shouldn't smell like this"—but I wasn't listening to her. When I fell over she tackled my ankle and pulled me out straight away. But it took us ages to get you out.' Lily glanced at him and must have seen scepticism. 'I did think at first that I'd fainted from low blood sugar,' she said. 'But it didn't feel like a faint. And there was a weird smell.'

'There's something stopping us leaving?'

'A kind of no-go zone. It makes you pass out. I did try twice to be sure. The second time I was crawling, so I just slumped.'

There were house lights here and there in the settlement and the streetlights had come on.

'Where am I going?' Lily said, as one more corner brought them to the intersection of Bypass, Haven, Beach, and Peninsula roads. The Mercedes headlights showed them two bodies lying on the intersection, both with diluted blood puddled under them.

'I live along there,' Sam said—and William had to tear his eyes away from the bodies to look where she was pointing.

'Isn't Peninsula Road a dead end?' Lily said.

'You mean we'll be trapped?' William and Lily stared at each other, considering their options.

From the back seat, Sam said in a musing tone, 'It got dark.'

'Didn't you notice it getting dark?' Lily asked.

'I'm always home at this hour,' Sam said. 'I never work the night shift. I'm not licensed for it.'

'Sam?' William said. 'We need directions.'

That brought her back to herself. 'My bach is number 37. Three from the end.'

'"Bach" is Kiwi for beach house. That's what it says in my *Lonely Planet*,' William said.

Lily turned onto Peninsula Road and drove slowly along it, peering out over the hood so she'd see any bodies before they went under her front wheels.

'Guidebooks are so useful,' William went on, 'though they could have included a bit more on local epidemics of madness and murder.'

'I don't know how you two can make jokes,' Lily said. 'People are dead, and it's horrible.'

'Was I making jokes?' Sam asked.

'Grappa,' said Lily.

'Grappa,' Sam echoed, sounding more puzzled than chastened.

Their headlights turned the kowhai at the gate of number 37 into a beacon of yellow. William reached out and switched them off. He and Lily sat still, watching the dark house, but Sam jumped out and hurried through the gate. She fished a key out from under a pot plant and unlocked the ranchslider. She turned on the light and stood waiting for them.

Lily said, 'You know, despite being slow, that girl has plenty of practical savvy.'

'She kept her head?'

'Yes,' Lily said, then changed her mind. 'Except that, when things were at their scariest, she started talking about herself in the third person.'

'Like how?' said William.

'She referred to herself as Sam.'

'She does that.'

Lily swivelled in her seat to face him fully. 'The no-go zone was so strange that I kept shoving Sam's weirdness to the back of my mind. But, look, when she stopped seeing to the old people and came to wait with me—she was a mess. Hiccupping from too much crying. *Not at all* the type to take charge.'

William shook his head.

'No. Listen. We went to look for you and found you lying on the road. I rushed in and passed out. Sam pulled me out, but then she's all snotty and weepy and hopeless. She keeps wringing her hands and saying she has to *do* something. I said that we needed some kind of grapnel. She goes, "What's that?" And I say, "You know, like in the movies, when they have a hook on a rope for climbing walls?" And then—get this—she says: "Would the supermarket have one?"'

William laughed.

'So I decide she's a bit limited and figure I'm pretty much on my own. I couldn't tell whether you were still alive. Your eyes were partly open, and drying out by the look of them. I was wracking my brain. That was when Sam began acting really strange. She got a paper and pencil out of one of her pockets and started writing furiously. She was holding her pencil the way clumsy kids at my primary school used to. You know? Making holes in the paper. She finished her note, and covered the paper with one hand, then put her other hand on the big patch of blood on her shirt—like someone taking a pledge. She was pressing really hard. She went dead white and fresh blood oozed through. By that time I was yelling at her, then I lost the plot for a bit because I got another whiff of that weird smell. It's a little like medical-grade alcohol. When I started paying attention again I see she's dropped the note. She's wiping her nose, and looking at the blood and snot as if she hasn't noticed it before. Her expression was so strange, William—displeased, and really cold.

'Then she spots her note, and picks it up. She reads it, screws it into a ball, and throws it at you. It bounced off your cheek. I guess she was trying to check if you were alive. You looked awful. Your skin had gone kind of yellow.'

'How do I look now?'

'Terrible.'

Sam loomed out of the dark again. She tapped on the driver's window. Lily jumped, then collected herself and made a 'give us five' sign. Sam didn't go back up the path, only hovered by the car, looking chastened.

Lily turned back to William and went on in a whisper. 'She took charge, found a tow rope in the kit in your trunk and made a big knot in one end. She said something like, "Apparently we need a grappa. I could sure do with a drink about now, but I guess what she meant was a grapnel.'"

'*She* who?' said William.

'Exactly.'

William frowned at Lily.

'That expression better not be sceptical, mister. We saved you. And, you know, trying to do that wasn't a done deal. Sam wondered whether you were dead—like she was going to give up. But then it started raining, and a raindrop plopped into one of your eyes, and your eyelid twitched. We kept throwing the rope and shaking it to make a loop around your foot. It took forever. Whenever something wasn't working Sam would change tactics. I just did what she told me to.

'And look at her now.' Lily jerked her head at the patient, abject figure by the car.

'She's odd. Practical with problems, but paralysed when she interacts with other people. One of *those* people.'

'Maybe. Or maybe she only got a small dose of whatever it is that drove everyone else mad.'

'I promise I'll keep a close eye on her. But we should go in now.'

They got out of the car. Sam looked relieved. She hurried ahead of them up the higgledy-piggledy paving path. Her outdoor light switched itself on. William came up behind her and found its switch. He shut it off. 'We should show no lights,' he told them. He drew them indoors—then locked the door.

Sam Waite was the only one of the survivors in Kahukura during the deadly moment—the moment when everyone went completely and comprehensively insane. Sam went insane too. Then she went away. When she came back she found herself sitting at the big pine table in the kitchen of Mary Whitaker Rest Home, her place of employment. The windows of the long room were all open. There was a film of smoke at the ceiling, and the fluorescent lights were wrapped in its pale grey gauze. The extractor fan above the range was switched on and running full. The cook's big paella pan had been removed from the heat and was on the stainless steel bench, smoking and sizzling. The kitchen stank of charred meat, a sweetish meatiness, like honey-cured bacon.

There was a broom leaning against the table beside Sam, and on the tabletop were two of the ceiling-mounted smoke alarms; both were smashed. Also on the table were two packages from the first-aid trolley. One was a dressing, and the other a sterile wipe.

And there was a note.

The paper lay under Sam's right hand. The sleeve above that hand was thickly soaked with blood. Sam's chest and left shoulder were in pain—a fiery, pulling ache. Her scrubs were daubed with blood, and her T-shirt wet with it all the way to the hem.

Sam touched her chest. The ache became fierce and focused. She gasped and called out—to Angie, the registered nurse. Then she shouted for her fellow caregivers. No one answered. The cook should have been in the kitchen. The kitchen clock said that it was almost lunchtime.

The note was one sheet, folded in the usual way, in half, all its edges meeting with mathematical neatness. As Sam read, her lips moved.

I think you must be injured. Don't look at your wound. Try disinfecting and dressing it without looking at it. You can get someone else to change the dressing for you later. Don't go in the dayroom. Go down to the road and find help.

I'm not coming out again.

What have you done?

Don't, don't, don't—that was all the other one ever had to say.

Sam crumpled the note and jumped up. Her chest exploded with pain. She steadied herself against the table, then gingerly lifted her shirt. She saw that her cotton camisole was rucked up under her armpits, and her breasts were bare. Sam looked, as she had been advised not to. She saw a raw, hacked-at patch of flesh.

Sam fainted and, as she went down, her chin hit the edge of the table. The pain of the blow revived her, and she caught herself on her hands and knees. She stayed on all fours for a time, sobbing with fear. Then, for lack of anything else to do, she followed her instructions. She knew she could have faith in that note. The other one was always better at emergencies. The other one had a cool head.

Sam groped along the table top till she located the sterile wipe. She opened the packet, lifted her shirt, and held its hem with her chin while she dabbed at the meaty patch. She opened the dressing with her teeth and fastened its tapes to the smooth skin around the wound. Then she carefully rolled down her camisole, hoping it would help hold the bandage in place.

Sam decided to disobey the note. She couldn't bring herself to leave the building without checking on its residents. It was her job to look after them. If she was softer than the other one, at least *she* appreciated the responsibilities of having a job.

She climbed to her feet and hurried out of the kitchen. As she went past the paella pan she glanced into it. At first she thought she was looking at some kind of fried dough tartlets, left on too long and burned black at their edges. But her nose was telling her that the tartlets were meat. Then she saw that what the pan held was a dozen or so charred human nipples. Large doughy female nipples with spreading aureoles, and wizened male nipples. One scrap was neat and taut—and Sam could see that it had belonged to someone young.

She was on the floor again, retching. She let her body finish. Vomit had soaked her trousers. She climbed to her feet and left the kitchen.

This close to lunchtime the dayroom was usually full of people. It was almost empty. The few residents were slumped in their chairs, their clothes pulled about, and their laps full of blood.

Sam stumbled in, trampling the blood-soaked apron that was on the floor, a pair of kitchen scissors nesting in its folds. She checked the old people for signs of life, but none had a pulse.

Sam tried to go away then. She waited to feel what she always felt when things became too much for her: deep lassitude, a feeling like mild exposure, then nothing— nothing till there was something tolerable, like her warm bed in the bach on Matarau Point.

But nothing happened. She was still here. It was still now.

Sam looked about her. The TV was all static. That was the sole noise, and it served only to fatten the silence.

The fourteen found one another. They formed little groups and sought shelter. They hid, and shivered, and hugged themselves.

The light failed, and birds were falling out of the sky. But this wasn't a movie. There was no subharmonic rumble of cataclysm.

We have experiences that push us out of the flow of time. We react as if the worst hasn't already happened. We are creatures who learn, and something we learn is to fear for what we love. After the worst has happened our fears are retrospective. We keep trying to warn ourselves. Our now useless fears come and fly around our heads. They circle us, crying. The island they might have landed on, to roost, has vanished beneath the waves. What are our fears? They're the only birds left in the air. The birds of drowned nests.

Theresa sat in the cramped shelter of the *Champion*'s cabin, trying to control cascades of trembling, and watching Bub. It seemed he'd found a way to steady himself. He was going to feed people. He set up a Primus on the deck, scaled, gutted, and filleted a fish, and put several mugs on the cabin roof to catch the rain. 'I'll fill the billy and make a brew too.'

Theresa said, 'Can you give me something to do?'

Bub had her hold up a tarpaulin over the frying pan while he cooked. The tarpaulin kept the rain off, but smoke gathered under it and set them coughing. As Bub shook his pan over the burner, he told Curtis where he kept his first-aid kit, and got Curtis to disinfect the scratches on Theresa's neck and face.

Curtis had refused to leave Adele's body behind in his car. When they crammed into the shelter of the cabin to eat, they were sitting with their toes pressed against the blanket-wrapped bundle. Now and then Curtis would reach out to brush dropped flakes of fish from the blanket.

After they'd eaten, Theresa and Bub went to the bow to check the anchor and have a whispered consultation.

'We'll need that blanket if it gets any colder,' Bub said.

Theresa shook her head. 'I'm not going to ask him for it. Look, we'll take turns keeping watch—you and me. Whoever is up can have your jacket and my gun. Mr Haines can make do with the tarp.'

'Fair enough,' said Bub.

Theresa radioed Belle, who took her time picking up. By the time she did, Theresa was tramping in small circles in the *Champion*'s stern, setting the boat into a mild rolling motion.

71

Belle said she'd shut herself in the reserve's storage shed. It was windowless, and there was no room to stretch out, but it was dry. She'd drifted off—she said—and didn't know where she was when the radio woke her. 'I've opened the door now. It was getting stuffy.'

Theresa explained that she was on Bub's boat, and said she'd be up to fetch Belle come morning. 'Just keep the gate locked.'

Belle promised, and then said, 'Why isn't there any sign of help?'

Theresa considered her response. She watched Bub, who was leaning over the side, rinsing his frying pan. He straightened, seawater dripping from his broad forearms and making a pool on the deck. The water was black in the radiance of the sharp white running light at the top of the short mast. Only the boat and a circle of choppy waves were visible. Beyond that there was nothing till the lamps, shining like safety among the sleek flaxes along the shoreline walkway. There were very few houselights—but of course none of them would have been on in the late morning when all this started. But as Theresa watched, a light shone, then went out, in the windows of a house on the point.

Bub came to stand beside her. 'There's someone over there.'

Theresa lifted the radio to her mouth and pressed the talk button.

'Listen,' said Bub.

Theresa released the button and strained her ears. She thought she heard a faint droning sound. It was very far away. She glanced at Bub and saw a spark of green in his dark eyes—a reflected light. She turned to where he was looking and saw the plane, or at least made out its shape from the port and starboard lights on its wingtips. She held her breath.

The droning stopped, and the lights winked out. A moment later, beyond the headland to the west, flames bloomed in the air—billowed out, and then retracted. For a few seconds the headland was sharply delineated by the fire's glow. Then—all at once—the fire went out, as if smothered by a great, invisible hand.

'They'd better not try that again,' Bub said. Then, 'That's our help.'

'That was pretty far off, I think.' Theresa hoped she sounded just as calm as he did. 'What was it? An Air Force Orion?'

'I reckon. Poor bastards.'

The radio crackled. 'Tre?' said Belle. 'What was that?'

'I think that—*thing*—I told you about has us completely cut off.'

'*You* got here,' said Belle.

Theresa said to her friend, 'I'm in the dark, Belle. But I'm coming to get you first thing tomorrow. Till then just stay put, and keep warm.'

'She's right, you know,' Bub said, once Theresa had signed off. 'You got in.'

'Perhaps I was the last,' she said. Then, 'I'll take the first watch.'

William prowled about the house for a time, before stretching out in the bach's only bed, beside Sam, but on top of the covers.

Sam didn't quite cry herself to sleep. She lay on her side, her back to William, and alternately wept and held her breath. William supposed that, in her silences, she was trying to suppress her tears, trying to get a hold of herself. He could feel her ferocious concentration, feel her summoning her strength. Or summoning *something*. 'Perhaps she's praying,' he thought, though he couldn't

73

hear words, or detect the little breaths and wet clicks of supplications only mouthed.

The rain stopped. Somewhere further along Matarau Point an outdoor security light activated. It illuminated the mature kowhai at Sam's gate. The kowhai's bright yellow blossoms were drenched, closed, hanging heavy in their sockets of bronze.

Sam stirred and rolled over, whimpering in pain. She sat up and pulled off her camisole, making small gasps and whines of distress.

'Be quiet, would you?' William hissed, and she froze. William watched the window. The sky beyond the glass was the warm grainy grey of streetlight reflected on low cloud. He thought he heard someone out on the road. Then the light switched itself off again.

William turned to regard Sam. Her head was free of her top, though her arms were not. Her lean form looked surprisingly strong, but at the same time abject and vulnerable, her shoulders folded forward and arms bound.

William pulled the top free. He looked at the blood-darkened bandage that entirely covered one of Sam's small breasts. There was a long streak of dried blood running from the bottom of the bandage onto her flat stomach.

'Lie back down,' William instructed. 'I'll see to that once it gets light.'

Sam lay down. 'I was told to have someone help me change the dressing,' she said.

She was told, so had injured herself *before* everyone went crazy. 'Were you already injured?' William asked.

'No.' Sam's voice came out as if wrung tight. 'I saw what I did,' she said. 'It was me.'

'You're not making any sense.'

'I don't have to. I'm not ever to try to.'

William frowned at the patchily lit blur of bare flesh that was the young woman beside him. 'You've had quite a few instructions, haven't you? I do hope you're not still getting them.'

'No,' she said, despairing.

Lily, for all her fright, simply slept. She'd run thirty miles and her body—attuned to its frequent crises of overexercise—seemed to decide that fear was just another crisis, like a hundred-kilometre race.

But her sleep wasn't dreamless. In Lily's dream it was an early autumn evening. She and her boyfriend were on their way to a dinner party, in Pukerua Bay, in one of the houses right on the beach. They were on the path that went along the top of the sea wall, which ran between the beach and the low breeze-block fences of the little houses. There'd been a storm three days before, and floods in the Manawatu and Horowhenua. The sea was still wild, frothy with river mud. The floods had stripped the fertile plains and carried the crops out to sea, before depositing them on shores further south. The beach was littered with carrots and onions, and dead sheep, stiff-legged like grisly piñata. In her dream Lily turned to her boyfriend to remark, 'Here's the makings of Irish stew.' Then she felt a pang of guilt for the poor people whose job it would be to bury all those bloated fleecy bodies—

Lily woke, and cried out in horror. She remembered what had happened, but didn't know where she was. There was a lumpy foam-chip cushion beneath her head. It smelled faintly of perished rubber. She fumbled about her for her phone. It was 4:30am.

Once there was enough light, William went to Sam's bathroom in search of a fresh dressing. They'd all managed to find the toilet in the dark the night before, and Sam had brushed her teeth. But now William was able to see that the bathroom was as clean and tidy as the kitchen. Sam had horrible stuff—William had woken up to find that the duvet cover he'd sweated under all night, through a medley of mad dreams and convulsions of panic that bounced him up into consciousness again and again, was a nasty pink polyester thing with swallows and roses. Sam's furnishings were vile, but everything in her house was scrupulously clean.

William pissed, washed his hands, and turned to the bathroom cabinet only to be confronted by the spectre of a prisoner, a haunted, hollow-eyed face behind black bars. He flinched—and the face did too, because of course it was his own reflection in the cabinet mirror. His bottom lip was swollen and scabbed from the mad child's bite. The prison bars were on the mirror. William touched its surface, and felt ridges. Black gaffer tape had been smoothed onto the glass in evenly-spaced, vertical strips, with the effect of forming bars over whatever was reflected there.

William opened the cabinet, found a dressing, closed it again, and regarded his face, sectioned by bars. He thought, 'Who—or *what*—is it Sam wants to keep imprisoned?'

When the rain let up, and the bush stopped dripping, Belle emerged from the storage shed and went down to the gates of the reserve. She stood, her forehead pressed to the wire, and listened. The little settlement was quiet; quieter than it had been when she'd come to work shortly after six the previous morning. Then there'd been the odd car, and all the scarcely discernible noises from indoors, a sound made of boiling jugs in kitchens where the mothers of small children were perhaps already assembling bigger children's school lunches while the two-year-old sat in pyjamas in front of a softly chattering television. Belle thought of the cumulative whisper of all that, of sleeping people, and morning showers, and cats plucking at the blankets near their owners' heads, wanting breakfast.

This morning Kahukura was as awfully still as a cooling baby in a cold crib.

Belle unlocked the gate and went out into the clearing to get a better look at the town. The streetlights were still on. As she watched, Belle saw a new light come on in one of the streets near the garden centre. Before it went off, another illuminated. They were outdoor security lamps, a relay that showed someone present in the silence, someone walking in the twilight across other people's properties. Belle heard a dog rouse to challenge the presence with frenzied barking. It continued to bark long after the last light had gone off.

PART TWO

When the sun came up, Bub started the *Champion's* engines, and a number of survivors emerged from hiding, rallied by the sound of the trawler's throttled-down gargling.

Three people came from the bach on Matarau Point, where the light of a carried candle had shown briefly in the night. A man, armed with an axe, was followed by two slight young women, one wearing a thick bandage around her otherwise bare chest.

Bub raised anchor and slowly motored in to the pier. The small group made its way around the shore and waited there.

Theresa stood in the *Champion's* bow, one hand on the blistered rail. The reflective checkerboard pattern of her hi-vis jacket caught the light. In her unspectacular police livery Theresa looked like help, and one of the women— the skinny blonde in running gear—began to wave, with the businesslike jubilation of someone greeting a rescue helicopter.

A car pulled onto Beach Road, and the small group from the bach quickly rearranged themselves, the women moving to put the man, and his weapon, between them and the car.

A guy with a topknot—whom Bub picked as Samoan— got out and approached the group at the pier. He came slowly, holding his hands out before him, open and empty.

Bub cut the engines. The *Champion* coasted to a halt, wallowing in low, steep waves, about five metres from the pier. Bub examined the people, narrow-eyed. The axe-man's flash shirt and trousers were fouled with blood and his bottom lip was swollen and scabbed. He was coppery dark, and had pale eyes, like a malamute. He called out, 'You're not really help, are you?' He had an American accent.

The Samoan said, 'Give her a chance.' He went and stood by one of the pier's bollards. 'Throw me a line.'

'Are you all okay?' Theresa called.

'Well, I'm not crazy,' he answered. 'And you'll notice I've turned my back on these others, because they seem to be fine too.'

Bub was tired of straining to hear what the people on shore were saying. There was room aboard for all of them, and he was prepared to put in and pick them up, if only that bowlegged gingery guy who was hanging back by the car would get all the way out from behind its open door—where Bub hoped he didn't have a gun concealed—and get over here with the rest of them.

Bub swung the wheel, pushed the throttle, and let the *Champion* glide forward. Then he gave the helm to Curtis, told him to hold her steady, and went forward to throw the line. He had to straddle the sailboarder's body to do so. The night before, they had shrouded the dead man in plastic, but had left him where he lay.

Bub's gaff was gone, so once the Samoan had the mooring line, he and Bub had to pull the boat in to the pier by main force. The hull's buffers ground up against the pier and Bub shouted, 'Get on board!'

There was no hesitation. The American very diplomatically left his axe behind. He jumped nimbly aboard. The Samoan then handed the women up onto the gunwale, and Bub helped them down onto the deck. The gingery guy slammed his car door and hurried over. All he'd been hiding were his trembling hands. The survivors balked a moment at the wrapped body, but stepped over it and made their way to the deck. Bub walked though them to the wheelhouse, nodded at the Samoan to cast off and watched the guy try to coil the rope—with good heart, but not a lot of skill. Bub backed the *Champion* out from shore, then cut her engines. It was quiet again. Or almost. The sounds of human activity had stirred up Kahukura's dogs. They raised their hoarse, exhausted voices again, to bark in rage, in hope, in warning; to call out for people who were *late, late, late*—who wouldn't come, who had gone and left dogs *alone, alone, alone* all night.

The Samoan dropped the rope and came to join them. He said, 'Warren and I left two people in a truck outside town. Dan and Oscar. Oscar's a kid. And—sorry—I'm Jacob.'

'How old is this Oscar?' said Theresa.

'About fifteen I guess. And there are two women in a car stuck up in the hills back there,' Jacob pointed. They could in fact see the small blue vehicle, but not the people in it.

The bandaged woman raised her pale, very pretty face and said, 'Was one of them an old lady?'

'Yes.'

'That might be Mrs McNeal. Her daughter was bringing her back yesterday. She was on the list for lunch.'

'Back to the rest home, Sam means,' William said. 'Sam works there. Sam Waite. I'm William Minute. And this is Lily Kaye.'

'Jacob Falafa, and this is Warren Kreutzer. We came in this morning to check on Warren's Aunt Winnie. She runs the bed and breakfast.' Jacob pointed at the villa one along from Sam's bach.

'I think she's dead,' Warren said, his voice soft and hollow.

'I'm Bub Lanagan,' said Bub. 'And this is Constable Grey.'

'Theresa,' said Theresa. 'And this is Curtis Haines.'

Jacob turned to Theresa. 'Is it over? Are they finished?'

'And is this it?' Lily said. 'I mean, are we it? Us, Dan and the kid, and the two women on the hill?'

'No, there's Theresa's friend Belle, too,' Bub said. He looked around the variously bleak, bruised, bloody faces.

'They can't all be dead,' said Jacob.

'The whole of Kahukura—as well as my aunt?' said Warren.

Lily began to tremble like a racehorse.

'How many are we talking about, anyway?' said William.

'I guess the daytime population is about five hundred,' Theresa said, looking at Bub for confirmation.

Bub didn't know. People had jobs. The people of Kahukura, and Ruby Bay, and Mapua. They got in their cars and drove into the city. He'd be out in Tasman Bay, fishing, then he'd come in and touch first one place then another—making his quick daily landfalls. And sometimes he'd think about the rest of them, commuters, regular folk, earthbound, going out wide on the roads, surrounded always by places people lived, like little birds that live in gardens, not like him, on his boat, out over the water, like a gull or a gannet. So, when Theresa looked at him, Bub just shook his head.

Theresa's face suddenly crumpled and she began to sob. She made a start for the water as if she meant to jump in and swim to shore. Bub was appalled and paralysed; it must be his fault. But the American had quick reflexes. He intercepted her. Curtis then took hold of her more gently. 'What is it?'

'There's an Area School,' Theresa said, sobbing. 'I didn't think of it yesterday. It has a roll of about thirty. I forgot them!'

'You'll have to go later,' Bub said. 'First we have to get your friend Belle, and the other survivors we know about.'

Jacob upturned Bub's empty bait box and sat Lily down on it. She was shaking hard, and her teeth were chattering. Next, Jacob tried to take Sam's hand and lead her to the shelter of the cabin, where there were seats. It was then he noticed the blanket-wrapped bundle—Adele Haines's body—and stopped, aghast.

Theresa roughly wiped her eyes. She pulled herself together. 'Look, she said, 'I know I'm not really better

84

qualified than anyone else to take charge—'

'You have a gun,' said William.

She only glanced at him, then went on. 'But Bub is right. We need to make plans. Plans based on what we know for sure. And what we know is this: we are trapped here, for the time being.'

'Quarantined,' said William. 'Shut in with whatever turned the town murderous.'

Theresa kept her cool. She just raised a hand and made gentle hushing motions at William. 'We have to think about what we can do to make ourselves safe.'

'Safe where?' said William. The man wasn't about to be silenced, Bub saw.

'Why can't we just stay here?' Warren said.

'*Champion* is too small for all of us,' Bub said. 'Plus she's too exposed to the weather. The crazies are terrifying, but a cold southerly will kill you just as dead.' He looked into their faces again and regretted talking about killing. Tears were coursing down Lily's cheeks, and Warren looked like he was about to throw up, though Bub doubted the man had anything in his stomach.

In the pause Sam said, almost inaudibly, as if speaking only to herself, 'I should be writing this down.'

Bub gave himself a moment. He went up to the bow to toss out his anchor. The tide had turned again. The *Champion* would swing bow on to the swell once she was moored, then they'd all feel a little more comfortable. Bub could tolerate the rolling, but he was positive the others would get motion sickness. Who needed that misery on top of everything else?

When he rejoined them Theresa said, 'Lets not get tied up just yet with explanations. Right now there isn't much point in speculating about how many are dead, or what killed them. Or the—thing.'

'Lily's named it the No-Go,' William said.

Bub thought it was good to have a name for the thing. He'd started to feel that the indispensable word 'thing' was being spoiled for all its normal uses. No-Go was like Never Never—odd, and descriptive. Last night, when he'd been on watch, he'd tried 'anaesthetic zone' and 'inertial field' in his head. Science fiction terms. They'd felt wrong—slippery, and *used*.

'We have to gather the others,' Theresa was saying. 'I'll get Belle to take her quad bike up through the scrub to the subdivision and help the old lady down.' She touched Sam's arm. 'You know this Mrs McNeal. Can I get you to go with Belle and help reassure her?'

Sam nodded.

Jacob said, 'What's under the bandage, Sam?'

'Never mind me. Let's just go get Mrs McNeal,' Sam said.

William said, 'She's being a stoic. It'll need sutures.'

'I'm a nurse', Jacob said, like a punchline, and gave them all a brief sunny grin. Then he blinked and his smile faded. Bub caught Theresa's eye and saw her look of immense relief. *A nurse.* She said, 'Jacob, would you go with Sam and Belle? I think retrieving Mrs McNeal might be a bit of a challenge.'

'Sure.'

Theresa turned to Warren. 'Will you go with me to get Dan and Oscar?'

Warren's eyes looked black in his pale face, but he nodded.

'Join us *where*?' said William. 'I have a count of thirteen. We'll need space.'

'Fourteen,' Bub said. 'There was a guy who helped me put out a fire yesterday, then took off. So—fourteen we know of.'

'I was staying at the spa,' William said. 'It was only half full, and my party checked out when I did.'

'Were they in the helicopter?' Theresa asked.

William nodded. 'Didn't they get away?'

'No. Sorry.'

William looked sober, but not cut-up. Bub guessed his 'party' weren't actual friends—as George had been Bub's friend.

'So, William?' Theresa recalled his attention to her. 'Can you be told what to do?'

He laughed. 'Not really.'

'How about you go check out the spa? Take Bub.'

'Sure.'

Theresa looked from face to face, her gaze firm and steadying. 'Are we all set?'

'What can I do?' Lily asked.

'Perhaps you can help me with my wife,' said Curtis. 'She's here on the boat. If no one comes in the next few days we'll have to bury Adele. I want to be able to choose a good place. And I want her with me till then.'

Lily looked scared, but said, 'Yes, of course.'

'Are we all ready?' Theresa repeated. Bub saw how she made sure to meet every eye. The survivors made signs of assent. They braced themselves.

'Bub and I will clear as many—' William hesitated, then got a haughty look and went on as if delicacy were contemptible, '—bodies as we can before you arrive.'

'Good.' Theresa told Bub to fire up his engine and take them in to shore.

Sam and Jacob parked the Captiva beside the unfinished visitor's centre, about a hundred metres from the predator-proof fence. A small woman in a Department of Conservation uniform was waiting at the gate of the reserve. 'Sam and Jacob,' she said. 'I'm Belle. Theresa called me to say you were on your way. Before we leave, I should quickly fill the hopper.'

'Okay,' Jacob said, not knowing what the hopper was.

'You can come with me if you like.'

They stepped inside the gate and Belle restored its padlock. Belle was a little pale, but she looked untouched. Jacob had only had brief glimpses of yesterday's mayhem. He may not have seen the worst of it—like Lily, William, Sam, and Theresa, all of whom had bloodstained clothes. But he had entered the No-Go, had felt it wipe the vitality out of every cell in his body, so he did have a feeling for the non-negotiable strangeness of the trouble they were in. Looking at Belle he could see that she hadn't quite got it yet. He didn't resent that. In fact Belle's businesslike ordinariness soothed him, and he was content to follow her up the track through the glistening bush. Sam obediently tagged along after them. They stopped at the shed and Belle picked up a bag of feed. Then they all went on up the hill. Before they'd gone far Belle stopped them and said, 'Shhh,' and, after a moment, Jacob saw the hunched green shape of a kakapo.

The bird stood on the trail ahead of them, peering at the ground. It was large, rounded, big-headed, and its feathers were several shades of green, some dulcet, some vivid, and some tipped black, as if they'd been flocked with black velvet. The kakapo stretched out a claw to pick up a twig and move it from his path. Then, path cleared, he moved on—still stooped and peering.

Belle whispered, 'That's Tutira. He's very stealthy. He hates to make any noise when he's walking.'

They waited till the bird had passed out of sight, then went on to a sunny clearing dusted with tobacco-brown beech leaves. A plastic hopper stood in the centre of the clearing, above a timber feeding trough. There was another kakapo perched on the hopper, dozing in the sun. This one was even bigger, and had a venerable halo of whiskers, like an Amish patriarch.

'This is the All-Father,' Belle said. 'He's fathered fifty chicks and he's so old we don't even know how old he is.'

Belle ripped open a bag of feed and the All-Father woke up. He partly opened his wide green wings and dropped down onto the lip of the trough. He landed clumsily, but not hard, his weight incommensurate with his bulk. He sidled back and forth along the trough as Belle lifted the hopper's lid and shook the feed into it. Now and then the bird opened his hooked beak and nipped Belle's vest. 'Watch it,' Belle said to him. The kakapo made a few deep rattling remarks in reply, then put his whiskery face down into the pellets. Belle rested one hand lightly on his back for a moment. Jacob would have liked to do that too; the bird's feathers looked thick, springy, and alive.

They went back down the hill. Belle returned the sack of feed to the shed.

'Have you got plenty?' Jacob asked as she was locking up.

'Yes. Why?'

Jacob didn't answer, but she read his expression. 'Are we really stuck?'

'I don't know. But if anyone could come in they would have by now.'

'We're not supposed to think too far ahead,' Sam said. 'We're only supposed to help Mrs McNeal and her daughter.'

Belle straddled her quad bike. 'Who wants to ride and who wants to follow?'

There was a way up through the meadow and along one edge of the old arboretum, the collection of exotic trees planted by Richard Stanislaw, a nineteenth-century runholder whose twelve-bedroom homestead formed the core of the spa. There were times when the going was steep, especially on the trip back down, when Jacob and Sam waded through ferns while holding Kate steady on the back of the bike. Kate rode side-saddle—the only position her hips could manage. Holly scrambled after them. Holly was near collapse when they finally reached the spa in the early afternoon—scratched, bleeding, trembling with exhaustion, less from the walk than the effort of suppressing her anxiety since noon the day before. Jacob carried Kate into the spa past the sheeted shapes that lay in a row on its terrace. He put her down in one of the armchairs in the double-height glass atrium.

When William and Bub arrived at the spa they went from room to room checking for signs of life. They found three yellowed, pitted corpses in the greasy-walled sauna. And two more in one of the treatment rooms, one whose head was a pomander pierced by a dozen scissors and nail files, the other with her face encased in plastic wrap—its box still clutched in her cyanotic hands. They found the manager in his office, dead on his feet, with the top of his smashed skull pressed into a bull's-eye of blood on his office wall.

It was in the manager's office that William picked up a ruled pad and began to make notes. He wrote down where each victim was found, how he thought they'd died, and who they were—easy in the case of the staff, who were wearing name tags.

Bub asked William, 'How can you be so clinical?' And William replied that this wasn't his first dwelling full of dead people.

After they'd been at the Spa about forty minutes, Warren turned up with Dan and Oscar.

As soon as they came into the lobby Dan spotted the smears of blood on the floor. He grabbed Oscar and turned the boy towards him. Dan was a dad himself—though of younger children—and it was his instinct to press Oscar's face into his chest, to enfold and blind him. But Oscar was so tall that Dan was only able to set his hands against the boy's temples. He made blinkers. 'Don't look,' he said.

Oscar stayed obediently still, eyes wide and nostrils flaring.

William came out of the manager's office. 'The Business Centre is uncontaminated.' He pointed the way.

Dan was impressed and rather reassured by the man's use of 'uncontaminated'. It made him sound like he'd found himself in similar situations before—crime scenes perhaps, Dan thought. Warren had talked about a police officer. But the police officer was a woman and not an American, Dan recalled.

'The business centre is open for business,' Oscar said, still wide-eyed.

Dan marched Oscar into the room and told him to stay put.

Oscar was still there hours later when someone finally remembered him and sent Holly to find him. She found him sitting staring at one of the computers and its error message—'Server not found'—like, Holly said later, a cat waiting at a mouse hole. She introduced herself, and took the boy into the kitchen, where her mother was busy cutting onions and peeling potatoes for a stew they had underway.

Jacob climbed up onto the table in the conference room and prodded the swivelling halogens till their light converged on the tabletop. He got down and spread a duvet and sheet over the table's polished surface, then plugged in a desk lamp and set it on the table.

William helped Sam up, and eased her back against the sheet.

Jacob put on the plastic gloves he'd found in the spa's beauty salon, and began to pick at the tapes on the edge of Sam's bandage. Once he'd removed the last layer of gauze he winced at what he found underneath it. He lowered his head and peered till he felt the heat from the desk lamp on his scalp and smelled singed hair. He said, 'Oh—darling,' and studied Sam's face. Surely this real show of sympathy would give her the cue she needed to cry. 'How did it happen?'

'I did it with scissors, I think,' Sam said.

William said, 'She said to me that she'd been told to get someone to change the dressing for her. So I thought maybe it happened before everything else. I mean, when there was still someone to tell her what to do.'

Jacob frowned at William and shook his head. He was pretty sure William had just stopped Sam telling her own story in her own words. He asked, 'Did you do this to yourself before the Madness?'

'I don't remember doing it. And I think I did the same thing to other people.'

'I think she was mad,' William said.

'She's sane now, so let's leave it at that.' Jacob placed a square of cling film over the raw flesh and then put a packet of frozen peas on top of it. 'I searched the spa, and found only a weak local anaesthetic,' he explained. 'So the best I can do is numb the place by making it cold. You're going to have to be brave and hold very still. I have to join skin to skin for it to heal. It's going to be a rough job, honey, and I'm sorry. But a plastic surgeon will be able to fix it for you properly once we get out.'

Sam blinked at him. She held still, breathing shallowly to minimise the movement of the icy packet on her chest.

'I'm not going to start till those pills I gave you kick in.'

William wanted to know what kind of pills Jacob had given her.

'Tramadol, and anti-inflammatories. I went through the guest's rooms. Tomorrow I'll search the pharmacy.'

'And how will you tell the difference,' William said, 'between everyday Sam and stoned Sam?'

'Don't be an arsehole.'

William shrugged. 'I wonder whether she's the only

exception to the Madness. Whether anyone else was crazy and came through it.'

'You mean, are there people still out there, hiding from us, and horrified at themselves?' He looked into Sam's hazy eyes. 'Why do you think you came through it, Sam?'

'I went away,' Sam said.

'You went unconscious?'

'Yes,' Sam said. 'I suppose I did that too.'

Jacob lifted the packet of peas and watched watery blood swimming under the plastic wrap. The sight of the wound made him want to weep with pity. 'Okay. I'm going to start,' he said. 'I want you to slide your arms up over your head, so that your hands are by your ears. I'm going to ask William to hold down your arms and shoulders and I don't want him standing in my light. Do you understand?'

'Yes,' Sam said, and followed his instructions.

Jacob told William to put his elbows on her shoulders and take hold of her wrists.

William bent over Sam and pressed her arms down. 'Look at me,' he told her. She did, her gaze fearful and fascinated.

Jacob adjusted the light. He picked up tweezers and a sewing needle. He pinched the edge of the wound closed.

Sam pulled a sharp breath through her nose. The muscles in her jaw rippled. Her eyes filled with tears and the tears spilled down into the hair at her temples.

The locks on the doors of the spa's bedrooms worked with swipe cards, and no one knew how to program the machine. But William found a card, in the pocket of a dead housekeeper, that seemed to open every door. He began opening them while Bub followed him to tape down the latches.

So far the only room in use was the one Curtis had commandeered to lay out his dead wife. William and Bub had secured that door first, working hurriedly, fumbling and hushed.

Some minutes later and several doors down, Bub was breaking off a length of tape while William kept his thumb on the steel wedge and the little light on the lock flashed at them angrily. In the middle of this fiddly task William said, 'I'm not normally intimidated by other people's grief.'

Bub didn't respond. He pressed the gaffer tape to the latch while William wriggled his thumb free. Bub smoothed the tape, and air crackled in its folds.

Two doors on, Bub began to feel William's silence. William was expecting a response. Bub bit his lip and stayed quiet, but the pressure eventually got to him. 'Do you mean you expect to feel *less* upset?'

'Nothing happened to me,' William said.

'You were covered in blood, man,' Bub said. 'So I'm guessing you either tried to stop someone from being killed, or to save someone badly injured. *I* had to throttle a guy. And then I found my friend George with his head in a deep fryer. You can't say "Nothing happened to me".'

'But I'm not feeling it.'

'You're in shock.'

'Are you?'

Bub thought about this. After a time he said, 'Well, I guess I must be.'

William shook his head, but didn't make any further remarks till they'd reached the end of the corridor and the door to the fire escape. Bub pushed it open and stepped outside. The night air was cool. He could hear barking. 'Tomorrow I'm going to round up those dogs,' he said.

William said, 'The dogs didn't go mad.'

'Neither did the seagulls. What's your point?'

'Nerve gas would affect animals too. And what else could have done this?'

Bub stepped back indoors and waited for William to

join him. William opened and closed the emergency exit several times to check it was working properly, then stood, his manicured fingers curled around the bar latch. 'We witnessed other people's mad behaviour, but we didn't go mad. Don't you want to know why?'

'Look,' Bub said. 'I respect that you're a thinker, but I'm going to go along with Theresa's recommendation that, rather than analysing all the data, we make ourselves safe and comfortable. She's right, you know. We should just batten down the hatches.'

William looked at Bub for a long moment, then said, 'Unbelievable,' and set off along the hallway.

Bub pursued him. For some reason he didn't want this guy to think badly of him. 'Do you want to be responsible?' he said. 'If Theresa calls the shots then *she's* responsible.'

William rounded on him, but at that moment, the lights went out.

Downstairs someone shrieked.

The blackness made the hallway seem stuffy. Bub's heart had split in two and was trying to bash its way out through his ears.

One of the women called out in a shaky voice, 'Has anyone got a lighter? There are candles on these tables.' Bub thought it sounded like the DOC worker, Belle. He'd last seen her sitting in the dining room.

After a moment the general blackness turned grainy, and William's shape reappeared, black, against it. Someone downstairs had switched on a flashlight. Its beam was swooping about crazily.

'That's your responsible constable,' William said.

William went towards the light, and Bub followed. They made their way back along the hallway past all the open doors. Bub collided with someone in the dark and yelped. It was Curtis, who had come out to see what was happening. 'Stay put,' Bub told him.

95

In the lobby Warren began shouting, demanding to know whether they were under attack. Theresa called for quiet. Bub and William reached the head of the stairs, and Theresa flung the beam of the torch up into their faces, dazzling them. But not before Bub had seen that her face was clenched with fear.

Curtis hadn't stayed put. He spoke from behind Bub. 'Constable Grey,' he said. 'Hold your light on the stairs and keep it steady.'

She did, and Curtis gave Bub a little push and said quietly, 'We should all go down and join her.'

Everyone had crowded into the reception area—everyone but Sam, who was still in the conference room, oblivious and asleep.

The candles in the dining room were all alight, and Belle was carrying one in a glass tumbler. Its light made her round-cheeked face look sweetly cherubic.

Theresa drew her gun and used her torch to push the front doors open. She went out onto the terrace. The others followed.

The whole settlement was dark. Far off, across Tasman Bay, the lights of the small settlement of Glenduan glimmered, watery silver, above the rim of the horizon.

'Maybe the officials have turned the power off,' Curtis said. 'I mean, whoever is in charge out there has decided that the No-Go is pulling power off the grid. That *that's* how it works.'

'Wouldn't they know if it was?' Theresa said. 'Couldn't they tell without leaving us in the dark?'

'They're probably desperate,' Bub said.

'And experimental,' William added.

Then Dan appeared carrying a bottle and shot glasses. He set them up in a row on the rail of the veranda, and filled them. He passed a glass to Bub. Its sides were wet with spilled liquor.

William took a glass. 'I can smell peat. That's a good one.'

'Laphroaig. Twelve years, it says,' said Dan.

'Booze and bravado,' said Holly.

'If it's *them* they'll soon realise cutting the power isn't going to making any difference,' Theresa said.

'How do you know it isn't?' That was Warren. He took a whisky, slugged it back, and ran down the steps to the Captiva. Jacob darted after him shouting, '*Sole*! Do you really want to go on your own?'

'I'll just go nose the car into it,' Warren said. 'And if it's down, I promise I'll come back to tell you.' With that, he drove off.

Behind Bub, William said, softly, 'I don't know that I would.'

Theresa told them she'd follow Warren. She too promised to come back for them. She took her patrol car.

They waited. Bub sipped his whisky. Belle came out and took a glass. She went down to the lawn and stood looking up, her hair almost phosphorescent in the starlight. It was so dark the Milky Way was visible, a long skein of shining fleece stretched across the sky.

Someone lit a cigarette. Someone else asked the boy, Oscar, if he was okay. He said he was and, a moment later, Bub heard a tinny whisper of music leaking from his ear buds. It was a homely sound, but one that, under these circumstances, Bub found somehow objectionable. He decided to join Belle. He stood as near to her as he could without being obtrusive, and turned his face up to the heavens too. The stars were bright and far away. They were the big picture. They were everything already over. They were pretty and apparently tickled, apparently laughing in the distortions of the atmosphere.

'Think big,' Bub said, and made a sweeping gesture at the stars.

'I'm thinking about my kakapo,' Belle said. 'They're

small. But sometimes small is big.'

Bub waited for her to go on.

'I should have gone with Tre,' she said. 'I'm her friend and she's got *all this* on her plate.'

Bub said he got that. He got that they were Theresa's kakapo.

Belle gave a little laugh. 'That's right.' Then, serious, 'I guess certain kinds of people become police officers. I never thought about it before, but at some point Tre must have made a decision to take things on, and be someone people turn to in emergencies.'

Bub saw that the two cars were already making their way back along Bypass Road, carving a green corridor in the blackness, lighting up the trees. They arrived together and Warren got out, came up the steps and, without a word, resumed drinking. Theresa followed Warren, looked at everyone, and simply shook her head.

Theresa convinced almost everyone to try to sleep. To find a room—they were all empty—and a bed. Jacob chose to sit with Sam, who hadn't stirred. William hunkered down at the head of the stairs, just behind Theresa, who'd posted herself there, on sentry duty. When she looked at him he said, 'I'm keeping you company,' then, overcome by a sense of mischief, 'Or maybe I just don't trust you to watch over me.'

'You're such a dick.'

William laughed.

After a little while Theresa said, 'Do you have any idea what things are going to be like for us without electricity?'

'So, now you're asking me to take a look at our situation and think things through?'

Theresa turned to him, studied his face. Then, 'Arsehole,' she said, disgusted.

'I'm trying to cheer you up,' William said. 'When the back wheels of this cataclysm roll over us, at least you'll be able to think that it got me too.'

'Why are you sitting here?' Theresa demanded.

'I can't sleep.'

She made a dubious sound.

'I bet you didn't sleep last night, Constable Grey.'

'I doubt any of us did.'

'Sam did. And Lily. Dan said Oscar did. Holly said Kate did.'

'I hate you,' Theresa said. There were tears in her voice. 'You've remembered everyone's names.'

William slid down a couple of steps and put his arms around her. She tried to shake him off, then finally submitted to being held.

'Let's make a deal,' he said. 'I'll follow your lead. I'll be useful. And, for a time, we'll see how that goes.'

Theresa was still. William could almost hear the cogs whirring in her head. Eventually she said, 'Are you saying that you'll *let* me be the leader?'

'That's right.'

Again she tried to shake him off—but, he noticed, not very hard for someone who must have been trained in how to get out of grips when grabbed. 'They wouldn't follow you!' she said. 'No one likes you!'

'People mightn't like me, but they're always trying to please me.'

Theresa shivered. She stayed still in his arms. He suggested she try to sleep. He told her to relax, rest her head on his shoulder. 'And we can present a united front to the open door.'

'It's open so I can see when the lights come on.'

'They'll come on in here too.'

'I want to see them come on out there, in Kahukura.'

'All right, Constable. But watched pots never boil. Close

your eyes. I'll stay awake and keep an eye out for all that stuff stories have made us expect—the blowing leaves, the lightning flashes, the shambling zombies.'

'Jesus you can talk,' Theresa said, and William thought he could detect some admiration in her exasperation. 'Are you some kind of writer?'

'I'm a lawyer. A trial lawyer.'

'Right—A. Arsehole, Attorney at Law,' Theresa said, then giggled.

Theresa's hair smelled of smoke, and perhaps it was this that suggested a memory to the drowsy William. A memory that melted into a dream.

From Los Angeles all the way up to Monterey the sky was stained, as if it had hung for twenty years in a bar filled with cigarette smoke, or for 300 in a church full of candles. The fire behind Big Sur was still burning, and the Pacific Highway was closed. William was on his way back home— San Francisco—and didn't want to take the detour inland to Paso Robles and the 101. Instead he followed the tour buses north to San Simeon, then went on past the colony of elephant seals, where the last few cars had stopped. After that he had the road to himself. He drove on between the sea and sudden hills with their aggregations of brown stone slopes, and tin beach shacks, and rusty remnants of small-scale coast industries—everything held together by white sage, its leaves damp and softened by sea mist. It was chilly on the coast, but as soon as William turned onto the last exit—the only way around the fire—it got hot. For every twenty feet he rose above the blue whey of water, it was another degree hotter. Nacimiento-Fergusson was open, but each time he came to a road leading into Ponderosa National Park, its entrance would be barred and locked, and posted with a sign saying, 'Be warned.'

It was fifty miles of narrow winding road. William's air-conditioning took care of him, but he did once touch the windscreen and snatched his hand back because it was burning hot. He went over the mountain, and came down a road so sunk in trees—live oaks and pines—that he had no views of the countryside. As the road dropped, the sunlight thinned, but didn't pale. Instead, the splashes of sun on the road grew gradually more brilliantly orange, till finally William pulled off into a rest area and stepped out into hot silence, tangerine sunlight, and air full of drifting white ash. It looked like some hellish afterlife.

Out again on the flat he had only to watch for the turn he must take. He couldn't tell from the map whether it was before or after Jolon. He kept thinking he was asleep. The country was all strange. There had been a back-burn, and one side of the road had foaming yellow grass and oaks in green, while the other was scorched and balding, the trees alive but dirtied with soot from below.

From the map he knew he was near Fort Liggett, and, in the burned fields, he saw shelters with gun slits, and a tank, stained by smoke but otherwise unperturbed. There was the road, and there were people's things—though they all looked left over. He was alone. He kept driving, and kept on being alone.

Finally he reached a checkpoint manned by state troopers and national guardsmen. They were all huddled in a deep gateway erected over the road, an aluminium frame hung with heavy sheets of clear plastic. William slowed at this gate, and let his window down. He drove through a curtain of icy air. There was another vehicle within the gate, the first he'd seen in an hour, a UPS van, facing the way he'd come. A trooper was writing down the details of the UPS driver's licence, and explaining something about looters, and Big Sur's three thousand empty houses.

William found his licence, and stepped out of the car.

The sky to the northwest was white and bruise brown. A guardsman beckoned him further into the glassy obscurity of the tent. 'Come in out of the heat, Sir,' he said. 'It's nice and cold in here.'

There was a phone ringing—the happy fanfare of the Nokia ringtone.

Theresa pulled out of William's arms so fast he almost tumbled down the stairs after her. It was dawn outside, and the lights were burning in the atrium. The power was back on.

Theresa paused only a moment indoors, then rushed out onto the veranda, following the sound of the phone. Her lips were pressed shut and William knew that, if she weren't listening so intently in order to find the phone, she might be sobbing with relief.

Lily arrived. Then Bub and Jacob. They all stood very still, only swivelling their heads to locate the sound. Lily had her own phone out and was peering at it, puzzled.

The phone continued to chime.

'It's been dropped out here somewhere,' Theresa said.

They began to search the grounds. Before long others joined them—everyone except Kate and Sam.

It was Belle who called an end to their search. She gave a shout—and they all rushed towards her before registering that her shout was one of despair. She was doubled over, as though someone had kicked her in the stomach. She was keening at the ground, then, as they joined her, she began to laugh too, wild and hysterical.

'Belle, be quiet,' Theresa said, because the phone was still ringing, and so close now. She began to search the ground near Belle's feet. 'We must be right on top of it,' she said. Then again, 'Shut up, Belle!'

Belle straightened and pointed. Up.

And there, over their heads, in the branches of the jacaranda, was a bird—a bird of a kind clearly familiar to everyone, though William hadn't seen one before. It was iridescent black, with a little bunched cravat of white on its throat; and it was gaily, flawlessly imitating the Nokia ring.

They all watched it awhile. No one disturbed it. No one threw a stone. No one said anything either. The gathered people simply drifted apart. They moved away from under the tree, some staggering, oblivious to one another.

There had been a phone call—they'd thought—someone looking for them, someone who'd tell them what to do. There'd been a reprieve, and now there was only the sun coming up over the ridge at the top of Stanislaw's Reserve, and a day to be got on with somehow.

After the Nokia ring tui had raised then dashed their hopes, Oscar, like the rest of the survivors, sat for several hours in shivering despondency. But eventually he felt hungry, and his legs were restless, and he decided to find something to eat.

Halfway through a packet of Mallowpuffs Oscar decided to deal with his feelings, as if his feelings were what he had to fear. He told himself that he'd felt like this before—not too long ago—and it had turned out all right.

In January of that year he'd first noticed he was being kept awake at night by a new sensation. It was as if there were a lump in his mattress, or something caught under the fitted sheet, like one of his mum's nylon knee-highs that had perhaps got mixed up in the washing and ended up in his bedding. He took his bed apart to look for whatever it was, but couldn't find anything. He lay back down—and the lump was still there. He ran his fingers down his back, then went to peer at himself over his own shoulder in the bathroom mirror. There was something beside his spinal

103

column—a patch of highlighted skin. A lump. He touched it. It was flat and firm, but not hard.

Oscar made his discovery on a Saturday and had to wait till Monday to see his doctor. His parents spoke reassuringly to him, but went around all Sunday with a strange stark look in their eyes.

Anyway—it turned out that the lump was a lipoma, and was made of fat, and the doctor said that although it might grow and need to be drained, it would almost certainly shrink and vanish. So—Oscar had had a sentence and a reprieve. He already knew what that felt like. He knew that just because things looked bad and you felt doomed it wasn't necessarily the case. And he remembered that, while he was waiting to see the doctor; he'd kept himself from going crazy by doing what he normally liked to do anyway, only with more intensity. He'd watched a whole season of *Lost*; played *Oblivion*, and *Bioshock*, and *Mass Effect*—nothing online because he didn't want to have to talk to anyone, even strangers. He had really gone into those games, had let them close over his head.

That was what he was going to do now—he was going to go back into the bright worlds, the dark worlds, and let the games carry him through this too.

Oscar slipped out the kitchen's delivery door and hurried off down the spa's driveway. No one seemed to notice him leaving. And they wouldn't miss him if he was quick.

Sam came awake, and struggled up, ready to fight or flee. Her first step was bigger than she anticipated; it took her off the tabletop and onto the floor. Several duvets tumbled after her.

The table she'd been lying on was long, highly polished rimu. The chairs pushed back to the walls of the room were those fancy black mesh ones. The sunshades were down, and the room was full of filtered sunlight.

There was no one in the room with her.

Sam touched her chest. A thick pad of fresh dressing covered one nipple, and a bandage was wound tight around her rib cage, keeping the dressing in place. Sam's top was bare, but she was still wearing uniform pants. She slipped her hands into their pockets and found a hair tie, a pencil, a limp stick of chewing gum, but no note.

Because she had to leave so many things to chance, Sam was constantly double-checking what she already knew. Yes, the dressing was on her left side, so the other one would still have full use of her right hand—her writing hand. There *should* be a note.

Sam listened. What she could hear she didn't like at all— the stifled weeping of a number of people, like the sound under the music at the end of a funeral service.

A woman appeared at the door. She was wearing khaki shorts and a green T-shirt. She had short blond curls and handsome, if incongruously dark, eyebrows. She was pale and tear-stained. She said, to someone beyond the door, 'Sam's awake.'

'You're not Lily,' Sam said.

'I'm Belle. Remember? Would you like me to fetch Lily?'

Sam shook her head. The pill bottles on the tabletop caught her eye. Codeine phosphate, tramadol, naprosyn. Painkillers and anti-inflammatories.

Taking her cue from the bottles, Sam hunched and folded her right arm across her chest. So, she'd been right, and had *seen* right, despite the smoke, and the smoke alarm shrieking in her ear. That taut little nipple in the paella pan had been—

Sam shook her head. 'No,' she said.

A man appeared behind Belle. An Islander with a topknot. He looked exhausted. He wheeled one of the chairs towards Sam, got her to sit, and knelt before her. 'We have a bed ready. Once you're lying down I'll give you some more painkillers and inspect your wound.'

'I can help you get her to her room, Jacob,' Belle said. 'And—oh—she was asking for Lily.'

'I wasn't.' Sam wondered how long she could postpone the moment when this man unwound the bandage on her chest. How much she could discover in the time she had.

The sound Sam had woken to had gone on, unabated. A sound of private lamentation, but without a funeral's solemn or uplifting music, or the bad guitar, ragged singing, and glassy chatter of a wake.

'Why are those people crying?' Sam asked.

'Don't bother yourself about that now.' Jacob helped her up. Belle draped a duvet around her—a flash one, of crackling cotton and thick down. It dropped onto Sam's shoulders and, at the same moment, she recognised the view through the gaps in the sun blinds. She was at Kahukura Spa.

Belle and Jacob put their arms around her and led her from the room.

In the atrium a guy with a shaved head was nursing a bottle of whisky—though judging by the sun it couldn't be later than eight in the morning. An old lady was sitting beside another woman with an expensively streaked blunt-cut bob. They were holding hands. The younger one was crying. The old lady looked drawn and remote.

They reached the foot of the stairs. Sam tried again. 'I was writing something. Where is it?'

'Were you? We don't know about that, darling,' Jacob said. 'I suppose you left it at the rest home.'

So they knew about Mary Whitaker. 'Have you been up there?' Sam asked.

'The rest home? No. Why?'

'Perhaps you should carry her, Jacob,' said Belle.

'I don't want to risk disturbing those sutures. I've only ever *watched* suturing, Belle, so they're not very professional.'

'Hospital can do it properly,' Sam said, and then she started to tremble. It was involuntary. She was a patient person. She was accustomed to the time it took to get on top of the situations in which she found herself, used to having to bat bits of information out of the air, as if she was a blind cat who'd fallen through the roof of an aviary full of startled and innocent birds. If Sam was at a disadvantage, other people were at a greater disadvantage, and she knew how to work that. But she wasn't making any progress. And back at Mary Whitaker it wasn't an aviary she'd fallen into, it was a slaughterhouse.

'Just one step at a time,' Jacob coaxed.

'Only a little further,' Belle added.

Their tenderness was ferocious. And Sam understood that she'd given them something to do—get her up the stairs and into bed—and they were grateful for it because it meant that, for a few minutes, they weren't with these others, the old lady and her daughter, and the man with the bottle.

She practised another question, silently, in her head. *'Does anyone know what happened?'* Then she asked it, hedging her bets by adding a modifier. 'Does anyone know yet what happened?'

Jacob said, 'Don't worry about that now.'

A moment later Sam was sitting up in bed, and Jacob was laying out bandages and scissors and surgical tape. Then he remembered the medications and hurried off downstairs. While he was out of the room another man looked in. A tall, well-built guy with black hair. His eyes were a clear tawny brown and made him look fierce and hyper-alert. Sam recognised him. It was William, of course. William, fully conscious and not helpless. Sam found herself blushing. She crossed her arms over her chest and said, 'Nice to see you up and about. Now how about you piss off?' She'd had enough of being examined, and of the draughts of mysterious misery. She couldn't get any traction with her questions. Why was she in a hotel room being patched up? Surely they weren't all still trapped?

When Jacob returned he found Belle standing at the bathroom door, alternately knocking and calling. She said to Jacob, 'William looked in, and Sam got all flustered and locked herself in.'

'Did you send him away?'

'He tried to coax her out, but she just kept saying "In a minute, in a minute." And Jacob—she took your roll of surgical tape.'

Jacob pressed his forehead against the door and spoke very gently. 'Come out, Sam. That dressing really needs to be changed.' He listened to the silence within, then added, 'It's okay. William's gone now.'

The door handle turned and Jacob stepped back. Sam emerged. She was trembling and there were beads of sweat on her top lip. 'It really hurts, Jacob.'

'I have the pain pills.' He told her to get back in bed, and asked Belle to get a glass of water. Belle went into the bathroom and emerged with the water, and Jacob's roll of surgical tape, and a very odd expression on her face.

Jacob gave Sam two codeine tablets. He sat down on her bed and held her hand till she began to look a little dopey. Then he changed her bandages. The wound site was a healthy colour, and wasn't weeping, and he was able to sound sincere when he told her she'd be feeling better soon.

Once Sam had drifted off, Belle took Jacob into the bathroom to show him what Sam had been doing with his surgical tape. They stood staring in incomprehension at the vertical strips of tape which were stuck on the mirror, till eventually, Jacob caught sight of his own perplexed face past the strips. It was only then that he saw that they represented the bars of a cage.

Belle said, 'What the hell is that supposed to mean?'

William caught up with Bub, who was heading into town on foot.

'Do you think it's safe for us to be out?'

'I've no idea. But some of those dogs we can hear are still on their leads, or shut indoors. I can't just listen. And, anyway, I'm not unarmed.' Bub hefted his jack handle.

The streets back from Haven Road and the waterfront hadn't been busy on the morning of the deadly day. They were clear of traffic, and Bub and William might have driven down them without encountering any obstructions. But there were a few cars run up onto the curb with their doors hanging open. One had crossed a lawn and demolished an elaborate ornamental dovecot. Its driver was face down in a flowerbed, almost hidden in a thick patch of blue match heads.

Bub regarded the body. 'It seems wrong to just leave him lying there.'

'Yes, but I guess the whole town is a crime scene.'

'That's one way of looking at it,' Bub said. Then, 'Have you finally started doing that? Looking at all this in ways that will just do for now?'

'I'm trying not to. I still think being practical and being thoughtful aren't mutually exclusive.'

'That's not what I'm saying—' Bub stopped and shook his head. 'Let's just get these dogs.'

They had some difficulty deciding which dog was nearest. There was one regular, hoarse bark, and another intermittent yipping. The sounds were equidistant and seemed to cancel each other out. Bub said, 'We could just go one way, and see which gets louder.'

It turned out that the yipping was coming from behind

the door of an internal garage. They circled the house, trying doors. Eventually William positioned a wheelie bin under a bathroom window, and Bub stood on its lid. He broke some louvres, and eased the broken panes out of their rubber seal. Then he boosted himself up and slid inside.

The yipping changed to snarling. The dog was approaching at a run. Bub scrambled back out the window. The wheelie bin toppled, and he fell into the shrubbery. The terrier launched itself upward to hang scrabbling on the sill, its eyes popping in its comical face.

Bub got to his feet, backed off and tried to speak to the dog to calm it.

William went to find something sturdier to stand on. He returned with a patio chair, set it under the window, and stepped back with a 'be my guest' gesture.

Bub climbed up onto the chair and spoke soothingly to the dog. Then he tried speaking roughly to it. It subsided, whining, and Bub ventured back through the window again. There was a second eruption, then a stifled yelping that moved through the house. William followed the noise. He met Bub at the back door. Bub had the terrier clamped under one arm, his big hand wrapped around its snout. He said, 'Could you go in and look for a lead?'

William found an extendible lead and a nylon muzzle, both hanging on the back of the laundry door. He brought the lead out and clipped it to the dog's collar. He showed the muzzle to Bub.

'Okay,' Bub said. 'Have you ever put one of those on a dog?'

'No. But this is a week of firsts for me.'

The dog seemed happier once she'd lost the option to bite—relieved of the burden of choice. Bub let the lead out, but she stayed pressed against his leg, quivering.

William went back into the house to see if there was any sign of the owners. But the doors had been locked, and there was no car in the garage.

As they were leaving, William paused at the gate. 'This is a house we know is empty. Perhaps I should leave some sign. To save time and trouble later.'

'Whose time and trouble?' said Bub.

'Whoever comes.' William hesitated, then ventured, 'Don't you think it's quieter today than it was last night?'

'It's been quiet since they all finished killing one another. Apart from the plane.'

'Shouldn't there have been more planes?'

Bub picked the terrier up. It wriggled and nuzzled him under his jaw. 'What are you trying to say?'

'I think the air feels kind of deadened. It's as if they—' William made a sweeping gesture at the hills '—are further away. As if the No-Go is getting thicker.'

Bub took a deep breath, let it out, and said, 'So, you want to make a mark to say "No bodies in this house". How about something simple, like a zero on the letterbox?'

William patted his pockets. He turned around and went back indoors. He found a marking pen in a mug by the phone, uncapped and tested it, making a black spot in the centre of his palm.

The fridge shivered into life.

William flinched. Then he lifted the phone and listened for a time to the urgent beeping of its out-of-order tone.

Bub had moved along to the next intersection and was standing with his hand around the terrier's muzzle to suppress even its whining. William used the marker to draw a zero on the letterbox.

The other bark was coming from a house somewhere beyond a fenced field. They set off that way. But when they reached the field they stopped, frozen. Bub's grip loosened, and the terrier leapt out of his arms. It took off, the plastic cartridge of its retractable lead skittering along behind it. The dog sprinted for a short distance, then doubled back to savage the cartridge—or to try to, though hampered by the muzzle. Bub bore down on the dog and swooped it up again.

William joined him and they stood in silence, staring at the three weatherboard classrooms and newer school hall and office buildings. William finally spoke. 'Let us just go and look,' he said.

Bub was thinking that *this* was the reality of their situation. He wished he'd thought to ask Theresa for her radio before he set off. He wanted to share this with her and see what she had to suggest. He'd been doing all right on his own so far this morning. Well—he was with William, but was on his own inasmuch as he was following his own agenda.

Setting out to see to the wellbeing of Kahukura's dogs was a small, reasonable, progressive task. He was going to locate them, collect them, and take them back to the spa and human company. He was going to feed and reassure them. He was going to make the dogs his business. But his task had taken him out into the town—to be confronted with a silent school building. He felt as if he was standing on the shore of a vast ocean of possible duties and responsibilities. He felt paralysed, but when William said, terse and somehow formal, 'Let us just go and look,' Bub followed him.

When they got onto the school grounds Bub left the terrier tied to a playground sun shelter. William stepped up onto one of the long benches under the classroom windows, and looked into a room. He jumped back down and said, 'There's no one there.'

They walked up the wheelchair ramp to the school offices. There was a notice on the door. *Attention parents. The bus won't return the children till 4pm.*

Bub put his hand on William's arm. 'They weren't here,' he said. 'Thank Christ.'

William pulled the door open. The hallway was full of the smell of frying circuitry. A printer could be heard complaining about a paper jam. They went into the office and saw that it wasn't paper that was jammed. Bub switched the printer off at the wall and William found some scissors to cut the woman's hair and free her from the machine. He laid her down on the floor.

Bub then crossed to the principal's office, took a look, and muttered, 'What is it with these people and scissors.'

They went back out. William produced the marking pen and wrote '2' on the glass of the door.

They left the school and followed the sound of the hoarse, bass barking. They found a medium-sized dog with a deep chest and curly black coat. It was pressed against the gate of a yard whose lawn was marred by a long drag mark, the flattened grass blackened by blood.

Bub tried to calm the dog, then realised that the dogs might do a better job of calming one another. When he opened the gate, they began to circle and sniff. Then the terrier flopped onto the ground and exposed her round, nipple-studded belly.

William followed the blood trail. He disappeared around the house. Bub looked after him and thought, 'He has an appetite for that.' Then he felt ashamed of himself. He was being squeamish. He wasn't usually, and maybe he and William were only doing the same thing in different ways— beginning to see what they might have to deal with if no one came to help, if it turned out that burying the dead wasn't someone else's job, but theirs. The only difference between him and William was that whereas the idea of having to think about doing something with all these bodies made Bub want to postpone thinking about it for as long as possible, William seemed to be trying to get some sense of the size of the task.

William reappeared with car keys and a remote for the

garage door. He pointed it, and the door rolled up to reveal a four-door Holden ute. 'This'll be useful,' William said. He unlocked the ute, got in and backed it out into the driveway.

Bub opened its back door and the curly-coated dog leapt inside and settled on a ragged blanket. It looked relieved. This was its blanket and vehicle—never mind the change in drivers. Bub put the terrier in the back seat too and climbed in beside William.

William let the windows down so they could hear. He drove slowly. Now and then they stopped to listen.

Within another hour they'd found three more dogs—one who called out as they passed by, another that they spotted sulking in a doghouse. The last was a Bichon Frise, which they discovered near a crashed car, cuddled up to its dead owner. It had been covered in blood, but the rain had rinsed it, and its white coat was now pink. Bub took off his jacket and bundled it up. 'We should go back now. This one needs seeing to. I hope Jacob can do dogs as well as people.'

Before they'd gone far they heard the loudhailer, and Theresa's voice. She was repeating her name and a message: there were people gathered at Kahukura spa, and any other survivors should join them there.

They pulled up alongside her. Theresa craned to look at their backseat and the now docile dogs. She asked about Bub's bundle. 'Is it injured?'

'Yes.'

'I left Jacob and Warren foraging for supplies at the pharmacy. You could go straight there and give them a lift. Haven Road is choked with wrecks, so cut through the supermarket carpark.'

'We went to the Area School,' Bub told her. 'It was empty. The kids were all off in Nelson at a play.'

Theresa paled. 'I forgot the school. I thought of it yesterday then forgot it again. How could I?'

'No harm done,' said Bub.

William said, 'There were two bodies. The principal, and another woman in the school office.'

'He's started counting,' Bub said.

Theresa had completed several circuits of the bypass and waterfront when she spotted someone in a side street. She slammed on her brakes, threw the car into reverse, then drove forward so rapidly that the gears gave a thump. However, by the time she'd turned into the street, she'd recognised the person. It was Oscar, plodding along, burdened by a white plastic box piled high with DVDs. When she pulled up beside him, he said, 'What's got you all excited?'

'Couldn't you hear me calling for any survivors to come out?'

'I am out.'

'Yeah, and you shouldn't be.'

He set his jaw. Theresa saw that it was a console he was holding. And games. 'Couldn't you go another day without plugging in?' Then she noticed that he had tied a ribbon around his neck, and on it he'd hung a house key and every component of his broken phone that could be strung on a ribbon. He was glaring at her like the standard defiant teen, but he'd made a talisman out of the key to his home and an object he'd punished for its failure to put him in touch with his family.

Theresa reached over to open her passenger door. 'Get in.'

Oscar put his games in the backseat and climbed in beside her. Theresa rested her arm on the seat behind his head. She instructed herself to show an open body posture.

Oscar seemed to instantly spot her strategy. He gave her a look of scorching scorn.

She went on regardless. She was calm and firm. She told him that he should be patient and cooperate with their efforts to keep him safe. She said that town wasn't cleared. She said that, for instance, Bub and William were making sure the dogs were all accounted for. 'You do get that I'm the police force, and Jacob is suddenly the whole medical profession, and that Bub and William are weighing in as dog control officers?'

Oscar didn't answer.

She said, 'The dogs might be dangerous.'

'I know most of Kahukura's dogs.'

'What about the people?'

'The only person who isn't up at the spa with us is Bub's firefighter, and he's a good guy. I went to check on our neighbours, and my friend Evan. He was home too because of the teacher-training day.' Oscar paused and breathed hard through his nose. Then he went on. 'They were dead. We're only alive because we were all outside its influence at the moment it started—the craziness, I mean. Everything was normal when I went off on my bike, and crazy when I came back. Think about it.'

Theresa thought about it. William had said he got partway to Mapua but had come back because he'd forgotten his phone charger. Dan, Warren, and Jacob had been just behind her as she sped into Kahukura. Curtis and his wife had been just a little ahead of her. Lily had said she'd reached the cutting about three minutes after William drove back through, and maybe only seconds after the fence collapsed under the weight of the old people trying to climb it. 'Where were you, Oscar?' Theresa asked.

Oscar said he had gone for a ride along the marine walkway and was over the other side, he reckoned, when it happened. 'And while I was riding I saw Bub's boat, before it came in past Matarau Point.'

'What about Holly and her mother?'

'It wasn't possible to reach them by road once the No-Go activated,' Oscar said. 'I think Kate and Holly were out

116

of the range of influence of the craziness when it started. I think the subdivision is closer to the town than the road *up* to the subdivision. The road loops in behind Cotley's orchard. Maybe Holly and her mum went *out*, then back *in*, and got caught inside when the No-Go activated.' Oscar glanced at Theresa and blushed. 'You do see what I mean, don't you?'

Theresa could see that this would all make some sense of that terrible nagging question: *Why us? Why were we spared?*

'I think there was a kind of window of time between when the craziness took hold, and when the No-Go went up like a fence,' Oscar said. 'Everyone either arrived in Kahukura for the first time in that window or, like me, Holly and Kate, and William, we went out and came back.'

Oscar was looking at her anxiously. He needed to be believed. But Theresa could see the flaw in his theory. 'Wasn't Sam here the whole time?'

Oscar looked crestfallen.

And—Theresa thought—Sam had admitted to Jacob and William that she'd been mad and had mutilated her own breast.

Theresa looked at Oscar and, after a brief moment of delicate consideration, said, 'Sam was under the influence of the madness. She was here in the deadly moment—and survived it.'

'Shit,' Oscar said.

'If she survived there *must* be more survivors. And you just about had me convinced that what I was doing was futile.'

Oscar said, 'I'm sorry. I guess you're following protocol.'

'Inasmuch as there are protocols for this.' She started the car. 'I'll run you back to the spa, then do a few more circuits.'

Oscar kept facing rigidly forward throughout the ride. Theresa guessed he was suppressing tears. But when they reached the end of the Waterfront Road nearest Matarau

Point, he looked at the beach. The tide was coming in. Theresa saw what she hadn't when she went by on earlier occasions—Oscar's handiwork. He had written, in letters several metres high: 'MUM AND DAD THIS IS OSCAR. I AM OK.'

Theresa pulled over and waited till she had her feelings under control before she spoke.

Oscar was blushing. 'I smashed my phone,' he said. 'I was going to tell them that too. Stupid, eh.'

'No,' she said. Then, 'When you wrote it were you thinking of satellites?'

He nodded.

'You're a smart cookie,' she said.

That afternoon Bub went to the garden centre and then to the service station. He came back to the spa with a bag of flashlights and batteries, several rolls of packing tape, and a bundle of bamboo garden stakes—plus a clutch of cans of spray-paint. He went looking for Theresa. He found her and Belle standing in the atrium before a framed historical map of Kahukura. Or, rather, a map of Stanislaw's Station, the late nineteenth-century sheep run, and its environs.

Theresa looked at Bub's clattering collection of salvage. 'You've been out again,' she said, disapproving.

Bub shook a bag. 'I'm going to tape these torches to the stakes, facing inwards. We can switch them on then go poke the No-Go. We should start figuring out its boundaries. And we can use paint to mark the ground a few feet back from where it begins, just so there won't be any more accidents.'

'Can we start in the reserve?' Belle said. 'I was just telling Theresa that I think the No-Go might cut across it.' Her chin quivered. 'And that means I will have lost some birds.' She drew a circle on the map with her finger. 'We can expect the No-Go to be symmetrical, can't we?'

'Help me assemble some pokers, and let's go see for ourselves.'

Belle spun the tumblers on the combination lock at the gate of the reserve, and the padlock clicked open. She unchained the gate.

They walked up through the forest to the clearing with the trough and hoppers. The All-Father was sitting in the trough, dozing.

'Wow,' said Bub. 'An actual kakapo.' Then, 'Are you sure he's okay?'

'He's elderly,' Belle said.

They paused to switch on their torches, then continued on towards the ridge, holding their bamboo stakes out in front of them, going slowly and keeping their eyes on their sun-paled lights.

'It's hard to tell whether they're on,' Theresa complained.

'We should start collecting little radios and MP3 players,' Bub said. 'They'd work too, and better in daylight.'

The highest point of the ridge was a limestone bluff, part of which curled over to form a long, barrel-shaped cave—a cave like a breaking wave, its crest fringed with stalactites. They had slowed right down. They crept around the bluff, crossed the shoulder of the ridge, and came out the other side.

Below them the forest was full of bird calls.

'It's not there,' Belle said. She leaned on a tree, weak with relief.

'Maybe it's not there at all!' Theresa said. Then, gabbling, 'Which trail leads to the back gate, Belle?'

Belle pushed past them and ran. They followed her, Bub shouting, 'Not so fast!'

But it was hard not to hurry. Every so often Belle would halt and they'd all bunch up, hold their breath, and listen to the birds.

For a long time there was birdsong ahead of them. Then, suddenly, they weren't quite so sure it was ahead and not just flanking them. They were close to the back fence by then. Bub took the lead, his stake held out straight. After another quarter hour they reached the gate. Belle opened it, then unlocked and opened the second gate. All of Stanislaw's Reserve's gates were like airlocks. There were always two, so that neither enterprising pests nor endangered birds could dash through from their respective sides.

Bub ventured out onto the stubbly grass of the cleared strip that ran beside the fence. The forest beyond the strip was utterly silent. Bub took a couple of steps, and then his torch went out. He put the stake down, produced a spray can, shook it, and sprayed the grass at his feet.

It was then that Belle cried out in a broken voice. She dropped her poker and hurried away along the outside of the fence, her hand on its mesh.

Bub lunged after her. 'We don't know that it's safe that way!'

But Belle had stopped. She dropped into a crouch, her hands pressed to her mouth. She was looking at a bronze and green parrot, which was sprawled, wings flung wide, on the fern-shaded ground where the forest began again.

Bub hunkered down beside her and put his arm around her.

'Most of the kaka fly out every day,' she said, and gestured at the felled bird. 'They have a huge territory. People in Nelson say they hear them going over at sunset, on their way back here. They don't all fly out, but many do, especially the adolescents.'

'They're rare, aren't they,' Bub said.

'Yes. Rare, but not endangered. And my kakapo can't fly, and won't get themselves into trouble.' Belle was talking calmly, but tears were streaming down her face. 'The kaka are lovely. When it's really lousy weather and even the seagulls roost I've seen them flying back here into the teeth of the storm, talking to each other the whole way. Flopping about. What I mean is, when they fly they flap and flop and it looks clumsy. But they're very, very strong fliers, and they only flop because they're always looking around, not just for food, like gulls and gannets, but for *fun*. They're always out for a good time.' She scrubbed a hand across her eyes. 'I'm sorry. They're just birds, I know.'

'It's okay. You've been crying over people too.'

Belle looked into his face, her blue eyes red and spoiled. 'Not that much,' she said. 'But the things the people did makes it hard to see them as people. It's as if their deaths—the manner of their dying—stopped them *being* people, at the end, anyway. The corpses don't make me sad, only scared. I mean, so far. I expect that'll change.'

'Yes,' Bub said. He took her hand and together they edged back along the fence to the gate.

Theresa gave Belle a hug, then Belle locked the outer gate, closed the inner, and they went back through the reserve.

After a while Belle said, 'The kaka are smart. The No-Go won't get them all. They'll work it out.'

'I'm sure you're right,' Bub said, kindly. And who knew, she might be.

'The No-Go isn't symmetrical,' Theresa said. 'It bulges to take in the reserve.'

'You mean it's formed so that it doesn't cut across the reserve?' said Bub. 'As if it recognises the kakapo are important?'

Theresa frowned. 'Or as if whoever made it couldn't climb the fence, or unlock the gate, and had to go around the outside.'

Bub gazed at Theresa, trying to make her acknowledge what she'd just said. Theresa—who kept telling them to put off thinking about what everything meant. She held his

121

gaze, but didn't say anything. Finally Bub asked her if she was listening to herself. 'You said "whoever made it". You said "*who*ever", not "whatever".'

The first person they buried was Adele Haines. Jacob and Bub dug a grave for her under the big jacaranda on the lawn below the spa's terrace. The tree was in bud, but not blossom—though spring was well underway, and the kowhai by then had as much bruised gold pooled under them as bright gold above.

They started to dig in one place, but worked too close to the jacaranda and found their spades confounded by its root system. They began again, further out, but were only able to go three-and-a-half feet down until they hit thick clay. They kept apologising to Curtis.

Curtis sat on the lawn by his wife's body. Adele was tightly swaddled in two sheets. He'd finally had to cover her hair. In a week it would be her sixtieth birthday, and he had promised their children he'd have her home for the big day. The kids had been planning something, and he was charged only to deliver her. They all had Adele's habit of treating him like a vague creature, an artist, the guy who always burns the soup. They'd said, 'All you have to do, Dad, is get Mum home by the sixteenth.'

When the grave was finished, Jacob and Bub lowered Adele into it, and climbed out again. Jacob had a Bible and offered to read.

Curtis said, 'Adele wasn't religious, but she always had a strong sense of occasion.'

Jacob commenced, but after a moment Curtis stopped him. He put his hand over the page. He couldn't speak.

'Is it the wrong thing?' Jacob said, distressed. 'Is there a passage you'd prefer, Mr Haines?'

Curtis was finally able to say that the 23rd Psalm was

never wrong—but what Bible was that?

Jacob showed the cover. It was *The Good News Bible.*

'Adele would have wanted the King James.'

Jacob looked confused, but then William started up. 'The Lord is my Shepherd, I shall not want, he maketh me to lie down in green pastures, he leadeth me beside the still waters, he restoreth of my soul. He leadeth me in the paths of righteousness for His Names sake. Yea, though I walk through the valley of the shadow of death I shall fear no evil. For *Thou* art with me . . .' word perfect, even to its emphasised 'thou'. Grand, personal, universal.

Once William finished, Jacob sang *Abide With Me.* He was used to singing, and good at it. He kept his composure, but almost everyone was in tears. All the women except Kate were crying. And all the men except William—that cold, or cauterised, man. Curtis wept for Adele, and they wept for his loss—but their grief was also anticipatory.

Oscar began to cry so hard he was hiccupping. Belle hurried to embrace him and everyone tried to rein themselves in.

Curtis asked for a shovel. He wanted to bury his wife himself, or at least to make a start. Bub handed Curtis his shovel. Curtis filled it with wet clumpy soil and dropped it onto Adele's shrouded form. And, at every shovelful, Curtis said his wife's name. He spoke over the sound of the falling clods. 'Adele,' he murmured. 'Adele. Adele.' He wanted to make her another promise, but couldn't imagine what she'd want for him now. And then he realised that what she'd most want him to do was to hold each of their children for her once again—their grown-up children, and their grandchildren. He had to find his way back to them, and give them the news.

Curtis could no longer feel the handle of the shovel. He was walking away through the air. He was going to go away, and find his family, and renew that old, warm pact.

Jacob took the shovel from him. Sam put a hand under his elbow and helped him sit down on the damp ground.

And then the dogs began to howl. Warren covered his ears. Bub and Jacob kept filling in the grave. Belle said, 'I'll go and see to those animals,' and went off towards the pool, the spa's only fenced area, where Bub had put the dogs he'd taken into protective custody.

Sam stepped away from Curtis, raised her hands from her sides, and, face upturned, began to spin slowly like a child enraptured by an early snowfall.

'Sam?' William said, in his hard, incisive way. 'Why are you doing that?'

'It's the wind,' Sam said.

There was scarcely a breeze, and still Sam went on turning in her private whirlwind, seduced by something none of the rest of them could see, or hear, or feel.

Four days after the catastrophe, no one had come to their aid, or communicated in any way. The No-Go appeared to have thickened. The survivors could still see the rough flanks of Pepin Island across the mouth of Tasman Bay, but its base was blurry, as if some giant had dipped a finger in clear oil and carefully wiped along the join of land and sea. The whole horizon was smudged and streaky and, at night, no lights showed across the bay at Glenduan.

No one was coming, so they got on with what they had to do.

Theresa, Bub, and William broke into a succession of garages, looking for cans of spray-paint, collecting only pale colours. They painted a message on the school field, the town's largest open area.

'We can always revise it,' Theresa said. 'If we do find more survivors.'

'Only if we mow the grass,' said Bub, rattling his can. He

stooped and began the long line of the first numeral. Bub wrote *14 survivors* and then a list of their names, plus *one unidentified man.*

Bub, Theresa, Dan, and William moved all the bodies from the section of Haven Road between the pharmacy and supermarket, and both buildings. They moved the bodies slumped in wrecked cars, and lying broken on the lawn around the old bank building, and sprawled on scorched footpaths. They took them to the school hall and laid them out under sheets.

While that was happening, Warren, Holly, Jacob, and Belle shifted the supermarket's meat from the fresh section to the big chest freezers. They filled the Captiva's boot with cans of beans and bags of rice. They stockpiled as if they meant to winter over—although the others were only moving bodies out of sight for later, for their rescuers to deal with in due course.

All those who foraged, or moved bodies, had moments of insight. They kept seeing what they had to do. Yet no one said, 'Let's sit down together and talk it over,' even on the day when the wobbly wheel on a trolley caused Jacob to spill his load of lotions and antiseptics onto the oil-soaked surface of the road. He and Belle were picking it all up when she said, 'You know there's a digger up by the reserve. There was going to be a ground-breaking ceremony for the Visitors' Centre. We could use that digger to move the wrecks off the road and use cars instead of these blasted trolleys.'

'That's a good idea,' Jacob said—and thought, 'A digger. Yes. We'll need one of those.'

It turned out that Dan could operate a digger, and that Belle had a pretty good idea where the man who drove it would have been shortly before noon on the deadly day. She and Theresa went to the Smokehouse Café and searched the pockets of the men from the construction crew. They fumbled one-handed, faces pressed into the crooks of their arms, to shield them from the stink. And even then the subject wasn't broached.

But the next day, when they were all having breakfast, Oscar shifted to a seat beside Theresa and said in a low voice, 'I'd like to bury Evan, that guy from my school. Can you help me?'

Warren overheard. He said he wanted to lay Aunt Winnie to rest too. 'I'm sure she'd like to be under her flowering cherry tree.'

Before Theresa was able to respond, Kate said, 'And I'd feel much happier if I could think that my fellow residents at Mary Whitaker weren't just lying about like so much lumber.'

Sam looked up. 'I went and put some blankets over the poor people on the road. But that isn't good enough. It isn't right.'

Theresa held up her hands. 'I promise we'll make a start today. Certainly we must with your aunt, Warren, and Oscar's schoolmate. But I think perhaps me, William, Bub, and Jacob should sit down and talk about how to tackle the old people's home.'

'Why William?' said Warren. 'I get that Jacob is kind of health and safety, and Bub's got more muscle than the rest of us, but it's Dan who knows how to drive the digger.'

Dan said, 'I'm happy to be told what to do.'

'Well, yeah, so am I,' said Warren. 'I only want to know why William.'

William said, 'Bub, Theresa, and I have already moved bodies to the school hall. We've even checked to see where the buried cables are on the playing field.'

'Whoa,' said Theresa to William. Then to Warren, 'Don't worry about him. He keeps getting ahead of himself.'

Bub was looking grim. His eyes settled on Belle. He said,

as if it was only her he had to convince, 'Just let us work out all the details. Okay?'

'That's right,' Theresa said. 'We're not going to rush into anything. I'm asking these guys to help me nut out the details. If that's okay.'

'Sure,' Belle said. 'That's fine.'

'For now,' Warren added.

At the end of their meeting Theresa said, 'We are going to have to get everyone together at some point and present this as a plan.'

'It is shaping up as a plan, isn't it,' Bub said. He sounded gloomy.

William said. 'We should wait and see how we go with the rest home, before committing ourselves to anything further.'

'The rest home is a huge job,' Bub said.

'Sam and Kate actually knew those people. We have to do it.' Theresa tapped her pen on her teeth. 'If we discover we can't cope, and have to stop, then we'll be dealing with flies and rats and disease instead. We're between the devil and the deep blue sea.'

'Only if no one comes,' said Jacob.

Bub said, 'We have to make a start. We're *living* here. And if Mary Whitaker proves too hard—well, we just have to toughen up. People do. I know this.'

Theresa said, 'You were in Afghanistan, right?'

'I dug drains and helped build a school, but there was tough stuff, and we got shot at.' He went on, 'My only rule when it comes to burials is that whoever handles bodies doesn't prepare food. Kate and Holly are already doing the cooking so it makes sense to say that's their job. And Oscar can give them a hand.'

'Okay. That's good,' said Jacob.

'So you agree that we have to start?'

'I keep hoping we'll be rescued.'

Theresa closed her eyes and pinched the bridge of her nose. 'Being rescued—that's Plan A. Plan B is we take care of ourselves as best we can.'

Warren and Jacob were seeing to Mrs Kreutzer's burial, and Bub had insisted on handling his friend George by himself—probably because he wanted to spare anyone else a sight that had so horrified him. So Theresa dispatched William and Dan to find the digger, and set off herself with Oscar to his friend Evan's house. She told the boy just to point her to the right place. He did, and she wrapped the teenager's body in his own duvet, before calling Oscar in to help her carry the wrapped body out into the back garden.

Theresa hadn't done any spadework since she was about fifteen, when she would help her father dig over the garden before putting in potatoes. Oscar told her he'd once helped dig a hangi. Later, after he'd managed to scratch another foot down into her two-foot-deep hole, he admitted that, with the hangi, his whole class had taken turns digging. Then he looked at the shrouded shape, and his legs folded, and he sat down hard on the pile of earth by the hole. 'I'm sorry, Evan,' he said. 'I forgot you were there too. I'm sorry I'm so shit at this.'

'Look,' said Theresa, 'how about I send you back to the spa and you get Jacob to help me finish?'

It was then that William turned up. He was pale with excitement. 'You know that loud bang I told you about? The one we all heard when you and Bub and Belle were off in the Reserve? I know what made it now. You've got to see this.'

Oscar got to his feet.

William said, 'Not you buddy. This is pretty horrible.'

Theresa had another of her contained, icy thoughts. She thought it was interesting the way they were onto *grades* of horrible now.

It took Theresa a few moments to see that the black spray was blood, dried and oxidised, spread widely, in a fine coating on the driveway, the blades of grass, the stove-in steel roof, and the buckled door of a garage on Bypass Road.

The body was dressed in a neoprene coverall, and was wearing boots with hard-ridged soles. The metal on the parachute harness was still bright. The blood had erupted laterally, sprayed out in blades—there were distinct stripes of it on the roof behind the body. The tough fabric of the suit had split rather than torn, and the shattered flesh *inside* the suit was split too, as deeply fissured as a pumpkin dropped on a concrete path. A pumpkin in a bag—because the suit still contained the sectioned flesh.

The body's helmeted head had made a round dent in the roof, but the back of the helmet was flattened. The man's cheeks and jaw looked as if they had been carefully cut away from his skull and spread out, like a circle of raw dough. The mask of the helmet was still in place across the eyes and nose, but the eyes were pushed out of their sockets and pressed against the goggles like pickled eggs in a jar.

Because the corpse was that of a military man, Dan had fetched Bub while William was fetching Theresa.

Bub said that it looked as if the man had made a high-altitude parachute jump. 'His parachute would have one of those devices that allow a chute to deploy only when it reaches the right altitude—like the parachutes on a fighter pilot's ejection seat.'

'But it didn't deploy,' William said. 'The man wasn't conscious. And the mechanism didn't work.'

'Because it's a mechanism, I guess,' Bub said. 'And the

No-Go is hostile to them.'

'How do those things work? The parachute devices?'

'I think they're triggered by changes in air pressure.'

'Does that mean the No-Go is tens of thousands of feet high?' William asked. Then, 'You know, we thought we heard two or three distinct sounds. This guy won't have been alone.'

'The others might have landed inside the No-Go,' Bub said.

Theresa said, 'Or we might yet find them.'

'Shouldn't we look through his clothes for information?' Dan asked. 'There might be a message saying what they're up to—the people out there. What they know about what happened, and how they plan to help us.' He sounded desperately eager.

'I'll search him,' Bub volunteered. He tried to prise the military man's shoulder out of the folded roofing steel. The man had a gun under him, but it was bent out of shape.

The man had identity tags. He had a name. A name, a knife, a gun, a first-aid kit, two flashlights, one normal and one with a light so bright it was hot and impossible to look at.

'What's that for? Starting fires?' William said.

'It's for signalling, I think,' said Bub. He switched the torch on and aimed it out at the bay.

'At night,' said William.

'Yes,' Bub said, then switched the torch off again. He sighed. 'When I went into the army they'd stopped teaching signallers Morse.'

'Were you in the Signal Corps?' Theresa asked.

'No. Armoured Corps. A LAV unit,' Bub said. Then, 'I'll do some meaningless flashing tonight. Just to remind them we're here.'

★

Curtis had plugged his digital video camera into a computer in the manager's office, and was reviewing footage. He'd been filming some of what went on day-to-day: Bub and Belle standing on a street banging spoons against tins of pet food till the cats came running; Jacob changing Sam's dressing; Warren ploughing up and down the pool, after dark, when little wisps of steam came off the heated water; and the shimmering stillness of the town at morning, every morning.

Curtis was a documentary filmmaker. When he'd picked up his camera he was reverting to the habit of a lifetime in order to find his way forward. But he was having trouble imagining himself, even a year later, looking this over and finding anything that made sense, or was worth seeing.

William came in and stood watching over Curtis's shoulder. They'd got to Curtis's long shots of bodies lying in the street. Of Theresa and Jacob searching them for identification, then draping them with sheets. Curtis said, 'All this is problematic. I have to consider the feelings of relatives, then weigh them against the idea of having some direct evidence.'

William said, 'And I've been mentally composing opening arguments for someone prosecuting the case in which those relatives are the plaintiffs. My arguments are all about the carelessness and callousness of corporations. With references to Bhopal and Union Carbide.'

Curtis's years of documentary-making had inclined him to just listen to people and let them run on. He swivelled his chair and looked at William—his bruised eye sockets, his very clear eyes.

'But making a case is just a habit for me.' William nodded at the images on screen. 'And so is your thinking about what you should and shouldn't film.'

'So you're not going with the nerve gas theory?'

'How could something like that be so selective? How

could it drive people mad but not animals?'

'Theresa keeps telling us to put all that aside for now,' Curtis said. 'She's right.'

'She's right to get us to focus on the things we can do. But I'm not sure that's all we should be considering. You're a *thinker*, Curtis. I need you to think.'

Curtis had begun to feel that his habit of facing life with a camera in front of his eyes was a curse. He'd lost his wife of thirty-eight years, and here he was still filming things, and being wooed by the group's leader for his moral qualities, and by its maverick for his imagination. But Curtis didn't want to be reminded of his worth. He wanted to go on being the man he was in Adele's eyes. He wanted to be left in peace to think only about Adele. He said, 'If you're trying to enlist me into pushing Theresa to discuss things, don't bother. I don't want to be a part of any of this. Part of the group or the group's decisions.' Then, 'Excuse me,' he said, and left the manager's office.

He went and sat on the leather sofa in the atrium, where Oscar was sitting, grimly hanging on to his controller and glaring at the big plasma TV. 'Hi, Mr Haines,' said Oscar, then, explanatory, 'The red line is my health. I'm taking too many hits.'

The following day, Theresa, Bub, and Curtis went to the supermarket. Theresa asked them to stock up on things they needed in order to tackle Mary Whitaker. She grabbed a shopping trolley and went to the start of the toiletries aisle. 'I'll fill this with hand sanitiser.'

Bub said, 'I'll collect rubbish sacks and packing tape.'

'And rubber gloves. And twine, if there is any.'

Bub wrestled the trolley out of the cue, and went off pushing it with his belly.

Theresa looked at Curtis. His eyes were red-rimmed. His

skin seemed thin and bluish in the light of the fluorescents. 'I know I can trust you to judge what we will and won't need right now,' she said.

He grabbed a trolley and set off down the aisle.

Ten minutes later Theresa ran into him again between the canned fruit and breakfast cereals and, glancing into his basket, saw that it was full of single-serve food products. She nosed her trolley up to his. He was peering over the top of his glasses, reading the fine print on a small tin of tuna. He tossed it in, and pushed his glasses back up the bridge of his nose.

'What are you doing, Curtis?'

He regarded her, his expression strained. 'I think it would be better for me to be on my own.'

Theresa opened her mouth, but stopped when he held up his hand. 'Hear me out. I can't be with strangers right now, Theresa. It's harder than being alone.'

'Has someone been disrespectful?'

'No, not at all.'

'We want to look after you,' Theresa said. 'And if you go off alone I can't guarantee your safety.'

'Bub might be obediently filling his trolley with rubbish sacks and rubber gloves, but don't you see that you can't keep asking people to handle corpses?'

'We only have to make a start,' Theresa said. 'Of course police and coroners are going to come along after us. And I know that even making a start will be a hard, horrible task. But we have to, for sanitary reasons, never mind anything else. Obviously I'm going to exempt Oscar and Kate. Oscar's too young and Kate's over eighty and kind of off-duty.'

Curtis said, 'If you start, where will you stop?'

'There are satellites watching us right now. The people monitoring them have to see hostages, not hostage-takers. They have to see survivors, not perpetrators.'

'Sanitary reasons I understand. But you can't get people

to dig mass graves because you're worried about a bunch of remote and invisible watchers, and what they're thinking.'

Theresa heard Curtis concede the sanitation point. She decided his concession was a lever, and leaned on it. 'I wouldn't ask you to do anything more than photograph bodies for later identification.'

'No. Listen. You have to know that you're not representative. You're a very tough person.'

'But you've been *filming* stuff.'

'And I've discovered that I don't want to.'

Theresa looked across their kissing shopping trolleys, and the different declarations of their contents. Her heart was pounding. 'This is just a difference of opinion,' she said. 'You're over-thinking everything.'

'You're the one who's imagining she's being watched and judged,' said Curtis. He turned his trolley and went on hard-headedly gathering his meals for one.

That evening, when dinner was over, Theresa explained to the others that Curtis had decided to leave them. She emphasised what he'd said about missing his wife more when he was with people. She tried not to let on that she felt she'd failed him.

Belle touched Theresa's arm and said, 'I guess that's where he is right now in the process.'

'Where is he now?' Sam asked.

Belle looked baffled.

'Belle means where he is in the grieving process,' Bub said, helpful.

'I think Sam's asking where Curtis actually is,' said Theresa. Then, to Sam, 'He's been to the garden centre, and he's out there in the dark planting petunias on his wife's grave. I wouldn't bother him. I think it's a private ceremony.'

★

'What do you want, William?' Curtis said. He was working in the light of Bub's big storm lamp. It was drizzling, and the soil was cold.

William unfurled an umbrella and held it up over him. 'Are those petunias?'

'Yes. Why?'

'I'm surprised Theresa knew what they were. The model and make of cars maybe—but flower names, not so much.'

Curtis grunted. He pinched a cell in the tray of seedlings and extracted another plant. Its roots resisted and tore. He said, 'I trust you're going to support her. Theresa has a hard row to hoe.'

William crouched. He kept the umbrella positioned above Curtis's head. 'If the madness was a disease and you were asked to make a list of its symptoms, how would that list go?'

'Okay, you tell me. What's your list?'

'One—' William began, 'it switched on all of a sudden and—two—seemed to communicate itself to everyone simultaneously, except—three—all of us, excluding Sam. Four—it went on for forty minutes to an hour. Five—it had an end stage, that passive going-away period just before each of its victims died. That's what we know about it.'

'But we don't know what caused it.'

'No. But I know a bit about insanity. And the insanity I've known has had a kind of logic to it, as if the crazy person's only problem is one of perspective, or a sense of proportion. For instance, a woman I knew used to say that her roof was leaking but that it wasn't rain that was coming in. She'd climbed up into her roof to look at the holes rusted in its iron and, while she was up there, she noticed a lot of pipes that seemed to have no purpose. So she decided that of course someone had put them there. And though liquid ran down the walls either when it was raining or shortly after, it was *obvious* that it wasn't rain, it was from these pipes and it wasn't water, it was something else, something sinister and bad for her family's health, worse for their health than a leaking roof.

'What's going on there, with that madness, is that the woman had built a logical scheme of thinking based on a false premise. Her premise being that everything was about *her*. There was no point asking her why anyone would go to so much trouble with a rundown house, and impoverished occupants, to put pipes between roof and ceiling to periodically release some mysterious liquid. "Why would someone take the trouble to do that to you?" wasn't a meaningful question. Crazy people can't consider probability. Of course everything is about them. They are a constant—and it's the world that has changed. They're in the know—and everyone else is in the dark.

'Most mental illness is like that. There are problems with a sense of proportion. And it's *internal*. The way in which the Madness was different, apart from its coming on all at once, was that the logic of some of it was like something imposed from the outside. As if there was someone overseeing what happened. Someone saying, "Okay, this woman is a shopkeeper. Shopkeepers take money from customers in exchange for goods, and the money puts bread in their mouths. But this shopkeeper is going to give her customer money, is going to *feed* her money, post each coin between her lips until she chokes." That's a total mad reversal of the normal relationship between shopkeeper and customer.' William paused and said, 'Sorry, Curtis.' He clenched his teeth, and a muscle rippled in his jaw.

'That's all right,' Curtis said. 'Please go on.'

'My point is that it was as if some intelligence examined the normal relationships between people—including fairly superficial, social relationships—then did something to flip them. The Madness worked completely differently from the way madness normally does. And, contrary to popular

136

belief, madness has a kind of normal in it. The only real mystery in madness is how hard it is to fix, and the usual, ordinary mystery of where people go when they disappear while still standing in front of you.'

Curtis sat back on his heels and looked up at William. 'You said "some intelligence examined". That implies a point of view, an agent of evil, not just psychosis-inducing nerve gas.'

'A narcotic that caused psychosis would produce behaviour that was distorted, but characteristic. The mad acts would come out of private fears or anger. But with some of what we saw it was like the *public* person went mad—the person seen from the outside, as if by some evil puppeteer.'

Curtis cast the empty seedling trays into the hedge of oleanders. William helped him up, then looked at the grave and remarked that the earth was settling already. Then, 'Where will you go if you're not staying with us?'

'I thought I'd take a room at the bed and breakfast. I couldn't go to a private house. Even if it was empty the bedrooms would all seem to belong to somebody. Someone dead—or out there.' He gestured at the world lost behind the rain.

'Doesn't it seem strange to you—staying beside Warren's aunty's grave and not your wife's?'

'I've lost my sense of things being strange.'

'That's just grief, Curtis.'

'Yes. But, William, you're only saying that to reassure yourself. To reassure yourself *about* yourself.'

William said, 'Yes,' very quietly, and Curtis moved to pat his arm, before remembering the mud on his hands. He patted the air instead, and said, 'You're afraid of losing your mind.'

'I always have been. Or at least from the moment it occurred to me, at six or so, that my mother's ways were mad ones.'

'Then at least you've had a lifetime of policing your thoughts. That should help you. You can keep a close eye on everyone else. And stay a step back from them.'

'Meanwhile, you're a mile off.'

'It isn't a mile. It's scarcely three minutes by car.'

'Close enough for daily visits.'

Curtis shook his head. 'Please don't visit. I won't feel so alone if I actually am. I explained this to Theresa.'

'And she passed it on. But, Curtis—I don't think we *are* alone.'

Curtis thought that William might well be right, but he couldn't bring himself to care. He could see William's fear, and his courage—but what he saw was drained of significance. Adele was in the ground. The rain was tamping down the disturbed earth with its gentle fingers, and rinsing blots of mud from the furry leaves of the petunia plants. But Adele was here too, beside him, alive to him—much more alive than he was to himself. He said, 'I must go. The Volvo's packed. I thought I should eat a first supper in my new place, even if it's only a can of soup.' He wiped a hand on his pants and offered it to William, who took it. 'I can't help you,' Curtis said. 'But please—you help Theresa. Look to her. And look after her.'

Theresa, Bub, William and Jacob paused in Mary Whitaker's carpark to put on protective clothing. Jacob had gloves and three hazard masks from the garden centre, plus two surgical masks from the pharmacy. He had a bottle of eucalyptus oil they could dab on the cloth beneath their nostrils. He was uncapping the oil when Sam broke away from the group and hurried inside. Jacob raised his voice. 'Wait, Sam! You're going to want some protection.' She didn't hear him. There was too much noise. Daniel was bringing the digger up the driveway. It came clanking and grinding, and left a white

138

striated track on the paving stones.

William ran after Sam, fastening his mask as he did so.

Theresa and Bub waited till Jacob had dripped eucalyptus oil on the bits of gauze that would rest just below their noses.

The digger had reached the carpark. Daniel turned its engine off and got out. He said that he should inspect the lawn and check for buried cables, sewers, and stormwater drains.

Theresa gave him a thumbs-up and led the others into the building.

William caught up with Sam in time to see her upend a large pan into the kitchen bin. William was about to say that if they were cleaning, the stovetop seemed a very strange place to start. Then he saw what it was she was getting rid of—human nipples, burned at their edges and adhered to sticky oil. Sam bashed the pan on the rim of the bin. Her foot slipped off the pedal. The flap clanged shut, and a scrap fell out onto the floor with a stiff little filliping noise. Sam dropped the pan. The front of her shirt was blotted red. She had torn her stitches.

William went to her, and moved her gently aside. He put on his rubber gloves, let his eyes go out of focus, and felt for the thing. He picked it up and put it in the bin, then pulled out the full bag and tied its top. He opened the back door, found a dumpster, and stuffed the bag into it.

When he came back Sam was rinsing the pan under the hot tap—and scrubbing it with an already blackened pot scrubber.

William removed both from her hands. He led her outside and told her to sit down for a minute. Then he joined the others.

They were frozen at the door to the dayroom. Bub held a bloodstained pair of scissors, contemplating them rather than the figures sprawled in the armchairs, and on the floor.

Theresa stooped and righted a fallen walking frame.

Jacob said, 'It's hard to know where to start.' Then he removed the scissors from Bub's grip.

'We should identify everyone,' Theresa said. 'That's a logical first step. Where's Sam? She knows who all these people are.'

'She's popped her stitches.'

Jacob said he'd have a look, and followed William out onto the porch. He lifted Sam's bandage, frowned, and asked if she could give them half an hour to identify the residents in the dayroom. 'So we can make a start,' he said. 'Then you and I can go back to the spa, and I'll fix you up.'

Sam nodded.

Jacob produced another mask—already sprinkled with oil. He fixed it over Sam's mouth and nose.

William put his lips to Jacob's ear and whispered, 'Sam told us that *she* did it. Remember?'

Jacob took Sam's hands. 'Sam—what makes you think it was you who hurt the old people, and not someone else? If you were unconscious, like you said, couldn't someone else have hurt both you and them?'

Sam shook her head.

Jacob said, 'If you don't remember, how do you know it was you?' He showed Sam the scissors. 'Did you have these in your hand?'

Theresa appeared in the middle of this interrogation and asked whether Sam was up to the job. 'I'm not going to sanction the burial of anyone we haven't identified.'

'I'll come,' Sam said.

Jacob supported her under her elbow while they walked into the dayroom. Sam baulked and leaned on him. She began to cry. Jacob patted her back and murmured in her ear. He said that this was something she could do for her old people. It would help their families. They'd get these poor souls cleaned up, then hold a service and do everything properly. He turned to the others. 'My pockets are contaminated with that bloody oil. Have you got a clean tissue?'

Theresa took off her gloves and fished about till she'd found a handkerchief. She wiped Sam's eyes.

'When you're ready, sweetie,' Jacob said.

'I can look now.'

Jacob put an arm around her shoulder and led her to the first lounger. They stopped short of the black mat of dried blood. Everyone peered expectantly at Sam, while Sam studied the swollen and discoloured face. After a moment, 'This is Snow,' she said. 'Mr Abbot.'

They had begun.

On the second day they were working up at Mary Whitaker, Sam got something nasty on her shirt. Theresa drove back to the spa to fetch a change of clothes. On the desk in Sam's room Theresa noticed a collection of pages covered in a laborious scrawl. It seemed Sam was making notes. Theresa glanced at the pages, and was taken by their dogged attention to detail. Sam's writing was ungrammatical and had poor spelling, but it went on, grimly, page after page.

Theresa stood with Sam's fresh shirt in her hands, reading Sam's account of that first day and night. *We went to my bach. We all had a banana. William said no lights. In the morning he fixed my bandage. . . .*

Theresa couldn't imagine why Sam would feel the need to write notes. Theresa's own writing in her little police issue notebook made sense. Sam's didn't. Sam just didn't strike Theresa as someone with any instinct to put pen to paper in order to sort her thinking or soothe her nerves.

Theresa got to the last page to find that Sam had left off her account after the third night. There was only one further sheet of paper. It contained a kind of list:

Oscar Brice is <u>15</u>. His mum and dad work in Nelson. Warren Crootser <u>smokes dope </u>all the time. Jacob F? is nice. He is an <u>Islander.</u> Kate is Mrs Mcneal from Mary Whitaker. <u>She knows me</u>. Holly is Kates daughter. She has <u>glasses</u>. Belle works with the kakapo. She is the one with <u>curly blond hair</u>. Bub Lanagan is a fisherman. <u>Maori</u>. He is a good person. William Minute is not a good person. He is <u>American</u>. Theresa Grey is a <u>police officer</u>. She lives in Nelson. She is very <u>pretty with red hair</u>. Dan Hail lives in Christchurch and has a wife and kids. He is <u>bald</u>. Lily Kay runs races. She has been on TV and is <u>thin</u>. Curtis Hanes is <u>about sixty</u>. He is gone to live at the bed and breakfast. There is another man who is <u>black</u> and does not speak English. He is not with us. I have not seen him.

I like Jacob and Bub and Bell and Kate and Oscar. I liked Curtis but he is gone. I have not decided about Holly and Dan and Lily and Theresa. I do not like Warren and William.

Thats everything. Its 2 hard.

Theresa didn't know what to make of this. Why the underlining? Why *those* words—words that provided the briefest possible description of each of Sam's fellow survivors?

PART THREE

When they had finished dealing with Mary Whitaker, Theresa called a meeting, and put it to the others—what they should do. They had a vote, and Theresa got her majority.

After that, for nearly three weeks, they went from house to house collecting bodies for burial.

There were two teams, and they followed a planned procedure. On each there were those who wore gloves and overalls, touched bodies, turned them over, and looked through their clothes for any identification. On one team Bub, William, and Sam did the job, and on the other it was Theresa, Jacob, and Warren. They were the ones who spread the shrouds—bed sheets lined with slit garbage bags—and moved bodies, rolling them off their damp shadows, the darkened ground.

The others didn't have to handle the dead, but cleaned up—mindful of the flies. Belle was the cleaner on Bub's team, and Lily on Theresa's. The cleaners also had the job of taking photos, of the bodies, and of objects that might help identify them later. They'd sort through letters tucked behind the phone, or bills fastened by magnets to fridge doors. They'd write down the names they found: the name on a power bill, or on a summons to jury duty, or names spelled out in candy-coloured letters glued to a child's bedroom door.

On their second week Lily announced that she had to get back to her training. There was a world championship in March of the following year, and she *had* to hope she'd be free by then. Thereafter the others would sometimes see her running a street away from where they had parked their rank vehicles, wherever they were plying their buckets and Spray 'n Wipe, their sheets, their binder twine and ziplock bags. They'd glimpse Lily only as movement; a blur of coloured smoke.

Though Lily stayed away, Curtis began to appear, sometimes waiting outside a house while a team finished up, sometimes standing at the edge of the mass graves. He didn't offer to help, only filmed what they were doing, panning from the ute to the grave, then away to the settlement of Kahukura, pretty in the pink evening light.

Theresa challenged him once. 'I hope you realise that what you're filming is going to be pretty upsetting for these people's families.'

He lowered his camera. 'I'm not filming the bodies, I'm filming you. Tight shots of Sam's hands, and yours. And Bub's bearing. How he handles himself at the edge of the pit, and keeps a leaking sheet away from his legs. I'm making a memorial of *your* bodies. Your capable graces.'

'I thought you said you didn't want to record any of this.'

'I'm doing it for posterity. It turns out that posterity won't leave me alone. My sense of it has always been so solid. It was never on a cloud above me, or gathered worshipfully at my feet. I've always had it by the hand, and gazed into its eyes.'

'I see. You won't give us a hand, because your hands are all tied up grasping at posterity.'

Curtis seemed unmoved. 'I'm filming for my usual imagined audience, people who know and understand me already, and who'll be interested in what I'll have to show them.'

'Wrong-headed Theresa and her misled crew?'

Curtis just shook his head and raised his camera between them.

★

146

After a time the survivors were so used to what they were doing that they scarcely reacted to anything they found. They didn't shed tears or shut their eyes, but they never stopped being shocked by these illustrations to grotesque stories. The greater their puzzlement, the more a cold forensic need to know would kick in, as if, by unravelling the events at 16 Bowen Grove, or 71 Haven Road, it would be possible to come to some understanding.

Theresa in particular kept thinking that if only she could keep her cool, she could make a pact with the parade of horrible facts. If her gaze remained unflinching and her head clear then the catastrophe might explain itself—for these corpses were its piecemeal speech, and perhaps it was possible to piece everything together and understand what it all meant.

While the teams were moving from house to house, car to car, street to street, Dan was busy using the digger to make graves. He was forced to dig at widely separate locations, for there was a shortage of flat, open, and unsealed land in Kahukura. He dug one long trench in the lawn at Mary Whitaker, and another in the little park behind the public restrooms; another was in an empty lot, two more on the school's playing field.

They gave up their wariness after only a few days on their grisly job. Bub stopped carrying his jack handle. Theresa holstered her gun, and then took it off altogether. It turned out that Bub and William had managed to gather all the dogs, and there was only one occasion when Theresa's team went into a house and was startled by a trapped and maddened cat. After all, houses had cat doors. The cats were often to be found still at home, sitting in a favourite chair with their feet tucked under them, too distraught to curl up and sleep, too hungry and exhausted to prowl about—and waiting patiently for something to change for the better.

So—there were the cats, but apart from that the houses

were quiet. If the front door was locked the team would assume the house was empty. Since the power was on, any alarms would be armed and they didn't want to have to deal with that. Those houses were left undisturbed. There were one or two places where the smell of death was accompanied by a scent of scorched metal, and they would find some overworked heater, though it had been a sunny spring morning. All these things provided signs if not of life then of things still happening—a heater creaking as its thermostat switched it on again in the cold breeze from a newly opened door; a refrigerator shivering into its cooling cycle; a cat jumping off a chair and running under a couch to cower while someone coaxed it, making kissing noises through their mask, and beckoning with gloved fingers.

Bub traipsed back and forth through the house, opening cabinets. Belle told him to mind his feet, she'd just cleaned there. Bub said, 'We've got more bodies than heads,' and started looking behind the cushions on the couch.

Belle watched this for a time, wondering at it. What was he seeing that she couldn't? The house was tidy, pristinely clean, its furnishings colour-coordinated, haphazard only in one square metre—the crowded corkboard in the kitchen. There was a place for everything, and—Belle suddenly understood—that was why Bub was searching for something tucked out of sight, at the last minute, as if at the sound of a knock on the door of the kind of dinner guest who arrives too early.

Bub was checking behind the curtains now, moving them with his elbows. His hands were gloved, but the gloves were spotted with gore. He said, 'I'll look in the bedrooms again,' and set off upstairs.

In the living room, William was picking up teeth. He gathered them in the palm of one gloved hand and tipped them into the shroud, where they made a small pile that nestled up against the neck of the body.

Belle stepped up to take a photograph of the smashed face. She put her camera down and wrote the woman's name and address, and the names of her two children—Ashley and Oliver—on a sheet of paper, using an indelible marking pen. She opened one of the ziplock bags they'd salvaged from the supermarket, and slipped the paper inside. She gave the bag to William, who fastened it to Robyn Clark's shirt with a safety pin.

Belle stepped back and got Robyn Clark framed again, making sure the woman's ID was visible. She took another photo.

Upstairs the small unfussy amount of noise Bub was making stopped altogether. There was a short, contemplative silence, then, 'Okay. I've got it.'

Sam carried the woman's smaller child into the living room and laid it on her lap, feet touching her knees and head resting on her belly. William and Sam carefully closed the sheet and fastened it with pink binder twine.

Sam and William picked up the bundle and carried it out to the ute. Bub followed with the body of the older child—one part bundled in a sheet, the other in a knotted pillowslip.

Belle finished wiping down the kitchen and used a box cutter to remove the patch of sticky, darkened carpet. She pushed the stiff square of hacked-off carpet into a rubbish bag, twisted the bag's top, tied it, and set it down by the gate as they were leaving. They would come back later for rubbish, which they were burying separately. Belle retrieved her bucket and rags and cleaning products, closed the front door and took a photo of the house, with the letterbox clearly visible in the foreground. In the evenings, she and Warren would load the data from their cameras onto two separate computers. Each file of images had a name. A name like *Haven Road, numbers 31–77.*

Lily flashed across a distant intersection. Bub looked up and stumbled. One of the bundles he was carrying came apart in his hands and dropped with sodden thumps onto the road. William, without comment, fetched another sheet and spread it on the ground. He and Bub got down on their knees to gather up what had fallen. They filled the sheet and lifted it into the tray of the ute. The tray was full so they drove off to the latest grave—an empty swimming pool at the Bayside Motel.

Theresa's team was there already, unloading. Theresa drew Bub and William aside, away from the margin of the blue-painted grave. She removed her goggles and pulled down her scarf. 'We got to the last house on Orchard Road,' she said. 'How about you?'

'There were only two houses on Stanislaw's Close with bodies in them.' William indicated the ute's burden. 'Plus a few in the street.'

Theresa pulled her hand-drawn map from her pocket and they bent over it together. Sam and Belle joined them. After a moment William said, 'That leaves the daycare centre you found on day four.'

It was one of those private early childhood education centres, which is why Theresa hadn't been aware of its existence, as she had the Area School's. When she found it she had hurried through its rooms and seen only scattered toys, and no bodies. But there were a couple of dead adults lying in the backyard.

'Let us take care of it,' William said. He turned around and signalled to Jacob, who left off what he was doing and came over. 'Can you and Warren help me and Bub with the bodies Theresa found in the daycare centre?'

'Let's not ask Warren. He's been stoned for days. It's his way of coping.'

'You mean he's not?' Theresa said.

150

'Not really.'

William said, 'Three of us will be enough.'

Sam began wiping her eyes with her gory gloves.

'Don't do that,' William told her. She didn't seem to hear him, so he gently pinned her arms and held her still.

'I'm not crying,' Sam said, though she was. She had been a steady, stalwart, tireless worker. She'd sometimes needed to be reminded what she was about, but she hadn't shirked or cracked—till now. 'Have we finished?' she asked.

'We have,' Theresa said.

'Go home to the spa,' said Bub to Belle. 'Have a nice relaxing bath.'

Belle gave a cracked laugh. *'Home.'*

The daycare centre was in a quiet cul-de-sac and looked like any other house, but with sturdier fences and, in its front yard, a wealth of brilliant plastic playground equipment.

William went in first, Bub and Jacob following. William opened the front door, immediately flinched from the smell, and stepped onto Jacob's foot.

There was always something new, some further subtle initiation into the job they had set out to do. William took a whiff of the air indoors, and despite the Vicks VapoRub coating his top lip he discovered something that seemed to fly to the centre of his skull and roost there—evil, soft, silent, usurping.

The smell of decay was thin and different, sweeter, as if what was spoiled was more vegetable than meat.

They retreated, tearing off their masks. Jacob draped himself over the plastic slide and hid his face in the crook of one elbow. Bub retched a few times, then kicked the playground bark chips over the patch of watery vomit. William hung on the fence and sucked in cold air scented with the gingery perfume of a flowering magnolia.

Someone was standing across the road watching them.

'Look,' William said. He didn't turn to the others—didn't dare take his eyes off the figure in black clothes. 'Hey, Bub,' he said. 'It's him, your firefighter.'

Bub wiped his mouth and came over. 'Where the hell has he been hiding?' It was four weeks since the man had helped Bub put out the fire on Haven Road.

The man crossed the street. He stopped at the gate, pushed it, then, when it didn't yield, he looked at the childproof catch and—after a moment where it seemed he was working it out—he lifted the catch's sprung plunger, pushed the gate open, and came in. He took in the sheets laid out ready on the ground. Then he looked into each of their faces. His expression was compassionate. It made William feel feeble, then grateful—then very suspicious.

The man went up the steps and into the building.

They followed him, and found him standing in a quiet, stinking room. He looked puzzled.

The room was redolent of decay, but there were no bodies visible. The floor of the main room was littered with books and blocks and scattered Duplo, and flat cars, trucks, trains, cakes, cows, and every other category of thing from spilled wooden puzzles.

William leaned through the kitchen hatchway. He saw that the floor was covered in pots, pans, broken crockery.

The man opened the door to the nursery. More sweet bad air billowed out. The tangle of bedding and mattresses appeared unsullied. The room was silent. The building's windows and doors had been closed and the flies hadn't got in.

For a moment or two they stood, exchanging looks. And then the stranger stooped, hooked his finger into the catch of a cupboard and pulled it open.

The children had been tidied away, like their toys. Everywhere, what belonged in cupboards was on the floor, and what didn't belong was stuffed into cupboards, and into the big pot drawers in the kitchen, into the pantry, and behind the sliding doors where puzzles were normally shelved.

William looked in horror, then mercifully remembered then that no one had suffered long; how, after that first hour, everyone who wasn't killed had simply keeled over as if at a signal. *A signal*, he thought, and his brain started up again. He recommenced thinking where he'd left off three weeks before, when they'd embarked on the urgent and reasonable task of taking care of the dead.

The black man was carefully prying a body free. He handled it gingerly and gently.

'You probably shouldn't be doing that with bare hands,' Bub said, and then, when he didn't get a reaction, he went out and found a pair of rubber gloves and offered them to the man. The man laid the little body down on the piled toys, and pulled the gloves on.

Back at the spa the others did what they always did at the end of each day: they trooped into the industrial laundry and stripped. Holly used tongs to lift their overalls and masks into the washing machines. She set about rinsing their gloves. They put on the spa's thick white towelling robes and picked their way through rain puddles to the side door. They went to their rooms and showered, soaked, shampooed, showered some more. They washed the menthol rub from their raw nostrils, then went downstairs and poured themselves drinks. Except Theresa, who went straight to bed, flanked by a hot water bottle, and the big labradoodle.

Oscar posted himself at the foot of the stairs. When Belle appeared he followed her into the dining room, talking.

'You're back early. What's up? Warren is wasted, and Theresa looks squashed flat. Sam came in from feeding cats then went out to the garden—she's still out there, floating about. Where are the other guys?'

Kate came to the door of the dining room and said that dinner was ready—then went to the foot of the stairs to call.

Oscar followed Belle into the dining room and pulled out a chair for her.

She said, 'Bub, William and Jacob are doing what, with any luck, will be the last horrible job. Don't crowd them when they come in.'

'Am I what passes for a crowd around here?' Oscar felt he was being fobbed off. The adults were all forming shells. There were times now when they wouldn't just postpone talking to him; they'd not even meet his eyes.

It was after midnight when the men returned. Oscar was on the veranda, waiting for them, eager to count them all in, like bombers after a raid. Holly had waited up to wash their clothes, Belle to serve them dinner. And Sam was just there, in the shadowy atrium, awake, and sometimes spinning to inaudible music.

When the headlights of the Holden showed on the driveway, Oscar hurried out, for it was his job to hose down the ute. He uncoiled the hose, but the men got out of the cab and stayed, leaning on the side of the tray in a way that made Oscar think, for an icy moment, that they were hiding something there.

'Sorry we're late,' Jacob said, nonsensically.

'That's okay,' said Oscar, and continued to wait for them to move.

Bub said to Jacob and William, 'No one else needs to know what happened to those kids. We've buried them—okay?—and we can burn the building down.'

154

'What happened to them?' Oscar asked, but they wouldn't even look at him. 'Hang on, are you talking about that daycare centre? I thought there weren't any kids there.'

Jacob continued to ignore Oscar and said to Bub, 'If anyone asks we can make stuff up.'

Belle came down the steps and told them to please come in out of the cold. She tried to take Bub's hand, but he drew away from her. 'Don't touch me. I'm covered in filth.'

'Was it bad after all?' Belle asked. Then, when she got no answer, 'For heaven's sake, come indoors.'

Jacob slogged off in the direction of the laundry and, after a moment, the other two followed, Bub stumbling with tiredness.

By the time they'd stripped and wrapped themselves in robes they were docile, and half asleep. They went upstairs, showered, and Bub went straight to bed. Jacob and William reappeared and sat in the dining room, and Holly served them. She spooned chilli into bowls and passed them buttered wedges of cornbread. Jacob's hands were shaking. 'It's just as well this is spoon food,' he said, and smiled at Holly.

Oscar went into the kitchen to make coffee. The espresso machine was off, but there was a six-cup Moka on the back of the stove.

Belle came in with dishes. She said, 'Perhaps I should get into bed beside Bub tonight.'

Oscar's ears began to burn.

Belle went on, musing. 'This isn't just exhaustion. He's climbing inside himself. Theresa's coming down with something, but her spirit isn't going to break. She'll get sick for a bit and we'll make her stay in bed. Bub isn't going to get sick. He's too tough for that. Instead he's going to go all remote, and we can't have that.'

'Whereas it's perfectly all right for Lily to be doing laps of the bypass, rain or shine?' said Oscar.

155

'Staying in shape is Lily's bottom line—it was *before* all this.'

Oscar asked Belle what her bottom line was.

'My kakapo. They're eight per cent of all the kakapo in the world.'

Oscar filled a milk jug and grabbed a handful of paper sugar straws. He looked around for a tray and asked Belle if she knew where Holly was keeping them now. 'She keeps reorganising stuff. It's a nervous thing, I guess, but I worry about it. If you were here all day like I am you'd be worrying about it too.'

'People have different ways of coping,' Belle said, then went back to what was on her mind. 'So—do you think I should climb into bed with Bub?'

'Um—yes,' said Oscar. He didn't want to discourage anyone from asking his opinion.

Belle relaxed, then said, 'Last time I looked the trays were in that skinny cupboard by the dishwasher.'

Once they were back in the dining room and Oscar was pouring coffee, Belle said, 'You should hit the sack, Oscar.'

He went off, walking backwards, saying he'd be up early and he'd see them at breakfast.

As Oscar climbed the stairs William called out after him, 'We're sleeping in.'

'Quick save,' said Jacob.

Belle realised that William and Jacob had been making a pretence of having recovered their spirits. She could see the strain of it in their eyes.

Jacob pulled her down into the chair beside him.

Holly had begun to clear away. William invited her to sit too, then, when she misinterpreted his invitation as politeness and shook her head, he said, 'Sit *down*, Holly.'

Holly looked put-upon, but pulled out a chair and perched.

Jacob told them that Bub's firefighter had finally appeared. 'He turned up at the daycare centre, and helped us, and then once we'd packed them all in the motel pool, he removed his gloves and walked away.'

Belle sat still, feeling the aftershocks of 'packed them all in'. Jacob hadn't volunteered any information about what they'd found at the daycare centre—apart from Bub's firefighter.

'I asked him whether he wanted to join us,' Jacob said. 'He listened, and then went on his way. Bub followed him, and apparently he's living on Bub's boat. Bub's been too busy to notice what's going on with his boat. *Champion* is the only sizeable vessel anchored out there, and I guess it's a safe place to choose to live if you're someone who's decided to keep himself apart.' Jacob stopped to catch his breath. His speech had accelerated steadily while he was telling his story. 'Even if I couldn't speak English I'd still be here, bunking up,' he said. 'I don't understand why he's avoiding us.'

'Curtis avoids us,' Holly said.

'It's not the same.'

Belle suggested that maybe the man was a deaf mute. Then she said, 'Sorry. That's a bit feeble.'

Jacob said, 'He looked at us whenever we spoke to him. He was listening. Only he didn't answer.' Jacob couldn't seem to stop shaking. His teeth were chattering. William put an arm around his shoulders and leaned into him. He said, 'Did you see fear when you looked at him?'

Jacob shook his head.

'Horror? Hysteria? Any kind of evasiveness?'

'No. He just didn't talk.'

William said, 'That's right. He gave us a little ration of his attention. He helped us as if he was taking pity on us after having judged our efforts to be truly determined and sincere. He handled the little corpses as if he'd handled little corpses before. He came down from his mountain with its

157

icy, airy summit still shining in his face, and helped us.'

Jacob was nodding. His expression was a mix of distress and gratitude.

Holly frowned furiously for a moment, then her face cleared. 'Maybe he's from some war-torn country and he's been plunged into some kind of *state* by all the bodies. What's it called? Post-Traumatic Disorder?'

William looked at Holly. 'Post-Traumatic Stress Disorder. Actually, that's plausible. And here was me thinking I'd found someone to blame.'

From the doorway to the shadowy atrium Sam said, 'I have to go.'

Everyone looked at her.

'Where do you have to go, sweetie?' Belle asked.

William got up. 'Well, *I'm* going to bed. So you can join me.' He scooped Sam up and walked away.

Jacob was quiet for a moment, apart from the chattering of his teeth. Then he said, 'By the way, how do we feel about that?'

'William and Sam?' Belle said.

Jacob nodded, and looked from her to Holly.

Belle bridled. 'Just because we're female that doesn't automatically mean we *get* what Sam's doing.'

'Or that we're any more qualified than you are to interfere,' Holly added, primly.

'But when did it start?'

Belle shrugged. 'He was always kind of proprietary about her.'

'Why don't you try talking to William about it? Since you're so concerned,' Holly said.

'He's my mate,' Jacob said. 'He's a great guy—in his own way.'

Belle said, 'He's your mate so you *won't* talk to him?'

'It's William that needs the talking to, Jacob, not Sam,' Holly said. 'Sam is—what do they say these days—

intellectually challenged?'

'I guess *I* could take care of it,' Belle said, in the interests of peace.

'Thank you,' Jacob said.

William told Sam he just wanted her warmth. She could keep her clothes on, but would she please clean her teeth.

Sam went into the bathroom. William took off his robe and got into bed. His dinner was repeating on him. He wondered whether he'd be able to keep it down. The food was just matter—like other matter. Kate was an old-fashioned cook. She made casseroles and stews, and William was off wet food. Or—it would be better if she used more chilli. Tonight he'd been able to taste the mince. The meat.

William threw off the covers, hurried to the bathroom, pushed past Sam and dropped onto his knees over the toilet bowl. Everything came out. The vomit had an undertone of decay, as if the air that had surrounded him all day had seeped right inside him and impregnated his digestive juices.

He got up, flushed the toilet and cleaned his teeth again, then scrubbed his tongue and the lining of his cheeks.

William was sure that everyone else involved had undertaken the burials because it was the right thing to do, and because they'd just moved by degrees into the task. Of course Adele Haines must have a funeral. Of course Warren's Aunt Winnie must. Of course they must lay to rest Bub's friend George, and Oscar's friend Evan, and Kate's fellow rest home residents. It was the right thing to do, and they'd all gone on doing the right thing.

For the first couple of weeks Theresa had even clung to her belief that the satellites could see what they were doing, and they must therefore be mindful of what those people thought of them. She went on imagining they were being watched and judged—as if, for her, the satellites were surrogates for God.

Theresa's persistence wasn't entirely unreasonable. Over the weeks the No-Go had continued to thicken. The horizon had vanished as though clear oil was rising there, roiling, so that when the sun was low in the sky the laminar movement of the transparent barrier would interrupt its light, sometimes magnifying it, sometimes making it dim. It had been a while since they'd seen the sun as a point of light. When it descended the sky it showed rather as a cloud of melting fire. Yet, on clear nights, the stars at the zenith were visible, a little blurred, but each one discrete. And Theresa's satellites were still apparent, passing over.

William had done his part, but never as a demonstration of goodness. He was a pessimist. When he wrapped and buried bodies he was only cleaning a house he had to live in. They'd finally finished the job. Shouldn't he feel better? Relieved? Acquitted? He was clean, so why did he feel dirty? He was alive, so why did he feel dead?

William got back in bed and hauled Sam into the curve of his body. He held her tight, pressed her buttocks into his belly, thigh and groin. He dug his fingertips into her upper arms. He wanted to crush her body into his own, to dilute himself with her, and be dim and absent like her.

Sam whimpered, a tiny bitten back sound.

William said, 'Do you let me do this because you're trying to help me?' He didn't hear her answer. His ears were full of a black buzzing. Then he heard her ask a question. 'Who did it?' Sam said. 'Who did bad things to the children in the daycare centre?'

'There were two adults by the back fence. Teachers, I guess. They had clawed their way out to the edge of the property. Their feet were—'

'Were what?' said Sam. He didn't reply and, after a moment, she said, 'I really do have to go.'

'No. Stay here with me.' William leaned up over her.

160

He brushed back her glossy hair and cupped one smooth cheek. Sam's eyes were troubled and puzzled—the person there inoffensive, but inadequate. Yet, still, her face was somehow unearthly. She looked like an Ariel from some ideal production of *The Tempest*.

'What happened to you?' William asked, amazed again by the way she looked.

Sam was stricken. 'I told you. I hurt my old people at Mary Whitaker and then hurt myself. You saw what I was doing with—' She hesitated. 'With the paella pan.'

'Sam, I don't mean what happened at the rest home. I mean—did something happen to you when you were younger? Some kind of head injury?'

'It wasn't my head.'

'All right.' William tried to think how to rephrase his question. The buzzing had receded. Sam's face was in sharp focus, her skin glowing like honey in radiance from the lamp with its parchment shade. She sighed, then said, 'This is what happened, if you want to know. One day, when I was by myself, climbing up a bank, I pulled on a bush and a stone about the size of a basketball came out and knocked me down the bank. They said it tore a vein in my liver. I bled so much my heart stopped. But not till I was at the hospital. Sam went to the hospital and left me there.'

William frowned. 'You said "Sam". What do you mean "Sam"?'

'The other Sam. She went to the hospital and told them she thought something terrible had happened. And then she left me, and the nurses and doctors saw what was wrong and rushed me into surgery. But my heart stopped. I had to learn to talk again.'

'How old were you?'

'Twelve.'

Brain damage from the oxygen starvation of severe blood loss, William thought. And whoever she was before the accident had already shaped her face, already conferred a momentous and eloquent beauty on her now dispossessed flesh. He asked, 'What did this friend of yours—this other Sam—call *you*?'

'Sam,' said Sam.

'Wasn't that confusing?'

'No. I don't usually call her Sam. When I'm talking to her I call her "You". One of my old ladies once said to me that everyone has a "You". Sam is my "You".'

William reflected that he hadn't ever had a 'You'. Furthermore he couldn't even imagine what his 'You' would be like. 'You must miss her,' he said.

'She should be here.' Sam gnawed her lips then met William's gaze and, for the first time, kissed him. She acted with initiative, and staked a claim.

That night William was able to sleep for a few hours, till a dream played him the recording his imagination had made that day in the preschool. In his dream he heard a thin, terrified crying, then a series of thuds, then squealing cut short by cracks and crunches and the innocuous not-quite-timber noise that custom board makes when you thump it with your fist. He woke up. It was as if he'd been dropped from the height of the ceiling. The room seem to quake. The bedside lamp was still on. All the shadows in the room were motionless, empty and clean. He was safe.

William slid his hand along the covers, but Sam wasn't beside him. He closed his eyes. After a moment, he felt the pressure of her attention. He raised his head from the pillow. She was sitting at the end of the bed wrapped in a throw rug. She flipped her hair behind her bare shoulders, an uncharacteristically nervy and self-conscious gesture.

He patted the bed next to him. 'You're very pretty,' he said.

She didn't move. 'Is that why you like me?'

'And very sweet,' he added. He closed his eyes and waited for her to nestle up. 'So,' he thought. 'This is what they mean when they say "bone-tired".'

The bed shook as Sam climbed off it. When next William looked, she was at his desk, her back to him, still robed in the rug. Her hair lay in shining waves—it looked washed, combed, carefully dried. When they went to bed it was clumped with sweat at her nape. He said, 'You washed me off.'

'I washed off the day.' She lifted a book. She showed him its cover. 'Are you reading this?'

'Jeeves and Wooster,' he said.

'Is that the sort of book you like?'

'I was enjoying it, when my mind was still able to settle. And speaking of settling—why are you roaming?'

Papers rustled, then, 'Is this your work?'

'Those are documents I was taking to a man in Granity, on the West Coast. Most of my work is on my laptop.'

And backed up, sent into the cloud, thank goodness. William hadn't thought about the case—even at first, when he'd still hoped to escape and continue his journey, as if the first hour massacre was just a hitch in his schedule, and as if continuing would have been allowed. He hadn't thought about the things he had to do, or the loss to his firm, the difficulties for the plaintiffs. But it was a relief now to remember that his work was accessible to his colleagues, and that the machinery of the suit would go on at its own slow pace, representing someone else's billable hours.

'Do you like to read books?' Sam asked.

He wondered whether she hoped he'd say no, he wasn't much of a reader. Perhaps she hoped to find he was more like her. But she didn't wait for an answer. 'Is your job important?' she said. 'Do you make a lot of money?'

'Other people could do my job,' he said. 'So I don't know

that it is important. But, yes, I make very good money.'

'Do you have a house?'

'Yes.'

The bed jostled again. She had resumed her seat, this time a little nearer to him. He reached out, and she took his hand. Hers was smooth, soft, lightly muscled. He caressed it, his calluses scratching her. He rolled her relaxed muscles against her little finger bones. 'Are you trying to get to know me better?' He continued to fondle her fingers. This was familiarity. And in a moment her hand would feel familiar again. It felt odd. Wrong.

'I told you about my accident, didn't I?' Sam said.

'I see. Your accident and my house are equivalent?'

Silence.

William tightened his grip to retain her fingers—but she didn't pull away. 'Sorry,' he said.

'Do you mean that my accident is *personal*, and your house isn't?' she said.

This was uncharacteristically astute. William said, 'If your aim is to get to know me better you can't have wanted to talk about books. Books aren't sufficiently personal.'

'That's why I asked you about your house.'

William yawned. He dropped her hand. 'Okay. Let's see. My house. Well—it has an amazing kitchen, but I never cook. When I want dinner I walk as far from my place as it takes to end up somewhere where men's cologne won't have too much olfactory impact on my enjoyment of my meal. What does that tell you?'

Sam didn't ask about 'olfactory impact' and William imagined she took in sentences with the phrase 'skipped words' in place of those she didn't understand, like a bad transcription of a wiretap. He went on. 'My books are still in boxes. I had an idea about putting them all in one room in built-in bookcases. But I have yet to find a cabinetmaker I like. And it all seems too permanent.'

'You mean you don't really want a house?'

'That's right. Because I blamed the house I lived in as a kid for things that went wrong with my family.'

'Why?'

William laughed. 'That's the time-honoured default question.' His eyes were closed again. He heard Sam take a deep breath and let it out slowly. Was she annoyed with him? He made an attempt to explain. 'I blamed the things that went wrong with our house—instead of taking issue with the reasons my mother found for those things having gone wrong. Her explanations of what must have happened when the roof leaked or she found a rat in the oven.'

More silence from Sam. It was a kind of busy silence. William shifted his head on the pillow so he could look at her. She was poised, radiant. He took hold of her wrist and pulled her into his arms. She went stiff, her elbows braced between their bodies. She said, 'I need to go to the bathroom.'

William released her.

She was gone for a while and he dozed off again—only roused when he felt her slip a hand between the covers, not to touch him but to smooth the sheets on her side of the bed. The hand withdrew. He watched her circle the bed, trailing her palm along the top of it. She stopped where she'd been sitting and stroked the covers. She looked like someone discovering a damp patch where a cat has done something illicit. She bristled with annoyance.

William opened his arms. Sam grinned, and clambered up the bed into his embrace. They kissed. Then she said, 'We were talking, right?'

'I don't mean to start again,' he said. 'Talking is done, for now.'

'So—you *don't* like me better when I talk?' She sounded hopeful.

'You don't have to talk to make me like you, Sam—if

that's what you're worried about.'

She considered that for a moment, then looked mollified.

'Was I being tested with conversation?' William was amused. He kissed her some more.

When he drifted awake again some hours later William discovered that Sam had taken herself off to her own bed. Sam—who would let him do to her pretty much whatever he wanted, and would sweat and tremble and gasp and sigh like she wanted it all too but, it seemed, would never ever let herself fall asleep beside him.

Out in the dark, on the steep shingle beach of Matarau Point, Curtis was making a kayak ready. He lifted its rudder so that it stuck out straight like a flag on a rural mailbox, then hauled it down to the water. He got on his knees to check its cargo, his camera wrapped in many layers of plastic and stowed in a water-tight container. As he tucked the package into the hull and closed the seals of the hatch cover, Curtis said to his camera, 'We'll make it.'

That's what Adele would always say to him, at any setback. 'We'll make it.' There was the film that failed, the bad reviews, the funding that dried up. He'd been fifty then—too old to learn how to do anything new. 'We'll make it,' Adele had said. It turned out that she was right— and he couldn't make it without her.

Curtis slid the kayak into the water. It coasted off, and he followed it. He eased it out between the rocks, walking till he was up to his waist in the sea. He began to push the kayak along the point, parallel to the shore. The water was very cold, and before long he was shivering.

Near the tip of Matarau Point he stopped and stood still, till the kayak's nose nudged back in towards land.

The tide had not yet turned.

Curtis waited. He would do this. He would let his camera go. If he didn't put it beyond his reach, he wouldn't be able to stop pointing it at people—living and dead—and pointlessly trying to say something by simply filling its data card. He didn't want to follow the old impulse that had shaped his whole life. He'd come to hate that impulse, and his hate was the kind that infects the past with the present. He'd had so much self-belief—and what use was it now? It was just noise in his head. It was his own voice harping back to old arguments he'd had with himself, when wounded by criticism. With *himself*, because who could argue with critics? You had to bite your lip and then endure the internal soundless fury of suppressed indignation and pointless reasoning. The critics were the canny ones. They had their say, then fanned their words away. And the artist was left to argue it out with himself. Barking, and barking, but only in his head, like a nuisance dog in a shock-collar.

Had he ever been equal to anything he'd tried to do? Curtis Haines and his camera; his boom like a boathook, grappling salvage to him, none of it really his.

He was tired of all that. Tired of thinking and planning and executing everything with care, and purpose, and full engagement—and that being never quite enough. He was tired of putting himself back together again, a little differently each time, hoping that this time he'd pass muster.

And now there was this. He had tried to film the things people really should know, like how the teams had never thought to use the digger to push the bodies into their graves, how, instead, Jacob and Bub would climb into a grave, and Dan and William would hand the wrapped bodies down to them. But people wouldn't want to see that, even if they should. How then could it be told? How could he refrain from horrifying an audience and still show how good, and tender, and civilised, the survivors were, despite the accepted wisdom about mobs, and riots, and the dissolution of the social contract that sets in whenever disaster strikes. Curtis had filmed things—long shots, dusk, the blue-painted swimming pool grave lit by car headlights; and close-ups, Bub's hands gripping the end of a gory shroud, or the tray of the ute before it was washed. Tasteful things, suggestive things, the *wrong* things—and all because he couldn't bear to be called immoral, or dishonest, or insufficient again.

He'd exiled himself from the others. Now he'd put this part of him—his past, his work—out of reach. He was in retirement.

It was very cold. His teeth were chattering so hard that he was worried he'd chip them. The slack tide went on and on, as if the sea had nowhere it needed to be.

When he was in his twenties, before surfers habitually wore wetsuits, Curtis had once stayed out for hours on a big break. He didn't quit when he got cold, and after a while he stopped feeling it. When he did come in—because it was getting too dark to judge the oncoming waves—he found he couldn't warm up. For hours he was sluggish and depressed and chilled through. It wasn't until the middle of the night that his body reached a normal temperature. Then he found himself unable to sleep because he was jacked up on adrenaline.

Curtis had had exposure and survived it, and he knew the worst of it. So he rode out the shivering as the chill seeped into his core. Eventually, the cold lost its bite, and his jaw stopped its spasms. He was almost comfortable.

The tide began to go out, and the kayak swivelled to lie at an angle to the shore. Curtis held it still in the current. He meant to make sure that, when he let it go, it would leave Kahukura and drift far away, and through the No-Go.

The moon was out. It was about sixty degrees above the horizon in air that wasn't quite clear. There were pits and snags in the transparency. Looking through the No-Go up close was like looking through a sheet of gritty ice.

When he was a boy in Invercargill, Curtis would arrive at school on frosty winter mornings to find ice on all the puddles. The kids would be elbowing one another aside to be first to scoop it up—a sheet of ice, rough with grit. They'd hold the dripping ovals above their heads and squint through them at a melting and wavering sun.

Curtis dropped his chin onto his chest. The moon reappeared, floating beside the kayak, sometimes wobbling and breaking apart like a drop of mercury. He closed his eyes. He felt serenely accomplished, as if he had paid back everything he owed the world.

He released the kayak, and his camera, then turned around and slogged back to shore.

Bub was up early. The first thing he did after putting on his clothes was let out the labradoodle, who was whimpering inside Theresa's room. The labradoodle followed him to the swimming pool enclosure where the other dogs were. As Bub swam lengths, several dogs charged up and down beside the pool, barking at him. 'This just won't do,' Bub thought. He got dressed, had an apple for breakfast and returned to the pool. He let the dogs out, then recalled them by shaving chunks off a dog roll and scattering the chunks around the lawn. The dogs wolfed the meat, then stood about, expectant, stiff-legged and trembling.

Bub regarded them with exasperation. He had hoped to have a proper breakfast, to sit down in the dining room with hot coffee, the heat pump making its slithery whisper as its vents opened and it got going. He wanted to see Belle. He had woken in the night and found her there beside him, wrapped in a coat on top of the covers. It was a man's wool coat, with shoulder pads that flared up around her ears and bunched her blond curls. He wanted to stroke those curls.

He wanted to thank her for staying with him, and see what her face did when he thanked her. But he hadn't wanted to wake her, and in the morning she wasn't there any more.

The dogs watched Bub with eager attention. Bub sighed and walked away, whistling them to him. He set off through the arboretum behind the spa, the cavalcade of canines trotting after him, tails up, each stopping now and then to sprinkle a ration of urine on this tree or that. Bub found a stick, and when he got to the meadow he threw it and the dogs raced away, the terrier and boxer reaching the stick almost simultaneously and tussling with it, the others turning back to watch for more sticks. The tiny Bichon Frise only floated off in the stick's approximate direction, moving blindly through the long grass like a blob of blown foam. Eventually, after several sticks had been shredded, Bub and his canine entourage continued on to the predator-proof fence, then walked beside it, where the going was easy because the grass had been mown and was still short, for the surge of spring growth had so far only conjured the thistles, dandelions, vetch, and soft sprigs of broom.

The bush inside the reserve was loud with birdsong, mostly tui making their combined noises: of waterfalls, ice falls, breaking glass, a truck backing, and steel reinforcing rods rolling on the tray of a truck. The Nokia ring tui was there too. Its song brought tears to Bub's eyes. He said to the dogs, 'Would someone please answer that bird,' and they regarded him with looks that seemed to say they were confident they'd understand him one day, once they knew one another better.

Bub walked the dogs all the way to where the No-Go came up to the fence near the reserve's eastern boundary. It was there he found Sam.

Sam was flicking lit matches over the line of fading fluorescent spray paint, and watching them fall, quenched and almost smokeless, into the dry grass. She was laughing in a sweet, shiftless way. Bub realised that he'd never heard Sam laugh.

Stoical Sam, who, throughout the burials, had followed orders without equivocation, only very occasionally needing a reminder to reinforce what she'd learned. Who had worked tirelessly, never complaining, and without seeming to need anything at all but a shower and meal at the end of the day. Sam, who was, in fact, the most low-maintenance female Bub had ever encountered, since even tough ones like Theresa and nice ones like Belle must be respected in a certain demonstrative way—bless them.

Bub was surprised by Sam's private mirth, and how comfortable she looked, as if the thing that was keeping them all imprisoned was an occasion of delight, like warm summer sun or fresh snow. 'Hey!' he said, incensed.

Sam stopped what she was doing and put the matchbox in her pocket. 'It's not going to hurt me,' she said, then stood very still, examining Bub and the dogs, who he had gathered to him, their collars in his hands, except the Bichon Frise, who was tucked under his arm. Sam pressed her lips together till she was smiling a sort of upside-down smile. 'How are you holding up, Bub?'

'I'll be better for a day off,' Bub said. 'Do you think you can help me sort out these dogs? We can't keep them shut up by the pool. I hate the poop. And the other day I saw Warren thoughtfully flicking his cigarette lighter at the collie's tail. I say we clear out that shed at the back of the laundry. You know—the one where the ride-on mower is stored? We can scavenge some blankets from one of the houses we've cleared, make beds, and put all the dogs in there.'

'Sure.' Sam looked once more at the strip of painted grass that marked the No-Go, then came over to Bub. One of the dogs butted its muzzle into her hand and licked her fingers. It let out a small nervous whine. Sam caressed its ears.

'I need my breakfast,' Bub said. 'An apple doesn't go

very far.' He let the sensible dogs go and set off downhill, whistling to them, and to Sam.

She caught up with him. 'What will we do today?'

Bub handed her the Bichon Frise. 'Apart from sorting out a dog run? Probably the *first* thing I should do is have a word with that guy who is living on my boat. My firefighter. He seems to understand English. And once I've talked to him I guess we fill in the motel swimming pool.'

'Uh-huh,' said Sam—this time sounding dubious. The Bichon Frise was in squirming ecstasies. Sam tilted her face up to avoid its licking. After a moment she said, 'Swimming pool?'

'Are you suggesting that the swimming pool was a bad idea? I don't get it, Sam. Since when did you have an opinion about things like that? *I* think it's been brilliant. What else were we going to do? Dig a series of smaller and smaller graves in people's back lawns? Try the school again and hit the water mains?'

'Oh, I see. Swimming pool,' Sam said.

Bub felt guilty. Sam was normally so passive and compliant that it seemed wrong to discourage her from expressing an opinion. Bub stopped and set his hands gently on the young woman's arms. 'Sorry,' he said. 'It's okay to ask questions.'

'I'm going to have to,' she said. She set the dog gently on the ground.

Bub examined her. How did she manage to look so fresh? Sam was healthy and good-looking and—despite her injury—had always had the sleekness that goes with all that. But she looked better still today—better than yesterday. She looked really beautiful.

'How's your chest?' Bub said.

'It's okay.' She moved away from Bub's touch and they went on down the hill. Bub had to recall the dogs, who were nosing at the graves by the wrecked helicopter.

Sam said, 'I've forgotten—do we know who they all were?'

Bub had given her permission to ask questions and on their way down the hill he explained who the people in the helicopter had been and what kind of lawyer William was—a litigator—not that Bub knew anything about that.

Did Bub think William should be running meetings since he was a lawyer? Sam asked. Well, Bub said, if we *had* meetings we'd have to decide who should run them. 'We've been so busy with the burials that we haven't really stopped to talk things over.'

Then she wanted to know whether Bub could call a meeting. Could he do it today?

Bub dealt with this barrage as best as he was able. He supposed that it had just occurred to Sam—a person probably used to letting others do her thinking for her—that there was next to no sign that anyone else was thinking. Sure, they were using the ziplock bags to protect papers they placed on each body to identify them. They were using empty swimming pools as mass graves. They had gone to work as if work was an act of supplication to the civilisation beyond the No-Go. They felt they were being watched and judged. They *hoped* they were being watched and judged. But none of this was exactly thought. Sam probably couldn't understand why there was so much they'd never talked about. She'd been waiting for someone to show her the way.

They returned the dogs to the enclosure. Warren was in the pool. He'd finished swimming and was now hanging by his elbows at the deep end and smoking his morning joint. Bub told him that he and Sam were going to sort out some more suitable accommodation for the dogs.

'After you've talked to the man on your boat,' Sam reminded Bub.

Bub took the young woman's arm and led her to the dining room, where breakfast was in full swing. As he came in Bub saw the cleaned coveralls and scarves and gloves draped on the room's empty chairs. He stopped dead. Then he found himself yelling. *'You said we were finished!'* He hadn't meant to express himself at volume. He was startled by it, and by the surge of panic, resentment, and distress behind it, pushing forward into his body. He began to shake.

His yell was followed by a pulse of stillness; people froze with spoons dipped and cups raised and stared at him.

'Okay,' Jacob said, cautious.

Theresa emerged from under the blanket draping her head. She was hanging over a steaming bowl, her nose red and running. 'We are. Holly was on autopilot this morning.'

'Sit down, Bub,' Belle said. 'Have some breakfast.'

Bub had alarmed himself. His ears were ringing. This wasn't *him*—he never lost it like this. He sat beside Belle and fumbled around under the table till his hand found hers and clasped it.

Sam took a seat opposite him and, much to Bub's bemusement, continued to stare at him, as if he were the only illuminated object in a field of darkness.

Holly bustled in from the kitchen and shunted plates across the table till Bub was surrounded by bacon, sausages, toast, and grilled tomatoes. 'Enjoy,' she said. 'We're coming to the end of the tomatoes. I had to clean out all the fruit and vegetables at the supermarket. I was able to leave the potatoes and yams and onions and so on. They're still fine.'

Bub took some tomatoes and some black pudding and a slice of bread—Holly baked it fresh every day.

Sam sighed. 'Those people out there—why don't they talk to us?'

Theresa coughed and retreated under her blanket. She complained that her nose felt as if someone had been at its interior with a bottle brush.

'We haven't any idea what's going on out there,' Jacob said. 'We can see the satellites, but that's all.'

'The satellites would be there even if no one was monitoring them,' said Belle. 'Even if the No-Go had engulfed the whole planet they'd still be there.'

Theresa sneezed, and said in a muffled voice, 'If the No-Go had wrapped the world there'd be way more dead fish washing up on the beach—just for a start. What I think is this: either they can't see us, or the only way they can is from directly overhead, and they can't signal us from space.'

'But you still like to imagine we're performing for the satellites,' said William. 'Being our best selves.'

Holly said she was going to make more coffee.

Theresa frowned at William, then got up from the table. She left, trailing her blanket, and looking like a cowled spectre.

Bub regarded his scarcely touched food and pushed his plate away.

'Are you sure you're finished?' Belle said, concerned.

Bub waved at Sam's place. Sam hadn't had anything but coffee, which was odd, since Sam was usually a dogged eater, possibly following the example of her Mary Whitaker people who, whenever they were off their feed, would still have made an effort to eat, being of that generation raised to waste nothing.

Bub told Jacob about his plans for a dog-run. Jacob said, 'Good idea,' and, 'Are you going to help Bub, Sam?'

'Sure.' Sam assumed a look of almost comical enthusiasm. 'Does anyone know Morse code?'

Again everyone stopped what they were doing and stared. Bub thought how often they did this—like a herd of deer lifting their heads at the scent of danger. On this occasion, though, there was a striking difference. Usually there was one person who had gone on doing whatever it was she was doing—with a kind of dutiful attention to the material, to whatever was immediately before her—and that person was Sam. This time Sam was exempt from the pulse of stillness, because she'd caused it.

Belle said, 'None of us knows the Morse alphabet.' Then,

'What on earth made you think of Morse, Sam?'

Sam didn't answer.

Jacob said, musing, 'I wonder if there's anywhere we can go to look for Morse, since we can't use Google.'

'There's bound to be an old set of encyclopaedias somewhere in Kahukura,' William said. 'Or a CD with Encarta. Remember Encarta?'

Dan suddenly thumped the table. 'We have to do something more than just dig graves. Don't we have—like—a *duty* to try to escape?'

'As if this is Stalag 17,' said William, amused.

Dan glared at him. 'You've got brains, try using them instead of being a dick. I hate the way you get super calm whenever anyone else is upset.'

Belle said, 'That's true. When we're freaking out you do tend to get above it all.'

'It does come across that way, William,' Jacob said. He looked uncomfortable, and added, 'You know—as a failure of feeling.'

William listened to this criticism and reflected that perhaps it was just that he was simply better at coping with uncertainty. After all, he had been here before, very early, waiting for someone more powerful to notice his suffering and take his part—just like Theresa waiting for a sign from her unfeeling satellites.

William had been eight and his sister thirteen when they were taken from their mother. After a short time apart in different foster homes, they fetched up with their father's family. The arrangement was better for them—though, after phoning once or twice, their father never did show.

They had one happy summer playing in the woods, or the scrubby mess of broken-down cars and tossed refrigerators just off the dirt road to their uncle's house. William's biggest cousin taught him how to shoot—then went into the army. William broke down and clung to him at the bus stop, while the adults and other kids laughed in that casual, mocking, meaning-no-harm way they had. Fall came and William toughened up to the mockery, and to the periodic alarms of all-night drinking sessions.

When the aunties and uncles got their cheques they went on binges. They didn't hurt or even yell at any of the kids— but William and his sister were alarmed by the raucous jokes and the heady stories that seemed a game of gruesome one-upmanship. They were frightened by the arm-wrestling and smashed furniture and all the reddened faces.

William was sleeping in a packed bunkroom with his boy cousins—three older—two several years younger. Sis was in with the single girl cousin, sleeping in a long room between the roof and ceiling. The cousins could sleep through the noise, because they were used to it—but William was scared, so, Friday nights, Sis would pick him up and take him out, bundled in his bedding, to sleep in one of the wrecked cars. When winter came he took to going to bed in his clothes so he'd be warm enough to sleep once he had to move.

Then, midwinter, there came a bitterly cold night— the first clear following a solid week of snow which stayed on the ground despite their proximity to the sea. After an evening when the drunken shouting melted into dreams that also shouted at William—that he must wake up!—he woke with his head tucked under the stinky plastic steering wheel of the old Chrysler truck, as usual, though he couldn't remember his sister carrying him out of the house. He was shivering and his feet were freezing, even in his boots and socks. He got out of the truck and gathered his blankets around him so that they wouldn't drag through the puddles. He hurried to the house.

The air indoors was thinly misted, and it made him dizzy. The house was silent. One uncle was on his back on the rug. Another was in a recliner, his head at an uncomfortable angle. All the doors were closed but the air was almost as cold as it had been outdoors.

William knew not to disturb the adults—they'd still be drunk—but he went to his bed to warm up, and, as soon as he entered the bedroom, he knew something was very wrong. His cousins' faces were flushed and pink, but they seemed not to be breathing. No one in the house was breathing. William didn't know what to do—but he did what he first thought he should. He dragged the two smaller kids outside. Then he went back and opened all the windows before climbing into the attic. His sister and his girl cousin were breathing. Maybe. He wasn't entirely sure. He scrambled back downstairs and searched his uncles' pockets for car keys, then drove to a neighbour to ask them to call an ambulance. He couldn't reach the brake pedal properly and had to bring the car to a stop by running it into some scrub.

What had happened was that his inebriated uncles had been feeling the cold, and had carried the gas barbecue indoors. Within a couple of hours the adults had succumbed to carbon monoxide poisoning.

One of the little cousins lived—the other might have, except it was too cold where William had left him, wearing only his pyjamas on the open porch. No one told William that though—he worked it out later.

William's sister lived—but she never woke up. The last time he visited her in her miserable long-term care facility, he found her curled up in bed. She hadn't had enough physical therapy and her tendons had shortened, drawing her limbs up so that her fists were bunched under her chin and her knees were tucked up by her stomach, so that she lay like someone sleeping in a cold room. A year after that she was dead.

William was a big healthy guy. Their mother hadn't stinted on food—only she'd never taught him and Sis to clean their teeth, so almost every tooth in William's head was a crown. She sent them to school, but had papered over every window in the house. She'd said, 'Don't believe what anyone else says'—but also believed that sinister out-runners of *everyone else* were creeping around outside all day and night, so that a person couldn't even hang out washing unobserved, and washing could only be done when it was absolutely necessary and then dried indoors in a room so perpetually damp that its white ceiling tiles were not just spotted but piebald with mould.

There was that life, with his mother—a life of intricately rationalised disorder—and there was the periodic feckless havoc of his uncle's household. And then there was silence, his mother gone—living rough somewhere far away—and a house full of stifled people. What had William learned from it all? That sometimes you just had to wait—and sometimes you had to walk away, never letting your feelings follow you.

Belle took a seat in the back of the dingy. Bub pushed out from the shore, hopped aboard, and let the dingy glide before running out its oars. They were quite close to the *Champion* before the man heard them and raised his head at the distinctive booming rattle.

Bub pressed on a few strokes then pulled the oars back in and let the dingy drift. There was no sound but that of drips falling from the blades of the oars into the sea. Bub hailed the man. 'Thank you for yesterday,' he said.

The man didn't answer. He put down what he'd been holding—a can of spaghetti and a fork.

Belle called, 'Can you understand us?'

Bub touched Belle's arm, said, 'This is Belle. We're wondering if you'd like to join us? We promise we won't put you to work—if that's what you're worried about.'

The man set one foot on the low rail beside him and dived into the sea.

Belle saw something she didn't understand. The man entered the water and her eyes anticipated the sight of his hands, arms, head, cleaving the waves, but instead something just ahead of his hands made a wedge of air, so that his arms and head first sank into an airy hollow in the sea. Then his feet disappeared and the water cracked back in a big inward-folding splash. The man surfaced some distance off, wet, the water touching him and bearing him up as water always does.

Belle shut her eyes and shook her head.

'Hey!' Bub yelled, and began to row.

The man accelerated. He struck out towards the shore. He pulled well ahead and by the time he'd clambered out onto the beach Bub had abandoned pursuit. They watched the man hurry away along the shoreline track—with Oscar drifting half-heartedly after him.

Bub called out, 'Leave him, Oscar!' and the boy came down the beach and helped them haul the dingy up past the high-tide mark. Bub stowed the oars and stood, hands on his hips, watching the man jog towards the Smokehouse Café.

Lily came into view, running. As she approached the man she broke stride and, once he'd gone by, she ran backwards for a few steps, looking after him. Then she continued on towards them. However, when she reached them she didn't stop to ask whether they'd managed to speak to the man, what he'd said, why he'd fled—instead she gave only a little salute and ran on.

'Do you think she's always been that hardcore?' Oscar asked.

Bub and Belle exchanged a look.

'Isn't she thinner?' Oscar said. 'And she runs like something is chasing her.'

Belle said. 'We don't really know what Lily's normal training programme was.'

'Don't worry about it, Oscar,' Bub said. Then, 'I think I might pull the *Champion*'s batteries and remove my Primus—just to give that bloke the right signals.'

Oscar gave a great huffing sigh and swung the dinghy around to run it bow-first down the beach, complaining as he did that Bub kept changing his mind all the time.

'Why don't you go back and fill Theresa in?' Bub said. 'She'll want to know that the guy wouldn't speak to us, and that he ran off.'

Oscar looked disappointed. He peered at Bub, then Belle, blushed suddenly and mumbled that—okay—he'd go.

Bub called after him, 'Thanks for your help.'

It seemed to Belle that it was by mutual consent that she and Bub postponed what they had to say to each other until after he'd rowed back to the *Champion*, disconnected the batteries, placed them in the stern, and stowed the Primus behind his seat.

Belle held the dingy steady against the *Champion*'s flat stern. When Bub got back in he was carrying a couple of empty sacks. 'I feel like a feed of mussels.' He ran out the oars, aimed the dinghy at the end of Matarau Point and, with several strokes, set them skimming across the water. Halfway there Bub met her eyes and said, 'Thank you for last night.'

'You're welcome.'

'Look. I'm okay,' he said.

'Yes. But if I keep an eye on you that's not going to make you start worrying about yourself, is it?'

Bub shook his head.

Half an hour later they were both in the water. Belle was standing up to her thighs and feeling along a fissure thickly clustered with mussels. Small waves were washing in and out of the crack, causing trapped air to sound a solid, metallic *bloop!* deep in the rock. The mussels were firmly anchored, and Belle was finding it difficult to slide a hand in among them in order to twist any free.

Bub had stripped to his boxer shorts and was floating above a submerged rock several metres from where she was. The water was very clear and Bub's body looked paled and flattened. He was holding on to the rock with one hand and fishing with another, both his forearms concealed in a waving garden of deep burgundy and bright green seaweed. He freed another mussel and pushed up, plumping out as he emerged from the sea, the water running off his smooth brown back. He looked at Belle over his shoulder and showed her what he had, a mussel nearly a foot in length and stippled with barnacles.

'Aren't those ones always tough?'

'We're going to make chowder. If you heat them gradually and cook them for a long time they stay tender.' He put the mussel in his sack and ducked under again, showing Belle the soles of his feet, which were broad, with deep, arched insteps.

It took Bub fifteen minutes to fill his sack. He swam to shore and emerged, his closely curled hair audibly sizzling as the seawater ran from it. He picked up Belle's sack, which was only a third full. 'That'll do,' he said. He went and stood in the narrow strip of sun at the top of the beach, shaking his arms and head, then hopping on one leg to dislodge seawater from his ears.

Belle pulled her shorts back on, with difficulty, since her skin was wet.

Bub said, 'I'm just going to stand here a moment and dry off.'

Belle came and stood beside him in the sun. She tried not to let him catch her looking at him. The curls against his neck kept pulling straight with the weight of each fresh drop, then springing up again. As she watched, surreptitiously,

Belle could see his hair apparently recoiling against his skull as it shed water. He had gooseflesh on his arms. She wanted to shave the drops from him with the flats of her hands. She wanted to warm him up.

'So many mussels,' Bub said.

Belle giggled. 'And very shapely,' she said.

Bub looked surprised then burst out laughing. They laughed together for a bit then Bub said, 'Yeah—well,' stupidly. Belle thought he was going to say something like, 'Let's talk about this,' which is what men had always said to her. Belle was twenty-seven. She'd had boyfriends, but not for years. The men she'd liked would always come out with some version of, 'Let's talk about it.' Or they seemed disbelieving. Of course Belle's problem was that she would insist on declaring herself—frank, and self-respecting, but somehow defended. She didn't know how to brush up against a man; tuck in her chin and thrust out her chest; stand twisting her curls. Somehow all those skills had passed her by. She wasn't one of those very fierce women who are only ever pursued by masochists and egotistical conquistadors. It wasn't that she *frightened* men. Her problem seemed to be only that she had somehow set up a sexually neutral personhood between herself and them. It wasn't a shield. It wasn't there for any reason. It didn't have any biographical explanation—Belle hadn't ever been hurt. It was just the way she was, she supposed, friendly, egalitarian, reliable, neither repulsive nor attractive, but simply without a charge.

Belle was waiting to hear Bub say that they should talk about it, then he surprised her by saying, 'If I give you a squeeze, I'll get your shirt wet.'

'Oh.' Belle thought about this for a bit, then turned to him and put her arms around him. She was immediately damp and momentarily chilled. But the chill was superficial and, after a moment, everywhere they touched they were warm. Bub smoothed her hair and gazed into her eyes. 'Hi,' he said.

'God, you're tall!' she said.

'Sorry.'

'No, it's—' She laughed. 'It's great!'

They stared at each other—eye to eye—she was a good ten inches shorter than him but the beach was steeply sloped. It was wonderful having permission to stare.

Bub said. 'Mostly when you get to know people you have to go through all that "What's your name? Where are you from? What do you do? Who are your people?" stuff. But I *know* what you're like. What you're really like.'

'Yes, you do,' Belle agreed. She moved her gaze and squinted past his shoulder at the sun. 'How long will your chowder take?'

'Well,' Bub said. 'First you have to chop plenty of onions and garlic, and fry it so it's soft. Then put in a little saffron. Or turmeric, but saffron's better. The mussels have to be steamed open. You rinse them to get out any barnacles and tiny crabs, then you chop up the big ones, and put the whole lot in water with some salt and pepper on a low heat—so that the liquid doesn't get hot before the solids. That's what makes mussels tough. You simmer it for a couple of hours. Then you add potatoes, bite-sized, and cook till the potatoes begin to get that peach fuzz look. And that's it.'

'You just gave me the whole recipe.'

Bub looked sheepish; then resolute. 'I'm not going to say, "Let's go somewhere." Sorry, Belle, I don't know what you expect.'

'I don't know either.'

Bub said, in a rush, 'And that's what I love about you. You never say something just for effect. You have the patience to actually pay attention to what's going on with the other guy.' Then, '*Yeah*,' he said, as if he'd finally worked something out to his satisfaction.

One of the bags slumped with a rattle as a mussel moved, perhaps sealing itself off more firmly.

'I'm a geek,' Belle said. 'That's why I'm not saying let's go somewhere.'

Bub put his salt-sticky palms against her cheeks. 'It isn't that I'm shy,' he said.

'No. It's how long chowder takes to cook.' She gave him a sceptical look.

'No, seriously, it's—it's that this is *serious*. I've been rattling about since Dad died. *Champion*'s a trawler, but I haven't been trawling because I'd have to hire a guy to help with the nets, and I don't want anyone else on the boat. And I can't sell *Champion* because that would be like selling Dad. And, anyway, I shouldn't sell my quota because it's a living, and I'm lucky to have it. So I'm burning my savings slowly in fuel and sundries, and catching a few fish then selling them as if I'm only going to sell to people who *care* about fish, or who care about me. I'm not making business decisions. It's like I'm trying not to—not to be in the world.'

'As if you're saying the Kaddish for your father,' Belle said.

'That's Jewish, isn't it?'

Belle nodded.

'Well, yes, it is like something religious. As if it's something to do with a tapu. But that's just me. I mean—it isn't really anything like that. Dad was Pakeha, anyway. It was Mum who was Maori. She's been gone for over ten years. When she got sick, I basically ran away from it. I joined the army. I'm only just out. When Dad got sick I came back and fished with him, then for him when he was having chemo. Then he died. And it's like I've been in a *nothing*, just drifting about as if I'm under a curse because of all the stuff I should have done for Mum and didn't. And what I couldn't do for Dad anyway.'

Belle was so moved that, without quite meaning to, she

interrupted him. 'Did your dad do that stuff for your mum?'

'He did. And her brothers and sisters. And my cousins. Everyone did what they should. Things were seen to properly, so I don't get why I'm stuck.'

'You've been grieving for your dad,' Belle said. It was obvious to her.

Bub blinked at her. The thick flesh on his forehead didn't so much furrow as form deep uneven rumples. 'But Dad and I got to say goodbye. He had a rough time, but he was brave and patient and never lost his sense of humour. He made it *easy* for me.'

'*And still*—' Belle thought, but didn't say it. And still, death, like the icy phantom of fable, had reached into Bub's brave, kindly father, and pulled him out of himself.

Bub was biting his lip. His eyes brimmed. 'Belle, the way I feel about you is the best thing that's happened to me in ages. But I'm scared that it'll be the *last* thing too. I just can't bear to bury another person.'

She told him to *shhh* and stretched up to kiss him. She kept kissing him, not coaxing, only tender. She trembled from the strain of being up on her toes. Eventually he took her weight and they leaned together in the sunlight, in a warm fug of evaporating seawater.

When Bub was putting his footwear back on he remarked that he wished he could show her something.

'You know, you can change your mind about that at any time,' she said.

'Now you're just being lewd, as Kate would say.' Bub shook pebbles out of one of his boots. He pulled dry gorse prickles off the bottom of his socks. 'Have you ever looked at the old pa site?' He jerked his head at the slope behind him.

'The Department of Conservation maintains the track,

so of course I've looked at it.'

'Right,' Bub said, and Belle worried that—once again—she'd stopped him from saying something he needed to. She watched him grooming his sock. He was thorough. 'How many pairs of socks do you own, Bub?'

'About four I suppose. Why?'

'Four.'

'Yes. Why?'

'You're a miracle of anti-materialism.'

Bub stopped what he was doing and frowned at her.

'Go on,' she said. 'What about the pa site?'

Bub said that, while they were smooching, he happened to be staring at the bush on the Point and he'd remembered the pa site.

'I should have given you something else to stare at,' Belle said.

Bub was unperturbed by her teasing. He went on. He said he thought about the mystery of the pa. 'You know there's a mystery, right? You know how Te Rauparaha came over from Kapiti and attacked settlements all around Tasman Bay, but not the pa on Matarau, because it was already abandoned. They reckon about four hundred years ago.'

Belle knew all this, but didn't say so.

'Archaeologists were up on Matarau Point in the fifties, digging in the midden, looking for adze heads and stuff. That Stanislaw bloke hadn't ever grazed the Point, and it was still all virgin bush. The earthworks were overgrown. But archaeologists poked about and found the pa—remnants of fortifications and storage pits. Do you know about the storage pits?'

Belle knew what storage pits looked like. She'd taken a good look at some in the Marlborough Sounds. The ones she saw were shallow oblong excavations with built-up lips. The lips were foundations: all that remained of huts with frames of manuka branches, and raupo walls and roofs. The walls were designed to overlap the lip of the pit—that way, rats were kept from the stores of kumara, and yams, and dried fish, and gourds packed with preserved kereru. Belle had an odd feeling that there was something particular she should know about the storage pits on Matarau, something she had skimmed over while reading about something else.

Bub was completely dressed now; his boots were on his feet and his shirt buttoned. He'd paused for a moment to discover how much or how little he'd have to explain to Belle. When she looked at him he went on. 'There are five pits on Matarau Point. They were filled in, but the archaeologists could see what they'd been. Besides, there were stories. They had a local, Bill Waiti, helping on the dig. The old fellow said the pits had been used as graves. Back then, in the fifties, they didn't think twice about digging up graves. So they excavated one pit and it turned out that it was true. Altogether, between the five pits, there were over a hundred skeletons—men, women and children.

'The most plausible story the archaeologists came up with about what happened was that, around four hundred years ago, one group of people had attacked another—they were possibly all Ngati Tumatakokiri, the people who were here when Abel Tasman arrived. Anyway, the attackers killed mostly everyone in the village, and took their stores. And, since they were so few, the survivors chose to abandon the pa and to bury their dead in the empty storage pits. Possibly the survivors wanted to make it hard for the raiders to come back, settle, and use everything.

'So,' said Bub, 'that's what they reckon happened. That's what I've heard and read.' He stopped speaking and regarded Belle, expectant.

Belle, of course, was thinking of how they'd thought to use a swimming pool as a mass grave. And then, all at once, she thought of the rock drawings under the curling limestone escarpment at the highest point of Stanislaw

Reserve. She felt herself flush. Her face and neck flashed red, not with embarrassment or shame, but as if her body was driving her to run or to fight. *'Jesus!'* she said. Then, 'You have to come with me now.' She jumped up, grabbed a sack, and scrambled down the beach to the dingy.

Bub was up too. He shoved the boat into the water and put the other sack on board.

'We should stop by the spa,' Belle said, and added, practical, 'Drop the mussels off and get someone to start steaming them open.'

Bub picked her up and put her in the boat. Belle was in turmoil—she needed to take another look at those rock drawings before saying what she thought she knew—but she *knew*, she *knew*. She was adrenalised and distracted, but being scooped up and swung in the air and placed in the dinghy's bow made her dizzy with infatuation.

The sun was low and the bush made runnels of shadow on the ground. As they climbed, the track branched and diminished. The forest thickened till it was the sun that was the intervention, sunlight in streams and splashes, then splatters, and finally only a fine dappling on the brown confetti of fallen beech leaves.

Belle's hair was a beacon, brightening as the day got darker. Once she turned back to say to Bub, 'I hope there'll be enough light.' Another time she came to a halt and caught his hand and pointed till he too could see the substantial but somehow buoyant kakapo flutter several feet up on to a log and stand, hunched and peering. Bub put his hand over his mouth to stifle a laugh.

There were kaka in the trees along the ridge, taking off two by two, squawking, as if they were offended and making their exit shouting abuse over their shoulders. Bub watched some drop into a treetop farther off, not settling, but just coming to a dead stop like jets landing on an aircraft carrier, arrested by cables. They snatched at branches and stopped, bobbing back and forth, one horizontal and fluttering, the other upside-down and apparently comfortable with that.

The crest of the hill and the curling escarpment had sun on it still. The rock looked like a breaking wave. It was almost a cave, its interior coated with a beige and velvety marble, its outer rim fringed by vestigial stalactites.

Belle led Bub in under the overhang, and they clambered across tumbled stones to reach the back wall and the rock drawings. Bub had never seen these drawings in actuality, but as soon as he laid eyes on them he knew he'd seen them reproduced somewhere—perhaps in a magazine.

'Look,' said Belle, and pointed at one drawing.

It was circular, as if in a frame—something Bub hadn't ever seen before in a rock drawing. The frame contained figures painted with a red pigment. Thin, semi-squatting human shapes. They were in a ring, their hands raised and pointed outwards. They were like the decorations around the rim of a plate. There was no up and no down in the picture. There was only the frame, and people pointing at it. Bub counted nine figures. Then Belle touched his arm and drew his attention to another drawing, to the right of the first and further down the wall.

Bub crouched to take a closer look.

This drawing too was framed. Again there was a circle, but whereas the first had been rendered in red pigment, this one was black. Again there was a rosette of figures, arms raised to the frame. But at the centre of this drawing was a larger figure, a man, not in a partial squat, as the others were, but straight-limbed. This alone struck Bub as unusual. Human figures in rock drawings usually had postures similar to those of tekoteko in a wharenui—braced as if load-bearing, yet twisting and supple. This central figure was rigid, and isolated, despite the way it dominated the drawing. It looked foreign. And it was rendered entirely in black pigment.

Behind Bub, Belle was silent. It was almost as if she'd disappeared. When he turned to her, he saw that she had been holding her breath. She lifted her arm and pointed at the black figure. 'That's him,' she said.

Bub's eyes wandered. Nine red figures in the first frame. Five in the second—only five, and the black man. The figures were facing away from the black figure. They were pointing at the line, as if warning: 'Yes, it's here too.'

'That's the No-Go,' Belle said. 'Those are the people who buried their dead in holes already dug for them—in their case not swimming pools, but storage pits. Those are survivors. And that's *him*.'

PART FOUR

The first morning of the hunt they set off eager and early. Theresa had her Glock, Bub and William had rifles they'd taken from one of the cleared houses, and which they carried on their shoulders, safeties on, pointed harmlessly up. Dan had a shotgun. He bore it comfortably cradled, like a Hollywood Apache. He told everyone that he was used to guns and that, every May, he'd be in some maimai on the south bank of the Raikaia River, duck hunting with his mates.

Oscar followed the hunting party as far as the arboretum and watched as they cut up through it. The morning was misty, and the hunters faded away, watercolour figures between watercolour trees.

They came home late that afternoon, and Theresa announced that she was going to institute a curfew. The hunting party were watching for movement and had been distracted by the sight of Lily on her run.

'How about I confine myself to Bypass Road and the waterfront?' Lily said, and Theresa reluctantly agreed.

'What about me?' said Oscar. 'I take my bike out most days. I need exercise too.'

Theresa looked at him and simply shook her head.

For five days it was just the four of them, and their searches were thorough and determined, and they'd be worn out when they came in. They'd sit, the men with whisky and Theresa with a glass of wine, and give an account of where they had been and what they'd seen. Oscar would perch at their feet and listen. Eventually he made a suggestion. They liked his idea, and on the sixth day of the search they sent Belle up to the edge of the subdivision with a pair of binoculars and her radio so that she could call Theresa if she spotted the man moving away from them.

Despite their organisation, they could find no sign of the man in black and, by the end of the week, they were feeling discouraged. They began to set out later, once everyone was up—everyone except Warren, who would be nursing a hangover.

'Nursing a hangover or opening another bottle,' Bub said.

'Don't ask me to talk to him,' Jacob said. 'There's no point in getting into all that. When you find this guy, we're going to get answers.'

'And we'll blow his kneecaps off if he doesn't give us any,' said Dan.

'Please don't. I'm not up to treating gunshot wounds.'

Theresa handed Jacob the binoculars and Belle's radio. It was his turn to keep watch.

Warren appeared, sat beside Oscar, and casually ruffled the boy's hair.

Holly brought them their packed lunches. Jacob pressed his packet to his nose and made a loud, pleased exhalation. 'Banana bread!'

'That's the last of the bananas,' Holly said, then, 'You're going to be hearing that a lot from now on. It will be the last of this and that. And, in case no one's told you, Jacob, you're doing Belle's job because she's out scouring the houses we've cleared for macadamia nuts, which she tells me her kakapo will accept at a pinch.'

Bub said, 'She's low on feed?'

Holly nodded.

Jacob turned to Oscar. 'There's no need to see us off, buddy. Warren can pick up my game.' They went out the door.

Oscar had let Jacob use the wireless controller, so now Warren had it. Oscar played *Halo 3* and *Gears of War* with William, Bub, Jacob, and Warren—whose playing was amazingly unimpeded by his being drunk or stoned. He played with Theresa, who was good, but always got bored within about twenty minutes.

They were playing campaign *Halo*. Oscar tried to get into the game, but his attention had wandered off after the hunting party. He wasn't allowed to follow them. Theresa didn't want anyone extra out there with all the firearms.

Oscar did appreciate the way they all looked after him, but someone should think to *use* him. They were searching a map, basically, and he was good at figuring out maps. Like the map in this game. Sure he knew where he was because he'd done it before, but even if this was his first time he'd still be several hills ahead of Warren and waiting, like he was now, his avatar—the Arbiter—dancing in place while Warren struggled to shake off his fog and catch up.

'I'm over there, under that green arrow,' Oscar said, pointing at the top half of the split screen—the landscape from Warren's point of view.

'You're teaching your grandmother to suck eggs, kid.'

The Arbiter danced around under his arrow. No one was shooting at him just yet, though Oscar could hear the Australians-on-helium voices of Grunts coming his way. 'Hurry up then, Granny!' he said.

On Warren's screen the Arbiter came into view, spinning about for a second longer then taking off to lead the way.

Suddenly Oscar got the scary air-in-his-stomach feeling he'd have whenever he realised he'd forgotten something— left his phone at a friend's place, or his favourite jacket on the back of a chair at Burger King. There was something he'd failed to notice. He looked away from the screen and around the room. What was it he'd missed?

Lily was on her way out, heading off for her run. She

was limping, and the tights that, weeks before, had clung to her lean form, now flapped as she walked. Holly was at the long dining table sorting packets and pill bottles into various filing boxes, apparently making an inventory of the supplements from the health food section of the chemist shop. Her expression was grim and harried. Sam was out on the lawn throwing a stick for the dogs—they too were confined to the spa while Theresa and the men were walking about with firearms.

That was it. It was Sam. The sight of the Arbiter reminded Oscar of how Sam would dance, spinning, in her invisible 'wind'.

Warren recalled Oscar's attention to the game. 'Now you're the one lagging, buddy!'

On Oscar's half of the screen the Master Chief was showing the Arbiter his heels, sprinting down the hillside and into the crossfire of a couple of plasma cannons, the green arrow above his head just there to say 'He's here' to Oscar—because the arrow was nothing in itself, was only the game being helpful.

But if Sam's strange dance suggested an arrow to Oscar what would that arrow indicate? Would it be just, 'Look at this mad chick', or would it be pointing out something that was invisible, but *there*?

Bub, William, and Theresa had set off along Matarau Point, leaving Dan posted at the intersection of Beach, Peninsula, and Bypass Roads. While he waited for them to work their way back to him, he kept his attention on the bush behind the houses on the point. He watched for movement—their quarry creeping away from this latest sweep.

One house had a terraced back section, and its washing line was up on the top terrace. There was a wash someone had put out that last morning. The clothes were flapping and, try as he might, Dan couldn't make his hyper-alert brain eliminate them and only watch for *other* movement. He had his gun at the ready, and he longed to let off a shot at those taunting, twitching clothes.

The shadow of a gull slid over the intersection, and Dan shuddered. He wanted to blast everything back into stillness. It was windy and the sun was catching the sides of choppy waves in a way that seemed to make slits of white open up in the sea, as if the water was a tattered material through which a light was shining. A light that, as Dan stood there, began to represent to him the energy behind the thing that was keeping them all its prisoner, that was keeping him from Faye and the kids, with Christmas five weeks away now and the six-day holiday he'd booked in the camping ground out at Sumner Beach. It was time to clean the barbecue. It was time to take the training wheels off Kayla's bike. Where was the man hiding? The man who was behind it all, who was like a switch they could throw that would turn the No-Go off and make everything go away—the sheeted shapes stacked in the motel swimming pool, the blobs of soured milk that had splattered onto the road when Dan had finally thought to empty the milk tanker—the mess, the stench, the hours and hours of work left for them to do the job right, and the waiting, like he was now, here, while some dead person's clothes made crippled gestures at him, and the few trapped gulls gathered where they knew sooner or later someone would appear with scraps, with vegetable peel, and bits of those too-sweet frozen muffins that no one would eat.

Dan detected movement out of the corner of his eye and whirled to face it. But it was only Lily, running along Bypass Road.

Lily raised a hand to acknowledge him, and turned down towards the beachfront walkway. She was favouring her left knee.

Dan thought of a boar he'd once clipped with a bullet. It had staggered away through the bush, and he'd had to chase it to finish it off. Dan found he had the shotgun stock against his shoulder and that he was staring across the black notch of its sights at Lily's receding figure. He stroked the trigger. The trigger was an open quote mark. 'Open quote,' he thought, 'and then the gun says something.'

Dan lowered the gun. He was trembling. He was horrified at himself, at what had just gone on in his head. It was true that he felt sorry for Lily, the poor woman running herself into nothing, as though if she was thin enough and fast enough she might slip away somewhere. And it was true that he was as tired of other people's misery as he was of his own. But he wouldn't have pulled the trigger, would he? And whose thought was that anyway—about the trigger being an open quote? Dan might occasionally use air quotes, but he wasn't very confident about how to use quote marks on paper.

It wasn't his thought. It was malicious and perverted and savage and clever, and had come as a soundless whisper from the centre of his skull as if there was something inside him, something that wasn't him, stirring like a hatchling in an egg.

As for Lily: she passed Dan and ran on, ignoring the twinge in her knee. All she was thinking was this: that after a long run she'd feel euphoric and pleased with herself. She'd have discharged a duty. Her first duty, which, despite cold mornings or that reedy feeling following a bout of illness, despite injuries that had dogged her, remained a simple duty. Get out, hydrate, warm up, run, stay hydrated, warm down, rehydrate, eat plenty. Every day she'd face forward and go. That was how it worked, and it had always made her happy. No one but she knew where her barriers really were, not her trainer, or doctor, or physiotherapist, or the sportswriters who watched her career.

Lily ran through the pain in her knee, she ran past exhaustion and into crisis and the exultation of her body trying to save her life. She would swear she could feel her cells at work, and she was reminded of this thing her brothers used to do at Guy Fawkes.

The day after bonfire night her brothers would gather up the squibs, the crackers that hadn't gone off, and snap them open to empty the gunpowder from their paper barrels. They'd make a little heap of salvaged gunpowder and put a match to it. It would fizz, and seethe, and spark, every grain igniting, each with its own fierce voice. Lily felt her cells were doing that, they were on fire, but it wasn't just combustion, how things ran—the cellular motor of life—it was how she alone could run, it was a slow explosion, and as she went on it would be something else, a detonation, with a thunderclap like the boom of a jet breaking the invisible but audible barrier of sound.

Lily ran on, so whittled down now that the air scarcely resisted her. She ran through it. She ran through it.

Curtis was spending the day in bed. His curtains were closed, so he didn't see Bub and William go past with their guns.

His extremities were feeling strange. His hands and feet were cold, and had been since the night he'd stood in the sea at the end of the point, waiting for the tide to turn.

Curtis could feel his big toes, but not the others. It was what used to happen when he'd been swimming too long. His feet would be fine when he was actually immersed, but afterwards, when he was walking up the beach, he'd find that ordinary sensation terminated where his sole joined his toes, and intensified there, as though every time he set his foot down he was stepping on the edge of a dull blade. But, on those occasions, his feet had always warmed up again. Now they wouldn't. Nor would his hands.

Curtis got out of bed. He went into his bathroom, switched on the lights, and stood before the bathroom mirror. He took a good look at his feet and hands. Then he pulled his boxers down and his shirt up.

There were deep bruises on his torso and thighs.

Curtis peered. The marks looked like something *worse* than bruising. What he had first seen as the discolouration of blood seeping into damaged tissues was, in fact, an interior rot beginning to show itself. Rot rising to the surface and shining darkly through flesh that was still alive.

Curtis fingered his side. Didn't that dark patch feel a little pulpy?

He checked his arms, and saw a darkening there too, a kind of purplish webbing, deep in his muscles. And—now that he thought about it—weren't there areas of diminished sensation in his arms, a sort of chilly insensitivity? Were his muscles not a little less firm and elastic, as if he'd aged ten years in the last few days?

Curtis stood pinching his biceps, fiercely and repeatedly, his nails making red crescents on his skin. He kept it up till his skin was stencilled with marks like fish scales. He was brutal, and yet his arms still felt numb.

He did have sensation in his hands. He put them together and wound one over another as if washing them. Yes—he could definitely feel his hands. The problem was his arms— he could see them, but they weren't there. And his legs, they were numb too, and mottled. And his feet were bloodless.

Curtis gazed in the mirror and turned his palms out to his reflection, beseechingly. They seemed to float beside his body like shining lotus flowers in a Hindu devotional painting.

Clearly something was wrong with him, something terrible, and without remedy.

The next day the hunters weren't due to set off till eleven, so Holly sent Sam to the supermarket to find pearl barley, lentils, and bulgar wheat.

Sam was stopped in an aisle, anxiously checking and rechecking Holly's list against the label on a packet, when Warren joined her. He put one hand on the small of her back. 'Holly told me that you could probably do with some help,' he said, then pried the packet out of her grip and dropped it in her canvas shopping bag. 'Yes, that is the thing Holly wants. See, I am useful.'

'Thank you,' Sam said. She waited for Warren to remove his hand. He didn't. He was drunk, and breathing fumes on her. His hand drifted down to the top of her buttocks. 'William is a very lucky man. Do you think he knows that?'

Sam didn't know what to answer. She had always supposed that lucky people were the happy ones, not just those who won Lotto or 'lots of dosh on a flutter on the gee-gees'—as Uncle would say. Uncle, the man who raised her. Uncle, who used to have the odd flutter and would tune in to the racetrack broadcasts and shout at the radio, seeming to urge it on as if it might jump off the kitchen counter and gallop out the door.

Sam looked hard at Warren to try to determine what he meant about William being lucky. She saw that he had pinpoints of sweat under his eyes. Years ago there'd been a boy who worked with Sam in the storeroom of this very supermarket who had looked like that, and sometimes smelled funny, like the engine of Uncle's old Falcon when its gearbox casing cracked.

Warren took her hand. She tried to pull away, but he held her fast. 'Sam, come on. I just want to be your friend.'

Sam delivered her practised reproach. 'You shouldn't take advantage of someone just because they're slow.' *Now* he would let her go. It mostly worked that way. But instead of letting her go he began shaking her hand, as if they'd just been introduced. 'I wouldn't take advantage of you. I'm not like that,' he said. He dipped his head to peer into her face. It was an exaggerated stoop, because really he wasn't much taller than her. It was what people did when they were trying to get a child to meet their eyes and be talked out of a sulk or something they wanted and couldn't have. 'Anyway,' Warren added, 'you're not as stupid as William thinks. None of us could *possibly* be as stupid as William thinks.'

'I don't know what William thinks,' Sam said, 'and I said slow, not stupid. Stupid is when you don't try to think about things. I try all the time. I'm just not as good at it as I once was.'

'Okay—I've offended you. At least tell me you forgive me.'

Sam wondered if she should give him a bit of a shove. She was stronger than he was. Strong from helping people out of bed, lifting them into their bath chairs. Strong from loading bodies into the ute, and carrying them from the ute to their graves.

Warren looked pouty and squinty like a kid pretending to be sad. 'I didn't think you were so *fussy* about people. I mean—William isn't a very nice person and you like him.'

'You shouldn't drink so much, Warren,' Sam said.

'Another wowser,' he said, and flicked a finger against her cheek.

Lily ran past the supermarket, her ponytail swinging. Sam dashed out and ran after her. She ran for a time in Lily's wake. But Lily didn't slacken her pace or turn her head to say 'Hello' or ask, 'Is everything okay?' And Sam couldn't keep up for more than half a circuit, so eventually came to a stop and watched Lily float away.

★

During the time they were searching for the man in black, William would wake up in the middle of the night to find Sam wanting a conversation.

They'd have gone to bed, always in his room, not hers. They'd make love. He'd fall asleep and would wake later to find that she wasn't beside him, but was perched on the end of the bed, just out of reach. As soon as she saw he was awake she'd start asking questions. They were very simple questions, and her manner was oddly constrained. Perhaps she was rehearsing. Not that her questions sounded rehearsed as such—but neither did they seem spontaneous.

Finally William decided to take Sam's need to know him a little more seriously. He began to vet his answers carefully to make sure there was nothing she wouldn't understand. But instead of being grateful or even stimulated by a conversation conducted at her level, Sam became visibly displeased. She chafed and fidgeted.

William lost patience. 'Would you rather we go back to discussing books?'

'But you're still reading the same one,' she said.

'I'm not reading. When you're not here with me I'm doing the same thing I do all day—only with my ears. I *listen* for the man in black.'

Sam was silent. But the air seemed to vibrate.

William said, 'I was making an effort with you, Sam. I can't think what you want. What these questions are for. It can't be flattery, because whatever else you are, you're an honest person.'

Sam didn't respond, didn't thank him for the compliment. He was agitated, and that was unfair on her. He modified his manner. 'To be absolutely honest, this thing you've taken to doing creeps me out. It's like—' He considered for a moment how he could make the comparison he wanted in a way she'd understand. But she wouldn't like it if she sensed him making adjustments in order to accommodate her simplicity. She clearly thought he was talking down to her.

'Okay,' he said. 'What I tell myself is that you're getting to know me, and being dogged about it. You've compiled a list of questions and are working your way through it. I've heard that the Queen of England, when she's taking one of her little walks shaking people's hands, always asks: "Have you come far?" That's what it's like with you. Your questions are so *general* that it's as if you haven't taken in any of what I've already told you. As if you're only asking questions in order to pass on what you learn to someone else.'

'Sorry,' Sam said.

William sat up so that he could meet her gaze full on. 'We're having a kind of relationship,' he said. 'And it's a relationship with some certainties. Do you know what I mean?'

'Yes,' she said. Perhaps she was too afraid now to admit she didn't.

'I'll tell you something about books,' William said, and waited for her reaction.

'Okay,' she said, neutral.

'When my mother finally went right over the edge, she was still trying to save, or comfort herself, with the things that always worked before—like rereading her favourite books. She had an early edition of Joe Haldeman's *The Forever War*, signed by him. She was very proud of it. But one day she confided to my sister that someone had changed her copy for another one with exactly the same cover. She'd discovered the substitution when she was trying to read it again, and found that all the words were subtly different. My sister asked to see the book. Mom produced it, and my sister pointed out Haldeman's signature and his personal inscription. But Mom didn't want to be reassured, she wanted to be believed, and colluded with. She'd say, "People are jerking us around!"'

William stopped talking—he'd quoted his mad mother and her favourite saying had scorched his mouth. After a moment he went on. 'She said someone had come into the house, taken her book, and left a replica in its place. A physically exact copy, right down to Joe Haldeman's signature.'

'Am I like a replica?' Sam said.

William shook his head, impatient. 'Where did you get *that* from? What I'm trying to tell you is that the weird way you ask questions is doing my head in, partly because I keep wondering whether I'm being like my crazy mother and imagining a difference that isn't there.'

Sam apologised again.

'I don't want an apology.'

'Do you want me to get back into bed with you?'

'Yes.'

'I'll be a minute,' Sam said. She went into the bathroom. This time William wasn't overtaken by sleep. He waited. Sam couldn't have understood much of what he'd just said. She'd decided he was telling her off, and that she had to make peace with him. He couldn't talk down to her—but he couldn't talk *to* her either. He couldn't conjure a simpler past for himself, or simpler feelings about his past. He wondered why it mattered anyway. Because one of the certainties of their relationship was that it was temporary. After all, he could hardly fall in love with a brain-damaged caregiver, could he?

And then he had a moment of insight. Of course he could. Sam—tolerant, responsive, loving—was someone who would have taken his mad mother just as she found her, and managed to be simply, steadily kind. He *was* falling in love—with someone right now very suitable—but someone who would never fit into his life. A life he could scarcely imagine resuming now, though it was his *real* one.

Sam came out of the bathroom. She had washed her face

and her hair was damp. She tried to disguise it, but she'd been crying. She climbed into bed and pressed her hot, wet face against William's naked chest. She muttered, 'You like her better than me.'

'Excuse me?'

'You were arguing.'

'I didn't hear what you just said, Sam. I thought you said that I liked someone better than you.'

'You argue with Theresa and Bub, and you like them.'

'I like you. We weren't arguing, Sam. I was just being—' Over emphatic. 'I was just fussing,' he substituted. He uncovered her face and wiped her tears. 'Don't cry. Look. Here we are. The two of us. Together.'

Skin to skin.

Sam bit her lip and made a brave attempt to stem her tears. She managed it eventually, and they nestled, and she went to sleep, damp, warm, relaxed—leaving William worrying about himself, worrying that he'd felt more or less intact till now, and didn't any more.

On those nights, the nights of the hunt, Theresa would lie in bed and imagine the satellites. She'd continued to believe they were being watched, and had visualised various foiled attempts people on the outside might have made to get to them. On the night following the power cut they'd heard one short burst of what Bub said sounded like an RPG—but only the roar of the rocket, he said, not the detonation of the grenade. Theresa imagined unexploded ordnance lying in the transparent thicknesses of the No-Go, somewhere below one of their hill horizons. She speculated about high-flying drones, till remembering how engines stalled whenever they entered the No-Go. She thought about giant catapults. She thought about slow-tunnelling rescuers.

Theresa understood something of what the people

out there—those in charge, of whom she was a lost foot-soldier—would so far have tried to do. She believed they would make every attempt to communicate, to take charge from afar. And she still believed they would talk, once the survivors found that helpful encyclopaedia with an entry on Morse that included the code.

Theresa lay in bed and thought what message they might send first. The people out there would already have a list of the missing, Kahukura's weekday daytime residents, and travellers on Highway 60. The survivors might have already been identified, and differentiated from the dead, the bodies layered in the motel swimming pool, wrapped in their own bed linen. The satellites could see them—the survivors—and so people would know that the red-haired woman who sometimes still wore her checkered high-visibility vest was Constable Theresa Grey; and the woman who regularly passed back and forth through the locked gates of Stanislaw's Reserve was the Department of Conservation worker Belle Greenbrook; and the woman who ran laps of the bypass and shore reserve was ultra marathon champion Lily Kaye.

As for the rest of them, surely whoever was missing someone in the vicinity had been called in to look at the satellite pictures of the gathering at Adele Haines's graveside; Bub and William's team around their ute; Holly on the Spa's lawn, lifting sod to make vegetable beds. Hopefully Oscar's parents had recognised him from above. Maybe they'd all been positively identified, and any messages they sent would only confirm what was already known. Surely if they'd been identified, their names had been released, and her mother and sister and her police colleagues were watching her doing what she'd said they must all do, and *be seen* to do, and were proud of her.

'Those people out there,' Theresa thought, 'poring over our most recent remote portraits, proud, pitying, anxious. Police, military, scientists, the media, all thinking and talking and making moves and—probably—lying awake, just like this, trying to imagine how it is on the quiet side, for *us*, with the cats crowded once a day at the boat ramp, heads down and tails up, eating, with all the gulls who've learned not to try to fly.'

Every night Theresa would lie awake imagining the satellites, then she'd fall asleep and dream. She'd dream that she was trying to find a parking space at the Port of Nelson and every bare bit of asphalt was covered in military vehicles and she couldn't see the water past the grey walls of ships. Or she'd dream she was visiting her mother and they were in the garden and her mother had asked her to hold a hose—because there was a ban on sprinklers and she was watering by hand—and then her mother had gone inside and Theresa was left standing there, drenching the garden, while the twilight thickened, and the indoor cooking smells grew fragrant, then acrid, then ashy, and then it was dark, and there were no lights in her mother's house.

Theresa was hauled up out of sleep by the sound of a fight. She was out of bed and in the corridor before she was properly awake.

The yelling was coming from William's room. Theresa tried the door handle. It was yanked out of her hand. Sam erupted from the room, knocking her aside. William followed Sam and, when she turned to defend herself, he pushed her up against the wall opposite his door. He grasped the blanket she had wrapped around herself and, strangely, had retained, even though it was hampering her flight. William gathered a fistful of blanket under her jaw. He threatened a slap, and then did slap her.

Sam made no sound. For moment, there was nothing but the slap and a thump as her shoulders slammed back into the wall. Then Theresa shouted, 'Stop!'

Sam let go of the blanket, but it stayed in place, pinned by one of her arms.

William landed a volley of slaps on Sam's shoulders, and her free, defensive, hand. Then he dropped her and stepped back.

She fell to the floor and finally made a noise—a yelp of surprise, as if she'd only just registered what was happening to her.

Theresa grabbed William's arm, but when he advanced on Sam again and raised his fist he lifted Theresa off the floor. She jabbed her knee into his hip and he staggered.

Bub and Jacob arrived and, with difficulty, wrestled William away from Sam. Theresa let go of him. Bub wrenched William's arms up behind his back and forced him down onto the carpet on his knees.

Sam was now sobbing, fearful and heartbroken. There was a strange smell in the corridor—as if someone had opened the door on a freezer used to store something inorganic. It was very like the scent Theresa sometimes got a faint whiff of whenever she was near the No-Go.

One of Bub's elbows was jammed against the back of William's neck, forcing his face towards the floor.

William began to shout. 'You crazy bitch! Before you fucking started in with your manipulations you should have done some reading! No one believes in fucking Multiple Personality Disorder any more. It isn't even in the DSM Four!'

William was articulate even when nakedly enraged. He tried to buck Bub off and they both collapsed sideways onto the carpet. Bub threw a leg over William and got him in a chokehold. Theresa hesitated, looking for a safe place to lay a hand on to help, and chose to grab a handful of the thick hair on his crown. 'Easy,' she said.

Just about everyone else was, by that time, standing in the doorways of their rooms and looking on.

Jacob picked Sam up and carried her to an empty chair

in an alcove. Belle darted in to pick up Sam's blanket and return it to her.

Bub said, through gritted teeth and grunts of effort, 'I'll let go when you let up, buddy.'

William stopped fighting. He lay still.

'Are you going to be good?' Bub said.

William stayed quiet and Bub loosened his hold. He let William straighten, but didn't release him.

Sam was sobbing. She was trying to say something too, her voice so broken and mushy that it took Theresa a while to work it out. 'What did she do?' Sam asked, apparently in an agony of confusion. 'What did she do?'

'What did *you* do,' William said—correcting Sam, not questioning her. '*You* did it.'

'No. You did, buddy,' Bub said. 'And you'd better not do it again or I'll give you the bash!'

William ignored Bub. He concentrated on Sam. 'You should've read the latest research before you came up with your little bit of theatre. The current view is that Dissociative Identity Disorder is a creative strategy a damaged person uses to try to express the painful truths of their history. But I think it's all histrionic attention-seeking. What did you think I'd feel?'

'You are so out of line that you're out of orbit!' Theresa said. She poked William in the sternum with her index finger. 'You have issues.' Jab. 'You can keep your issues to yourself.' Jab. 'I take a very dim view of partner abuse.' Jab. 'So watch it!' Jab, jab.

William ignored her too. He glared at Sam's slack, miserable face. 'Are you following me? Or have you conveniently reverted to the Sam who hasn't a hope of following me?'

'*William*,' Sam sobbed. She was pleading.

'Stay away from me,' William said. Then he looked down at the floor and became still, haughty, inward.

Bub continued for a time to pester William with threats, then pleas for promises—'Promise you're done. Promise to behave'—till finally he ran out of anger, or self-confidence, or whatever had carried him through the confrontation, and let William go.

William straightened his clothes and, without another word, stalked through the gathered onlookers into his room, slamming the door.

'That guy has fucking lost it,' Belle said. 'Perhaps we should shut him up somewhere.'

Bub gave a whoop. 'Yeah, and feed him meat on a stick!'

'And hose him down when he's dirty,' Belle said.

They began to laugh, semi-hysterical.

'Would you two just chill,' Jacob said. Sam had her face against his neck and was lost in noisy grief.

'Let's get her into her bed,' Theresa said to Jacob. They led Sam to her room, speaking to her gently, Jacob saying, 'Are you injured?' and Theresa saying, 'You should just stay away from William.'

A few days later Curtis arrived at the spa and asked if he could please see Jacob in private.

They retired to the treatment room. As Curtis undressed, he explained his problem. He was careful to use the word 'bruise' instead of 'rot'. He felt confident that Jacob would see for himself what the problem was. He didn't want to inadvertently provide Jacob with cues and stop him seeing what was actually there to be seen.

The room's lights were all soft-toned, recessed halogens—not the best for an examination—but there was a magnifying glass framed by a fluorescent tube which, presumably, had been used by the spa's beauticians to inspect sun damage, enlarged pores, wrinkles, and spider veins.

Jacob asked Curtis to take a seat in one of the recliners.

He positioned the magnifier.

The room wasn't cold, but Curtis found he was shivering. It was difficult to suppress his disgust at the sight of his own reflection in one of the room's kindly mirrors. His skin was darkened by a puce webbing of diseased flesh. He said, 'The thing that alarms me most is the absence of pain.'

Jacob moved the jointed arm of the magnifier to another position. He peered closely at Curtis's thighs.

'When I run my hand down my leg the flesh feels quilted, as if there's stitching along all the dark places,' Curtis said. 'As if someone *made* me.'

Jacob, his head down over the lens, said, 'Honestly, Curtis, all I can see are one or two bruises. Their persistence might be due to a lack of vitamin C. Stress will make your body chew through vitamin C and B. And we're not getting enough fresh fruit and vegetables. I can't wait till Holly's garden starts producing. Tell me—have you been eating canned fruit with your cereal?'

'I've been off my food. That can be dealt with. But, Jacob, is it really a good idea to just reassure me about the other thing?'

Jacob straightened to look him in the eye. The man seemed perplexed. 'Your circulation might be a little under par. But are these bruises of yours really bad enough to be giving you all this bother?'

The darkening on Curtis's legs seemed to swarm, as if he was seeing something without substance, like shadows cast on a sandy streambed by the twists and dimples in the current. He rubbed his eyes.

Jacob noticed this and asked, 'Have you got floaters? Dark motes in your field of vision?'

'I'm not sure.'

'That could make you see blotches where there aren't any.' Jacob sounded hopeful. 'The blotches would move. Are they moving?'

Curtis watched the darkness ooze. It looked like bloodied water moving in a vacuum-sealed meat pack. 'Yes.'

'Well—there you go,' Jacob said. He explained that floaters near Curtis's optic nerves could be another result of stress. 'Stress has vascular effects. Perhaps you're only noticing and minding because you're such a visual person.'

'You talk as if I'm complaining about a poor-quality print of one of my films,' Curtis said.

Jacob laughed. 'Look. I'll give you some multivitamins. Get dressed now. You should probably spend the day sunning yourself on your porch. But stick to the Bed and Breakfast. We'll be out again today with our guns.'

Jacob walked Curtis to the front door. As they passed the dining room Holly spotted them and hurried out, wiping her hands on her apron. 'Curtis! How lovely to see you. I was about to bring you your bread. If you wait a moment I'll go get it.'

'I'm sorry to deprive you of an opportunity to visit.'

Jacob glanced at Curtis. There was something unpleasant in the man's tone, something smug and sly.

Holly blushed. 'Oh—that's all right—I'll just go get your loaf.' She set off towards the kitchen.

Jacob was puzzled. It seemed that Curtis wanted reassurance, but not looking after.

When Holly returned, with the bread wrapped in a clean tea towel, Curtis accepted it from her but didn't say thank you. Instead he looked at Jacob and said, 'Holly is wooing me.'

Holly stiffened. Her blush drained away. 'I'm not,' she said. Then her eyes filled and she muttered, 'Excuse me,' and bolted up the stairs.

'Why on earth did you do that?'

'She keeps turning up with baked goods. She fusses about my kitchen, sniffing the butter, and saying inane things like, "A man shouldn't have to cook for himself."'

'She means well.'

'You think so?'

'Of course.'

Curtis said, 'You all want something from me.'

Jacob gaped. He couldn't think of a reply.

Curtis walked off with a limp, hugging his loaf of bread.

The first thing Jacob did when he came in from the day's hunt was go to find Holly.

She was at a table in the dining room, spreading tomato seeds on paper towels. She glanced up. 'I'm drying them for planting. I'm going to make another vege bed. And I've been foraging further afield, not just taking my daily—Theresa-approved—trip to the supermarket. I've been making an inventory of freezers in the cleared houses. We have to organise our provisions. For instance, we should save all the canned food. Within twelve months everything in the freezers will have gone off. Theresa thinks I'm being bizarre, talking about twelve months. But since it's my job to feed everyone, I'm obliged to think that far ahead. If you people fail to find the man in black, or he turns out to be no help, then at least there'll be some plan in place to keep everyone from malnutrition.'

'Fair enough,' said Jacob. Then, 'How are you?'

'Don't fuss, Jacob.'

'Curtis was totally out of line.'

'He's grieving,' Holly said. 'It's understandable.' She paused a moment, then added, 'And forgivable.'

Jacob went away to wash up and Holly sat wondering how she was really.

When she was a girl the news sometimes used to make her cry. Her mother would switch off the television and say, 'Don't get so carried away, Holly. You may have strong feelings about what is happening in Somalia, but when you sit crying in my living room you're only imposing those strong feelings on your family.'

Holly was going to try very, very hard not to do that. She couldn't communicate her feelings, so she mustn't impose them. She had really felt for Curtis, but her mouth was always full of empty politeness. And Curtis didn't want to talk to her. He didn't want to talk to any of them.

'Holly is wooing me.' The shame of that! And it was the only thing he'd ever had to say about her. Curtis seemed to despise even the few things the other survivors had been able to do for him. Adele's grave. Her baking.

Holly wrenched her attention away from her feelings and concentrated on her task. It was a worthwhile one. She felt that she was being sane in her aims, and farsighted. But, as the days of confinement had gone by, she'd catch herself repeating herself, checking whether the oven was off over and over again, or making exhaustive inventories of Jacob's filing boxes of medications. Once, when Jacob caught her doing it and asked whether something was missing, she'd snapped at him. 'Aren't they normally locked away? Don't you and I have the only keys?' Then, 'Warren has had plenty of opportunities to go through houses for himself, looking for drugs, if that's what you're suggesting.'

Jacob had held up his hands, palms out, and said that he hadn't meant to suggest anything—certainly not that his friend had been dipping into their store of medications. He was only concerned to find Holly going through the drugs *again*.

Holly was worried herself about this panicky compulsion to keep checking things, to keep counting under her breath, her count a charm against disorder. She was doing it again tonight. Sorting. Counting. Trying to blot out the voice that kept saying, *'Holly is wooing me.'*

Jacob sat down on the couch with Dan and Oscar, who were trying to watch a DVD. Warren started to talk, trying to make sense of things, though nothing immediate, nothing on the screen. He spoke as if he and Jacob were alone in the room. 'Piri's tangi seems so long ago,' he said, slurring. 'Wasn't it shitty that only five of his old mates bothered to come? Hey—did you notice how the other guys all had big guts sitting on their belts?'

'Did they?' said Jacob.

'Yep, going to pieces. You know, I reckon Piri might have preferred a wake—something less solemn. Do you think it's right to be so solemn?'

Jacob rubbed his palm across his mouth, determined not to answer—because, of course, he did have an opinion. He kept thinking about the daycare centre. He kept waiting for the tide to recede, a king-tide of horror and disgust, of pity, and distressed tenderness. There didn't seem to be any way to *be* about the dead. Gentleness was useless. Formality was useless. Solemnity or celebration—it was all useless.

He'd escorted Belle that afternoon when she went to feed her kakapo. The reserve's fence would be very difficult to scale without a long ladder, so Theresa had thought it safe to assume that the man wasn't hiding in there. Still, just to make sure, she'd sent them to patrol the inside of the fence, checking for ladders or ropes. A full circuit took four hours and Jacob was pretty tired. Too tired to go on thinking.

Oscar complained that his legs ached. 'I need to go out for a bike ride,' he said. 'I hate being cooped up.' Someone suggested he make use of the stationary bike in the gym, and he pressed his lips together and set off around the building, peering out through the dark windows as if he hoped to catch the view at something illicit.

★

Lily was already in bed, worn out and asleep, her exhaustion a hammock she'd hung over the fizzing abyss of everyone else's sleeplessness.

William was in his room, a little drunk, his phone plugged into the room's stereo, listening to something sufficiently big and real—Schubert—and deaf to Sam who was standing at his door, alternately knocking and pressing her ear to the wood to listen.

Bub and Theresa were sitting on the terrace. It was chilly and they were wrapped in coats. They were trying to make plans about what might come next, if catching the man in black and asking him questions didn't solve all their problems. Theresa said that she thought they should move the last of the cars from the supermarket parking lot, and paint the concrete some pale colour—they could easily get enough paint by scavenging in people's sheds and garages. They could run a power cable out from the supermarket and set up some big lights, then use the lights and the reflector of painted concrete to send messages. If they didn't manage to find Morse surely they could devise their own code of short and long flashes? 'With the simplest combinations representing the most commonly used letters. Like SOS— three dots, three dashes, three dots.'

'That sounds right. Not much point us sending that though. I'm pretty sure they know we're in trouble.'

Theresa went to the rail and looked up. It was a fine night and the stars were visible, though blurred and melting. She picked up the pair of binoculars that lived on the terrace, and pointed them at the zenith. That part of the sky had a particular look; the air was like clear oil roiling in clear water. She moved her head to focus the binoculars on the place where the stars began to streak and run, then, further down the sky, where black space and bright stars smeared together into a dark glassiness. She said, 'I think we have to concentrate on the satellites.'

Bub fetched a blotter pad from the manager's office, and sat down to nut out some code.

Theresa finally took herself off to bed. As she passed Sam she said, 'For God's sake girl, have some pride!'

Kate put away her knitting and climbed the stairs.

Jacob asked Dan to give him a hand with Warren.

Holly told Bub that she would put out the lights; he should get to bed.

Bub found Sam still sitting on the floor of the hallway, her cheek pressed to William's door. 'I hope you don't mean to stay there all night,' Bub said. He was very irritated with her. How could she bear to be so abject?

Bub went on to his room, where Belle was waiting for him, the ends of her hair still damp from her shower. She was rosy, and smiling.

Sam let Bub shoo her back to her room, where she waited for everyone to go to bed so that she could return to her post at William's door. She paced her room, chafed by its emptiness. She wasn't thinking, only feeling. Her heart had stopped and she was still upright. She was her body and she hadn't known it. William's door was what kept her from him, but, in his absence, it acted as a surrogate for William. She could lean against it. It had a texture and a temperature and a taste—she had pressed her mouth to it. Without something to touch, something standing in for William, Sam was left with the memory of his rebuff—how he shook her hands off when she tried to touch him. His disdain, his pressed-together lips, wrinkled nose, squinting eyes. That was disgust—Sam had seen that look often enough on his face when they were going house to house, cleaning up.

Sam had liked her job at Mary Whitaker. Every morning Snow would say, 'Here's my girl!' and Mrs Craig would have a story about her grandson in Saudi Arabia. And Sam was sure that, even when changing Mrs Collins's bed sheets or wiping shit from poor partly-sighted Mrs Healey's bathroom light switch, *she'd* never have made that face.

William had held her, and held her down, and his body would go hard all over when he came. He did things to her she'd never dare to ask anyone to do, and other things she'd not dreamed people did, or that she'd like. Bits of her weren't her own any more. They were his. She'd showered many times—days had gone by after all—but she could still smell him. She was inside a ghost of him with nothing solid to touch, not even—while she waited for the hallway to clear and everyone to go to bed—his door to press and scratch and whisper at.

It was a mild spring night but eventually Sam got cold. She crawled under the covers. She could feel herself going, so sat up and opened a drawer in the bedside table. She took out a pen, and a pad of the spa's stationery, and wrote a note. She ripped her note off the pad, folded it small, closed it in one fist, and lay down again.

Theresa woke up. Jacob was shaking her. He said, in a whisper, 'I need your help. Get Sam, and maybe Bub too.'

221

And then he was gone from her room.

Theresa found Sam's light still on. Sam was lying looking up at her bedroom ceiling as if listening to movements in a floor above. (There was no floor above.) 'Jacob needs us,' Theresa said. She left Sam to sort herself out, and knocked on Bub's door. After a moment the door opposite—Belle's—opened, and Bub poked his head out. He put his finger to his lips and said, 'Belle's fast asleep.'

Theresa pointed down the hall, at the cracked door of Warren's room.

Bub came out, closed the door carefully and followed her.

Jacob was kneeling by Warren's bed. He'd rolled his friend to its edge so that Warren's face was turned down to the floor. There was a small patch of vomit on the carpet, and more smeared on Warren's face and in his hair. There was vomit filling his nose too, and the fluid in his nostrils bubbled with each breath he took. Jacob asked Theresa to get a wet towel, and she scrambled into the bathroom. She ran taps, soaked one towel and came out with two, one wet and one dry.

Jacob thrust his fingers into Warren's mouth and caught his tongue. Theresa passed him a towel. Jacob wiped his friend's face then pinched Warren's nose closed. He placed his mouth over Warren's and sucked. He spat vomit into the towel and wiped his own mouth. Warren was now making rasping and gargling noises. 'Help me roll him onto his face,' Jacob said. Bub and Theresa rushed forward as eager as racehorses from a starting gate. Together they rolled Warren back across the bed. Some more fluid trickled out his mouth and nose, and his breathing eased a little.

Theresa said, 'His skin is clammy.'

'I think he's only aspirated a little bit of vomit,' Jacob said. 'But he isn't gagging, which worries me. His reflexes are depressed. And don't you think his fingers are a touch blue?'

'Yeah,' Bub said.

Jacob fished in his collar and produced a key on a cord. He gave it to Bub. 'Unlock the top drawer of the filing cabinet in the manager's office. The drug I want is Revia.' Jacob spelled its name, and Bub hurried out the door. He passed Sam, who was hovering there helplessly as if waiting for instructions.

There were pill bottles on the bedside cabinet. Jacob picked one up and rattled it. 'He hasn't taken all of them,' he said. 'Only a dose—or his idea of one, since he's self-medicating. But he was probably foggy, and has taken it twice.'

'So you think it's a mistake?' Theresa gathered up the bottles and read their labels. 'Temazepam, and codeine phosphate. And this is diazepam—which is a form of Valium, isn't it?'

'Yes. It's a muscle relaxant. But it's the codeine I'm worried about. I've sent Bub to find a drug that's usually prescribed to wean people off heroin. It's not the best thing for the job. It's an oral medication and not very strong. There was some in the pharmacy. The best drug for this job is intravenous, but you'd only find it in hospitals.'

'Shouldn't we get him moving?' Theresa said.

Jacob nodded. 'Let's put him in the shower.'

Theresa darted ahead of Jacob into the bathroom. 'Run it cold,' Jacob called out. He got into the shower with Warren.

Theresa wanted to go after Bub and hurry him along, but when she went back into the bedroom to check the clock on the bedside cabinet, she saw that Bub wasn't being tardy—time was dilating.

Sam was still in the doorway. She must be able to smell the vomit. Changing Warren's bedding would be something Sam would do almost by instinct. She was used to cleaning up after people and did it automatically, with thoroughness and dispatch. But she didn't begin stripping the bed, only drifted closer to the bathroom, her eyes unfocused but her face tense. One of her hands was closed into a fist. 'What is that?' she whispered.

Theresa could hear the shower, Warren moaning, and Jacob speaking in a strangled, tearful voice.

Theresa felt faintly scandalised. She said, 'Perhaps you should get a mop and bucket. Sponge the carpet then put fresh sheets on Warren's bed.'

Sam's head came up. Her shoulders were twitching, as if she were bracing herself in a series of small adjustments. She dropped a hand onto Theresa's wrist. 'What *is* that?' she said again.

'Warren has taken too much of something,' Theresa explained. 'And it would be a great help if you could sort out his bedroom while he's not in it.'

The shower shut off, but Jacob went on, haranguing his friend. Theresa couldn't hear the words, only the tone of reproach and distress. 'Sam!' Theresa said, exasperated. 'Are you listening?'

'No,' Sam said, defiant and desperate. '*You* listen. What *is* that?'

'Jacob is upset. He's scolding Warren. Are you going to be of any use?'

Sam's eyes filled with tears—it looked more like rage than anguish. 'For God's sake!' she yelled. 'Can't you *feel* that?' Then, as though her anger had incited something else, something exterior to her, she jerked upright and threw her head back. Her jaw went loose, her mouth dropped open, and her face relaxed. It was then that Theresa noticed the bruise on her jaw, dark, definite, and in the shape of knuckles. 'Jesus, Sam! Did William hit you again?'

Sam came out of her trance. Her clenched hand opened and she dropped a small square of paper on the floor by the door.

Jacob emerged from the bathroom, dripping and

shivering. 'We need a couple of clean robes,' he said.

Theresa hurried off to the treatment room where there was still a cupboard full of fluffy, folded white robes. On the way she passed Bub, taking the stairs three at a time and carrying a packet of pills.

When Theresa got back, Jacob was walking his blanket-wrapped friend up and down. Warren's ankles were turning at every second step. Bub had stripped the bed and was scrubbing the floor with a detergent-soaked cloth. Theresa took Warren's weight while Jacob put a robe on, then they wrapped Warren in the other robe and continued to walk him.

Theresa said, 'Where's Sam?' She spotted the paper Sam had dropped and picked it up.

'I threw her out,' Bub said. 'She was being useless and weird.'

The paper was a sheet of spa stationery, folded palm-sized. Theresa opened it and read: *Pleese pleese help me with William.*

Theresa decided that the matter of Sam, her fresh bruise, and her note—her cry for help—was probably best left for another day.

Oscar waited a very long time for the hallway to be quiet and empty. He hadn't wanted to know what the sounds of hushed alarm were about. He just wished everyone would go to bed and get out of his way.

After another hour the noises had subsided. Oscar's clock said that it was two-fifteen. He'd had no trouble staying awake. He was of an age when he'd naturally rather get up at noon and go to bed in the small hours.

At two-thirty Oscar opened his door, checked the hall, and went out. He crept to the fire exit—pressed the latch, then jammed the door open with the ironing board he was carrying for that purpose. It was the fifth time he'd done it, and it was beginning to feel like an established procedure.

He stood on the fire escape and listened to the night. A ruru had come down from the reserve and was up in the arboretum. Oscar heard the owl calling, then saw it, a small silent shadow that floated across a glade between a stand of birches and a black beech. He lost it in the dark and, a moment later, heard a scream—a rat or rabbit. Then, as if a sluice had opened in the sky, a wind came across the ridges landward and the tall brittle European trees began to roar like surf.

Oscar clambered quickly down the fire escape. The steel shivered and rang, but he couldn't hear it over the wind.

He made his way around the back of the kitchen and started across the lawn, navigating through a dark crease near to the shrubbery by the lights on the driveway. The grass was damp and squeaked under his trainers. From where he was, the driveway lights made a yellow gauze in the air, before which everything showed black. There was nothing to see, till suddenly he was under the jacaranda. Its top was visible: purple blossom blanched pink in the light. Oscar only just managed to stop before he blundered onto the pale patch of ground by the tree—Adele Haines's grave, now covered with flowering petunias.

Oscar caught his breath and listened. The wind had dropped again. It was coming around, one wind pushing against another somewhere up there, passing back and forth through the No-Go as if it wasn't there, except that it was and would be sieving the wind of birds and beetles.

Something brushed Oscar's cheek and he jumped, but it was only falling jacaranda blossom.

He went on, keeping away from the driveway, in case the man in black was standing somewhere down in the town looking up at that channel of light. He pushed through the feijoa hedge and came out on Bypass Road.

All along that road were sodium street lamps, high on

their concrete stems. Oscar hurried across and plunged into another hedge. He paused, held his breath, listened, and continued on his way. He skirted one house. In the fingers of orange radiance coming through the hedge, Oscar saw its windowsills were black with dead flies.

He made his way through several properties, parallel to the road, scaling fences. But that was too noisy, so when the street dipped down, out of the long reach of the sodium lamps, he returned to the footpath. He stood still and strained his ears. Then he set out, heading for Haven Road and the supermarket. He made his way from gate to gate, drive to drive, ducking out onto the path then back into the shadows of front yard foliage.

When Oscar reached the supermarket he traversed the carpark by darting from car to car. He reached the glass doors and peered through them. Holly had switched off the overhead fluorescents, but there was still light gleaming through the glass fronts of the cabinet fridges and in the freezers, shining out from under the rims of their fuming interiors. Oscar went inside. The place smelled of spice and plastic and dry goods, and a musty smell from the emptied fruit and deli trays. Holly had wiped everything down, but still, there it was, the smell of mildewed lemons and sour milk, and the dirty dog smell of old luncheon sausage.

Oscar found the aisle with pet food, and left the supermarket, his jacket stuffed with cans and rattling faintly. He stuck to Haven Road where the streetlights were off for two-thirds of its length, put out by the crashed truck and subsequent fire. There was no light to see by, but it was easy going, the footpath wide and even, kerbs indented at each crossing. Oscar kept his eye on his reflection in the glass fronts of the shop—checking that it *was* his reflection. Then the plate glass came to an end and he was going by houses—a splash of red paint on the path before all those the burial teams had cleared. Now and then he looked

227

back, and once, when he did, he thought he saw something move, a long shadow intruding onto Haven Road from one of the side streets. Someone with a streetlight behind them was walking towards the intersection—in the middle of the street, not bothering to hide themselves, to blend their shadow with other shadows.

Oscar flung himself back into a bush, then poked his head out to take a closer look. The long shadow was motionless now, and featureless. It had seemed to have a distinct head and arms, but now it might as well be cast by a street sign. Oscar waited, watching till his eyes watered, but nothing moved. He was mistaken—he must have been. Still, it was some time before he was able to relinquish the shelter of the shrubbery. He continued on his way, running now.

He had left the porch light burning, knowing he'd be back. He let himself in and didn't turn on any of the indoor lights, only stood a while in the patch of radiance that came in through the pebbled glass of the front door. He waited till his cat came to find him, chirruping, eager. She ran at him and butted his legs, her back arched and long tail trembling. He picked her up. She wiped her jaw along his, talking the whole time, delirious and scolding.

'Sorry, sorry,' he said.

The morning after the night the power went off, while Bub and William were rounding up the dogs, and Jacob was raiding the pharmacy, and Theresa was going slowly around the streets in her patrol car, hailing whoever might hear, Oscar went home to fetch his games, and to feed Lucy, his family's svelte caramel-coloured Burmese. He'd been back almost every day since. Holly and Kate knew he took his bike out and rode around—getting some exercise, they supposed. But nobody knew that, of all Kahukura's orphaned cats, summoned every day to the boat ramp feeding spot, only Lucy got personal service. Oscar fed his cat at home so she'd *stay* home, because, if she didn't, he thought his heart would probably break.

Lucy had always been a homebody; she stayed indoors or in the yard, though she liked to climb the trellis on the back porch, cross the spine of the roof, and clamber down onto the front fence. Sometimes now she'd be sitting on the fence waiting for him and would scramble down and trot along to meet him, making her way as he did, confidently in the centre of the road. It was amazing how quickly she had adapted to the lack of traffic.

Oscar didn't just feed Lucy and leave. He'd sit with her. He had carried his console and games off to the spa but, at home, he was rereading all his favourite books—*Harry Potter* and *Ender's Game* and *The Bartimaeus Trilogy*—but not *Sabriel* because he couldn't cope with the idea of walking corpses. He'd sit for an hour or two most days with Lucy curled in the crook of one arm and a book in his other hand. He'd put on one of his dad's CDs. Nothing with vocals in English, because if he could understand the lyrics he'd listen to them instead of the phantom reader who always appeared somewhere at the back of his skull whenever a page of print was in front of his eyes. Oscar played his father's music. He washed the duvet on his parents' bed when the gritty hollow where Lucy slept each night got too oily and dark. He came home because it had to still *be* his home. He fed his cat so she'd stay put and hold a place for him, for his mum and dad, for when they'd all be home together.

Lucy was acting normal, so the house was safe. Oscar left the lights off, went into the kitchen, gathered up the cat bowls, wiped the floor, and put down fresh water and food, canned and dry. He put the bowls in the dishwasher and turned it on to rinse—then immediately turned it off again. He needed to be able to hear. There would be no music tonight, and he didn't dare turn on a light to read. Instead he pulled the duvet off his bed and settled on the couch where he could see the front door. Lucy sat

229

in the middle of the living room and washed, all the time making her bubbling pot purr. Then she jumped up onto the couch, climbed on Oscar's chest, tramped about in a circle kneading for a minute, and settled, her nose nearly touching his chin.

Lucy purred as Oscar patted her sleek head and pulled her cool ears. Her purring seemed to spread a pool of sleep over him and, after a few minutes, his eyelids began to droop.

Then someone knocked on the door.

Lucy launched herself off his chest and ran under a chair. Oscar clutched his duvet and peered at the figure behind the pebbled glass. He held his breath. The knock came again. This time Oscar saw the hand, knuckles pale against the glass. Pale, not black.

'Oscar?' said the person, who was female.

Oscar got off the couch and went to the door. 'Who is that?' he said, feeling stupid for not recognising the voice.

'Sam,' said Sam.

Oscar let her in. She dropped into a crouch and extended her hand to coax Lucy out from under the chair. Lucy emerged, minced over and smooched Sam's fingers.

'You won't tell Theresa?' Oscar said.

Sam looked up at him, and Oscar noticed the darkening along her jaw. A fresh bruise, still showing distinct finger marks. Seeing it like that, out in the open, was, for Oscar, like being the recipient of some shocking intimacy. William had hit her *again*.

'Why would I tell Theresa?' Sam asked.

'Because of the curfew.'

She nodded. She picked Lucy up and switched on the living room light.

Oscar quickly switched it off again. 'I had them off for a reason,' he said.

'And what was that?' Sam had her back to him now. She was carrying Lucy into the kitchen. Oscar found himself

230

noticing her ankles, strong, lean, smooth-skinned. She looked back over her shoulder. Oscar knew she was really quite young—early twenties—but at that moment she didn't look much older than he was. 'Where would I find tea?' she said.

'In those dusty boxes by the kettle,' Oscar told her.

Sam put Lucy down and filled the kettle. 'Do you want some?'

'Sure. So—you followed me?'

'I wondered where you were off to in the middle of the night. Also—' Sam didn't finish her sentence. The kettle began to bump and roar. It sounded as noisy as a car alarm to Oscar. 'I've been trying to keep quiet,' he said.

She was looking for cups and a teapot. 'In the cupboard above the fridge,' Oscar told her. Then, 'I'm sorry there's no milk.'

'I'm making green tea.' Sam inspected the leaves in a patterned tin. 'Or perhaps this is one of those fancy white teas—the leaves are whole and screwed up into little balls.'

It was Oscar's mum's Iron Goddess of Mercy. His mum never let him try it, said he wouldn't like it, though Oscar had guessed it was one of those things his parents wouldn't be able to afford any more if he were to decide he liked it too.

The kettle finished boiling and switched itself off. Sam filled the teapot and carried it and two cups back into the living room. 'Are you sure we can't have a light?'

'He's still out there. I only came out myself because I had to feed Lucy.' Oscar was angry with Sam for looking so unafraid, and graceful, and pretty. And for wearing her bruise without shame or defiance, as if it was just another part of her face. And he was angry with her because she'd found him out, camped here with his cat, a custodian of his old life.

Sam put the teapot and cups on the coffee table and sat

cross-legged on the floor. Oscar went back to the couch and pulled the duvet onto his lap. A moment later Lucy was there too, happily tramping.

'The packet said it should steep for five minutes,' Sam said.

'It said "steep"?'

'Yes.'

'And you get "steep"?'

'Yes, Oscar.'

For a moment Oscar only fumed silently, and then he broke out. 'You're horrible! And I've been feeling sorry for you! Even if you're not lying like William thinks, you still have this alternate personality who is like some kind of human shield, and you're *hiding* behind her. It's creepy.'

Sam watched him rage. She listened with sympathy, and warmth. It made Oscar even more furious. His eyes filled with tears. It was as if someone had topped him up past his high water-level mark. He tried to wipe them surreptitiously, but his nose started to run, and the low light wasn't going to be any cover.

Sam gave him a moment. She poured the tea before it was ready and got up to hand him his cup. 'I need you to talk to me, Oscar,' she said. 'I've got a pretty high tolerance for being in the dark, but there are things I must know.'

Oscar dried his eyes on his cuff, then sipped the scalding tea. 'You followed me to talk to me?'

'Yes.'

Despite himself Oscar felt pleased that he'd been chosen— that someone had finally given him something to do—that is, apart from the almost impossible thing he'd been doing so far, which was constantly reassuring everyone that he was all right.

The tea was grassy water and Oscar couldn't see why his mother bothered paying for it. 'Do you actually like this?' he asked.

'Yes. But Sam wouldn't,' Sam said. She said it quite matter-of-factly.

Which provoked Oscar into another outburst. 'I can see why William's pissed at you! Maybe you deserved to be thumped!'

Sam gave a little laugh. 'William feels cheated because he had supposed he was sleeping with some innocent. He's the victim of false advertising, the poor man.' Sam sounded self-possessed. She didn't seem crazy, but Oscar was suddenly scared of her. He didn't renew his complaints and, after another minute where the only sound in the room was Lucy's soft rumbling, Sam said, 'Why don't you feed your cat in the daytime?'

'Because of Theresa's curfew, and the man in black. You know all this.'

'Let's just suppose I don't.'

'You want me to play along?'

'Go on, indulge me.'

'Fine. Okay. Theresa and Dan and William and Bub have spent the last week hunting for the man in black. There's a picture of him up in the reserve, a rock drawing from like four hundred years ago, of him and the No-Go. And it turns out that the people who lived here then had buried a lot of bodies in their storage pits, because they were survivors and there were only a few of them, not enough to dig all the graves. Like us with the swimming pools. And at some point those people tried to tell their story by painting it on the cliffs up in the reserve. They painted themselves testing the No-Go. Apparently rock drawing experts thought the figures had tails, were kind of anthropomorphic. But of course the tails are actually ropes they've tied to themselves so they can pull each other out of the No-Go, like we've had to. And, in the middle of the drawings, there he is—our black man in black clothes. We all think he's the same man from four hundred years ago.'

Sam's face was glowing with interest. Oscar had never seen anyone look more alive. It made him feel a little less stupid for sitting there telling her things she was pretending not to know. He said, 'Theresa and that are out every day looking for him—with guns. To ask him questions. Theresa says they don't want the rest of us wandering around while they're hunting because they're keeping an eye out for movement. So I've been sneaking out to feed Lucy. No one knows I come here. I've been coming every day since the beginning.'

Now Sam was looking sympathetic. Oscar wanted to thump her, though he hadn't hit a girl since he was about four, and everyone had made it pretty clear to him that, being the size he was, he shouldn't ever hit anybody. Oscar kept looking at Sam and seeing someone who wasn't an adult. 'You look younger when you're not pretending to be stupid,' he said.

'I am. Younger, I mean. Sometime ago I decided to let her go first.'

'Who?'

'Sam. I'm letting her go first. She feels lost on and off anyway, so the discontinuity is worse for her. And besides, maybe I want to see who's right about global warming.'

'Huh?' said Oscar.

'If she goes first then I'm around for longer, and can see what happens,' Sam said, calmly explanatory. 'But enough about me. So—there's no sign of him so far?'

'Who?'

'The man in black.'

'He's gone to ground. First he wouldn't talk to us—though he helped Bub and William and Jacob bury the kids at the daycare centre. Then Belle took Bub to look at the rock drawings and they put two and two together.'

'Theresa and company are carrying guns to coerce him once they catch him?'

Oscar nodded. 'Bub wants to shoot him. But Theresa says there's no point doing that since he's probably got some kind of machine generating the No-Go, and he has to tell us where it is so we can turn it off. Dan said that when he saw the man—on the day everyone died—he thought the guy was carrying something small, heavy, and metallic, some kind of device. And Belle says she thinks the man has a personal force field. That when he dived off Bub's boat he made a hole in the sea.'

Sam used both hands to push back her heavy hair. She looked galvanised. 'What about the other thing?'

'What other thing?'

'Oh,' she breathed. She seemed about to burst into tears of joy. 'Could you really not feel it?' she said. And Oscar was shocked to see the sudden bright streak of a tear on one of her cheeks. She said, 'It's the first thing in my life that's made sense in the terms of my life.'

'What?'

'The monster,' she said.

'Huh?' Oscar didn't know how to articulate his confusion, but his whole body must be showing it.

'The monster,' she said again, then frowned in consternation. 'Could you really not feel it?'

'I don't know what you're talking about!' Oscar shouted, desperate. 'And you're scaring me!'

All the other adults got a certain look whenever Oscar was scared, a look that told him they were hurrying their own emotions away out of sight. Sam wasn't wearing that look, and Oscar found himself feeling kind of grateful that she was prepared to scare him—to include him.

She said, 'The monster—the thing that came when Jacob was trying to revive Warren.' She was attempting to be patient, but sounded rushed and mad. 'It must have woken you.'

'I was awake, but I was in my room. I didn't see anything.'

'It was bigger than the room, and invisible. But it was there.'

Oscar thought of the green arrow in *Halo*. 'What was there?'

Sam's eyes grew wide, she raised her hands and held them up and open, just above her head, like one of those old pictures of a saint in rapture. She grew radiant and still—then seemed to explode. Her words flooded out. 'It was like a whirlwind,' she said. 'Or a biblical column of fire—flaming, noiseless, spectral, sullen, and terrible. But it didn't have a self. It was just made up of everything it had destroyed—deaths—moments of miserable dying—' She paused, shivered, and lit up another notch, till it seemed to Oscar that she couldn't be breathing air, the same air he was, but something that went into her lungs and came alive in her blood. 'It was like a tower,' she said. 'A tower touching heaven, but every one of its building blocks a death. A tower built of deaths—and a whirlwind.'

Oscar lost his grip on his cup. It tipped and spilled warm tea into his lap, soaking the duvet and splashing Lucy's head. Lucy launched herself off him again, and this time bolted into the kitchen and out the cat door.

Oscar surged off the couch and blundered across the room, his feet tangled in the duvet. Then he was fumbling with the chain on the door. Sam was behind him. She grabbed his arms. 'Don't run away,' she said, sounding properly appalled.

Oscar couldn't look at her. She sounded normal again. His fear abated some, but he was still determined to get away, before—and then it was too late, he was sobbing hard, really howling, like a frightened little kid. He shook her hands off and yanked the door open. It bashed his toes. He plunged out through the mobile lacework of circling moths in the sheer curtain of light cast by the porch lamp. Sam came after him and, because she was less clumsy than he was, she caught him before he got up to speed. He was only three paces from the porch. But he was too big for someone Sam's size to easily stop, or hold. He shook her off again, and she was still coming after him, trying to take his arm, when they both collided with another body—the black man in black clothes—who was standing on the path beyond the reach of the light, perhaps attracted by the eruption of voices—Sam's rapture, Oscar's sobbing.

The man in black put his arms out and caught them, and they rotated, as if they were balls simultaneously tossed into a greased catcher's mitt. Sam slid out of the man's grip and sprawled at his feet, whereas Oscar, who was too tall to simply slither free, only continued to rotate. He was in the man's arms, against the man's chest and neck and face, but touching nothing and sliding around on resistant nothing like the puck on an air hockey table.

Then the man opened his arms and stepped back. Sam shouted at Oscar to run. 'Get help!' she yelled.

Oscar darted past the man and fled. He looked back once he was at the corner of the road, but the neighbour's magnolia tree hid his view of the front yard. He ran on, shouting for help.

Oscar was gone. Sam lunged at the man. She wrapped her hands around his ankle. Her fingers made a loose shackle three centimetres from his skin. Sam stared in wonder and disbelief. She fought her urge to let go and, while he was still within reach, to simply appreciate the slick skin of insistent impenetrable air that surrounded him. She held on—hopelessly—for his foot was slipping free. Though filled with a kind of lust of curiosity, Sam was still thinking, and, because she was *clever* Sam, she was thinking fast. She thought that if he had to turn his force field on to stop a bullet it would never stop a bullet. And she thought that if, however, it was on all the time, then how would he feed himself? There was only one way in which this could work. She considered all of this, then, while she still had him, her grip around his arch and instep, compressing the slippery nothingness so that he slipped faster, she used this last possible traction to yank his foot so that he toppled. He sprawled onto his cushion of air, and she shifted her grip back to his ankle—or the air around it. Then she hauled on him, and he slid towards her so smoothly it was as if he was moving on a bed of ball bearings. She clambered up over him, straddling him—or his frictionless casing—as best she could. She balanced, and once again made a shackle of her hands, this time around his right wrist. She found the limits of the resistance, rested there a moment, then very gradually and gently closed her grip. It never would have worked had he not been staring at her, through her hair, which had pooled on the air before his face. She saw his white teeth and the white lights in his black eyes. She read his expression—which was puzzled and speculative—and knew he looked like that because he was looking at her, and saw that she was calm, completely calm.

The circle of Sam's grip got smaller—slowly. It was like a gesture in Tai Chi. And then the skin of her fingers touched the skin of the man's wrist, and his eyes went wide with astonishment. He raised his arm and rolled, but she had him, skin to skin, her hands inside his force field.

He clambered to his feet and began to pull away, dragging her. She tried to get her feet under her, but he was a big strong man and he kept jerking her about so that she was down on one knee, then up on her feet, then hauled against him, and then hurled back so that she crashed into Oscar's letterbox. And while he shook her, she kept shouting at him, 'Stop! Stay!'

She knew that all he had to do to be rid of her was to push her forcibly into something unyielding—like the low wall around Oscar's neighbour's yard. Once, he raised his arm so that her feet left the ground and they were face to face, and she could see him considering it—considering hurting her—but he didn't. He fought hard, but with restraint, as if she were a robust child, and this a play fight.

Then light began to grow in the street and shadows lunged out at an angle from every bush and fence as they were backlit by the headlights of more than one vehicle, coming in fast.

Sam shouted, 'Over here!'

The man drew her towards him once more, and spun her into his arms. He clamped his free hand across her mouth and nose and crushed her into the invisible resistance that surrounded him. The skin of his palm didn't connect with the skin of Sam's face, and she could still breathe—there were still a few centimetres of compressed air between them. Then he closed his hand and that air went as dense as foam rubber. Sam's lips were pushed against her teeth. The force field slipped into her open mouth and was abruptly as unbreathable as a vacuum. Her nostrils were pinched closed. She struggled. Her heels slid along the grass. The man was hauling her away somewhere. Her field of vision snapped closed, as first the world vanished, then the green bristle of its afterimage. All sounds faded into a ringing silence.

The room was warm. Its floor was polished wood. The lights were low, the curtains drawn—glistening gold curtains, so long that they pooled on the floor.

Sam heard the flinty 'chop-chop' of a match struck twice before igniting.

The man in black was crouching by a firebox. There was a neat fire laid in the grate, split kindling heaped over a pile of fire starters. The man held a long match to the white cube of a fire starter until it caught. He watched till the kindling was burning, then he laid two dry manuka rounds on the flames. He closed the woodburner's door, opened its damper, and turned to Sam.

She had discovered that her hands were tied before her with what seemed to be a silk curtain cord. While the man's back was turned she'd been surreptitiously struggling to free herself. She stopped and recoiled as he came over. He scooped her up and put her down in a white leather recliner, then tilted the chair and leaned over her, peering into her eyes. He smelled of wood smoke, a friendly open–air smell. His gaze moved from one eye to the other as if he were trying to judge a difference between each. 'Which one are you?' he asked.

Sam gaped. How could he know that about her?

'What's your name?'

'Oh,' said Sam. 'Sam.' The muscles of her arms and shoulders were twitching with tiredness and strain. One of her knees was smarting.

The man said, 'You have my attention, Sam.'

Sam stalled. She asked, 'Do you have a name?'

He said something that sounded like the name of the space station.

'M–I–R?'

'I haven't ever had occasion to write it in your alphabet,' he said.

'Or is it like the gifts of the Magi—gold, frankincense, *myrrh*?'

'How can it possibly matter?'

'It doesn't.' Sam privately decided that she'd think of him as Myr—the 'million years' of cosmologists.

Myr sat cross-legged on the floor by her chair and pressed its footstool until it tilted upright again. He fixed his eyes on Sam's face and said, 'I need to understand how you know that the monster is there. You were telling the boy about the monster.' He took Sam's bound hands and held them gently, so gently that his force field didn't activate. 'Tell me,' he said.

'It's your monster, so you tell me.'

'You shouldn't be able to feel it. Or rather, you shouldn't feel it as an entity, only as a disturbance—restlessness, misery, suspicion, a dark compulsion, or evil urge. Feelings you would suppose were your own.'

Sam moved her hands, trying to extract them from his grip, or perhaps trying to draw him closer—she wasn't sure which she wanted.

He didn't let go and he did lean closer.

Sam bent over their clasped hands, closed her eyes, and settled into her own darkness. She could feel her breath warming the air between her mouth and his knuckles. Myr was real and bodily, and appeared to be human. But he was unlike everyone else in the world—the multitude of mavericks whose lives had been allowed to grow freely, unlike hers, which had been trained into an inscrutable shape. In his unlikeness, Myr was the only one like her. The only one she'd ever met. Her heart went out to him. But Sam hated her own secrets, and she didn't want to tell them. She said, 'So I should feel the monster's influence, but not sense it as a presence?'

'No one knows it's there until, perhaps, their very last moments, when they sense that something is salting them with other people's agonies before eating them whole.'

Sam put that aside for now. 'Do you feel it?' she said.

'I only know it's there because I have it quarantined.'

'Because that's what you do.' Sam opened her eyes and stared at him, thinking. Then she asked him to please tell her about the monster.

He remained silent. His patience was of a quality Sam hadn't encountered before. She dropped her gaze and began to worry at the cord around her hands.

He said, 'If I explain, you'll be required to give up certain things.'

'What do I have to give up?' Sam would offer whatever guarantee he wanted. She was confident that she couldn't be held to any promise she made.

But, as it turned out, it was *hope* she couldn't keep.

PART FIVE

Shortly before the sun came up, after three hours of fruitless searching, Bub spotted a smudge of smoke rising from the chimney of a house east of the settlement. He and Theresa went up its driveway, while William and Dan came at it through the gardens of an adjacent property. Theresa tackled the front door, while Bub went in the back. Dan and William burst through a set of French doors into a room coloured by the faint orange glow of a dying fire.

They searched the house, but it was deserted. And when they gathered in the living room, they saw the silk ropes lying in the seat of a white leather recliner.

Later that morning Belle went, as usual, up to the reserve to feed her kakapo. Theresa insisted on delivering her right to the gate. As they made their way through the arboretum, Belle riding pillion on her own quad bike, Theresa kept turning her head to shout instructions over her shoulder. 'It should take me twenty minutes to check the fence in both directions. Then I'll come back to the gate and wait for you.'

They arrived at the reserve, and Theresa issued her final instruction. 'Lock yourself in. We can't have anyone else taken hostage.' She gunned the bike's engine and set off along the fence line.

Belle watched her friend go, and turned back to the gate.

There was something wrong. The padlock was closed but the chain looked looser than she'd left it, as if someone had removed the lock from the links and fastened it again, leaving the chain a little slack. Belle hauled on the gate and

245

found it had more than its usual give. She stayed still for a long time, clasping the lock and listening to the sturdy putter of the bike receding up the firebreak. She pressed her face to the mesh. Its weave was so tight that up close every hole served as pinhole magnifier. What Belle could see through each tiny hole was super sharp. Fragments of the view jumped into life, rounded, jewel-like, and as inclusive as a reflection in a convex traffic mirror.

Suddenly, there was Sam, looking back at Belle, vivid and magnified, as if seen through a drop of dew.

Belle jumped away from the fence, backed right off so that the mesh became a semi-transparent smoke. She could still see Sam—Sam's glossy hair rippling as she bolted away into the forest. Belle called out, then rushed to the gate, spun the tumblers on the combination lock, and twisted the padlock off the chain. She pulled the gate open so fast that the chain sang through the bars and came loose, bashing her knee.

Belle limped up the track into the forest. She shouted Sam's name. Then she stood still and listened. She sensed that Sam was standing too, perhaps not very far off, her back pressed to the trunk of a tree.

Two adolescent kaka arrived, screeching and fluting by turns. Fat, forward, and nimble, they landed on a branch directly above Belle, snatched at the same perch, lost their balance, and swung upside down, eyeing her hopefully all the while. Only last week one of this pair had picked a hole in Belle's backpack to steal a muesli bar.

'Shhh! I'm trying to listen,' Belle told the birds—to no effect.

She went on into the forest, calling. She skirted the clearing where the hopper was and walked all the way up to the limestone overhang. The shallow cave was empty. The rock drawings looked sinister, revised by what Belle now knew about them.

She stood on the ridge and called for a time, then limped back down. As she was passing through the clearing on her way to get feed from the storage shed, she saw that the hopper was full already, and that several kakapo were perched on the trough, grazing. Boomer turned his mild, whiskered face to her, spread his wings, plonked down, ambled over, and picked playfully at one of her bootlaces. She submitted for a time to his attentions, then made her way back to the gate. She went through it and locked it behind her.

Theresa was waiting. She looked concerned. 'You never leave the gate open.'

'Sam's in there. She ran away from me.'

'She knew the combination to the lock?'

'She's been up here a few times, and she wrote it down. She writes things down to remember them. The desk in her room is covered with notes to herself.'

'Yes, I know,' Theresa said, and looked a little guilty. 'How did she seem?'

'She ran away from me, Tre! What do you suppose he did to her?'

They stood in silence gazing at one another, then at the dark bush beyond the fence. The kaka could be heard screeching and fluting, as happy and unperturbed as ever.

'Let's just wait for a time,' Theresa said. 'If she doesn't show, we'll come back later and call some more.'

'Oscar said that when he ran to get help he thought she was trying to talk to the man in black—to *engage* with him,' Belle said. She peered at the forest. 'Maybe he's in there too.' Her heart gave a lurch and her skin went cold. She hated to think of the stranger anywhere near her kakapo. 'Maybe she ran from me because she's protecting him.'

'You mean like Stockholm Syndrome?' Theresa said, and at Belle's frown of incomprehension, 'You know—when hostages become emotionally attached to the people holding them captive.'

'That sounds a bit dodgy.'

'Well, yes. But let's face it, Sam is already dodgy about William. He hits her and she camps by his door and pleads.'

'Maybe she is crazy, like William says.'

'He doesn't think she's crazy, he thinks she's pretending to be crazy.' Theresa leaned on the bike, crossed her ankles and folded her arms. She looked like someone settling in for a long wait.

Belle said, 'She fed my birds.'

'But that's her, isn't it? The dishonest, or disturbed, but ever helpful Sam.'

At noon Holly stood at the head of the long table she'd set for lunch and carefully counted the place settings. For several weeks now she had sometimes found herself laying fourteen places. Before Bub and Belle had uncovered the meaning of the reserve's petroglyphs she'd been able to tell herself that she was only anticipating a time when Bub's firefighter would join them. And Curtis would choose to come back. Then it turned out that the man in black was an enemy. Holly had tried to be more mindful. But she kept getting her head count wrong. She'd set about the task, and this would waylay her—this invitation.

Now the Man was revealed, and Sam was missing, and Curtis was still shunning them—so there were eleven for lunch. And yet when Holly took the cutlery from the drawer, despite her vigilance, she'd gone into a fugue and had, this time, set the table for *fifteen*. She'd wished Curtis and Sam back, had issued her usual forgetful invitation to Sam's captor, and then one more, to some other ghostly guest.

Holly looked around the dining room. No one had arrived yet. She gathered up the extra knives and forks, swiftly and discreetly, and returned them to the kitchen.

In the late afternoon, when Theresa and Belle had gone back to the reserve to call for Sam, William said to Bub that he wondered why no one had thought to look for her where she'd most likely hole up if she meant to avoid them, but still be out of the weather.

'Her bach?'

'Yes, her cottage.'

They went along Matarau Point and stopped just out of the view of anyone standing at the bach's front windows. They had a quick consultation about how to tackle Sam if they found her. Then William went in by the ranchsliders, while Bub went in the back. They converged in the living room. The rug Lily had slept under that first night—a homemade rug of brightly coloured peggy-squares—was neatly folded and draped on the arm of the couch, perhaps by Lily herself all those weeks ago. William looked into the bedroom. The bed was made. 'She's been back at some point,' he said.

'If it was your house, wouldn't you?' Bub asked. He drifted off in the direction of the bathroom.

William checked the wardrobe, then, for good measure, got down on his knees and looked under the bed. There was a file box there. It was labelled *Sams*.

William slid the box out, removed its dusty lid, and began to leaf through the papers. He found an insurance policy for house and contents. He found the last will and testament of one John Waite, whose beneficiary was his only niece, Samantha Pehipehi Waite. He found an employment contract for Samantha Waite, from Mary Whitaker Rest Home, and a certificate to state that Samantha Waite had attended a food hygiene course. He found tax certificates and tax returns for Samantha Pehipehi Waite. He found a student ID, for Waikato University, the year 2000, for a *Samara* Pehipehi Waite, whose date of birth was 1967. There were forms from the Department of Work and Income for Samantha Waite, whose date of birth was also 1967.

William upended the box and spread its contents on the floor—no longer simply browsing, but looking for something. Bub leaned in the doorway. 'What have you got there?'

'What does it look like? How about you? You were gone a while.'

'It's a nice place,' Bub said.

'Huh,' said William, casual and surprised. He'd found two birth certificates. And a notice of a change of name by deed poll.

Bub said, 'Belle and I have been thinking of finding someplace where we can have bit more privacy, and cook for ourselves—all that.'

'So you and Belle want to play house,' William said, and held out the two certificates and the notice of deed poll.

Bub took the papers, but didn't look at them. 'You have a knack for making everything sound trivial.'

'Trivial or insincere, dishonest or mad—I can make things sound all sorts of ways. I'm a lawyer.'

'But why are you on *our* case?'

'I'm not. Bub, please look at what you have in your hand.'

The birth certificates were pinned together with a rusting paperclip. They were for two infant girls, born the same day—the second of October, 1967. Their mother's name was Ngaire Catherine Waiti. Their father's name was not given. The notice of change of name by deed poll was also dated 1967, and was for a John Waiti, who had changed his surname to Waite.

Bub said, 'I didn't know that sad bastards were still anglicising their names back in sixty-seven. Not that that happened much anyway.' He looked at the birth certificates, flipping back and forth from one paper to the other. 'Okay. So this is the root of Sam's nutty shit. She's a twin.'

250

'Bub, who the hell names twins Samantha and Samara, and gives them the same middle name?'

'Giving your kids the same middle name isn't unheard of. I bet Pehipehi is their dad's family. And a fanciful teenaged mum in sixty-seven might have called her twins Samantha and Samara. *Bewitched* was on TV.'

'That was Samantha and *Sabrina*. And Bub, do the math. *1967*. Sam isn't in her forties.'

Bub frowned and scratched his head.

'But this *is* her.' William handed Bub the student ID card.

Bub studied Sam's beautiful face, her baleful expression. '2000,' he said. 'Samara Pehipehi Waite. It sure looks like her.'

'Check out the date of birth.'

Bub steadied the card with his other hand and peered at it. There was a short silence, then. 'Some people hold their age well.'

'Right,' said William, with no discernible expression.

'What else can it be?'

'Is Pehipehi just a name, or does it mean something?'

Bub screwed up his face. 'It might be, but it isn't one I've heard before. Waiti is a local name. There was a Waiti shearing gang who worked Stanislaw's Station right up to the time the Stanislaws gave the land to the crown. "Pehipehi" means something like "ambush".' Bub scratched his head. 'Yeah. You're right—this is very weird.'

On their way back Bub and William spotted Curtis sitting on the veranda of the bed and breakfast, wrapped in a blanket and sunning himself.

Bub said, 'We didn't notice you there when we went past before.'

'You were so busy searching for the man in black that I was invisible to you.'

251

William said, 'News flash—we're now looking for Sam, who is hiding from us since being captured and detained by the man in black. So that's progress of a sort. We've swapped one hopeless task for another.'

Bub thought that Curtis looked pale. 'Are you okay, mate?'

'You people always manage to miss the man in black, sometimes by just minutes. He was here a short time ago. He's often here. Whenever I come out to enjoy a bit of afternoon sun, he appears on the path and stands so that his shadow falls over my feet. He knows what trouble I'm having keeping them warm.'

Bub met William's gaze. William frowned, then said to Curtis, 'Are you feeling all right? Is there anything we can do?'

Curtis curved his lips at them. It was more a smirk than a smile. 'I'd be perfectly fine if I wasn't being bothered by people putting their shadows on me.' He looked down at William and Bub's shadows, which had combined with the stripes of the paling fence in a way that reminded William of his own reflection in Sam's bathroom mirror.

'Have you seen Sam?' William asked. 'Is she one of the people who has been bothering you?'

'She was over there, on the beach near the backpackers.' Curtis pointed across the bay.

The beach below the backpackers was empty.

'What was she doing?'

'Just standing there on her two good legs.'

William turned his back on Curtis and whispered, 'I think we should get Jacob to give Curtis a visit.'

Bub nodded. He gave Curtis a friendly wave. 'Do let us know if you see her again.'

'I don't know that I will tell you anything. I think people should be allowed to avoid others if that's what they want.'

'This is Sam we're talking about,' William said.

'Do you suppose that, because she's not very bright, Sam has no rights?'

'This *rights* business is always a balancing act,' William said. 'Sometimes people need to be looked after, even when it isn't what they want.'

'Your opinions on that subject are strongly biased,' Curtis said. 'You forget that I know a few salient facts about you.'

'Huh?' said Bub. 'What have you got on William?'

They ignored him, and William said to Curtis, 'Well, what *I* know is that there are miserable people—children for example—clustered under every freedom-loving fanatic's carnival float of privacy.'

Bub looked nervously at William. He was used to these occasional rhetorical flourishes—but there were times when it seemed to be more than just William saying something flashy to silence whoever he was arguing with. These glimpses of something passionate and personal in William's rhetoric were like spotting a Minotaur making its way through the maze of a formal garden. Bub put his hand on William's arm. He said to Curtis, 'We've got to get going. Enjoy the sunshine.'

Jacob walked to Matarau Point in the late afternoon, carrying his small bag of basic medicines. He found Curtis in bed. Curtis had beads of sweat on his forehead, and was shivering violently. Jacob was alarmed, but he didn't want to worry Curtis. He fetched another blanket and spread it on the bed, then sat down beside Curtis and took his hand. 'How long have you been like this?'

'I don't know. For longer than I've minded being like this.' Curtis looked aged and stricken.

'Did you have a fever when William and Bub stopped by?'

'Maybe a mild one. I think I was surly with them. Was I making sense?'

'Not entirely.'

'I haven't been myself for some time.'

'What do you think the problem is?'

Curtis shuddered. 'A long slide.'

'A decline? Because of Adele?'

Curtis shook his head.

'I think you're dehydrated,' Jacob said. 'For a start I'm going to make you a sweet drink.'

But Curtis would not release his hand. 'Something's here. I hoped it was my wife. That Adele was sustaining me, telling me that she was all I would ever need. But it's something else.'

'What?'

Curtis glared into the dim corners of the room. 'Something at the foot of the slide. Something with its mouth open. I thought I could fix myself. But look what I've done.' Curtis gestured weakly at his body, finally releasing Jacob's hand.

Jacob got up. 'I'll make you that drink. But I need to ask—did you take something?'

'No. I haven't been in my right mind. I wish I'd stayed that way. It would be better than lying here thinking what a fool I am, and what a trouble to you.' Tears filled Curtis's eyes and spilled onto his faintly yellow cheeks.

Jacob got up and turned on the overhead light. He took Curtis's pulse, which was fast and thready. He found his thermometer and slipped it under Curtis's tongue. The man's teeth were chattering. Jacob said, 'Please be careful, you don't want to break that.'

The thermometer gave a beep. Curtis had a temperature of thirty-nine. Jacob told Curtis that, for a start, he'd get some Panadol and water into him. Then he'd find some sweet soda. He popped the pills out of their blisters and pressed them into Curtis's palm. He lifted Curtis's head and shoulders and arranged another pillow beneath him, then went into the bathroom to get water.

The shower stall was splashed and puddled with blood. Jacob opened its doors and looked down at what he first supposed were crumpled masses of bloodied bandages. But then he noticed the dropped knife, and he realised that what he was looking at were three conical plugs of flesh—skin, fat, muscle—each around five centimetres in length.

Jacob hurried to the bed and flung back the duvet. He moved too hastily. There was a sticky ripping noise, and Curtis cried out.

Curtis's blood-soaked pyjama bottoms had adhered to his legs, and the bedclothes.

For a moment all Jacob was able to do was stare. It was like watching the sea retreat. There was only blankness before him, and anticipation, of the thing gathering itself at the horizon, the thing that would soon surge back in and drown him.

He found his voice—and a firm kindness, which failing all else had always stood him in stead. 'Right,' he said. 'I'll see to this. You just lie still.' Jacob let the covers settle again. He left the room to get busy, to find swabs, disinfectant, and dressings—and to hide his face.

Sam had gone to see Belle's kakapo because the birds were an Elect—*they* were going to be saved.

She fetched the kakapo's feed and filled the hopper, then sat at the edge of the clearing to watch the birds gather and eat.

When she heard the quad bike she went down to the gate and saw Theresa let Belle off and go on herself, the bike rocking away along the overgrown grass of the firebreak.

Belle saw her and called out, and, for a moment, Sam stood her ground. There was nothing threatening or frightening

255

in Belle's open face, but Sam didn't really know Belle, and she didn't know what to say to her, or to any of them.

She hadn't planned to run; she just did, swivelling on her heel and taking off. She plunged into the forest and jumped up onto a fallen log, her foot hitting the slimy spot where the bark was coming away from the wood. She slipped, and tumbled into a patch of bush-lawyer. She lay still in its clinging tangles, listening as Belle went by calling her name.

Her name—Sam—the name she had first learned to answer to. But not *just* her, for when Uncle would say 'Sam', they had both raised their faces from whatever had their attention, like their bath toys—the duck, the frog, the spouting fish—floating between their chubby legs. Uncle would say 'Sam' and they'd both look up at him—Samantha and Samara. Uncle would call them Samantha and Samara too, and they had distinguished each other with what they could manage with their soft infant palates, of 'Samantha' and 'Samara'. So—'Fa' and 'Wa'. They distinguished each other whenever they looked up and saw that the other one was doing something different. For instance, there were nights when Wa would wake up to see Fa across the room, standing in her crib, crying. Wa would get to her feet and cry too. Uncle would come in and he'd be annoyed because, of course, it was difficult for him to pick them both up at the same time.

Then, one day, there was another adult in the house—a woman with skin so dark that light scarcely bounced off it, so that her facial expressions were impossible to interpret. This mysterious stranger and Uncle had a conversation in the twins' bedroom. While they talked, the woman plucked Wa up out of her cot, and Uncle picked up Fa. The girls gazed at each other and shared a laugh, because this being held at the same time was delightfully different. And they'd never had visitors! Here, suddenly, was a visitor, and, for a little while, two adults to comfort two crying children.

And then—

—then Sam couldn't remember what. All she remembered was waking up knowing that something had happened. Something terrible. She was in her crib in their bedroom, and the air was white. There were new net curtains on the windows—white nets filtering the yellow blaze of the blossoming kowhai. Uncle was by himself once more. He was sitting on the floor. He had a screwdriver in his hand and was winding the screws out of Fa's crib. He was taking it apart. Its mattress and bedding were on the floor. Uncle drew out the last screw, and got up to press on the sides of the crib. Its floor swung down and it collapsed with a loud *clack!* The crib's bars came together to make a grill with such narrow gaps that a child would be unable to put its hand out, were there still space in which a child could lie, as Fa would lie, blinking sleepily at her sister.

Sam watched as Belle went past her hiding place a second time, on her way back down the hill. Belle was still calling now and then, but she sounded spooked and uncertain.

Sam heard Belle greet Theresa. She listened to their consultation—their words indistinguishable except when they called out to her.

Theresa, urgent: '*Sam!*'

Belle, tearful: '*Please*, Sam!'

Then the gate clanged, and the chain rattled, and they went away.

When the sound of the quad bike's engine had receded, Sam went back down the hill and through the gate, locking it after her. She walked away from Stanislaw's Reserve and skirted around the edge of the town until she came to Cotley's Orchard.

There were leaves on the apple trees, and vestigial fruit bubbling from the hard red-brown casings left over from

257

the buds of blossoms. Sam walked through the orchard to the cutting and followed the long white stain of the tanker's spilled milk. She left the road and clambered through the scrub till she hit the shore track. She walked back along it till she reached the beach, where she took off her shoes and went to stand at the water's edge.

The tide was coming in and the sand was wet. The sky was reflected in it. Sam's feet pressed the water out of the sand, and each foot had a dry halo, flaws in the reflection, so that it seemed Sam stood on stepping stones in the air above the clouds. The wind was pushing the waves. They broke diagonally along the shore, their percussion not a beat but a long drawing sound.

Sam had discovered why the man in black had kept away from them all. She was thinking of doing the same, and for the same reason.

She didn't want to share what she knew.

Sam could stay away. It wasn't as if she'd be lonely. She was accustomed to loneliness, had been lonely most of her life, ever since that first wound had left her so bereft that she didn't know who she was, or even *that* she was.

Uncle collapsed Fa's crib and carried it out of the bedroom. Where was Fa? The day came to an end and another day arrived. Where was Fa? Wa was hungry and thirsty, so she ate and drank. But where was Fa? The days succeeded one another and Wa forgot that she was a big girl and knew how to put the special seat on to the toilet then use the step to get up there herself and do what she needed to. She wouldn't do it. She wouldn't do anything Uncle asked her to till he gave Fa back. Wa's stomach became very sore and Uncle put her on the toilet and begged her to be good. Then he shouted at her. But she wouldn't. Where was Fa? Wa went out in the garden and ran around with the pain pushing her. Then the poo was coming out and it had knives.

Wa stopped that particular protest and would go, but in her pants, or in the bath. Uncle was angry and told her she was dirty, but he still wouldn't answer *where was Fa?* He wouldn't say, so she stopped answering him. She kept her mouth shut and stared at him to see whether he'd understand that she was being bad so that he'd want a good girl. Fa was always a good girl—and so was *she* when Fa was there.

Uncle packed up the house into their van, the VW with chalky paint. They left Kahukura, and drove to the ferry at Picton. They went to live on the other island, in a different house. Uncle unpacked the boxes from Sam's bedroom and slit the plastic wrapping of the mattress on Sam's new big girl's bed. He glued yellow-spotted red fimo caterpillars to the outside of the bedroom door. The caterpillars were twisted to make letters that Uncle said read *Sam's Room*. All the toys were hers now. Though she and her sister had never bothered to keep track of which was whose.

But then, after a while, funny things began to happen with the toys. Sam would dress the dolls in the morning and find them undressed in the afternoon. Or she'd wake up and there would be a doll's tea party. She was very angry at Uncle for playing with her toys. She hid her favourites, but he kept finding her hiding places. She'd come in from the sandpit and the toys would be out again.

Then Sam noticed that the weather was funny. It got cold too quickly. The grass grew too fast. This was so remarkable that she had to ask Uncle about it. It was the first thing she'd said to him for a long time. 'How fast does grass grow?' she asked. Uncle explained seasons. He showed her a calendar: Waimate at strawberry time; Nelson Cathedral with Christmas decorations; cherries on the trees at Roxburgh; Arrowtown with its leaves turning. Sam hadn't any other experience to measure things by, but would still stand in the garden, or the kindergarten playground, and think,

'This can't be right.' It couldn't be right that flowers flashed into life like fireworks—but never when she was looking. It couldn't be right that the ducklings in the culvert under the road—tiny compact masses of gilded brown fluff —would, overnight, become sleek, sturdy, and bold. And there were fewer of them. 'The cats get them,' Uncle explained. 'Sam,' he said. 'It's that cat from number 10.' 'Sam,' he said—and she answered to 'Sam'.

Then, one day, Sam found a picture clumsily taped to the wall above her bed. A picture drawn with crayons. It showed Fa and Wa, holding hands. And on either side of the girls were their toys—two teddies, in different hats, though there had only ever been one teddy; there was the black-haired doll and the fair-haired doll as well, but two of each, beside either girl. Everything was doubled. It was as if there were a mirror standing on edge halfway across the sheet of paper. Of every single toy there were two. And the girls; there were two of them. But that was *real*, and though years had passed, Sam hadn't forgotten that she'd had a sister, and that her sister was taken away. Sam knew that the picture had been drawn by her sister—and that Fa meant her to look at it and understand what had happened to them. The picture didn't say, 'I'm still here and where are you?' It said, 'I'm still here and you are too.'

Sam—Samara Waite—stood on the beach till the waves came up over her feet and her feet went numb with cold. She tried to think what she could do—how she could get through this next bit. If she didn't rejoin the other survivors then she wouldn't have to keep another secret. She was good at keeping secrets, but this one wasn't hers alone—or, rather, it wasn't hers and her sister's. It was a secret that concerned them all. And she couldn't join the man in black, who had only released her because he thought she was damaged. For, as soon as she had understood what he was telling her, the monster had come—and it had shown Sam her loneliness, all of it, a loneliness as vast and unquenchable as its own greed. It had drilled down into her, its revolutions ripping every feeling from the experiences to which they were anchored— the damp flats, and dull jobs, and night buses; the moments where she had stood stupidly before a cash machine with the wrong card for her PIN number; the coming home to an empty house and to someone else's unwashed clothes and dirty dishes; the terror of surfacing straight into arguments, or into some cop at the driver's window shining a light into her eyes, and the hailstone smear of safety glass on the road. That was her life—fragments scattered along the broken path, the crazy paving, of someone else's life.

The monster had whirled inside Sam, sucking the heat out of each memory till Sam forgot why—why she cared that she'd been left alone, left to explain things she didn't see happen, and things she hadn't done. She forgot why she cared. And then she was in her childhood bedroom again, and the air was white. Sam went away. The man in black must then have thought that the monster had broken her— because when she went away he'd been left with the *other* Sam, the frightened and incapable woman who couldn't remember a thing of all he'd just told her.

Sam walked out of the sea, sat on the dry sand and let the sun warm her reddened feet. She looked around Kahukura. By daylight she could see the brilliant greens on the trees of the arboretum. There had been no heat yet to dampen down the colours. It was late November. The last time she'd been out—and outdoors—the air was perfumed by blossom and it was early November.

Sam was always coming back to note the changes. This was the only scale she had to measure time—the time of other people, those with continuous daily lives. She was always looking hard at nature, and admiring it, the surprises it played on her. The loneliness in that was wistful. The monster couldn't have made use of it. It used the other sort, the loneliness of being left—over and over—without a plausible story to stand on. 'What happened here?' and 'What happened to you?' were questions that filled Sam with rage.

There had been a time when it was easier to explain. From early on she and Fa had had a system and could cover for each other. When they first learned to read and write—as soon as they went to the first of their four different primary schools—they devised their system. They were clever and able, and by then were used to the practical material loneliness of their lives. For in another way they were never lonely. They were each other's treasured secret. They would swap in and out, day by day, to lovingly examine each other's little notes about Uncle, the cat, about schoolmates and teachers. About who got the most medals on School Sports Day, and how Annette had pinched Colleen under the desk. Notes detailing what happened last week in *Doctor Who*—and Sam always liked her sister's explanations more than the programme itself on the occasions when it was her who was out and got to watch it. Fa was always there, in Wa's thoughts, the first person she had to tell everything to. And she loved to think that, when she was gone, Fa would be reading her letters, laughing at her jokes, wondering at her stories, and solving the puzzles she'd left. They'd bring double the energy and interest and character to any project. They'd make things twice as good. Their poncho-wearing teacher always told their art class, 'Leave no white space on the paper', and that's what they did—together they coloured right to the lines, they filled up their time, and filled each other's shoes. Sam's sister warmed her bed for her; she warmed her clothes.

All that came to an end when Sam was twelve. They had just moved to Hataitai, in Wellington. On an afternoon when Uncle was out, Sam went down to the bottom of their section and was exploring the wilderness where the garden ended. She was on a hillside looking out over the little isthmus of Wellington airport and she thought, at her absent sister, 'Take a look at this.' There was the familiar trusting lassitude of letting go. Then she came out again suddenly to find herself lying head down on a slope at the foot of a steep bank. A little avalanche of stones was pouring around her, and a boulder was still bouncing away into the bushes. She went back to the house to look for Uncle, and then wandered around the neighbourhood looking fruitlessly for someone, anyone, who seemed trustworthy. There was no urgency to her search, and she could well have sat down and simply waited for Uncle to turn up and make decisions. But her need to know what had happened pressed upon her, urging her on. She checked in the phone book, and walked though the noisy Mount Victoria tunnel, and all the way to Newtown, and the hospital. She walked into Accident and Emergency and told the woman behind the sliding glass door in the reception area that there had been an accident. Then she willed herself away again.

When she finally returned she found herself back in Kahukura. Uncle told her she must be gone again by this coming Tuesday. He tapped the calendar on the kitchen wall, and Sam saw that it was *months* later. He said, 'You have to be gone by Tuesday because I have to drive your sister to Nelson for her physical therapy.' Sam agreed. They ate dinner in silence. Then Uncle said, 'Stay indoors until I tell you you can go out again. We are going to have to work out how to handle this.'

Sam went to her room and looked for a letter from Fa. There were no letters. Uncle didn't know about the letters so Sam couldn't ask why the other Sam hadn't written to say what had happened, how she was, what hospital was like. She got their pyjamas out of the pyjama dog and put them on. She stood before the mirror and thought of questions, then wrote her own letter. She hid her letter in the place they always hid them. She went to sleep in their bed, enveloped in her sister's smell, and was obediently gone by Tuesday morning.

When she next came back she looked for a letter, and found her own, unopened.

Uncle never bothered to explain. When Sam asked, he only said, 'She's alive. Everything else is immaterial.' Sam didn't know how her sister was, but she deduced from the way that Uncle seemed—of all things—more relaxed, that the changes in her sister somehow made it easier to cover for the fact that they were both younger than they should be. They had been sharing a life and were not walking in step with children their own age. That's why Uncle would always say to people, 'Sam is small for her age.' It was why they were always moving schools and houses. Now Uncle told Sam she was done with school. And if anyone asked she was to say she was seventeen—a runty seventeen.

Months later Fa finally did write. She wrote that she didn't understand Sam's letters. She wrote that she couldn't write much—she was still learning how to again. The letter wasn't in Fa's handwriting. Fa's subsequent letters showed some improvement, but they remained *different*. And life was different too—the life they'd shared. People now spoke to Sam slowly and gently, and looked at her with smiling patience, or frowning practicality. They stopped including her in conversations—instead their talk would part around her as if she was a stone in a stream. She had lost her life. Her sister, and her life. Ever since then she'd been lonely—lonely and responsible, lonely and thwarted.

At noon Sam spotted Bub and William across the bay, on Matarau Point. It was only when they stopped to speak to

264

Curtis that she realised he had been there the whole time, facing her way.

Sam lay down on the sand. She made herself small. She watched Bub and William head back towards Haven Road. Once they were out of sight she retreated along the shoreline track till she could no longer see the town and point, only the large empty expanse of Tasman Bay and the far off Richmond Range.

Myr had explained to Sam why he was in Kahukura. And, although his explanation was strange, dislocating, and in translation, it was also at first oddly comforting. It gave Sam comfort because it made sense, and encouraged her to stop thinking of the monster as *hers*. The monster was Myr's; he was its keeper, its jailer. It had a provenance, and Myr had protocols for it. He might be an alien, but provenance and protocols were the world Sam knew.

Myr untied her, and then, as she sat ostentatiously rubbing her wrists, he settled by the fire and started to talk. He spoke slowly, choosing his words carefully. Sam listened and understood that he was taking pains in explaining to her, and that all his facts appeared to her detached from words and terms that were important to him. Using Sam's language, Myr told her about his monster. The Wake.

'I will begin in the traditional way,' he said. 'Once upon a time, my people had things—devices and ideas—which, for the purposes of this story, I will call Finders. These Finders were the glory of our civilisation. For, although our lives are short, too short for what your people would call "a life's work", we have always been able to do a great deal. If we had been confined to the culmination of many short lives of labour, then our civilisation wouldn't have progressed much further than a village existence, raising gardens, planting orchards, for—think—how much is studied, digested and reflected upon by any of *your* people within their first thirty years? Thirty years is an average lifespan for us. However, when my people sleep—which they do fifteen hours out of any twenty-four—they dream.'

'Oh,' said Sam. 'That's why we haven't been able to find you. You've been asleep most of the time.'

'Yes.'

'Sorry,' said Sam. 'I interrupted you.'

Myr drew breath to go on. But Sam had another thought, and interrupted again. 'So how old are you?'

'I don't know,' Myr said. 'But I haven't entered my late-flowering. You see—we have several years of brilliance before we die—then go quite abruptly. Our whole system collapses within a few days.'

'You must have some very strange traditions,' Sam said. 'And here you are indulging me with "Once upon a time".'

Myr gave a respectful nod. 'I am pleased to indulge you if it helps me persuade you to trust me with your own special knowledge,' he said, then continued his explanation. 'Insights would come to my people in their dreams. Understandings, formulas, and plans for devices that could "find" whatever we might want or need. Whatever we lacked, our dreams supplied. And what we came to believe about ourselves was that the universe was giving us gifts. That the universe came into our dreams like a loving mother coming in to kiss her sleeping children.'

Sam said, 'Sorry, I'm not quite getting these Finders.'

Myr gave examples. 'My people have water Finders that pull abundant clean water out of thin air—or, in fact, from some other part of the universe. We have energy Finders that open gaps through to some pure energy entity—a latently sentient thing that seems only to want an invitation in order to flow through and act kinetically and make things work, an entity that seems simply to delight in making things run in a solid material world.'

266

'All right,' Sam said. 'But my people only know about energy without a brain in its head. So this is hard to imagine.'

'Is it?' said Myr. 'Even though you have felt your energy leaving you when you walk into my quarantine field?'

He meant the No-Go. 'Your quarantine field isn't an entity, is it?'

'It's powered by one.'

'Oh,' said Sam. She was beginning to get an itch of understanding—and it frightened her.

'Then one day,' Myr said, 'someone by accident made a Finder that invited a monster to come through to them, a monster that worked on minds, and drove people mad, and fed on the resulting chaos. The monster killed almost all of my people—all but those who for some reason were undetectable to it. It seemed not to know they were there. These survivors were, for the most part, people who'd never been able to find things in their dreams, people who were, in the terms of my world, disabled.'

'You?' said Sam.

Myr nodded. 'We survivors, the disabled and the very few surviving able, might have chosen to go on as we had, making gardens and purposely playing away our lives, following dreams and finding further treasures. But, instead, we decided to locate the monster—which we named the Wake. We chose to find the Wake, follow it, and make sure it didn't do any more damage, didn't come back to finish what it had begun, or go somewhere else and do to other people what it had done to us. For my people understood that though the Wake had gone, it had *gone on*, making its way through all the invitations we had sent throughout our history. Invitations we made to a supposedly wholly beneficent universe.'

'So this happened in your lifetime?'

'No. I say "we", but I wasn't there. I'm a descendent of survivors. Many generations removed.'

'Your people have been following this monster for generations?'

'These monsters. Plural. My ancestors' decision to send volunteers out after The Wake to help other people on unknown worlds was less altruism than a religious response. The way they saw it was this—if for all those years they had been chosen and nurtured, then they should show gratitude by at least trying to mend their mistake. That's our mission—to mend our mistake. Only it has turned into damage control. The original Wake was almost impossible to stop. And, of course, there were other Wakes with the same singular vicious practices—monsters slipping through every opening my people had made.'

Myr paused and waited for Sam to meet his eyes. Once she had, he went on. 'Some years ago I relieved another of my people from the task of following this Wake. I pursue it, catching it up as it alights and begins to feed, and keeping it corralled so that it can't spread from its entry point to engulf a whole world—as its kin engulfed our world.'

Sam bit her bottom lip and stared at him.

'You have something to tell me,' he said.

'You were here before. We've seen the rock drawings. We know that you were here before.'

Myr nodded. 'This monster, my Wake, is moving through a string of linked worlds in the mathematical and material regularity that your people call "space-time". Or, more accurately, the Wake doesn't move its whole self between worlds, since only part of it touches down. The rest of it remains where it belongs, out in the "between", a place where there is no time, or possibly where there is *all* time. My people aren't sure which it is—no time or all time—because though we follow these monsters, or their incursive bits, from world to world, we aren't conscious in the between, and can't make observations.'

Sam recognised this 'between' Myr was talking about

as the place she went when she wasn't *here*. She imagined the monster in that place with her, brushing against her static, breathless body. A vast rapacious thing, with its glassy proboscis thrust through to dabble at the dark earth of Adele Haines's grave, like a cat searching its empty plate for any overlooked crumbs. Sam could see Myr was about to forge straight on with his explanation, so she interrupted again. 'Wait,' she said.

Myr didn't want to be interrupted. He tried to make himself clearer. He looked impatient. 'We don't know how this Wake got into this particular string of worlds.' He paused, then said, with an air of delicacy: 'Though you might prefer to think of them as "alternate realities" rather than "multiple worlds".'

'Might I rather?' said Sam.

Myr leaned forward, eager. 'When I follow my Wake I always find myself somewhere *like here*, in a place that corresponds to this place. This is where the connection is. This is where there was a weakening—an event, an invitation.'

'You really were here four hundred years ago?' Sam said, again, when he paused for breath.

'Yes. The Wake comes here, and other places almost exactly like here. An insular nation, remote from other landmasses, with these plants, this rain, these mountains hard up against the sea, this large shallow bay, and these birds singing these songs.'

It was near dawn and the birds were singing. There was light coming through a crack in the curtains.

Sam thought for a bit. There was a stealthy little tumble of coals in the firebox, and the light altered. She was forming a horrible suspicion, and she must make absolutely certain she understood him. If he was here four hundred years before, that didn't mean he was very old. He'd just told her that his people had short life spans. No—someone had opened a

269

door on what was outside of space and time, and the Wake had come in, and was now tunnelling along a series of worlds not just linked, but whose links were produced by that 'invitation'. The Wake originated in the between, the between where she was stored whenever she went away.

Sam knew about Myr's 'between'. She understood Myr and believed him—though, like him, she was only ever between for an instant, and unconscious when she was. She'd come back, and drops of water from Samantha's skin would settle on hers when she arrived. (Only, her hair would never quite take the wet in a natural way. Instead of dripping, it would look more as if she'd been buffeted by windblown drizzle.) There was a slight displacement of dust or water, sweat or blood, but no real sign of the change. And because there was no sign, no evidence, Sam would sometimes play tricks on the other Sam. For instance, there was the one time she'd been so angry with her blameless sister that she cut her own hair off. Samara did those things because *she* was the one who had to pretend, to pretend to be stupid, because the other Sam could hardly be expected to pretend to be clever. So Samara had played tricks on her sister, but when she arrived even her sister's sweat would accommodate her and *no one knew* and, of course, the whole thing was hateful to her so she stayed away, and let the other Sam live her inoffensive life—

—and then she had appeared in the smoke-filled kitchen at Mary Whitaker, in blood-soaked clothes, to find herself standing at the stove, tending a spitting paella pan full of fried human nipples, one of them as familiar to her as her own. She arrived with the chilly, inorganic smell of *between* on her, into Samantha Waite's suddenly untenable life. 'And now,' Sam thought. 'Before I lose my mind altogether, I have to make sure I completely understand what I'm being told.'

Myr was sitting cross-legged on the floor in front of the

white leather recliner, watching her. When she looked at him he said, 'Yes, I had expected tears.' Clinical, as if he were checking symptoms.

Sam wiped her eyes, and said softly to herself: 'It was what was done to us.' She meant that it was whatever Uncle and the woman had done to separate her and her sister that had opened the door for Myr's Wake.

But when she said 'It was what was done to us', Myr apparently thought that she was comparing the survivors' current situation to that of the Ngati Tumatakokiri who had buried their dead in storage pits. 'Yes, many of the same things happened to those people,' he said. 'They were in quarantine. It rained for three months, and they invited me into their homes.' He waited for another question, and in the silence a look of desperation crossed his face. He said, 'If the Wake isn't trapped it will spread everywhere, feeding on human madness, zeal, and ecstasy. If I don't trap it, it kills everyone.' He sounded as if he was pleading for her understanding.

'It was us,' Sam said again. 'We did it.'

He didn't—and couldn't—understand her. He said, 'You didn't do anything. You and your companions only survived because you all arrived *after* the Wake had finished its first feed.'

Sam's ears were ringing. She was thinking two things. One was immediate and relative: if the Wake had finished feeding, then why did Myr still have it trapped? The second was that she must find out for sure whether she was in any way to blame. She tried to formulate a question. She felt her life depended on the answer.

'Space and time are one thing—space-time—like Einstein said. So, am I right in thinking that, when the Wake jumps from world to world, it can move not just between worlds but between times? It can go backwards and forwards in time? And so the thing that invited it in needn't

271

be something that happened a long time ago, it might even have happened recently?'

Myr frowned. 'That is a very odd question—given others you could ask. To answer—my people don't know whether time travel to the past is possible. We haven't had any insights. All these monsters move forward in time, but between worlds, and sometimes they skip hundreds of years. This Wake has been on the move for much longer than I have been following it. And for much longer than the person from whom I inherited the job. It was once more robust. But my people have followed it vigilantly, and starved it. We have starved it from place to place. Sometimes we're lucky and it alights where there are no people. It can't get any sustenance from birds and reptiles, and it has to jump again without feeding. That has helped.'

Sam laughed, and Myr looked startled. It was a laugh of relief. She wasn't culpable. The Wake was going from world to world, but always *forward* in time. She and Fa, Uncle and that stranger—it hadn't been them, what they did, and what was done to them. Sam ground her fists into her damp eye sockets and laughed. 'Not guilty,' she said.

Myr must have supposed she meant him. That she was laughing at his attempt to exonerate himself, to say that although he had the survivors trapped and separated from their families, he was only doing his duty. Because that *was* what he was saying.

He was watching her, waiting for something. Sam couldn't tell what. Then she had a thought. She asked another question—and could see as soon as she did that it wasn't the one he was waiting for. 'Are all of your people like you?' she asked. 'Very dark?'

He looked a little disapproving. 'I have come to see over the years that your different skin colours inspire attitudes that cause social complications.'

'That's not an answer.' Sam scowled at him and gnawed

272

her lip. 'And, by the way, we have "attitudes" to *all* our differences.'

'Yes. The answer is that my people are all variations on this colour.'

Sam was thinking of the woman who had come to visit Uncle just before she and her sister were separated. She was making a connection, but had to check some facts before jumping to conclusions. 'Your life isn't continuous, right? I mean, because you're following the Wake, your timeline doesn't match up with that of any other world, even your own.'

Again he looked surprised. 'You are very astute. And the fact that my life isn't continuous is a matter of more significance than my skin colour.'

'You follow the Wake between worlds, skipping over years and sometimes even centuries. Am I right?'

'Yes.'

'So you're not in touch with your own people?'

'No. I can see that you are worried—but there are numerous possible points in this Wake's path where I can be relieved. My life will come to an end, but this Wake will not go unguarded.'

'But you are currently out of touch and have been for some time?'

'Yes, mine is a solitary vigil.'

Sam didn't reply. She was thinking that if Myr's people had come up with a new strategy for dealing with these monsters, Myr might not know about it.

If only Uncle had confided in her. But after the other Sam was injured and damaged he had become distant and dictatorial. Had he supposed the plan would fail—if there was a plan? Had the other Sam's mental impairment made him lose faith in *her own* ability to understand things?

She would never know. Uncle had died of a heart attack when Sam and her sister were in their mid teens. And she hadn't even been there to notice warning signs and start asking the questions that she needed answers to, *now* more than ever.

Sam had a feeling that there was something else she'd meant to ask Myr—something vital. She looked at the fire. The log that had tumbled in the grate had fallen apart and its coals shimmered, so hot that the smoke rising from them formed above their surfaces. Each coal lay in a halo of hot, smokeless air. These bubbles of clarity reminded Sam of the No-Go, and she remembered what it was she'd meant to ask. 'Why is your quarantine still in force? Why is the Wake still here?' Then, 'That's a translation, isn't it? "Wake" is just a word you've chosen—a word in my language.'

Myr nodded.

'Is it "wake" as in "wake of destruction"?'

'No, it is "wake" as in "a feast in the presence of the dead". And that should give you your answer. The Wake powers the quarantine zone—though it doesn't know it. The zone won't vanish till the Wake moves on. The devices that form the zone are deep inside it. The Wake leaves, and, without a power source, the zone disappears. I gather up the devices, and go after the Wake.'

Sam frowned at him. She was trying to imagine his life. 'Don't you get lonely?'

A spasm of feeling passed across his face. Sam was unsure what it meant. She said, 'You could join us. Look—you've explained. You've exonerated yourself. I can convince them not to shoot you.'

Myr shook his head. 'You haven't understood. I'm only talking to you because you're different. You know the Wake is here. That's unprecedented. That's something I have to investigate.'

Sam wanted Myr on hand—and safe. She thought she would probably confide in him eventually. But first she needed to think things over in private. She said, 'You're

274

interrogating me, so I can't be kind to you? Is that what you're saying?'

Myr moved forward. He took her hands. 'Think.'

Sam sighed and stirred as if she was trying to shield herself from a cold, ticklish breeze.

'The fact that you know the Wake is there isn't a hope,' Myr said. 'It's only something different. You ask which meaning of your word "wake" I'm using, and I say "a feast in the presence of the dead", and you still don't understand me. You ask me whether I'm lonely. Let me tell you, loneliness is better than the death-watch. The Wake comes, it causes madness and terror, and it gorges itself. That's its sustenance. Then it savours what's left. It cleans its plate. That's what always happens. The only differences are in what I do. And I've tried everything. I've remained aloof, and I've gone native. I've kept survivors company, and I've killed them myself. I've been kind and cruel. I've been secretive and confiding. I've seen survivals like long summers that run on into warm autumns. I've sat holding the hand of the last one left while they've said to me: "At least I still have you".'

Sam stared at him. 'Oh,' she said. 'We are the feast.'

For a moment she felt nothing. Then a sudden downpour of terror coursed through her body, and she was soaked and heavy with fear. And not just fear—also despair and pity and fellow-feeling.

And then the Wake came. It came hungry for her terror, but it wasn't ravenous, or mindless, and it came for the other feelings too, her despair, and her empathy. It wasn't moved—it only settled on those good human feelings with a kind of exquisite epicureanism that seemed not just sentient, but intelligent—and alien, inimical, hell-bent.

Sam could still feel Myr's grip, and a stabbing pain in her ears, because he was shouting at her. Then the Wake had her completely and there was a moment of stillness, when she lay dissolving in the hollow of its tongue. It was in the room

275

with them, and in all adjacent rooms, rising, basement, ground floor, first floor, roof space—rising and spinning like a whirlwind, but leaving the blond basement dust quite undisturbed. It was down under the earth too, spinning and drilling, like something that should be able to set off earthquakes. Its venomous whirlwind savaged Sam. She was on her knees beneath a waterfall of tears. The Wake's every revolution wound her out of herself.

But Sam wouldn't leave. She had, for once, to be some use to herself. She tried to struggle out from under it—but the monster went with her, still circling her as she pushed past Myr—slithering off his activated force field and blundering across the room. There was no place she could take shelter. She tried to organise her thoughts so that she could fight the urge to go, to be gone.

The Wake, the whirlwind—the other Sam had danced under it. On those occasions it had come to savour and suck on someone else. 'But it's different when it's me,' Sam thought. 'When it's *me*, not Fa.' She let Myr catch her, and they collapsed together onto the floor. The Wake was with her, but Sam no longer felt fed on or threatened with annihilation. For a moment she was simply a bystander, someone who steps up to a window and parts the curtains to look down on some commotion in the street. She was a detached spectator. Then she was gone.

Holly was unloading the dishwasher and putting away the dinner dishes when Jacob banged in through the back door, out of breath, and headed straight for the refrigerator. Holly had all the ingredients for tomorrow's lunch sorted and separated into bowls, and she didn't want any of her preparations disturbed. 'What are you after?'

Jacob closed the door and showed her a bottle. 'I've been keeping liquid amoxicillin in here.'

'Is Curtis ill?'

'He has a fever. I've got him into a bed with an electric blanket. But I shouldn't have left him. I'm hurrying right back; I'll take Warren's car.'

Holly asked him if he needed help. For moment he just looked at her blankly. She began to apologise. 'I know I'm not terribly useful, but . . .'

'I can't think of anything I need you for right now. I think it's best if everyone just stays clear.'

'Is he infectious?'

Jacob's eyes flickered down to her hands. Holly found she was wringing them. She said, 'At least let me bring you something to eat.'

'That would be good. I'll manage my own breakfast. But maybe if you bring lunch. You can just leave it at the front door.' He stuffed the bottle in his pocket. 'I'd better get back.'

He pushed through the swing doors, and Holly heard him calling out, 'Warren? Are the keys in the car?' and then she heard the steely boom of the filing cabinet in the manager's office where he kept drugs and other medical supplies.

Holly went back to what she'd been doing. She was concerned about Curtis, but comforted by the thought that perhaps, when he'd said that horrible thing to her, he'd only been coming down with something.

Jacob managed to get Curtis into a fresh bed in another of Mrs Kreutzer's guest rooms. He closed the door on the fouled bed and bloodied en suite. Before tucking Curtis up Jacob steered the man towards the bathroom.

'No,' Curtis said. 'I don't need to. Though I haven't gone for hours.'

Once Curtis was settled, the chills and fever seemed to come upon him in successive cascades. They weren't really mitigated by a change from over-the-counter to clinical analgesics. Jacob administered a big dose of the amoxicillin—that went down okay. Curtis was having trouble swallowing pills, was gagging on even average sized gel-covered capsules. Jacob took his blood pressure and was alarmed by the result. But there wasn't much he could do to control his patient's plummeting blood pressure without intravenous fluids. Curtis needed IV antibiotics. Kahukura's pharmacy had stocked several kits for an insulin infusion pump—kits with cannula, needles, and grey tube. But of course the pharmacy didn't have IV antibiotics, or normal saline.

However, when they were burying the residents of Mary Whitaker, Jacob had taken note of the oxygen pump in one room. He went to get it now, rushed up there, hurried through the desolate rooms, and manhandled the pump out to the Captiva.

Oxygen made Curtis more comfortable. His colour improved and he even managed a few hours sleep. But the following morning he became agitated and tried to climb out of bed. Jacob struggled with him, and fresh blood burst forth on the bandages binding his legs. Jacob held Curtis down and slipped him some tranquillisers. They were tiny, and melted to mush in his mouth.

Near midday Jacob left Curtis to answer a knock at the door. It was Holly. She was holding a covered basket. She said she couldn't just leave his lunch on the doorstep and go away without seeing if there was anything he needed.

Jacob stepped outside and shut the door. 'I have him on oxygen,' he said. 'Mary Whitaker had an oxygen pump. But it wasn't the sort of rest home that supported hospital level care.'

'Is he very bad?'

'I'm afraid it's septicaemia. He has a rash. And he's bleeding, because his body has used up most of its platelets.'

Holly stepped back. The wicker basket crackled as her hands tightened on its handle. 'This is very technical,' she said. Then, 'You say he's bleeding. Is he injured?'

'At this point he wouldn't have to be injured to be bleeding.'

'Dear God,' Holly said.

'He's wandering again. And his breathing is very fast.' Jacob paused. 'I'm going to lose him, Holly.' He took the basket from her. She was clinging and clumsy, and between them they nearly upset it.

'Can I at least spell you?' Holly offered. She was scared, and her voice sounded strangled.

He shook his head, and went back in, closing the door on her white face.

Jacob ate standing at a sideboard in Mrs Kreutser's sitting room. He was hungry and shovelled down Holly's bean salad, bread, and fried haloumi. While he ate he thought about the reading he'd done for a course he'd been sent on during the two years he worked in an ICU. He thought about 'protocols for determining futility'. The paper was about how you could tell when you'd done enough. Not 'exhausted all your options', but *done enough*. Jacob couldn't find this situation's 'enough' place—because he'd had so few options to start with. And, quite apart from the lack of IV fluids, and intravenously delivered broad-spectrum antimicrobial drugs, dialysis, and steroids—quite apart from all that, he had already failed at what he *had* been able to do. He hadn't recognised that Curtis was seeing things; that somehow, for a time, Curtis had been almost as crazy as the victims of the first-hour madness. Jacob wanted to understand what had happened, but how could he ever hope to, with Curtis slipping in and out of consciousness now? Curtis wouldn't be able to give him any answers.

Jacob wiped his mouth, washed his hands, and went back into the sick room.

For the second night in a row William was hiding, hunkered down in the shadows at the edge of the arboretum, waiting for some sign of Sam, or her captor. He stayed rigorously still, straining to hear. This was his life now: looking all day, and listening all night.

He hadn't slept for two days, but he was wakeful more from shame than worry. Sam had suffered. She'd been spirited away and tied up and who knew what else had happened to her, and now she wouldn't come in and be comforted by her community.

She had wanted *his* comfort. She'd waited weeping at his door. If her abduction and lonely roaming were to be what finally happened to Sam, a close to her story—one of hard work and stoicism and compassion for others—then his behaviour gave her story a horrible shape.

William allowed himself to change position. He eased himself onto his knees. He'd only just got comfortable again when a sound came from uphill, a swishing noise that seemed to originate from a place higher than the ridgeline, yet not beyond it, which was impossible. There was a dragging crackle, as if something heavy was being drawn slowly through the treetops.

William switched on his flashlight and pointed it up through the trees. He saw boles and branches and leaves, and behind everything a solid fretwork of shadows that plunged back and forth as he swung his torch. He pointed its beam at the ground and got to his feet. He set off after the lit spot, sprinting up the hill as fast as he could go, stopping at intervals to listen for that odd, aerial rasping.

At one pause he thought he heard something behind him. Footfalls, coming up the hill after him. Someone was following him.

William switched off his torch, and lay in wait. His

pursuer kept coming, not at all stealthy, but fast and fearless.

When the noises of pursuit came close—but not too close—William pointed his quenched torch downhill, at the trees, into their shadows. He switched it on.

A shadow moved in the blackness, then a form delineated itself in the torchlight, appearing at first like a chalk sketch on a blackboard. The shape came closer, rounded out, and became the man in black, pushing determinedly uphill, his gaze apparently fixed on something behind William's right shoulder.

William wasn't about to fall for that one. He kept his eyes on the man and made calculations. If the man's force field covered his feet then surely he wouldn't be able to run. He wouldn't be able to *keep* his feet.

William snatched his rifle off his shoulder. It fell into his hands, and into position. He flicked off the safety and set his eye to the sights. He didn't look at the man, his face; he only aimed at the man's feet and let the sights frame and follow one foot, and find its rhythm. He squeezed the trigger. The leaf litter puffed up right beside the man. William got off another shot—but not before the man threw himself behind a tree.

The man didn't stay under cover. Instead he made another dive, this one downhill. He tucked his knees up against his chest, wrapped his arms around his head, and began to roll. He picked up speed, skidding, sliding off trees, bouncing more like a beach ball than a body. William took another shot—and the bullet chipped a tree trunk. Then he hitched the rifle back onto his shoulder and gave chase.

Half an hour later Theresa was there to meet William when he emerged on the road through Cotley's orchard. The morning sun hadn't yet cleared the hill and when it did, it would come up behind cloud. The day was dull.

The sound of William's shots had roused Theresa and, when she looked out her window, she had seen the light of his torch moving through the woods. She was able to pretty much figure out where to go to wait for him.

'It was the man in black. I lost him,' William said. Then he noticed she'd been crying. 'Sorry. It was an epic chase. He lost me twice, and I found him again both times. The third time—I don't know—he accelerated as if he'd only been playing with me up until then. I think he can control the force field over his feet. Because he is able to get traction and run. Still, if he has an Achilles heel, it's his heels.'

'What?'

'Never mind. What's wrong, Theresa?'

Theresa bit her lip fiercely for a time before answering. 'Curtis died early this morning, of blood poisoning. Jacob said he got to it too late to treat it.'

William didn't say anything. He put his hand on her shoulder and then pulled her against him and held her.

Her voice was muffled. 'I helped Jacob move Curtis into the supermarket cool store. We don't think there should be a funeral till we've found Sam.'

'So we can hold two funerals at the same time? Yes, that would be more emotionally economical,' William said.

Theresa pushed away from him. 'You're lashing out. I understand,' she said, but she found she couldn't look at him. She took a deep breath. 'You do know that the man in black didn't grab Sam just because you pushed her out of your bed.'

'She followed Oscar to talk to him. Because she could trust the kid to be honest—but not us.'

'Or, she followed Oscar because she thought he'd be easier to manipulate.'

'Oh, so now you think she isn't crazy, but manipulative?'

'It's pretty crazy to pretend to be two people.' She took William's arm. 'Come back with me. Once everyone is up we're going to have to tell them that we lost Curtis. Holly wasn't awake to help us with his body—but she did know he was sick, and that Jacob thought he wouldn't make it.'

'Are you saying that because Holly knew how bad Curtis was, we don't have the option of hiding that he died?'

Theresa nodded, and briefly met his eyes. 'I wish we could hide it. I don't think we should have to process Curtis's passing till Sam's found. Jacob agrees with me. He's really worried about our morale. I've been on about morale for ages. But when I talk about it I sound like a rugby coach; Jacob sounds like the Chief Coroner explaining why the media shouldn't report youth suicides.'

William considered her words for a moment then said, 'Curtis didn't kill himself.'

'No. Jacob said it was a neglected infection.'

'So what exactly is it that we want to hide?'

Theresa shook her head. She was exhausted. William slipped his arm around her waist, led her to her car, and put her in its passenger seat. He climbed in to drive. As he started the engine, she said, 'Jacob didn't tell me everything.'

'So you do think it *was* a kind of suicide?'

'It was something extravagant.'

'Like the first-hour victims?'

'Not that bad. Or at least more gradual.'

'And gradual is better?'

Theresa had done crying. She just shook her head. 'No, it's not.'

Back at the spa William got himself a cup of coffee, and sat down beside Jacob. 'So what was the cause of death?'

'Blood poisoning,' Jacob said. He held his hands out, studied their backs then their palms. 'I washed his body. I haven't done that since before I trained to be a nurse. Back when I was working in an old people's home.'

'I guess washing bodies would be one of Sam's jobs.'

'Yes. You remember that she wanted to do it for her old people? And we discouraged her because it wasn't practical.'

'What caused Curtis's blood-poisoning?'

William watched Jacob's right hand wander up to his collar to touch his crucifix. 'Cellulitis. From a graze. It can come on fast.'

'Why are you whispering?'

'I'm tired. Why else?'

'You tell me.'

Jacob looked at him, his face bleak. 'Go away, William.'

PART SIX

William, in the course of his life, had sometimes camped in the desert. Whenever he crawled out of his tent to urinate, and the liquid splash of that was done, it would be so quiet that he'd imagine the hurtling satellites among the still stars were making a thin, continuous exhalation, as if they ran on steam.

In the small hours, Kahukura's quiet had a quality all its own, for it was made of some sounds—the low throb of the refrigerator units at the back of the supermarket, a window banging, a cable knocking against the aluminium flagpole far away in the school grounds—and not others: a car engine; a drain gurgling as someone ran a tap; a computer game's swordplay or gunshots; a sports commentator on the radio of some insomniac senior citizen; the progressive tenor roar of a skateboard going by.

William lifted his head from the pillow. He thought he heard the sound of the spring mechanism on the swimming pool's safety gate. After a moment there was a splash.

He got up, put on his sweatpants and went out.

The pool was lit and blue. Sam was swimming lengths. Her clothes were draped on one of the timber loungers; her shoes lay discarded by the pool fence.

William unfastened the safety gate and went into the enclosure. The water slopping over the pool's sides raised the faint lingering scent of dog from the tiles. Steam was lifting from the disturbed water, which now looked a little oily.

William picked up one of Sam's dropped socks; it was still limber with body heat.

Sam passed up and down the pool, fast and coordinated.

She flipped and pushed off at each turn like someone with training, one of those people who carries a constant perfume of chlorine. Her hair flowed back across her shoulders as she turned to breathe. Her eyes were open, her lashes thick and spiked.

William regarded Sam's painfully familiar body, her long toes, her narrow hips, the little lozenge of silky pubic hair that tapered up to her navel, becoming finer and fairer as it climbed but still there, almost masculine. He watched that compact boyish body cut through the water. Sam rolled her shoulders up on every fourth stroke to breathe, and when she did, William noticed something. He crouched to get a better look. A better look at the whole of her—sleek, symmetrical, unmarred—for Sam's nipples were intact.

She swam fifty laps. William had time to go to the laundry and fetch one of the robes. He was waiting for her when she finally came to a stop. She slapped the end of the pool and her wake surged up to break over her shoulders. She wiped her eyes, then kicked off and came to him, climbed out, and turned her back so that he could drape the robe around her. She worked her arms into its sleeves and tied its belt.

'He healed you,' William said. His voice was shaking. If the man in black had healed Sam's mutilated breast, then he must be benevolent. But somehow William couldn't imagine him that way. His mind refused it. The man's avoiding them seemed to weigh more than his having healed Sam. His staying away—and his being there before, preceding all of them by centuries, someone who wasn't subject to the rules of time. A demigod, like Superman, or the Doctor; one of those judicious, sequestered aliens of fiction.

'I need to clean up,' Sam said.

'Where have you been hiding?'

A small crease formed between her brows. 'I want to shower,' she said, and brushed by him.

William was in despair. 'What did the man say? You're

the only one who knows anything.'

Sam stopped with her hands on the gate. She kept her back to him.

William said, 'When you were with him, you were representing us—you do get that?'

Sam went on through the gate and up the path to the terrace.

'I'm not the only one with questions,' he called after her. Then he headed to the kitchen to make coffee.

A minute later Lily arrived. She went straight to the sink to fill her hydration pack.

William asked her if she'd seen Sam.

She nodded.

There would only have been time for a few words in passing. But William wondered what Sam had said that justified Lily's lack of interest in the fact of her reappearance. He said, 'She wasn't very forthcoming.'

'No,' Lily agreed.

William waited for Lily to repeat what Sam had said to her, or to ask some cogent questions.

Lily put her hydration pack on and adjusted its straps.

'I presume you're as relieved as I am,' William said.

Lily met his gaze. 'Oh—yes—of course. She looked well. I guess she's collecting herself. I don't expect her to talk to me. I never understand her when she does.'

'Did you tell her about Curtis?'

'No. It's not my place.'

Lily wasn't really engaging with him. William wondered whether Sam had said something to Lily about him— something detrimental.

'I have to get going,' Lily said. 'I warmed up in my room. Don't want my tendons tightening up.' She pushed off the bench, gave a little wave and set off. William watched her bounce down the driveway. Her knee had settled and her gait was good.

Sam didn't put in an appearance until breakfast was being cleared away. She filled a bowl with cereal and fruit juice, then went out onto the terrace and sat in a cane chair, her face hidden behind her damp hair, her feet tucked up under her robe.

The others clustered in the atrium, out of her earshot. They murmured and hissed at one another for several minutes, trying to figure out how they might tackle her. Not everyone wanted in on the discussion. Holly was in the vegetable patch making bamboo tepees for runner beans; Lily was still doing her circuits. Kate was loading the dishwasher and said she just couldn't take another bickering discussion, and that, for her, it was enough that Sam was safe.

The discussion was contentious, but brief. Everyone stayed in character. Oscar put up his hand when he wanted to say something; Belle did her best to keep the peace when Theresa once again brought up the issue of Sam's bruises; William fumed; Dan called the rest of them 'You people'; and Jacob kept saying 'Go easy' whenever anyone seemed particularly upset.

It was Belle who was eventually delegated to speak to Sam. Everyone else ostentatiously melted away, and Belle went and sat opposite Sam.

Sam looked good, her skin dewy, her eyes clear. 'I'd like to go for a walk,' she told Belle, without looking at her.

'You've only just returned.'

'I'm restless.'

'William says that the man in black healed you. I guess that means we have nothing to fear from him.'

'The man in black isn't a problem. And we really don't have to worry anymore about safety in numbers.' Then, as if that subject was done with, Sam said, 'I'm going to scavenge

290

for foil. We need something bright to reflect our lights when we send messages.'

'Yes, we should get back to that. Our plans got a little sidelined when you went missing.' Belle hesitated then said, 'How were you able to communicate with the man?'

'He speaks English.' Sam finally looked at Belle. 'Would you ask William if he'll go scavenging with me? I'm going to get dressed.' She headed off upstairs. When she was out of sight, Theresa sidled up to Belle. 'Well?'

'She wants William to go for a walk with her.'

'Do you think he should have reason for concern? I mean, it's not as if they've been getting on. You don't think she means to lead him into some kind of trap?'

'No! This is Sam. Well—kind of.' Belle took Theresa's arm and walked her back into the dining room. She found William and explained to him that Sam wanted him to help her scavenge for aluminium foil.

'And how did she strike you?'

'Different,' Belle said.

'So, she's *clever* Sam.' William made air quotes.

'I think so. And she isn't pretending. I think she really does have two personalities.'

'And you know this because of your extensive experience with endangered parrots.'

'Fine, be like that.'

Theresa said, 'Will you go with her, William?'

'Of course.'

'Good. But be careful.' Theresa turned back to Belle. 'Did you tell her about Curtis?'

'No, sorry. Should I have? Can't it wait?'

'I suppose so.'

'William can tell her.' Belle looked at him. 'He can *tell her off*, say that people are perishing while she plays her silly game.'

William looked at Belle coldly, then went off to find Sam.

291

They went through some of the houses that had been cleared, and several they knew were empty. They took rolls of foil from kitchen drawers, and from dispensers, and stuffed them into their backpacks. In one house Sam paused and studied the photographs on the fridge door. 'I bet that woman has something in my size,' she said, and went off to the master bedroom.

After a moment William followed her, and found her trying on clothes—a silk chiffon shirt, with buttoned cuffs and a flourishing bow. She glanced at William in the mirror and said, 'When I was a teenager I used to have this dream where I could walk into any house and take whatever I wanted.'

'Were the houses empty?'

'Empty and unthreatening; it never felt like theft.' She frowned. 'Come to think of it, in those dreams I knew that everyone was dead.' She had found a pair of jeans; soft, aged denim. 'Do you mind, William?' She made a stirring gesture, meaning 'turn around'.

'Seriously?'

'Humour me.'

William faced the door. He heard her stomping on the backs of her running shoes and kicking them off. 'I'm tired of wearing sweatpants,' she said. 'I think I'll just work my way through this woman's things.'

'You're not worried about her family? About afterwards?'

Sam laughed. 'I'm not going to be called to account.'

'So—tell me—which is the real Sam? This? Or the one who wouldn't use a phrase like "called to account"?'

There was a sly smile in her voice when she answered. 'You think that the man in black healed my breast. Couldn't he have healed my brain as well?'

'Did he?' William turned around.

Sam was admiring herself in the mirror. She rummaged in a basket on the dresser and chose a lipstick, put it on, pouted at her reflection, then pulled the shirt from her shoulder to practise a kiss, and study the print of it. She said, 'I bet her shoes won't fit me. That would be asking too much.' She got down on her knees and pulled the shoe tree out of the wardrobe. She selected some ballet flats and slipped them on. She got up to check the effect with her jeans. 'Wow. They're only about half a size too big.'

'Sam, if the man in black had fixed your brain you'd be like the protagonist in *Flowers for Algernon*. You ever read that story?'

'No.'

'It's science fiction. An intellectually handicapped guy takes part in an experiment, and his IQ goes up 150 points. Then the mouse dies.'

'I take it the mouse is Algernon?'

'Yes.'

'The difference isn't as much as 150 points,' Sam said. 'Though, if it were shoe sizes, I'd have to say that I do have much bigger feet than the other Sam.'

William stayed very still, and held his breath.

Sam posed in her new outfit. 'Do you like the way I look?'

'You know I like the way you look.'

She turned back to the mirror to preen. She used a finger to blot the lipstick at the corner of her mouth, and pulled a stray lock of hair out from under her collar.

'Is this a test?' William asked.

'No.'

'I *hit* you,' he said. 'Do you remember that?'

'Yes. Are you sorry about it?'

'It was wrong. But—'

'With *mea culpa* there's not usually a "but".'

'Having your brain healed wouldn't produce the habit

293

of thinking that comes up with metaphors—that makes IQ analogous with shoe size. Or, for that matter, suddenly have a grasp of everyday Latin.'

'There's an everyday Latin?'

'Per diem. Pro forma. In flagrante delicto.'

Sam retrieved her backpack and said she'd come back later and go through everything properly. 'I can go about refurbished. Body, clothes—' she glanced at William through her thick eyelashes '—and brain.'

'So you're sticking to that story?'

'It isn't a sworn statement, or affidavit—since we're doing Latin.' Sam breezed out past William, and he followed her to the next house. They cut across the school field, skirting the turned earth of its mass grave. They began their scavenging again in a row of houses they knew were empty—houses that had been locked when the clean-up crews first came along. In the second they paused again so that Sam could inspect bookshelves. She said, 'William, are there books that make you feel better?'

'Me?'

'People. Books that make *people* feel better. And I don't mean diverting books, or the Bible.'

William sighed. 'Sam. I've been delegated to question you, and I'm supposed not to alarm or alienate you.'

'You're doing fine so far.'

'I'm biting my lip.'

Sam went along a shelf, her finger tripping from spine to spine. It was a good library, housed in floor to ceiling built-in shelves. There was one whole wall of books, apart from two bays displaying big cast-glass bowls. Sam said, 'What would you read if you thought you needed a book like a boat to put out in?'

'A boat?'

Sam nodded. 'A book to sail off in, and set fire to, like a Viking funeral pyre.'

It took William a moment, but he finally understood what she meant him to understand. 'Are we going to die?' he said. 'Is that what the man in black told you?'

Sam didn't respond.

'Just say it. Go on. Deprive me of hope.' William looked at the set of her turned head and saw smugness. He saw everyone who had ever said to him: '*This is for your own good.*'

'I'm sorry,' Sam said, without turning around.

'No, you're not.'

She looked over her shoulder. Her face was clenched and anxious. 'I have to stay calm,' she said. 'Everyone has to stay calm.' She returned her gaze to the books, eased one out, and put it on the arm of the couch.

'I'm not sure that's what you want,' William said. 'There's transcendence and "transcendence". Try the skinny one in the middle of the shelf below.'

She looked at the spine. *Gilead.* 'I haven't heard of it.'

William hated people who'd say they hadn't heard of something, in that sceptical way as if the state of their knowledge was the state of knowledge itself. He said, 'Sam? Why do you think the man told *you*?'

'I don't know. Perhaps he cracks periodically.' She pulled out another book, then put it back again.

'You'd probably be better off with poetry,' William said. 'Fiction is all people and connections and, at its best, it teaches us how to live. But since you're saying we won't live, then try poetry. Poetry's all arias and no recitatives.'

'I don't know what you mean.'

'Arias are the big, dramatic, self-actualising soliloquies in operas. Recitative does plot, pretty much, or dialogue. You know—the Barber of Seville measuring his marriage bed.'

Sam gazed at William, her expression admiring. 'I wish I'd met someone like you a long time ago. But I kept having to come back to Kahukura.' She took William's suggested book and sat down holding it to her heart, as if making promises to it.

'Didn't you have a choice?'

'No. I've spent my whole adult life here. I've spent my life with my foot in the door, keeping it open, waiting for something to come along.'

'And this came.'

'And this came.' Sam echoed him.

'Okay. But what is "this"? Could you please be a bit more specific?'

'What's the point?' Sam said.

'No,' William said. 'I guess you'd rather nurse another secret and feel special. You obviously like feeling special.'

Sam leapt to her feet and took several steps towards him. The book she was treating with such tenderness had become her weapon. William raised an arm to ward off her blow. But then it was as though she was pulled up short. As if something above her tightened the strings that held her upright, so that she stiffened and stood very erect. Her hands fell to her sides. She dropped the book. For a moment she was blank and motionless, then she grew radiant. Her eyes widened, her lips parted, and she flushed.

There was nothing in the room with them. Nothing William could hear or see. But Sam was in the grip of something. Something godlike was there with her, caressing her.

William took hold of her, but she didn't feel his touch or turn her eyes. His rational brain began to make suggestions for things that could explain some of her behaviour. Cerebral lesions. Frontal lobe seizures. He considered all this, but he knew it was something else. It was the 'wind' that she had always liked to dance with. The wind that had come when the Nokia ring tui first made itself heard, and at Adele Haines's funeral, a wind intangible to everyone but Sam. It was there—*something* was there—and it and she were in communion.

When the Wake came, Sam felt, very remotely, William shaking her. His words were unintelligible, but his voice was as expressive as the Reserve's kaka, who would come every spring to squabble over the new growth on the kowhai at her gate. The monster was making a meal of their agitation. It spun faster, drilled harder, sang louder. It licked and sucked and savoured. It oscillated out from Sam to take William too, and coax him. Its voracious song and dance was making a kind of silence and stillness. Sam stopped breathing to listen to that, to what she had never heard, the perfect silence of that place she went whenever she wasn't here.

Shortly before noon, when Sam and William were still out, and Theresa was pacing the terrace and peering down the hill, the man in black came into view, framed by the spa's gateposts. He was carrying someone. He walked up the drive and Theresa hurried out to meet him. It was Lily he had in his arms, her body inert but not quite floppy. Theresa instantly recognised the not-quite floppiness as rigor mortis. She knew that Lily was dead, but when she reached the man for a time everything Theresa did was a denial of what she knew. She called Lily's name and tried to take her from him, which was impossible—Lily wasn't entirely in the man's force field but, because of it, Theresa couldn't slip her hands under Lily to lift her away. Jacob arrived and tried too, but retreated wiping his hands on his thighs as if he'd touched something nasty.

The man laid Lily on the driveway. Only then were they were able to get at her. Jacob checked her and then got up shaking his head, probably for the benefit of everyone else— Holly in the vegetable bed, and the others who had come out onto the terrace.

Dan stormed down the drive, shotgun in hand.

The man got up and backed off.

Bub intercepted Dan and wrenched the gun from his grip.

Theresa said to the man, 'Just wait.' She put up a palm and patted the air. 'Wait.' She wondered whether what she imagined was a universal gesture would turn out to be merely terrestrial. 'Where did you find her?'

'At the farthest point of the shoreline track,' said the man. 'I didn't see her collapse. She has been wearing herself out. That was her weakness.'

Theresa was surprised by the compressed coherence of his answer. Sam had told Belle that the man spoke English, but Theresa hadn't imagined his English would be so good.

'Why didn't you do something to help her?' Jacob asked.

'She wasn't warm,' said the man.

'Is that how it works?' Jacob said. 'For you to help her did she need to be alive? I thought—since you healed Sam—'

The man looked immensely surprised. 'What do you mean?'

'You healed Sam,' Jacob said, and touched his own chest. 'During the Madness Sam cut off her nipple. She had nothing here but a healing wound.'

'I didn't look under Sam's clothes.'

'Why are you lying?' Theresa was in despair. 'Why would you finally come to face us, then lie? Why would you run away from William only two days ago, but come now? It doesn't make any sense!'

Belle arrived with a sheet to cover Lily. Jacob helped Belle roll Lily onto the sheet, and they folded its sides over her body, neatly and expertly.

For some time the sky had been lowering, and the temperature falling. Now there was a scattering of fat drops that fell, *pock, pock*, on Lily's shroud. Then the air thickened with rain so hard that it activated the man's force field, until he stood in a halo of clear air from which the drops rebounded like sparks. 'The Wake changed Sam,' the man said. 'I'm sorry.'

Theresa was about to ask what he meant by 'the wake', but then Bub said, bemused, 'You're sorry Sam's fixed?'

'I'm sorry she's broken,' the man said.

'I get it that we shouldn't be surprised when we don't understand you,' Theresa said, 'given that you're some kind of alien. But what I'm asking myself is, should *you* be confused by us?'

'No,' the man said. 'But my experience doesn't encompass Sam's experiences. She knows that the Wake is there. No one ever knows. And you say she was mad. Only those who are present when the Wake arrives go extravagantly mad. And, mad or not, no one present when it arrives has ever survived. How did she survive? That's something I need to know. I kept Sam captive because I wanted her to explain. But before she was able to tell me, the Wake came, and made her hollow.'

'Huh?' said Bub. 'What do you mean, the wake?'

'You're sounding like a near miss in Google Translate,' Belle said. 'What is it you're talking about when you use that word?'

The man said, 'I told Sam. She would explain if she was able to. But the Wake changed her. She still functioned, only poorly. And she was afraid of me, as if we had not just spent several hours in rational talk.'

'Um,' piped up Oscar from nearby, 'there are two of her.'

'Oh—yes,' Jacob said, 'apparently there are two Sams. We don't know whether she's pretending, or has a pathology. There's a sweet, stupid Sam, and a smart, experimental one. The pathology is known as Dissociative Identity Disorder. There is some debate about whether it's a genuine mental illness, or some kind of extravagant self-dramatisation.'

'It isn't something I've encountered before,' the man said.

Then, 'Tell Sam I need to talk to her.'

Bub ventured near, and poked his finger into the man's blurred casing of rebounding rain. 'Buddy, we want to talk to *you*. But all you do is go on about some wake.'

'Sam knows what you want to know,' the man said. 'Ask her.'

'She might not remember,' Theresa said.

The man frowned. 'You are saying that there is one Sam *under* the other. And that one of them is prepared to know things and understand them, while the other is a refusing Sam who turns up any time she feels fear or unhappiness?'

'Man,' said Bub, admiring, 'you just put the nut in a nutshell.'

'The Sam who is prepared to know will tell you, if she isn't broken,' the man said.

'We'll ask her,' Theresa promised.

The alien turned his back on them and walked away. Bub said, 'Hey!' He raised the gun he'd taken off Dan. He sighted down the barrel at the retreating figure.

Theresa was positive Bub meant only to relieve his feelings by taking aim, but then the barrel jumped and she was deafened by the sound of the shot—Bub had let off both barrels simultaneously. She closed her eyes and clapped her hands over her ears and had actually to force herself to open her eyes again and look.

The man was much further down the drive. He'd been knocked over and had skidded off, and was now moving gingerly, not because he was injured, but because his force field wouldn't at first let any part of him resume contact with the ground. He was patient, and was soon upright. He paused a second to regard them, then continued on his way.

They were all frozen in place. Theresa was opening and closing her mouth to make her eardrums stop squeaking. Bub looked sheepish. The people who'd stayed on the terrace drifted down to stand around the insubstantial shape in the wet shroud. Holly sat down beside Lily—unmindful of the puddles. She put a hand on the shroud and gave Lily a kind of consoling pat.

'Let's take her inside,' Jacob said. He helped Holly up and moved her gently to one side so that he could lift Lily. Bub came to offer assistance, and Jacob scowled at him.

Bub apologised. 'Sorry. My trigger finger got angry.'

'We did this,' Holly said, staring at the shroud. 'We let her down.'

'Her running looked positive,' Theresa said. 'She wanted to stay in shape. There was a race she'd entered—in March, I think. She hoped to be out in time to compete in it.'

'We can't look after one another,' Holly said.

'We just have to try harder,' said Theresa.

'We treated Lily like an adult and let her run herself into the ground,' Holly said. 'We left Curtis alone, and he died of our neglect. We have meetings and take votes and talk things over and give one another space, but we can't manage the big decisions. We can't take responsibility. Someone needs to do that—take responsibility.'

'Yes. You're right. But all we can do is try harder,' Theresa said. 'I promise I will.'

Everyone went indoors with Lily, except Bub, who stayed out on the terrace and watched the gate expectantly, waiting for William and Sam.

Sam opened her eyes. Her pupils kept altering as her gaze wandered around the room. William picked up her hand and put it against his cheek. The hand was softer and less densely muscled than he remembered. Sam had the hands and arms of someone who did manual labour, finer than Bub's, but stronger than Jacob's.

She tried to sit up. William helped her, but kept his arms around her. She let out a small sigh and leaned on him, her soft head tucked under his chin. Her hair smelled of Pears soap. 'I didn't go away,' she said. She turned her face into his open shirt and pressed her lips against his collarbone. They were plump and hot, dry and scabbed. 'You're warm,' she said.

William sighed, and folded her in his arms. They rested, listening to the rain on the steel roof. William stroked Sam's back and watched the runnels of grey light on her face. She was completely relaxed, and present. She kept her eyes on his.

'What am I going to do with you?' he said.

'I think there's very little that can be done with me. I think I'm a single-use thing.' She looked at the scattered rolls of aluminium foil. 'We have to rig our lights and send messages.' She met his eyes. 'When a plane goes down with enough warning, people switch on their phones and call their loved ones. All of you will have someone you want to say goodbye to.'

'I don't,' said William.

'Me neither—no one I can, anyway.'

When they were walking, hand in hand, up the driveway, Sam noticed the open grave beside Adele Haines's flower-covered mound. She stopped and said, 'Is that for me?' Then, 'I hope that's for me. A precautionary grave.'

'Who does that? Isn't it always the other way around—people have every reason to believe someone is dead and they don't have a funeral till they find the body?'

'I don't think I have a normal attitude to those things,' Sam said. 'Because of my sister.'

'Your twin sister?'

'Yes. Because of her body.'

'Being lost?'

'Because her body is never beside mine.'

302

'Yes, lost,' William thought. He said, 'That grave is for Curtis. He died. It was blood-poisoning.'

'Why didn't you tell me?'

'I just did.' He led her indoors.

The spa was dark and there were none of the usual cooking smells. The place was so quiet that at first they didn't notice the figures scattered around the dining room, all of them except Belle and Bub sitting alone. There was candlelight shining through a crack in the door to the conference room.

A chair scraped, and Theresa came out of the dining room. 'It's Lily. She's in there.'

William put his arm around Sam's waist, and they walked into the candlelit conference room.

When the rain stopped, Jacob and William went out, hung a lantern in the lower branches of the jacaranda, and dug another grave. They took turns digging, and when Jacob paused and leaned on his shovel he registered the sound of katydids singing in the wet shrubbery.

So—it was summer.

At midnight Dan found Holly busy in the kitchen, kneading bread dough.

'It's for tomorrow. Lily and Curtis's funeral lunch,' Holly said. 'It seems I've been at this bench for months.'

Dan, sensing a reproach, reminded Holly that she'd always had help. 'Though we should probably make up a roster. Now that the heroes have let the rest of us off mass burials and manhunts.'

'The heroes,' Holly said, and laughed. 'That says everything, doesn't it?' She looked around at him. 'I'm fine, Dan. This just has to be done. And now is better than later.'

Dan gave her shoulder a friendly squeeze and left her to it.

Jacob decided to sit vigil with Lily. He carried some fresh candles into the conference room and saw that someone else had been there before him. They had surrounded Lily's narrow, shrouded form with damp foliage—oleander, though it wasn't yet in bloom.

At midnight Theresa finally decided to put herself to bed. On her way upstairs she ran into Bub and Belle, who were burdened with bundles of bedding and backpacks. Theresa took Belle's arm. 'Where are you going?'

'We'll be back tomorrow morning for the funeral,' Belle said.

'But only for the funeral,' Bub added, and clenched his jaw.

'We've decided to move into Sam's bach. We want to be together,' Belle said.

'Together alone,' Bub added.

Theresa released her friend.

Belle looked stricken. 'I think I can only look after Bub and my kakapo.' She gave Theresa a beseeching look. 'I'm not managing, Tre.'

'It's okay, babe, Theresa gets that,' Bub said. Then, to Theresa, 'We'll see you tomorrow.'

Theresa told them to keep safe.

There was a light shining under William's door. Theresa knocked and heard a muffled 'Wait'. She hovered, and after a time William opened the door and slipped through it. Theresa had a glimpse of the bed and the tumbled waves of

304

Sam's dark hair.

William took Theresa's arm and led her downstairs. There he turned on the light behind the bar and found a bottle of whisky, a few inches left at the bottom. 'Warren has certainly made a dent in the top shelf.' He sprawled in a chair, whisky bottle in one hand and two glasses in the other.

He had only put on jeans. Their knees were grass-stained. He was sweating, and droplets of moisture on his stomach trembled with every breath he took. Theresa could see that he was already a little drunk. He raised one eyebrow, proffered the glass, and shook the bottle invitingly.

Theresa took a seat and accepted the glass.

He raised his bottle to toast.

'What are we drinking to?'

His face looked congested; his eyes were gleaming. 'Nothing, nothing, nothing.' He put the bottle to his lips and tipped his head back. 'Look at you—' he said, '— businesslike Theresa. Any moment you're going to say, "I'm expecting a report, William."'

Theresa was silent.

William went on, 'Or you're going to put your glass down, wipe your mouth and say, "I'll talk to you when you're sober."'

Theresa tried to school her breathing. She'd wait this out.

'So,' William said, 'which is it to be?'

Theresa shrugged.

William mimicked the shrug.

'Curtis and Lily are dead,' Theresa snapped. 'Where's your sense of decency?'

William subsided into his chair, arms hanging. 'Do you imagine I'm civilised?' he said. He dropped the bottle; it landed upright, spilling nothing, but the life seemed to go out of it, as if his touch had given the greasy glass some extra brilliance. 'Go on. Tell me off. Relieve your feelings.'

Theresa clenched her teeth and tried not to fume too visibly.

William went on in a musing tone. 'Though, you know, I don't actually *enjoy* listening to you. I mean—I hate the way most of you sound. Kate has that crisp British pronunciation—very refined and ladylike. And then there's the rest of you Kiwis, with your blurry, unforthright voices. Jacob's shrinking defensiveness, the way his voice always rises at the end of every sentence as if he's constantly asking for affirmation. And Bub with his cute syncopated accent—a big tough guy who sounds infantile.' William paused for a time and Theresa could see that he was checking the truth of his own feelings, as if he'd only understood them once he'd articulated them. He met her eyes. 'You're all children,' he said. 'Moral infants.'

There was a long silence. Theresa finally got up, retrieved the bottle and poured herself another drink. She put the bottle back into William's hand. 'You're baked,' she said.

William laughed.

'The alien brought back Lily's body. He wants to talk to Sam.'

'He told her—' William paused and looked away.

Theresa made a winding motion. 'Go on.'

'I think what he told her is that we're all going to die.'

Theresa wondered what her face was doing. She felt that her body had thickened, and gone stiff, like cooked egg.

'Take a moment,' William said. He suddenly sounded very professional and Theresa realised that, like her, his work sometimes involved giving people horrendously shocking news.

'I'm okay,' she said. 'You can go on.'

'That's it. That's all I've got. She wouldn't confide in me.'

There was another long silence. Theresa wasn't actually sure how much time passed before William continued. 'I said, "Tell me, Sam." I said, "It's okay, you can tell me. I

306

have a hard heart." But that only made her cry.'

Theresa was postponing feeling anything. She'd wait till she had all the facts.

'What *I* think is this: there is something trapped in Kahukura with us, probably by the man in black. I think Sam has always known. Kind of.'

'The man said something like that when he brought Lily. He was talking about something he called a wake, which caused the madness.'

'A *wake*?'

Theresa nodded.

'Remember you told me how, when Warren overdosed, Sam kept saying, outraged, "What is that?" I think that was *clever* Sam's first time with the thing. *Simple* Sam calls it "the wind". It comes when we're in despair. It was there when we buried Adele Haines, and the night we came in after clearing the daycare centre, when simple Sam was twirling on the terrace. She was *dancing* with it.'

'Yes,' said Theresa. 'What interests the man in black is that Sam knows it's there.' She picked up her glass and took a big swallow. 'After the funeral tomorrow we should have a meeting. See if we can't persuade Sam to treat us like adults and fill us in.'

The funeral was subdued. It was raining on and off—that sodden early summer weather that comes into Tasman Bay from the southwest. Nobody had an umbrella. They all stood bareheaded in the rain.

Oscar shuffled to the back of the group. Since he'd grown tall and begun to block people's views he habitually stood at the back. Besides, he didn't want to look at the shrouded forms, or anyone's face. Instead he gazed at the feijoa hedge downhill, and the wall of macrocarpa on the far side of Bypass Road. The hedges and road reserve were blurred and lumpish, and it occurred to Oscar that the road reserve hadn't been mown, and was sprouting thistles and blue borage, and that normally it was about now that the Tasman District Council sent their hedge trimmers, the marks of whose blades would show for months in the fleece of the roadside hedges.

Kahukura was going to seed, and had ceased to look like Oscar's hometown.

Oscar thought about Lily, and how bogus he felt standing at her graveside. He knew he had spoken to her often—but never about anything much. At that moment he could only recall her swinging ponytail and receding back. He tried to summon Curtis—whom he'd actually *liked*—but couldn't remember anything concrete about him. It occurred to Oscar that he didn't really know any of them. And then that he didn't really know anybody, and wasn't close to anyone any more. Sure—he'd had schoolmates he used to meet every weekday on the bus to Nelson Boys, and friends he'd chat to in a sidebar while playing *Heroes of New Earth*—but if he met one of those kids now he wouldn't know how to start a conversation. He gave it a go. At the graveside, under his breath, he practised an imaginary greeting. 'Sup?' Oscar said, to the drizzle, and everyone's backs.

What was up? Not him. For the rest of his life he was going to be one of those gloomy, seen-it-all people—a special kind of loser.

Oscar extracted himself from the gathered mourners and dawdled back to the terrace. He sat on the steps. A moment later Holly arrived with Kate and said, 'My mother is feeling a little under the weather. Could you see her upstairs, Oscar? I've got to go get lunch on the table.'

Oscar took Kate's arm and they went slowly upstairs. 'I don't know what's got into me,' she said. 'I'm so sleepy. It's as if I took a pill.'

When they got to her room Oscar helped the old lady

308

remove her shoes. He rolled the duvet down and left her to get into bed.

Jacob appeared. He had come to take a look at Kate. Oscar hovered a moment to see whether Jacob looked worried, but Kate and he were talking comfortably, so Oscar went downstairs and asked whether he could carry his food into the atrium and play a bit of *Bioshock* before the meeting. 'Theresa said something about a meeting, didn't she?'

When the meal was over Belle followed Holly into the kitchen with a stack of dishes. She was about to say, 'You'll want to go check on your mum. I can do these straight after the meeting.' But when she came in she found Holly emptying the bread basket by cramming the last few slices of today's none-too-successful batch of herb bread into her mouth. Holly caught Belle's eye and gave a grimace. She mimed that she couldn't talk, and Belle said, 'Well—I'm going to take my seat. They're all in a fierce rush.' It occurred to Belle that Holly's gluttony was perhaps a response to Lily's having effectively starved herself.

Holly swallowed hard and offered the final slice to Belle. 'No thanks.'

Holly said, 'Take it to Oscar. He didn't have nearly enough.'

Belle took the bread and put it down by Oscar on the arm of the sofa. 'Thanks,' Oscar said. His eyes didn't leave the screen. His thumbs flashed on the controller, and the fine muscles in his forearms seethed.

'Aren't you coming to the meeting?'

'Nah. I'm going to skip it. I've got this boss on the ropes. If he gets to that health machine he can heal. But he's not going to get to that health machine.'

Belle went into the conference room. The table was clear and smelled of wood polish. All the candles were gone from the room. Belle took her seat and gave Oscar and Holly's apologies.

Jacob was writing on the whiteboard—one bullet point, then, *Mental Health vs. Privacy*. He replaced the cap on the pen. 'We're going to have to talk about this.'

'Communicating with the outside—that's our first order of business,' Sam said.

'Our first order of business is communicating with each other,' Jacob said. He favoured Sam with a reproachful look. 'You talked to the man in black, and then stayed away for five days. He only held you prisoner for a single night, Sam. If you'd come back earlier with news—*any* kind of news—it would almost certainly have helped Curtis's state of mind. And Lily's. They would have had something to think about, instead of obsessing—'

'Hang on, Jacob,' Bub said. 'You told us that Curtis's death was natural causes. Some skin thing that got out of hand.'

'Jacob—Sam is the only person here with pre-existing mental health problems,' Belle said. 'You can't blame her because Curtis insisted on living by himself and had no help on hand when he needed it.'

'What I'm saying is that we can't lose anyone else like we lost Curtis and Lily,' Jacob said. 'We need some process in place to guard against it. We can't have people sliding unchecked into self-destructive behaviours.'

'Curtis didn't want us to look after him,' Bub said. 'He wouldn't let us. And what happened to him—a complication from a skin infection—could have happened in everyday life.' He gestured at the smeared blue of the bay. 'Only, out there he'd have had the safety net of a hospital.'

William said, 'Sam, you have to tell us what you know.'

'That'll be good for our mental health,' Sam said.

'Belle and I are sick of this,' Bub said. 'We want to get on with our lives!'

'So Belle thinks you're a safe pair of hands?' Warren said. 'I'm asking on behalf of Jacob and his mental health.'

'It's not my mental health I'm worried about,' Jacob said.

Warren said, 'That's right. You don't need to worry. You have faith. It's your drug of choice.'

Theresa put a hand on Warren's arm. 'We can do this calmly and politely.'

Belle bent over and clasped her arms around her stomach. 'Yes, let's not be angry. It's giving me indigestion.'

'Come on, Sam,' Theresa urged. 'You have to talk to us. There's no point in keeping secrets.'

'Yes, Sam. What is it we don't know?' Bub was loud and insistent.

Sam folded her hands before her on the table and stared off into space. She said, 'We're trapped inside the No-Go with an invisible monster that feeds on suffering and hasn't finished feeding.' She focused her eyes and looked around the table, and into each of their appalled faces. 'It cleans its plate,' she said.

The room was silent. Sam continued. 'The man in black follows the monster from world to world doing damage control by closing it in a quarantine. The No-Go is formed by machines he has, but is powered by the monster. The machines are inside the No-Go, which won't disappear till the monster leaves. And the monster won't leave till it's killed us. All of us, except the man in black, who is the descendant of people who survived an attack by a similar monster. He's invisible to it, and immune to the Madness. The Madness, which is like a marinade the monster likes to use.'

'Jesus, Sam!' Bub said, apparently as horrified by Sam's description as the information itself.

Sam continued, remorseless. 'The monster picks at people's loose threads—their faults, like Warren's fondness for mind-altering substances; and their virtues, like Lily's driven need to stay in shape.'

311

'Hey,' said Warren, 'I'm sitting right here.'

Belle abruptly craned forward and vomited on the tabletop. The people opposite her quickly pushed their chairs back and Theresa rushed to get a towel. Bub took hold of Belle's head while she retched, then, once she'd stopped, he sat on the floor and pulled her down into his lap.

'Oh shit,' she said. 'Sorry.'

Theresa returned with a roll of paper towels and several wet cloths. Sam took them from Theresa and began to clean the table, while Theresa wiped Belle's face and hair. Jacob knelt down by Belle, felt for her pulse, and started counting it against the second hand on his watch face.

'It's shock,' Bub said.

'I was feeling sick already.'

'Sorry,' Sam said. 'But you kept saying "Tell me", and it turned out that telling was a bit like vomiting—hard to stop.'

'I feel sick too,' Warren said.

'And I feel weak and grey and depressed—but that'll be the death sentence,' Bub said, acid. Then he looked penetratingly at Sam. 'The man wanted to know how you knew his monster was there. And after we'd talked to him he also wanted to know how you came through the Madness alive. He did ask, didn't he? When you were with him he asked you how you know the monster is there?'

'We didn't get to that.'

'The man doesn't know she's got two personalities— gentle Sam and shrewd Sam,' said William.

'He kind of does now, because when he came with Lily's body we explained it to him,' said Bub.

'But Dissociative Identity Disorder is psychological, not neurological,' Jacob said. 'The Madness was neurological. It killed people once it was done with them—just flat-out killed them. Sam couldn't escape being killed by switching to her type A personality. The man in black is just fooled by the coincidence. He thinks it means something, that it's fate, not just circumstantial. But I think it's like those plane crashes with only one survivor where everyone says God's responsible. And believe me—if I thought those things were God, I'd acknowledge Him. But it's science. Those sole survivors are all kids with low body mass, or skinny flight attendants strapped in near the galley—wreckage riders cushioned by the bit of plane they fall inside.'

'Okay,' Bub said, 'what's the science of Sam being spared going crazy?'

'I'm talking about chance and circumstance.'

'If anything can save us it'll be science,' Bub said.

Jacob said, 'No, Bub. I believe in the afterlife. I am never without hope.'

Bub frowned mightily.

'I don't get what you're saying either, Jacob,' Theresa said. 'You were explaining why the man in black was barking up the wrong tree and then suddenly you're all plane crashes and heaven.'

William said, 'Sam didn't survive by chance, Jacob. There's something about her that brought her through it.' He stared at Sam. 'What is it about you?'

'Actually, that's a good question,' Theresa said.

Jacob said, 'My point is that I don't need to think Sam's singularity represents an escape clause for us. If what you say is true and we're all screwed then *prayer* is the answer. We pray for salvation. Not the salvation of our bodies, but our souls.'

'Bro, I'm so disappointed in you,' Bub said to Jacob.

'Maybe people who are crazy can't go mad,' Dan said. 'Sam is crazy, right? Like the guy in *Fight Club*.'

'So if we all contrive to go nuts we'll be spared going nuts,' said Bub.

'We have our hope of Heaven,' Jacob insisted.

Dan gripped his shaved scalp. 'What about my kids?' he

said. 'My kids need their dad!'

Belle said to William, 'Are we all going to go mad?'

Then they were all shouting. Belle and Jacob and Dan were in tears. Then Dan got up and staggered out of the room.

The world had gone grey. Bub gripped his head. It was aching. His mouth kept filling with saliva. He'd opened it to say something, and had slobbered on his own chin. He was watching Sam, who had dropped the fouled wads of paper towel into a wastepaper bin and was wiping her hands on her shirt. He said, 'Wow. Sam. You have a halo. It's all around your body—a yellow light.' He looked around the table. 'Hang on. Other people have halos too, and so does the table. Hey. Is that it? Is that the monster?'

Several others panicked: 'Is *what* the monster?'

Bub: 'I'm not even scared. Shouldn't I be?'

Theresa: 'Jacob—my throat is bone dry. What's wrong with us?'

Jacob's tongue was burning. His upper arms and neck itched. He took Belle's wrist again and asked her how she was. 'I'll adjust,' she said. 'Does William mean to say we have no hope?' She looked apologetic. 'Sorry Jacob, I can't do heaven.'

Jacob turned to William. William was white. His eyes were closed. He was pinching the bridge of his nose. Jacob said sharply, 'William!'

William blinked at him. 'Fuck.' He swore succinctly and politely.

Jacob looked around the room. Sam had begun scratching fiercely. Warren was holding his abdomen and wiping drool off his chin.

314

Jacob took Theresa's arm. He pulled her to her feet and hustled her away through the atrium and into the manager's office, out of earshot. He told Theresa to find Holly. 'She didn't come to the meeting.'

'Neither did Kate. Or Oscar.'

Jacob said again that he wanted to speak to Holly. He opened the cabinet that contained his file boxes of medicines and almost immediately found what he was looking for. Ipecac. A single twenty-tablet packet.

'I had a bulimic friend who used to take that,' Theresa said. She pressed the back of her wrist against her mouth, belched, and swallowed. She said she had to go to the bathroom.

'Get Holly.'

Theresa nodded, her mouth clamped firmly closed. She headed out the door.

For a moment Jacob considered the packet—considered dosages. But he wasn't sure yet. He needed more symptoms. If it was food poisoning, ipecac wouldn't be any help.

He headed towards the conference room. Its doorway seemed to surge towards him like a wave. All the sounds grew louder. From outside he heard what he thought might be the summer's first cicada. Then the sound was sucked back, and Jacob staggered and doubled over. His stomach gave a heave, but he didn't vomit. Warren appeared beside him, helped him to a seat, then sat heavily beside him. 'I reckon we've been poisoned,' Warren said.

Jacob waited for the spasm to pass. He told Warren to go to bed. Promised he'd be up shortly. Then he noticed the dark, shadowy, expectant form on the screen of the big TV—Oscar's avatar, breathing but motionless—and the dropped controller. He told Warren to find Oscar, who was probably in the downstairs bathroom.

Jacob continued to the conference room. He saw that several other people had taken themselves off to a bathroom or to bed. William was next to Sam, a hand on her back. She had her head down between her knees and her hands clasped over her mouth.

Jacob asked Belle how her back was. 'You were the first to get sick,' he said.

'It's my stomach,' Belle gasped. 'And I'm woozy and cold, and I have a headache. I feel like a wet noodle. What about my back?'

'Do you have muscle spasms? Does the light seem very bright? Do sounds seem loud?'

'No. I just feel like shit.'

Jacob asked Bub how he was.

'Crook, bro.' There were beads of sweat on Bub's top lip.

Jacob opened the packet of ipecac and pushed a tablet out of its blister. He gave it to Bub. 'I think you should probably vomit.'

Bub eyed the tablet with distaste.

'Take it, and drink a couple of glasses of water.'

Theresa appeared at Jacob's side. She said that Holly was in bed. 'I couldn't wake her. She's clammy and her pulse is—I don't know—slow, or weak, or something.'

Jacob gave Theresa a tablet. Then he took one himself. 'Has Holly vomited?' he said. Then, 'Just take that, Theresa. I don't know what the poison is, but this is poison.'

'Food poisoning?' Theresa asked. She was still holding the pill between her thumb and forefinger with her pinky cocked. 'Do we take pills for food poisoning?'

'Just take it.' Jacob put a hand on Sam's back. 'Sam,' he said. 'Everyone will need a bowl or bucket and they should be in bed, keeping warm. Can you help me?' His guts gave a spasm, and he stopped talking and breathed through his nose. The packet of pills was removed from his hand. It was William. William pushed a pill out, and put it in his own mouth. He gave another to Sam. She began to make her

316

shaky way around the table, her hands resting on the back of every chair.

'Everyone needs to take one,' Jacob said. 'I think.' Then, 'God help me.'

'You'd rather wait?' Theresa said.

'I don't know. If it's strychnine then an emetic is the last thing we need.'

'Jesus!' Theresa said. 'Strychnine!' She wavered and drooped. Her face went grey.

Sam paused to put the tablet in her mouth. She said, very deliberately, 'I'd better go before I pass out.'

'Can everyone please get to their beds,' Jacob said.

Dan came and leaned in the doorway, clutching its frame. He had taken his shoes and trousers off—probably in the toilet off the atrium. He had streaks of shit on his legs and socks. 'Help me!' he said, looking at Jacob. Then he slipped down the door frame and onto the floor.

There was a little burst of cold beside Jacob, and a waft of some scent, as clean and astringent as isopropylene. It was a little familiar, but Jacob couldn't place it. The brain in his miserable, sluggish, chilled body tried to make sense of the scent as a new symptom, but he wasn't able to make olfactory hallucinations fit with any poison he knew.

He discovered that William was holding him. Sam had darted across the room to Dan. She looked Dan over—felt his pulse—put him on his back and checked his airway, then moved him into the recovery position. She turned to Jacob, her face pinkly healthy and stricken with puzzlement. She was looking to him for guidance. Then William let him go, and rushed outside to vomit. Jacob felt himself teeter, and lose his lower limbs, and then he didn't have a leg to stand on. Sam caught him. She was there, and capable. He said, 'Make sure everyone takes the ipecac. Make them vomit. They'll need Lucozade once they have.' He remembered that Kate wasn't at the funeral breakfast. 'Get Kate. She might not have eaten what we ate. She'll be able to help.'

'This box isn't full, Jacob,' Sam said. William had tossed her the box of ipecac before rushing out of the room. 'Has someone already had a pill?'

Jacob was sure that he'd just pulled a full, sealed box of the drug from his filing cabinet dispensary. He had a moment of absolute dread. Perhaps ipecac *was* the poison— and they were all only feeling the results of a big dose of a simple emetic. But twenty tablets of ipecac between twelve people would be a mild dose. Besides, he was sure the box was full before he handed some out. And Sam had taken one herself, so why was she asking who'd had them?

Jacob found that he couldn't count, couldn't think; he felt stupid and cold and hollow. He seized Sam's hand. 'Make them vomit,' he repeated, and passed out.

Kate woke up. Sam was leaning over her, shaking her gently. Kate roused herself and climbed out of bed. She contemplated her stockinged feet, and patted her hair into place.

Sam said, 'Everyone is sick.'

Kate couldn't seem to collect her wits. 'What was that, dear? Who has taken ill?'

'Everyone. How do you feel, Mrs McNeal?'

Of all the survivors, Kate thought that Sam was the one most likely to produce a dubious or garbled report of events. But Sam wasn't prone to over-dramatisation. '*You* look perfectly fine,' Kate said, sharply.

'I wasn't here. I came back, and everyone was sick. Jacob gave me some ipecac tablets and told me everyone had to have one. Except I won't give it to you; it's too rough for someone your age. How do you feel, Mrs McNeal? Do you feel like you want to be sick?'

'Not at all.'

'You have to help me then. I have to get everyone into

their beds. You can find bowls and buckets and towels and stuff.'

Kate held up a finger. 'One moment.' She located her slippers then went to find Holly. The door to Bub and Belle's room was open and Kate could hear their voices, urgent and distressed, interrupted now and then by stifled moaning. Kate stopped dead. She turned back to Sam and asked where Holly was.

'I haven't seen her. Shall I check her room?'

Sam ran along the hallway ahead of Kate and threw open the door of Holly's room. Theresa was sitting on the edge of Holly's bed, sweaty, pale, her mouth open and a string of drool hanging from it. She was shaking Holly. Holly's head flopped and rolled. Her mouth was blue. Sam hurried to the bed and pulled Theresa out of the way. She felt Holly's pulse—in her wrist first, but that limb was silent in a way that Sam knew very well, working in an old people's home. She touched Holly's jugular and waited a count of twenty, during which she felt only two sluggish heartbeats.

Kate had come into the room—she called her daughter's name, but didn't approach the bed.

'She has to tell me what she did,' Theresa said. She sounded drunk. Then she lifted her legs onto the bed and lay down beside Holly. Her pupils were huge and black. 'Oh shit!' she said, 'I feel like I did the time I passed out at my gym, when my blood pressure bottomed out. Where's Jacob?'

'He fainted.' Sam told Theresa she didn't know what to do. Then she asked whether she had thrown up.

'Not yet. Too tired.'

'Did Jacob give you ipecac?'

'Yes.' Theresa took Sam's hand. 'Do triage, Sam. That's what Jacob would say. Leave anyone who is too sick. But make sure Oscar's okay.'

Sam nodded and pulled away. She had to get moving. As she went past Kate the old woman said, 'Is my daughter dead?'

Sam said no. She didn't say 'not yet'. 'Mrs McNeal, could you go and get buckets and towels. I need your help.' She hurried out into the corridor, paused to listen, then rushed into Bub and Belle's room. She found them in the bathroom, sitting either side of the toilet bowl, wrapped in duvets. She asked whether they'd taken a tablet. She showed them the box.

'I have, but Belle hasn't,' Bub said. 'But we've both been vomiting. That's what Jacob wanted, isn't it?'

Sam helped Belle up and told Bub they'd be better off in bed. 'Holly's heart is going all funny,' Sam said, 'so I'm watching out for hearts.' Then she promised to be back soon and hurried off again.

She ran from room to room, checking. Warren was in bed. He looked very ill—was starkly pale, and the curly ginger hair on his chest was thick with blue. Sam tried to rouse him to ask him if he'd had a tablet, but he just moaned and pushed her away. She left him; she was doing triage.

She met William and Dan on the stairs. William was half carrying Dan. Both were salivating so copiously that their shirt fronts were soaked and opaque.

'I was going to get him into a shower, then bed,' William said. His tone was businesslike, but his expression was almost kind. Sam came and took Dan's other arm. She gazed at him and tears sprang into her eyes. 'You have to lie down, William,' she said. 'Take off your dirty clothes. I'll wash Dan. And do you mind if I put you two in bed together? It's easier for me to check on everyone if you're not all spread out.'

'Sure,' William said. They steered Dan into William's room. William staggered clumsily to the bed and climbed under the covers. He said his feet and hands were numb.

Sam manhandled Dan into the shower, lifted the shower head off its hook, and aimed it at the wall till the water ran warm. She rinsed Dan and his remaining clothes, then dropped the shower head and propped him in a corner, holding him upright against the slippery tiles by leaning on him. She pulled his sodden shirt off over his head. His arms were as heavy as two sides of lamb. She left him in his Y-fronts, hauled him out of the shower, and wrapped him in a big bath sheet. That was when he fainted again. Sam went down under his weight, half in and half out of the bathroom. Sam heard William moan and climb out of bed, then he was lifting Dan off her. She got to her feet and together they dragged Dan to the bed. William fell onto it with Dan. Sam got Dan's feet up onto the covers and helped William extract his arm out from under the truck driver's bulk. William was gasping. 'My—*chest*.'

Sam put her fingers flat on his neck and felt his pulse. It wasn't the pulse of the sick man who'd exerted himself. It was far too slow. 'It's like you took too many blood pressure pills,' Sam said. 'I've seen that happen at Mary Whitaker. But there I could just go to the nurses for help.'

Kate came in with a bucket. She looked older than she had only minutes before. Her complexion was papery, and her usual upright, definite stride had become a kind of aimless stumping. She placed the bucket on William's side of the bed and said to Sam, 'Could you please check on Holly again?' Then, coldly, 'If you can bear to tear yourself away from William.'

William fumbled for Sam's hand. His was slippery and icy. He said, 'If I die—'

Kate said, 'Heavens, here comes an apology.' Then, 'Mr Minute—people *are* dying. My daughter is, I think.'

'Look at me, Sam,' William said. He caught her gaze. 'Don't tell Kate about Holly.'

'I already know my daughter is as good as gone,' Kate said. 'I'm trying to get Sam to help her.'

William squeezed Sam's hand, he pulled her close and said, in a whisper, 'You know what I mean. For Kate to be of any use she can't know that Theresa suspects—'

'I don't know what you mean!' Sam wailed. 'I never do!'

'Oh God!' William cried, in despair. He practically threw Sam's hand from him. 'Why do you play this game? Why now?'

Sam clambered off the bed and ran out the door. Kate followed her, shrieking, demanding that Sam see to Holly at once, this minute.

Sam bounded downstairs and began to look for Oscar. She shouted his name till finally she heard a miserable croak from out on the terrace.

Oscar was lying on the wicker sofa—under its thin cotton-covered foam cushion. He had pulled the cushion over him for warmth. His face was mottled and tearstained. There was vomit on the tiles by the sofa. Sam felt Oscar's forehead, and his pulse, and asked a few simple questions. His answers were mumbled and disoriented. She thought for a moment, then flipped the mattress off him and onto the floor, and rolled him off the sofa and onto the mattress. Then she gripped the mattress by one end and dragged it indoors, heaving him over the doorsill. She dragged him into the atrium and found the mohair throw he liked draped over his legs when he was playing games. She covered him, neck to ankle—the throw was too short to cover his feet.

In the manager's office she found Jacob's store of Lucozade. She decanted some into a glass and went back to Oscar, sat him up, and got him to drink. Most of the Lucozade went into him. She laid him back down and explained that she had to go—she had to rouse Jacob and tell him the symptoms. Oscar murmured something. 'Wait, wait, wait,' he said. His eyes were rolling. 'Sam. The man in black,' he managed.

322

Sam didn't want to think about the man in black. She was afraid of him. The last time she'd come to she was in his arms, and they were both sitting on the floor of a room Sam had never seen before—a beautiful, rich, hushed room. Her head was lying against his shoulder and he was gazing at her face, and for a moment she saw him only as a shadow—a man, warm and strong, and she mistook him for William. She thought it was William's warm breath on her face. But then she saw the fire light shining on his smooth black cheek and she understood that it was him—the man Theresa and Bub and Dan and William (her William) had been hunting for days. The man tried to address her then, but she panicked, struggled out of his arms and crawled away. She tried a door—it opened—and he had followed her outside, trying to question her, or reason with her, and finally had caught her and quelled her, held her still. Then he tried to continue the talk he'd been having with the other Sam. He asked questions about whatever it was that had interrupted them, something that had made Sam's these-days-thoughtful sister just up and go in the middle of a situation that was dangerous or uncertain. He talked using braiding, beautiful words (he talked like William). Sam didn't understand him, but she understood his tone. He was getting things off his chest. He was sharing secrets. He was thankful, and his gratitude was like love. Sam was reluctant to open her mouth and spoil it for her sister. But in the end he stopped talking and turned her face into the light and looked at her properly, and his expression became horrified and heartbroken. And then he just let her go. She found her way out of the house and down the hill and ran till she was out of breath. Then it was as if her sister's phantom caught up with her and slammed into her and knocked her away into the other place, where she stayed—knowing nothing, doing nothing—till she came out and found herself in the spa conference room, with everyone around her distressed, and vomiting.

So, when Oscar said 'the man in black', Sam just patted him on the shoulder and went back to the manager's office. She collected a dozen bottles of Lucozade before hurrying back upstairs to report to Jacob.

Kate was standing in the corridor outside his room with her hands pressed over her face. Jacob was in the grip of a powerful simultaneous bout of vomiting and diarrhoea. The bout lasted for a further five minutes after Sam arrived. She sat by him, supporting him on the toilet and over the bucket Kate had dropped beside the bed. She kept saying, 'You'll be all right, Jacob.' And, 'I'll clean up once you're done.'

Though he was exhausted Jacob cooperated intelligently when she removed his clothes and gave him a quick wipe with the sheets, before rolling him onto his bare mattress. Only then did Sam spare a glance out the door. Kate had gone, and Sam hoped she hadn't gone to Holly.

Sam soaked a towel in warm soapy water and wiped Jacob off more thoroughly. She fetched a fresh sheet and made the bed up under him. He'd thrown off the duvet when the bout took him, so it was clean. Sam put it back over him, and got him to sit up and sip some Lucozade. She took his pulse.

Jacob said, 'How are you, darling?'

'I need Kate to help me. But Holly is dead, I think. Her heartbeat was so slow, she must be dead now.'

Jacob asked about his own pulse.

'It's not like Holly's, but it's not good.'

Jacob closed his eyes and leaned back on the pillow.

'When people are this sick their hearts go faster,' Sam said. 'I mean, when they're throwing up.'

'Yes, that's usually the case. But this is a poison that slows hearts. In hospital they'd use intravenous atropine to treat it,' Jacob said. Then, 'I have to think. You go check everyone's pulse again. Take my watch.' He took it off his wrist and gave it to Sam. 'It has a second hand. Write down the beats per minute. Can you do that? And Sam, tell me what else you notice. Look hard. Then come back as soon as you can.' She was at the door when Jacob called out. 'Wait! Can you find some way to contact the man in black? He's another pair of hands. We need him.'

Sam said, 'I'll try, Jacob. But I'm frightened of him.'

'Then get Kate to do it.'

Kate was with Bub and Belle. She had taken them Lucozade. Belle was sipping hers—Kate had found some straws. Bub was still, and limp, and pale. Sam took his pulse again. She had to wait a full minute because she couldn't manage to calculate beats per minute—could only keep her eyes on the watch face and count. Her own heart was banging. It was very hard to concentrate. When she'd done she scrambled around the room, found a pen and an old envelope, and wrote, 'Bub—45.'

She took Belle's wrist, said, 'Shhh,' and stared at the watch face, counting, her head nodding not quite in time—she was urging Belle's heart on.

'How is it?' Belle said.

Sam wrote: 'Belle—51.'

Belle turned to Bub. 'Is he sleeping?'

'Yes,' Sam lied. She looked at Kate and jerked her head towards the door. She wanted Kate to follow her into the hallway. There she asked Kate how they might call the man in black. 'Jacob says we need another pair of hands.'

'Jacob is right.' Kate frowned, then said, briskly, 'You go about your business and leave it to me. I'll think of something.'

It was some time before Sam was able to get back to Jacob. She had to help Theresa back into bed after finding her in the shower. Theresa was too weak to get out and dry herself. Sam wrapped her in a bathrobe and draped a coat over her. Theresa's pulse was, after her exertions, far too slow—the same as Belle's had been when she was resting.

Sam was with Dan and William again when she heard the howl of feedback from outside, then Kate's voice, vastly magnified: 'Please help us. We have food poisoning. Only two of us are caring for all the rest. Please come and render assistance.' Kate had worked out how to use the loud hailer in Theresa's patrol car.

As it got dark, it was Kate, coming slowly after Sam, who thought to turn on the lights. Not that Kate strictly followed Sam. Periodically she would take a detour to Holly's room—where Theresa was still suffering.

Theresa had removed herself from Holly's bed and had got as far from that bed as the room permitted. She was lying pressed against the wardrobe doors wrapped in a coat. Kate would see to Theresa, wiping her face with a towel, which she then stuffed into the rubbish sack she was dragging around with her. Then she'd go to the bed and look at the still form of her daughter.

Kate had been afraid to touch Holly when she was dying, afraid she'd hurt her daughter, or hasten the process, or see or feel something intolerable to her. She couldn't now understand how she'd been able to think any of that. What had she been thinking? That Sam could do better? Sam, who was only a caregiver, which was more or less what they called hospital porters, and who was on a par with all those peculiar modern notions about protecting people's pride, so that there were no more clerks, only administrative assistants, and no more secretaries, only personal assistants, and people were 'challenged' rather than 'handicapped'. So—Sam, a caregiver, and challenged—could deal with Holly in her extremity better than her own mother? Why, Kate thought, had she stepped back for Sam? Had her recent history taught her to be so helpless, or was it just that these last weeks she'd been exempt from all the horrible tasks? The rest of the survivors—except perhaps Oscar—understood in their nerves that they couldn't step back and wait for someone better qualified to help. They'd learned to cross lines and take responsibility.

Thinking on this, while stroking her daughter's cooling forehead, it struck Kate that she was exempt in another way. She'd felt under the weather—not ill, only drowsy—and on Holly's and Jacob's advice had gone to bed straight after Lily's funeral. Holly had brought her some cereal to go with her usual little handful of medications for her heart and blood pressure and thyroid—but that was all she'd eaten, two juice-softened Weetbix. Kate stroked Holly's hair, brooding about this, and when she was next downstairs, she visited the kitchen. It was clean. Oscar always cleaned up after every meal and, presumably, had after today's lunch. There was only the big stew pot soaking in the sink, a slick of fat on the surface of its water, and bits of transparent onion partially blocking the plughole. There was nothing unusual.

Later, when Kate caught up with Sam, and they had a quiet moment, Kate asked the young woman what everyone had had to eat after the funeral.

'I don't know,' Sam said.

'You ate, didn't you?'

Sam turned away. 'I don't remember.'

'And I suppose you don't recall who served either?'

Sam shook her head.

Jacob felt the cold, rough touch of a towel on his cheeks. He opened his eyes and discovered a piece of paper before his face. Light lanced around its edges. On the paper was a list of names, and series of numbers. Sam said, 'Their heartbeats are all too slow. I don't know what medicine to give them. Please wake up, Jacob, and tell me.'

Jacob tried to sit. He was helped. He told Kate to be careful of her back. Sam's clumsy handwriting swam in front of his eyes. Jacob saw that she had made a note of the time too. 'Good girl,' he said to her.

'There's a name for it, isn't there?' Sam said. 'For when your heart goes too slow.'

'Bradycardia.'

Sam looked relieved, as if learning the term might help fix the problem. Her curls were damp and matted. She smelled of vomit and Dettol. 'Your heart's slow too,' she said.

Jacob was having trouble thinking. Time seemed to stop with a little hitch then proceed again in a surge. 'We need atropine,' he said. There had been some in a weak solution—one of the Mary Whitaker residents had it to control excess salivation. But that wouldn't do; it was too dilute. 'Wait,' he said. 'I'm not a pharmacist, but I know this.'

He had spent several evenings going over the collected medications—sorting those he was familiar with from the others—alternative and weaker versions of the drugs used in intensive care and emergency medicine. The sorting had been difficult. He had kept looking at bottles and packets and flipping through the pharmacist's many manuals, trying to digest paragraphs of exhaustively informative small print. 'I know I came across something that worked like atropine.'

Kate raised the pen and paper she had ready. She looked like someone preparing to catch a fly ball.

Then Jacob had it. He took the pen from Kate and wrote *Orciprenaline*. 'They're tablets,' he said. 'They're in the third file box in the cabinet.' He dropped his head back on his pillow and closed his eyes.

Warren's feet and hands were cold and pale. Kate tried to warm them with hot towels. She worked at it assiduously for nearly an hour, but her efforts made no difference.

Eventually she left off and simply slipped several pairs of socks onto his hands and feet, then left him. She went outside to try Theresa's loud hailer once more. Later, near 10pm, she checked on William and found that his bucket contained only a little bit of grainy bile. The Lucozade bottle by the bed was empty. Kate shook him. When he opened his eyes she asked, 'Did you regurgitate the Orciprenaline?'

'Yes. But I swallowed it again, and it stayed down.'

Kate went and rinsed out the bucket. She looked at herself in the bathroom mirror. The lower half of her face looked strangely slack and sunken, like the face of a friend of hers who'd had Bell's Palsy. 'My girl, Holly,' Kate whispered to her reflection, trying to make Holly's passing more than a mere fact. Holly was down the hallway, dead, but all the other Hollys—the Holly who came back from a holiday in Vietnam and brought Kate embroidered silk pyjamas; the Holly who'd kept company with that nice but ultimately insufficient soil scientist Gavin; the Holly who had been to secretarial school, back when there were such things; Holly the schoolgirl, who'd played netball, goal-defence—all those girls, those daughters, though they weren't anywhere to be found, weren't dead. How was it that a plain fact could fail to be true?

Kate left the bathroom and took a seat on William's bed. She said, 'Sam isn't at all sick. Why do you suppose that is?'

'She was at first,' William said. 'She was pale, and had stomach cramps.'

'But she's not ill now. Might her earlier signs of sickness have been an emotional reaction? Or perhaps it was feigned?'

'You're not sick either, Kate.'

'I didn't have any of the funeral breakfast. Did Sam?'

'Yes. But this isn't food poisoning.'

'That's what I'm saying. The food wasn't contaminated, it was *poisoned*. I didn't have lunch. And Sam did, but isn't ill. Did she serve the food? Did she eat what you ate?'

'She helped Holly serve. She sometimes does, just as she often helps Oscar with the dishes.'

Kate said, 'There's a disease where a person will make other people sick in order to nurse them—to be a hero, and elicit sympathy. What's its name?'

'I think you mean Munchausen's Syndrome by proxy.'

'I knew you'd know.'

William shook his head. His hair was plastered to his neck and his dark skin was pallid yellow.

'My daughter is dead,' Kate said.

William reached for her hand. Kate snatched it away. She didn't want William's commiserations. She had imagined she could rely on him to follow her thoughts about who was culpable—Sam, on whom he had already closed his door. Sam, who was making a martyr of herself, and who refused to say who had served the food. Lying Sam, who had been mad, and who had mutilated half the residents of Mary Whitaker rest home. 'She's being shifty,' Kate said.

William shook his head again. And Kate cried, 'Why won't you listen to me?'

He tried to sit up. He was so weak that she was able to push him back against the pillow. She put a finger to her lips. She hushed him.

They both listened. Someone was coming up the stairs several at a time. Then they heard Sam calling in a fierce whisper, 'Kate!' She shot past the door then doubled back and looked in at them. She said, 'It's him. He's come.'

'Who?' said William.

Kate got up and edged past Sam.

'Yes, you go talk to him, Kate,' Sam said. 'I don't know what—what my relationship is with him.'

Kate regarded Sam a moment—her thin nostrils flared, her mouth clamped, then she walked out.

William called Sam to him, he drew her down so that their faces were level and close. 'Is this food poisoning, or

330

poisoned food?'

'You mean bugs or bad chemicals?'

'Accidental or deliberate, is what I mean.'

'Jacob said I wasn't to tell Kate. He said I needed her to help me.'

'Tell Kate what?'

'About Holly. Jacob said he thought it was Holly. She made lunch. Oscar said the bread tasted funny.'

'Kate thinks it was you.'

Sam's face crumpled; she began to cry. William tried to soothe her, stroking her arm and speaking to her gently. Finally she managed to choke something out. 'I don't know that it wasn't,' she said. 'I don't know what she's been doing. She hasn't left me any notes.'

'The other Sam?'

Sam looked at him, her eyes wet and desperate. Then she nodded.

'The other Sam was sick,' he said, reassuring her. But then he thought, 'How does that work? Simple Sam might be able to refuse knowledge, but how can she refuse the effects of poison?'

When the man in black finally arrived, Kate discovered that she wasn't afraid of him. She knew there was possibly information the rest of them had about him that she wasn't party to, because she'd missed the meeting, but she didn't mind. He couldn't hurt her. She was beyond harm. What did she have left that could make her vigilant about own safety? She had only to keep these strangers in decent order till they were well. She would do that. She wouldn't let any of them, or herself, down. And she had to defend Holly, who was dead.

'Sam poisoned us,' Kate said. 'She's making a meal of running around after us all now.'

He looked puzzled, and Kate realised that 'making a meal' was a rather problematic use of idiom when one was talking about poison.

'But she didn't poison you?' His voice was like his face, so dark it was indistinct.

Kate tried again. 'I didn't eat what she served.'

His expression was gently sceptical. He didn't believe her, but he thought her feelings were more important than the truth of what she was telling him.

'Just so you're warned,' she said. Then, 'Jacob asked me to call you. We need another pair of hands.'

'Tell me what you want me to do.'

Oscar saw that it was the man in black who had come to help him. He was embarrassed. But this was his opportunity to ask for assistance getting to the toilet. He tried to work up his courage, but all that came out was the first part of his pep talk to himself. 'In a crisis there's no time for embarrassment.'

The man in black said that it was his observation that there was always time for embarrassment.

'Even for professionals?' Oscar said.

The man in black put his hands on his hips and just stood like that, staring at Oscar. Oscar felt his priggish little thought being pursued and wondered whether the man was a mind reader.

'Do you need—how do you put it?'

'The bathroom, yes. It's way over there, and I'm wobbly.'

The man picked Oscar up using the firemen's hold. He carried Oscar into the bathroom, put him down by the door to one of the stalls, and waited till he was done. Then he carried him back to the mattress.

Oscar was having a strange time with his body. It was like he kept hitting a switchback—one of the 'sudden dips' of cautionary road signs.

The man knelt and repositioned the throw rug. Then he raised Oscar's head so he could drink. The Lucozade was flat and ferrous. Oscar pushed the glass away. 'What's your name?'

'Myr.'

'Is there a monster, Myr? Sam says there is.'

'Sam's talking about the monster?'

'She thinks it's not finished.'

'She said that?'

'I wasn't at the meeting. But I heard some stuff because they were all shouting. And, before you abducted her, Sam told me the monster was like a tower, where each stone was a death. A tower going up and up forever. I think she meant it's not finished.'

'I see,' said Myr.

'I've been worrying about it,' Oscar said.

Myr twitched at the blanket on Oscar's chest, though it didn't need any adjustment.

Oscar said, 'I've wondered whether this monster situation is something like when those guys playing *Dwarf Fortress* made a hole in the ocean floor so that the sea started draining into the fortress, and the game's physics engine couldn't procedurally generate enough space for the water at the rate it was draining, so it fatally froze the computer, which had to be returned to its factory settings.'

Myr sat down beside the mattress and took one of Oscar's hands. Then, much to Oscar's puzzlement, he didn't make a comment or ask a question. Oscar was forced to gather his strength and make another attempt to explain his fears. 'If the monster is making itself out of the people it kills, or at least out of their deaths, then it probably won't pass us over. I don't want to die, but actually, that isn't what's bugging me. I don't seem to be able to believe that.'

'You don't believe you'll die?'

'No.'

'Then what is worrying you?'

'Where the monster is going with all this? What say it's like what happened with *Dwarf Fortress*?'

'You mean—will it shut down the computer? The computer being the universe?'

Oscar nodded. 'If it goes on eating faster than the universe provides it with people to eat.'

'We have considered that. We've thought that these things might be a provision for the end of the universe. Or at least the universe of higher consciousness.'

Oscar relaxed. He was pleased that what was keeping him from getting some rest was something other people were thinking about and troubled by—even if those people were aliens. If someone else was thinking about it, then he didn't have to. He said, 'Do you think you could get me upstairs to my room?'

'Yes.' Myr took a careful grip of one of Oscar's arms, sat him up, tipped him forward, and settled the boy across his shoulders again. He straightened and, with great care, carried Oscar through the atrium to the staircase.

They met Sam on the stairs. She was going up with bottles of Powerade and L&P. 'We're out of Lucozade,' she said.

Myr said, 'Oscar will be more comfortable in his bed.'

'How's his pulse?'

'I haven't been briefed on that. But his hands aren't cold.'

'Tell her,' the upside-down Oscar said, from the thicket of his hair.

'Later,' said the man, and continued on up.

Oscar's bed was clean and cool. His door had been shut so his room was uncontaminated by the smells that were present everywhere else—of disinfectant and regurgitated soft drink. 'I'm going to have a sleep,' Oscar said. 'Could you tell Sam that my cat won't have had anything to eat. And the other cats will be hungry too.'

'Cats can wait.'

Oscar was drowsy. He closed his eyes. 'I still think you should tell Sam that end of the universe thing. Sam knows stuff.' There was no answer and Oscar felt his thoughts float off like spectres—the spectral Oscar who was worried, the spectral Oscar who was reassured that someone had listened to him, and the other one, no more solid, who had everything worked out.

His door was open and in a little while there was a new smell, one that made him smile in his sleep. Kate had washed a big load of towels and bedding and put them in the dryer, so that the spa was filled with the scent of detergent and steam. It smelled good. Homely.

Sam got Myr to carry Jacob in to see Warren. Myr deposited Jacob in an armchair then wheeled the armchair up to the bed. Sam lifted the covers. Warren's hands and feet were white, his nail beds were blackish. Jacob took one look and identified peripheral circulatory failure. He told Sam to put the blanket back. He lifted Warren's eyelids. Warren's eyes were rolled up in his head, but the eye muscles weren't trembling. He was deeply unconscious. Jacob closed Warren's eyes again and gripped his shoulder and whispered, 'Stay with me, *sole*.' He looked at Sam. 'There are two things we can try.'

Warren was Curtis all over again, except this time Jacob was fighting gangrene, not septicaemia. And this time he dared to try something that would hasten death if it failed. Forget 'first do no harm' and death with dignity. Jacob would gamble his friend's dignity and comfort for the smallest chance of life.

Jacob stayed with Warren to oversee treatment, but he couldn't remain upright. Sam expertly remade the bed

335

under Warren, and Jacob climbed under the covers too. He held his friend's cold hand—the one beside him, the one not tied up with the cannula and line. He massaged it gently.

The cannula and line were from the insulin infusion pump kits. They were hooked up not to real intravenous fluids, but to a bottle of sterile saline—for contact lenses—into which Jacob had injected a measure of some atropine eye drops. Jacob wasn't sure it was absolutely sterile, and he didn't know what effect, if any, the solution's preservatives would have on his friend. But, if Warren revived enough to swallow, Jacob could give him some phenoxybenzamine pills, which would dilate his blood vessels, and some antibiotics, to fight any introduced infection.

Jacob's thinking was fuzzy. He wished he was watching a drip, not this jerry-built thing. And he wished he could think of something further to try. He attempted once more to summon his knowledge, but everything he'd learned since being trapped in Kahukura seemed vague and distant. Everything, but what he'd learned to *feel*—a crushing sense of anxiety and culpability. And what he'd learned to expect—the worst.

At around seven in the morning Jacob got up to check on the other survivors. Warren wasn't any worse and Jacob had begun to hope he'd pull through.

Jacob gave a further dose of orciprenaline to William, who was taking longer than the others to recover.

Once Myr and Sam had settled Jacob in his own bed, he caught Sam's eye and said, 'You look exhausted.'

'Once you're better I'll go,' she said.

'You could catch a little sleep now. Kate's resting, isn't she?'

'She's sitting with Holly.'

'Holly was responsible for the poisoning,' Jacob said, to

Myr. 'I think she ground up oleander seeds and put them in our bread. If she'd been at the meeting where Sam passed on your bad news I'd be able to believe that she thought she was saving us by sparing us suffering. But she wasn't at the meeting. She didn't have any idea what we were facing. So—I think it was the monster. The monster made her crazy, right?'

Myr said, 'Perhaps she had some trouble the monster just pushed farther along.'

'What monster?' said Sam.

Sam made herself some instant soup and sat on a stool at the central bench in the kitchen. She ate, blowing on each spoonful. She was very tired, and for once her reflection in the kitchen window didn't look like her sister.

Sam knew that it all made perfect sense that she was the one who had been rushing from room to room, emptying buckets and wiping arses. Her job had fitted her for that kind of work. But she felt resentful. The other Sam had proved very good at avoiding trouble and effort. A few years ago the other had stopped trying to carry them off out of Kahukura, and then pretty much gave up putting in an appearance at all. She didn't have a job of her own and wouldn't share Sam's job at Mary Whitaker. (There had been a period in their mid-teens where she and the other had worked very profitably at two jobs, a daytime one stacking shelves in the supermarket, and a night-time cleaning job. Though being out wasn't as refreshing as sleep.)

For years now it was Sam who'd had the job—the life— and the other Sam would only come sometimes to read her difficult books and listen to her hardcore miserable music, at night, at home. The other would keep the house tidy if she found it that way, and would tidy up if it wasn't. Sometimes she'd bake—a lemon loaf or banana bread—and would leave it for Sam, warm and steaming, with only one slice gone. She wouldn't leave notes, because she didn't go out and nothing happened to her. She checked the mail and might answer Sam's questions about some notice from their bank, or the tax department, or district council. She'd get the modem going again (when it broke Sam was always at a loss as to how to fix it and she hated to ring the helpdesk, and really, it was mostly the other Sam's computer). The other periodically appeared, but these days she had nothing to say for herself, nothing to share. Sam had written to ask why she didn't want to come out any more, and the other Sam had only answered, 'You know why.' And she'd left the bathroom mirror sectioned by black tape so that when Sam looked into it she saw herself behind bars. Herself, and her sister.

William sat up and took a swig from the bottle of lemonade by his bed. It was flat but helped settle his stomach. He tried to get up—but once he had both feet on the floor he thought better of it and lay down once more. He opened a drawer in the bedside cabinet, found his phone, went straight to settings and sounds, turned up the volume, and pressed one field repeatedly. The airy wail of the theremin eventually brought Myr to his door. William flopped back onto the bed, laughing.

'What is it?' Myr said.

'My sci-fi ringtone,' said William.

Myr lifted William's legs back onto the bed and pulled off William's socks to inspect his feet. He pressed William's toenails. 'The blood is flashing straight back into them,' he said. 'You're going to recover.'

'Okay,' said William, warily. 'Who hasn't recovered?'

'Holly and Warren.'

'They're dead?'

'Holly is dead. Warren might make it.'

'And when did you arrive?'

'I came before sunrise.'

William looked at the window, which was black. He laughed again and then said, 'Why am I laughing?'

'Are you amused?'

William shook his head. He tried to examine his feelings. It took a while but he finally figured it out. He wasn't losing his mind—like Holly—he was just upset.

Before, what upset him was what was immediately in front of him: the cruel spectacle of the daycare centre; the treacherous changes in Sam's behaviour; the whole idea of this man, a powerful and paternalistic warden. He'd be upset, and fine again the very next moment. He should have felt *more*. He should have felt what he knew everyone else had been feeling the whole time—guilt and gratitude. He'd survived. Holly was dead. Lily and Curtis were dead. Before now, none of the dead people had been his. Even his Kiwi colleagues weren't *his*. When Sam and Kate had wanted to bury the residents of Mary Whitaker, and Warren to bury his aunt, Oscar his classmate, and Bub his friend from the café—William had coldly decided that it would look odd if he failed to insist that they gather up the charred remains at the helicopter crash site and give them some kind of the ceremonial interment. It was the done thing, so he did it. The whole town was full of corpses; disposing of them had been, for him, a matter of hygiene, and a public relations exercise. They were doing it—the Kiwis—so he did it too.

So, here he was, still a gravedigger and not a corpse. He had survived. Again.

William had a job where he got to talk to people about their problems—specific problems, their talk on-topic—and he'd almost always be able to say how he could help them. It was satisfying work. And sociable, too; he often worked as part of a team, and dipped his oar in time with others.

He was professionally competent and comfortable. He was witty and people would laugh. He was charming and they'd smile. But right now it seemed to him that he'd spent his life with his back to the sun and his face to a wall, writing on its white surface, working in his own shadow.

People had called William hardhearted, but they never asked him to account for it. He was always interested in other people's attempts to explain themselves. He'd listen with appreciation, if not empathy. But when it came to his own story he couldn't shape an explanation that didn't sound, to him, like an excuse. Even this: that he was the product of a final conscientious and caring foster home, but that, though the good things in his youth came in time to save his self-respect, they were too late for his heart.

So, he'd survived again, if only to dig graves and listen to eulogies. Meanwhile Bub and Belle would love one another; Kate and Jacob would mourn and still manage to tend to people; Sam would work her fingers to the bone, as dumbly faithful as a dog; Theresa would heroically soldier on; Dan would simply go on hoping; and Oscar would continue to chirp away like a lively bird, as entitled in his sweetness as the Gospels' lilies of the field. They'd all keep doing some kind of good, and he'd be left as lost as that formless soul, Warren. Only he wasn't formless, but badly-formed, armoured in ice, and no use to himself.

Myr was still there, watching him. 'Are you in pain?'

'What point would there be in that?'

'Pain is a stimulus that encourages us to avoid it. That's its main point, I believe,' Myr said.

'Fuck you,' William said. 'It's fine for you—you have a job to do.'

'Yes,' Myr said, quietly, 'I have a job to do.'

'Are you saying that it's *not* fine for you?'

'I volunteered,' Myr said. 'I'm supposed to be here.'

'I'm not.'

'None of you are,' Myr said, respectful, and sympathetic—
and then he frowned, as though something had just occurred
to him. 'Sam is a resident of this settlement, isn't she?'

'Yes.'

'Yes,' Myr echoed, contemplative.

'So is Oscar,' William added. He waited for Myr to
tell him why this might be significant, but Myr didn't say
anything further.

When Bub and Belle came downstairs, both were wan,
and Bub was faintly yellow. They found Jacob and Sam—
Jacob with his ear to the open top of one of the treatment
room's ceramic tea-light holders. He had the wide end of
the candleholder pressed to Sam's back. A number of funnels
and jelly moulds were scattered on the bench. Jacob told
Bub and Belle that he was trying to contrive a stethoscope.
He said to Sam, of the tea-light holder, 'I think this will
have to do.'

'Belle and I are going to inspect the kitchen from stem to
stern and make sure anything left over is thrown out,' Bub
said.

'That's a good idea, but I'd feel happier if I could have a
listen to your hearts before you exert yourselves.'

Sam got herself a drink of water. Belle saw that her hands
were shaking. 'You need to rest, honey,' Belle said.

'I'll go when Jacob is free,' Sam said.

'If everyone is in clean bedding there's nothing more you
need do for now. You've been a trooper,' Jacob said.

Sam stared mournfully at the three of them.

'Has anyone remembered to feed the dogs?' Bub asked.

'It was the last thing Myr did before he took off,' Jacob
told Bub.

'I couldn't answer his questions. He needs answers,' Sam
said. Then, 'You'll have to take care of Sam.'

Belle's scalp prickled. She touched Bub's arm. He had stilled and stiffened.

'Can you?' Sam said to Jacob, and, 'Is it really all right for me to go now?'

'Yes. Get some sleep,' Jacob said.

'I should sit down,' Sam said to herself. She went out through the swing doors into the dining room. Belle leaned on the doors and looked out after her.

Sam shuffled to the couch by the coffee machine. She sat down and looked up at Belle. Even from across the room Belle could see that Sam was smiling and that the smile was one of trust, and relief. Sam lowered her head so that her face was hidden by her hair. Then some change came over her. She was still in the same position, head hung, but her long hair seemed to fatten with static, and she began to shake. Her hands flew up to snatch her hair back from her face, and she stooped and vomited between her feet.

Jacob heard the sound and rushed out past Belle.

Belle told Bub to get some damp cloths. 'Or whatever.' She felt a little stupid. Sam and Kate had had a system. They'd been proficient: wiping faces and arses, bundling up bedding, sponging carpets, emptying basins.

Belle went to sit by Sam and took over holding her hair till the retching had tapered off. Bub appeared with a glass of water, and soaked, steaming dish towels.

Sam was trembling so violently she wasn't able to take the glass. Jacob held it to her lips and she sipped, and looked around at them, her eyes assessing. 'You're all okay,' she said—it was a statement, not a question.

Bub passed a hot wet cloth across her face.

She looked down at the floor and said, 'I've regurgitated the ipecac, Jacob. Does that matter?'

In the glistening mass on the floor lay the tablet, whole, its surface only a little furred by its time in stomach acid.

'Jesus, Sam!' Jacob said. 'Where did you get that? No

wonder you're vomiting. How many have you taken?'

'Vomiting is good though?' Sam said, and then writhed and clutched her stomach. Tears of pain sprang into her eyes. 'This is rough,' she gasped. She clutched Jacob's arm. 'Did you figure it out? Do you know what to do?'

'Let's get you lying down,' Belle said.

They helped her upstairs and put her to bed. On the way up she managed to ask whether Oscar was all right, then once she was lying down she asked after William.

'I still have to check everyone's hearts,' Jacob said. He produced the tea-light holder.

Sam looked at it in great puzzlement, which cleared when Jacob rolled her splattered shirt up over her head. He placed the wide end of the tea-light between her breasts and listened. He was still, listening. But, after a moment, his stillness altered in quality. His gaze drifted up to meet Belle's. He straightened. 'Sam, what have you had to eat?'

'That's why we should check the kitchen,' Bub said. 'There's no telling where else Holly planted her poison.'

Sam gritted her teeth and moaned. When the spasm passed she scanned their faces. She wasn't looking for help. She seemed reassured. 'You all came through.'

Belle said, 'Give me that top and I'll find you a fresh one.'

Sam sat up and pulled off her shirt and camisole. She said, 'So it's treatable?'

'What did you eat?' Jacob asked, more urgent. 'Was there any orciprenaline left over? Where is it? I hope there's some left, Sam, because you'll need it.'

Sam had flopped down and was trying to cover herself. Her movements were weak and uncoordinated and she was very pale. 'The bread tasted funny. I dissolved mine in the casserole.'

'There was some of Holly's bread left over? Why on earth did you eat it?'

Sam made a strangled noise; she was in pain, but laughing.

'The poison was in the bread!' Jacob shouted. 'I'd have thought even you would have sense enough not to eat anything unless it was out of a packet or tin!'

'Let me be,' Sam said. She pushed weakly at Jacob.

He gripped her and shouted again. 'Your heartbeat is too slow! Where did you put the orciprenaline—the second lot of pills I asked you to pass around? Where are they?'

Sam was still. 'Oh,' she said. 'I don't know. Why don't you look?'

'Try to remember.'

'This is the other Sam,' Bub said. 'She doesn't remember. Maybe the vomiting was psychosomatic. You know—they both have to have a turn at being poisoned?'

Belle poked Bub and shook her head. He should remember that Sam hadn't been ill. She had carried on and cared for them all.

'Get away from me,' Sam said. 'Go find the pills.'

Jacob told her that she had to snap out of it now. Her life depended on her putting herself back together this minute. 'Just step up,' he said. 'Right now you've got more to be scared of than whatever happened to you in the past to make you this way.'

'Shut the fuck up!' Sam yelled. 'Just fix me.'

Belle reflected that being furious was probably stimulating Sam's heart as effectively as Jacob's heart drug—albeit temporarily.

Sam reared up, leaned across Belle and vomited on the carpet—this time only thin bile. Belle put her arms around her. 'She is mentally ill,' Belle said. 'Shouting at her about what she can and can't remember is about as effective as telling an anorexic to eat. She is not going to suddenly stop being crazy, even to save her own life.'

★

Sam was weak and chilled. She wanted to be left in peace to sink back into the bed. She wanted to fall through the mattress, bed base, floor, through the whole building, and on through the earth itself. She wanted to lay down her flesh and bones and melt away; to be still, where she was; to stop, where she was. But she heard what Belle said, and knew that Belle was absolutely right.

Sam may have played games with people, hinting at her true predicament, but she wouldn't *tell*. She would rather die than tell. She was sick and cold and sluggish, she had sunk as low physically as she'd ever been; her heart was beating slower and slower; her cells were starved of oxygen; her consciousness had been hunted into a corner, and it seemed the last thing keeping her company was that old, powerful compulsion to keep their secret—her and Fa's.

For the first time in her life Sam turned to regard that compulsion. 'This isn't rational,' she thought. 'Why would I rather die than tell?' And then she thought, 'Why did Sam keep bringing us back to Kahukura, no matter what I did to punish her?'

Belle was still holding her, and Sam took hold too, as a way of remaining conscious. She gripped Belle's arms and dug her fingers in. Belle gasped as Sam's fingernails pierced her skin. Sam held on and pursued her thought, plunging like a freediver following the rope that measures her depth.

There are understandings that are summations of many experiences—the grass, rags, threads, and moss that magically shape themselves into a nest, into something for the future. Sam suddenly understood the only thing she had ever needed to understand.

The other Sam had kept them in Kahukura. She and the other Sam had concealed their nature, kept it a strict secret though it had been a tormenting nonsense to both of them. They had rules they'd rather die than break—because the rules had been *given to them* with what was done to them.

The rules, simply stated, were: 'Stay in Kahukura' and 'Stay hidden'. (Wait here. *Lie* in wait here. Lie in wait for what will come. For what will, one day, *come back*.)

Sam clutched Belle and swam up again so she could see them—Belle, Bub, Jacob—with the darkness bleeding in around their worried faces. 'Jacob,' she whispered. 'Either she'll know where the pills are, or you'll have time to search the pharmacy again.'

And she went away.

Belle snatched her arm out of Sam's grasp as soon as Sam relaxed. Frigid, astringent air blew up into Belle's face, and she closed her eyes for a moment, so was first alerted to the change by the silent flurry as Jacob and Bub leapt back from the young woman on the bed.

Belle opened her eyes.

The young woman on the bed looked surprised, then tearful, and very, very tired.

The young woman on the bed had a clenched, raw-looking scar where her left nipple should be.

PART SEVEN

A late equinoctial gale had swept into Tasman Bay and was blustering about, surging in short gusts from every point of the compass, like an attack dog looking for an opening. Those survivors who were fit for strenuous work were out in the weather, either rigging lights or painting the supermarket carpark. They had scavenged three long-handled paint rollers and a collection of paints—only pale colours. They were making a bull's-eye, its rings brightening towards a reflective centre.

First Oscar drew three concentric circles. Theresa stood still, holding one end of a piece of string, while Oscar circled her with a pencil tied to the string's other end. Then they began to paint. First they made a bright bull's-eye using spray cans of silver rust-preventer from the petrol station's shop. Then they picked up their paint rollers and filled in the next ring, using the contents of scavenged tins of ceiling-white. They rinsed their rollers and started the outer ring. They painted it with all the other whites they'd gathered; the yellow, pink, green, and blue-shaded whites. They didn't combine the colours, and the outer ring ended up a pleasing patchwork of pastels.

While the painting was in progress, Jacob and Bub were rigging lights and putting up reflectors—sheets of cardboard wrapped in aluminium foil. Only the supermarket and spa had power boards robust enough to handle the required wattage, and the repeated switching on and off of many lights.

The day turned dark early. The wind settled in one quarter, a rare easterly, and pushed a cloud bank across the hills. Most of the rain was already spent inland, but the cloud flowed out across Kahukura and filled Tasman Bay, dense and damp and accompanied by a surprisingly strong wind. The riggers and painters packed up and went back to the spa.

William and Warren had been allowed downstairs. Jacob was being careful about their convalescence. Warren was improving, but William was still pale and tired. He was permitted to go a little further every day and, that morning, had been as far as the gate and back.

He was now in the atrium, in his pyjamas, up only so long as he showed no sign of fatigue. He was helping Theresa compose a first, exploratory message in their improvised code, while Bub made a rocker switch for the lights.

Sam sat beside William, her mouth and nose pressed against his shoulder. This was the first Sam—Samantha. When she'd appeared, Bub, Belle, and Jacob had finally understood that the reason Myr had been so puzzled by their insisting that he'd cured Sam was because he'd done no such thing. There were in fact *two* young women, one who worked as a caregiver in Mary Whitaker, and was a bit slow, having never recovered from a brain injury caused by traumatic blood loss, and who had been in Kahukura when the Wake first arrived, and who had gone mad and attacked her charges and herself with kitchen scissors, harvesting nipples and frying them up till something—perhaps pain—made her go, and leave everything in the hands of the *other* Sam, her whole and competent twin sister Samara.

Bub caught on very quickly, because he'd seen the birth certificates. He was able to explain to Belle and Jacob—though he did it in a torrent of ungrammatical babble—that Samara and Samantha could of course have been born in 1967 and not be in their mid-forties, because they were sharing a life, and whenever one of them went *away* she wasn't present in the world where time was passing, so that Samantha was in her mid-twenties and Samara a little younger because Samara had spent more time *there* than here.

350

Bub paced back and forth thinking it all through aloud, while Jacob kept saying, 'Where, Bub? Where is *there*?' And Belle kept trying to question Sam herself, who stayed motionless as they flung themselves about the room raving at one another, her knees drawn up to cover her lopsided chest. She trembled and sobbed soundlessly, tears shining on her face. Belle fired questions at her and she flinched, but didn't answer, only asked one herself: 'Why didn't she stay?'

Jacob finally calmed down enough to tell her what had happened and to ask was there any heart medicine left? 'The—other Sam—needs it,' he said, and nearly lost his mind in the middle of his sentence.

Sam's face crumpled. 'When you said "give them another pill" I kept giving out pills until they were all gone.'

The three of them stood still and considered this. Then Bub said, 'Am I right about you?'

Sam tucked her chin behind her knees and squeezed her eyes shut.

Bub changed tack. 'Will—the other Sam—be okay while she's—not here?'

Sam nodded.

Jacob sat down on the end of her bed. He made an effort to collect himself. 'I think I can manage a single patient with bradycardia if I can find some more atropine eye drops. I used what I found in the pharmacy on Warren, but there might be some at Mary Whitaker. Atropine is used to dry up excess saliva.' He touched Sam's hand. 'Did any of your old people have a problem with saliva?'

'Annie had motor neurone disease,' Sam said. 'She had drops and a patch.'

Jacob considered. 'And I believe there are asthma inhalers with orciprenaline.'

'Sam didn't leave me a note,' Sam said. 'She was going to stay here for a long time, I think. She'd talked to the man in black.'

'We know that,' Bub said. 'How come there are two of you? Like—*how*?'

Sam shook her head.

'Does the other Sam know?'

'We don't know what they did or why they did it.'

'Who?'

'Uncle and the visitor.'

Belle, Bub, and Jacob exchanged looks.

'Visitor?' Bub said.

'The woman. She was very black, like the man.'

'Myr?'

Sam nodded.

'So your uncle and this woman who looked like Myr did something to you?'

'Before the visitor came we were sleeping in the same bedroom. Wa was in her cot and I was in mine. When I woke up Wa was gone. My cot was gone too and I was in hers. I never saw Wa after that. We only wrote each other notes.'

'Sam is Wa? The other Sam?' Belle said.

'I was little. I couldn't say "Samara", and she couldn't say "Samantha". I called her "Wa" and she called me "Fa". Once Wa was gone Uncle said it was better if we were both just "Sam".'

'Jesus Christ,' said Bub.

Jacob plundered the pharmacy again for alupent, the asthma drug. And, once Sam had rested, they went together to Mary Whitaker, unsealed the doors, and walked along a corridor carpeted with dead flies to Annie's room. The atropine solution was in the bedside cabinet.

Jacob made ready for the other Sam, but William talked Jacob out of asking his own Sam to let the other return.

★

William was the first person to whom Jacob explained what he and Bub and Belle now knew—William first, because he was involved with Sam, and because Jacob wasn't feeling strong enough to face a bombardment of questions he couldn't answer. He told William what had happened then said, 'Sam has explained as much as she is able to, I think. And I've told you everything we know. I'm making ready for the other Sam. I want to be sure she'll be okay.'

'Because if you lose one of them, you lose both.' William looked thoughtful. 'Do you think Myr knows that there really are two of her?'

'I don't think so. He was confused when we mentioned his having healed her. And William—there aren't two of her, there are two of *them*. Twins, separate people, Samantha and Samara.'

William was pale—too pale—and Jacob had a dark suspicion that, if they ever did get out of Kahukura, William might need a heart valve replacement, or a pacemaker. Jacob put his tea-light holder to William's chest and listened to his heart.

William said, 'Perhaps it would be better to demonstrate Sam to Myr. We want him to think through any significance, and the other Sam isn't going to reveal herself willingly.'

'Shhh,' said Jacob.

William kept quiet while Jacob listened. When Jacob straightened, turned away and began fussing with his first-aid bag, William went on. 'She knows more than we do,' he said. 'Can I get up and see her?'

Jacob shook his head. He wasn't going to let William get excited or argumentative till he had him well-established on some drug for arrhythmia. Treating William required research. He didn't say this to William. Bad news was of no benefit to him—and Jacob hated to be the one to tell this fit, cared for, spectacularly handsome man that he had a damaged heart. He only said, 'You're on bed rest till I tell you otherwise.'

William's scrutiny was exacting. Jacob began gathering up his pills and his contrived stethoscope. Then he thought of a distraction. 'If this Sam stays here for the next little while, that gives you a chance to—'

'Make things square with her.'

'She *was* deceiving you, only not in the way you thought.'

'Please send her in to me, Jacob,' William said.

'Okay. But take it easy.'

'On Sam?'

'No,' Jacob blushed. 'I'm sorry. I have to make this clear. I don't want you exerting yourself.'

'Sure, whatever you say.'

Jacob went to call Sam to her long-awaited reconciliation.

Sam sat beside William, her nose pressed to his shoulder, and her eyes closed. She was in a trance of animal happiness. She didn't mind that he wasn't paying attention to her right that minute. He was busy helping Theresa with their made-up code. He had a job—the jobs were all cause for happiness. Nor did she mind that, when they were alone, he seemed content to just let her lie beside him. She did want him to touch her everywhere again, and to watch her face the way he did as she changed colour and forgot to cover her scar with her cupped hand. But she had faith that would all happen. Jacob had told her that William wasn't fully recovered. He'd said, 'Don't worry. It's early days yet.' It was okay anyway, because William took a different kind of interest in her. He finally liked to talk to her, too. He asked her lots of questions, and she told him things that she'd never been able to tell before. She talked about those things the only way she was able to, from her point of view, and they seemed at last to make sense to someone.

For instance, she told him how she and Sam had contrived to *be* one another. She said that, for ages now, the other Sam hardly ever came out. That had helped. And they both knew it was sabotage to make any changes in their appearance. She never had—deliberately—and the other had stopped that nonsense years ago. If she—Samantha—had been gone, when she came back, she would make sure to loop her ponytail so no one would be able tell how long her hair was till she could figure out how long the other's was—she'd do that by pulling hairs out of the shower drain and measuring them against her own. And when she had got a little fat—because she was eating lunch and dinner at Mary Whitaker and only walking the short distance to work and back—the other Sam had taken to coming out on the weekends and leaving her miles and miles out along some local bush track so that she had to walk all the way home.

This was the sort of stuff William was interested in. Insights into her life, he said.

Theresa and William were still busy with their code when Warren stormed out of the kitchen swearing at Oscar. He and Oscar were supposed to be making dinner. 'The kid can't follow simple instructions. Apparently he's above that.' Warren took off his apron and tossed it on the floor.

Oscar appeared, and tried to say something in his own defence.

'Can't you be trusted to do the least little thing I ask?' Theresa sprang up out of her chair.

'Are you talking to me or Warren?' Oscar asked. 'And have you done the dishes even once since we've been here? Or don't *cops* do dishes?'

'Stop being a smart arse.'

'I've been helping in the kitchen for weeks and weeks. I'm not trying to get out of anything. But it's *my* kitchen now and I don't have to listen to *him*!'

Sam got up. 'I'll help you, Warren.'

Behind Oscar, Warren started shaking his head furiously at Theresa.

Oscar caught this out of the corner of his eye and gave Warren a look of disgust. 'If you're too nervous to share a kitchen with Sam, just bugger off.'

Oscar came and took Sam's hand in his own large one and led her off to the kitchen, saying, 'Yes, you can help me. It's nice of you to offer.'

A few minutes later Theresa followed them and apologised to Oscar. 'Warren is a grown-up so expects to be in charge. And, Oscar, I keep trying to limit your responsibilities. I know it aggravates you, but you must see why I do it.'

'You have the job of feeding the cats now,' Sam reminded Oscar, to cheer him. To Theresa she said, 'Everyone needs to feel they have a part to play.'

Theresa looked at Sam and did careful things with her expression.

'Don't be scared of me,' Sam said. 'I'm not dangerous.' She wished she knew what to do to make them all feel easier with her.

Theresa said, 'You're just going to have to put up with our nerves.'

'But I looked after you when you were all sick.'

'I know, Sam. I'm trying, okay?'

'When Jacob has his medicines worked out the other can come back. She'll help you. You'll see.'

Theresa patted the air between them—trying to push an invisible something back into its invisible box.

The kitchen door blew open as if another unseen entity had rushed to the aid of the one Theresa was trying to confine. Sam hurried to close it. She had been startled, but not spooked. The door had been caught by an easterly wind. Kahukura didn't get them very often. There was a porch at Mary Whitaker where they used to store stuff, and once or twice a year the rain would blow in and the manager

356

would say, 'We have to think of some more permanent arrangement.'

'Is that—?' Theresa's voice was watery.

'It's the wind,' said Sam.

'And by "the wind" you mean?'

'The wind.'

It was a wild night, and at midnight Bub and Theresa drove down to the supermarket to check on the lights they'd rigged. They made everything secure and climbed back into the car, soaked through. Theresa shouted to make herself heard over the rattle of rain on the car roof. 'My hair was blowing in my eyes. It's usually too short. Time is moving on but we're not.'

'First clear night we'll get to it,' Bub said, gesturing at the quivering array of lights. 'I'm sure they'll work out our code.'

The survivors' very first message would be the twenty-six letters and ten numerals of their contrived Morse-like code. They'd send it over and over till someone out there caught on and responded.

On their way back they glimpsed a faint fire glow from the house where Myr had held Sam prisoner.

'He's up there again,' Bub said. 'Shall we do a detour to talk to him?'

Theresa said she was too wet and cold for that.

The following morning was calm and clear. Oscar took his bike out early to feed Lucy and the other cats. Jacob's patients on bed rest got up and camped in the sunny atrium. When Sam saw Kate hadn't come downstairs she went up and coaxed Kate from her room, then carried a folding chair out beside the garden beds. She sat Kate in it, then fetched a hoe and began weeding between the seedlings.

Jacob brought Kate a cup of tea on a tray and left it by her chair.

Back in the atrium, William, Bub, and Theresa had their heads together and were trying to work out what came next.

William asked Jacob when he thought he'd be ready for the other Sam.

Jacob shhhed and came to join them. 'I can't take any chances. I have to be absolutely certain she'll survive. It can't be a coincidence that she's here. That *they're* here.'

Theresa said, 'Yes. The other Sam has that strange affinity with the monster. Which suggests they're here to do something.'

'What say "doing something" harms them?' said William.

Jacob took William's wrist. 'Take it easy,' he reminded.

William let Jacob check his pulse, but declared that he wasn't going to be ruled by some dumb glitch in his body.

'Buddy,' Jacob said, gently, 'you have heart damage. I'm sorry. I didn't want to tell you but I've got to get you to behave and give yourself a chance. When we get out of here you can go put yourself into the hands of some top-class cardiac surgeon and get it fixed.'

William had lost his colour. He looked appalled. He snatched his hand out of Jacob's grasp.

'I'm worried about Warren too, if that helps,' Jacob said. He wanted William to say something, and stop looking at him accusingly. 'You're really sick, buddy. For a time there you were losing your peripheral circulation, like Warren. I'm not sure why Warren came through with fewer ill effects. My professional guess is that he has the constitution of a cockroach.'

It was at that moment that Oscar came in with his pockets stuffed with sun-yellowed paper, and his arms full of plastic bottles.

★

The main cat-feeding place was below the high-water mark on the boat ramp at the western end of the beach. It was a good place, because whatever the cats didn't eat was cleaned up by the seagulls and the sea. Oscar had got to the boat ramp at ten, after spending a bit of time with Lucy. As he rode up on his bike the gathered cats got to their feet, and others jumped out through the broken windows of the shorefront properties and trotted across the road. Oscar leaned his bike on the district council's big sign about boat ramp use, and took the cat food cans out of his saddlebag. He walked down the ramp, the cats sauntering after him or contriving to trip him by making affectionate dashes at his ankles. The cats butted his hands as he worked on the first tear-top can. He got that can open and tipped the sausage-and-gravy out onto the sea-worn concrete. He left the first cluster of cats and walked to a new spot, followed by the smarter and more patient animals. He tipped out another tin, then stepped back to admire the two quivering scrums. Then he rinsed the cans in the sea and put them back in his saddle bags.

The beach looked different after the storm. In a westerly or northerly gale, the sand would be either heaped in huge ripples or beaten flat and hard. It all depended on the tide. But an easterly only moved stuff around. Oscar's father knew Kahukura really well and would say, after an easterly, 'You might like to do a bit of beach-combing today, son.'

The sand was covered in flotsam—the usual driftwood, plus skeins of seaweed, even bull kelp torn from its anchorage on the rocks around Pepin Island. There were a couple of faded orange fishing floats, and near the ramp a grey ironwood hawser threaded with torn rope, so weathered it might have been drifting for decades. And there were plastic bottles.

There were always a few plastic bottles—but today there were dozens of them, none buried in the sand or even concealed in the piled debris at the tide line. And, as Oscar looked at them, he suddenly understood why they were on top of everything else, and why they were familiar—not just a common sight after an easterly. They were familiar because he'd seen them before, sitting like giant bubbles on the mess of stuff in the cove below the shoreline track where flotsam always fetched up. The cove Oscar hadn't stopped to take a good look at on any of his rides since it stank so—having collected the bodies of seabirds the No-Go had killed. The bottles must have moved when the easterly scoured the cove. So—that was why they were familiar. As for why they were lying on top of the rest of the flotsam—that was because they were all sealed, and watertight.

Oscar jumped off the ramp and ran to the nearest bottle. It was a two-litre soft drink bottle, lid screwed down tight, and sealed with the same soft wax his mother used on her jars of preserved lemons. Oscar picked the bottle up and shook it. The paper inside it rattled drily.

Oscar employed his teeth to get the lid open. He tipped the paper out. He took his time unfolding it—it was brittle after long exposure to the sun.

The paper was a photocopy of a hand-written letter. Oscar recognised the handwriting before he was able to read a word. He sat down in the sand. His ears roared. He tried again.

Dear Oscar. This is Mum and Dad . . .

Oscar's eyes swam. He wiped them and went on reading.

By the time he finished the letter his sleeves were damp with tears.

Oscar's father had first put his message in a bottle into the outgoing tide at the mouth of the Motueka River seven days after Kahukura was lost to the rest of the world. He wrote to his son that local experts on the vagaries of Tasman Bay tides and currents all agreed that things drifting from the river mouth would eventually find their way with the tide to Kahukura, or Mapua, or Ruby Bay (or, in certain winds, across Tasman Bay and out to sea). *But you see*, Oscar's father wrote, *it was worth a try.*

The first letter Oscar opened was his parents' fifth. It—and ten other copies in ten different bottles—had been dropped off the wharf at Motueka six weeks before. Because Oscar's parents couldn't have been sure he was getting any of their messages, in each letter they repeated their story. They explained their decision to attempt to communicate this way, what the local experts said, and how they finally came to know that they *were* talking to Oscar every time they consigned a bottle to the tide.

Only four days before they wrote the letter Oscar first opened—number five—his mother and father had had a visit from 'the officials'. They were shown satellite pictures of their son. They were asked to identify him, and told that he was part of small group of survivors. He had been photographed riding his bike—which suggested to everyone that he was fit and well. Oscar's parents were also told that, on the day after that terrible first, their son had inscribed a message to them in the sand of Kahukura beach. *If we had been told that straight away it would have saved us weeks of agony.* His parents were clearly angry.

From the sample of their letters that Oscar found—letters written on the twelfth, eighteenth, twentieth, and twenty-sixth of October, and the third and ninth of November—plus a handful of other communications the survivors spent the morning gathering, they were able to glean that, after the event, there had been a seven-day news blackout, during which all the media was able to do was report with gnawing repetition on the bare facts about what they were calling 'the Zone'. They reported on its known casualties—the crews of an air force Orion and navy Sea Sprite.

The Orion's engines apparently stalled then stopped when it entered the Zone—which appeared to be some kind of 'inertial field'. Observers had seen the same thing Bub and Theresa had. The plane had gone dark and silent, then had reappeared, after banking without power out of the Zone. The pilot tried to restart the engines, but by that time the plane was too close to the terrain, and it crashed and burned.

Early interpretations of the crash opined that the Zone was a kind of soft solidity—people in boats on Tasman Bay reported seeing what they described as 'thickened air'. But scientists had soon scotched that opinion, simply by watching the waves come and go. It was only living things the Zone recognised, or anything with an engine, a *spark*.

Parachute drops didn't work because the jumpers became unconscious in the Zone—and, it was thought, possibly even dead in its depths, since the oxygen regulators on their breathing equipment would fail. The jumpers couldn't free-fall, because gauges designed to make their parachutes deploy automatically failed to work in the Zone. The two attempts at parachute drops—one manned and one unmanned—had been monitored by satellite. A man was lost in the first jump, and the unmanned payload came down hard, in the Zone, after being nudged off course by wind during its long fall. It was decided that any further unmanned drops would be attempted again only as a last resort for the survivors.

The Sea Sprite had an even more horrible fate. It too entered the Zone and stalled, and was low enough when it came down that the crew survived the crash and lived for some time. But they couldn't be retrieved. Another Sea Sprite had nudged up to where the Zone began, and its pilot watched the windows of the downed helicopter mist over with breath as night came and the temperature of the outside air dropped. But in the morning there was no sign of mist on the windows.

Those stories were available to the media—along with

stern cautions to venturesome yachts and kayaks, which had been caught trying to assay the Zone from the wide open water of the Tasman Sea. All this was reported. And also reported was what the government had to say, and the arrival in the area of the Australian frigates and submarine, then an international military task force, and various experts.

'Experts on what, exactly?' said William.

Theresa was reading from a feature published in the *Guardian* on October the twenty-second—which an anonymous person had thoughtfully stuffed into a big plastic pickle jar with other pages printed off the web. 'On "Zones of inertia", I guess,' said Theresa. 'They have to say "experts". And frankly, I pity the poor sods whose job it is to figure out what qualifies someone to make the No-Go their business.'

Bub had been quietly reading. Then his absorption turned into an agitated rustling. Finally he rose partway out of his chair and yelled, 'Hey! Hey!'

William said, 'Yes, Bub, please share your discovery.'

It seemed that, for fifteen days after Day One, the Zone had continued to spread—not beyond the ridges inland, but across the mouth of Nelson harbour, all the way across the isthmus of Cable Bay Road, and beyond the highest point of Pepin Island. It moved gradually, nudging sheep, wild goats, and the few people on that coast away from the coast. It climbed the steep weathered slopes, and didn't stop till its border was well out of sight of Tasman Bay. Nelson was a closed port. This extensive Zone of exclusion was less exclusive than it was elsewhere inland, for during the period when military personnel had been clinging to those steep slopes across the bay, the soldiers had been able to train their binoculars on tide pools and see movement—sea snails and healthy pulsing anemone. And insects had been seen penetrating space that was impenetrable to larger animals.

'This explains their tardiness,' William said. 'It wasn't just the technical problem of how to communicate, or the political problem of which of us was to be trusted. For at least three weeks the scientists and military would have thought Kahukura was ground zero for an invisible creature-killing force that, as far as they could tell, was going to continue to bulldoze its way across the face of the earth.'

For a minute the people around the table looked at one another, open-mouthed, while this sank in—all but Dan, who went on leafing noisily through a sheaf of print from another pickle jar. He was desperate for some good news. He said, 'Apparently we have web pages.' He smoothed a crackling paper and held it up. The caption was *Survivor: Curtis Haines*. The page had several photos of Curtis, including one with the Governor General pinning his medal for Services to Film onto the lapel of a dapper charcoal suit.

William gave a little 'humph' of cynical amusement.

Dan was still reading. He cleared his throat and read aloud, 'It is rumoured that a video camera was recovered from a kayak found adrift in Cook Strait. The camera is said to contain footage of the survivors, and a straight-to-camera eyewitness account of events by filmmaker Curtis Haines. Officials deny the existence of such a video.'

William asked when the kayak was found.

Dan did some slow figuring. 'Four weeks ago.'

Theresa stood to scrabble in the pile of papers in the middle of the table. 'So, anyway, we know from the thumbnail photos at the top of Curtis's page that there are other pages.'

Dan peered at the thumbnails. 'Yeah. This is us.'

William said, 'When did they publish our names?'

'Dad says the newspaper was all full of the Zone, and the Orion and Sea Sprite, and the kakapo in Stanislaw's Reserve—then for a while there was nothing much apart from the gathering of Military from Australia and the US, and unconfirmed rumours about how the No-Go kept growing. Then, he says, someone leaked a couple of satellite photos of the graves on the school playing field. Until then the public hadn't much idea about what had gone on here.'

'Have they published a death toll? They must have known almost right off that nearly everyone in the settlement was dead,' William said.

'There's a difference between a death toll and confirmed casualties,' Theresa said. 'We always prefer to have proof positive before informing relatives.' By 'we' Theresa meant the police. 'The officials would have felt they needed bodies, or a decent interval. Besides, they could see us walking around so they knew *some* people had survived. The question is, when did they identify us?'

'Why do you keep making excuses for them?' Dan said. 'We gave them our names in the first week.'

'They would've needed to confirm that with their own observations. Officials can't report people dead, or alive, till they're sure they've got their facts straight. Besides, Dan, we can't keep thinking we know better than they do,' Theresa said.

William asked why not.

'At least I'm not in the habit of thinking I'm smarter than everyone else,' she said.

'Yeah,' said Bub. 'I'm with Theresa. Think how those people must have felt when the No-Go stopped up the mouth of Tasman Bay and kept on spreading. That would have been terrifying.'

Oscar said, 'Dad says in his latest letter that the officials told them that, before they talked to next-of-kin, they had to run background checks. On *us*. They had to be sure none of us were somehow responsible.'

'See. I told you,' Theresa said.

Oscar muttered that these bloody officials could still have given his mum and dad their good news earlier. It's not as if *he* would have been a suspect.

'They just went all procedural,' Bub said. 'That's the

nature of the military and government. They have to put procedure between them and chaos.'

Oscar said, 'Dad reckons no one knows he and Mum are sending messages. He says my cousins do the drops now, and one of them saw someone else on the wharf with a bag, looking shifty.'

'Pickle Jar,' said Bub.

'From the different containers it looks as if there are maybe as many as five people doing it regularly,' said Theresa.

'And this is the first news we hear,' William said, 'the low-tech way, from ordinary folk, rather than anyone with responsibility, or power.'

Bub was still fossicking. He froze, then stood up, speechless with excitement. He held out a sun-yellowed and damp-dimpled sheaf of papers.

Pickle Jar had sent them the Wikipedia pages on Morse Code.

That evening William joined Bub and Belle on the terrace. The gale had purified the air, and the dusk was coming with subtle gradations of gold that faded quietly to darkness. When the light before them was less than the light from the windows behind them, William finally spoke up. 'Now that we have a real code, Theresa wants to file a very detailed report, on the monster and Myr—and Sam.'

Bub said, 'I'm not comfortable about outing Sam either. But here's another problem—if we let on that any information is getting to us, they'll want to know how, and we don't want them to muzzle the folks with the plastic containers. But if we don't mention the plastic containers, then Oscar's mum and dad won't know he got their letters.'

'It's a quandary,' William said.

'I think we should report everything,' Belle said, 'the plastic containers, Myr, the monster, and Sam.'

'We don't know in what way, if any, Sam's situation is relevant,' said William.

'You're not very convincing for a lawyer,' Belle said. 'Sam is as relevant as all get out.'

'Belle's right. We need the brainpower of all the boffins out there,' Bub said.

William turned in his seat to look Bub square in the face. 'Don't you have faith in your own brainpower? You're here, with your heart and nerves and gut. You can see things those boffins are never going to be able to see. Even if they had instruments that were somehow able to register the Wake as it roams about and occasionally concentrates itself.'

'How do you know that's what it does?' Bub said.

'You told me how Sam acted when Warren overdosed. How she kept asking, "What *is* that?" The Wake was there, making a meal of Jacob's misery, and only Sam could feel it.'

After a moment Bub nodded. 'Yes. You're right. The boffins can't possibly get what we do.'

'Even if they had some flash science-fiction instruments showing the monster whirling about like a weather system, they're never going to see how even *my* Sam can register its presence better than any instruments, or that the *other* Sam is like its high priestess.'

'We should tell them,' Belle said. 'They might know how to use the information.'

'How? Do you think they are going to want to control what she says to the monster, just in case she creates a diplomatic incident?'

'So, you're saying we tell them about Myr, and the Wake, but not about Sam. And we don't mention any folksy forms of communication.' Bub made a summary of what he and William agreed on, and then stuck out his hand. 'I can go with that.'

William took Bub's hand and shook it.

'Bub!'

'William's right, Belle. We have to make our own judgement calls, as if we're in a fire fight and the radio's broken and we're the ranking officers.'

'Theresa won't like it.'

'Theresa has left it to me to master Morse and compose our messages,' Bub said. 'She's not going to be able to keep a close enough track of what I'm sending to know what I leave out.'

'You can't exclude her like that!'

William said, 'Never mind Theresa. I have to protect *Sam*. I owe her that.'

Bub placed the rocker switch beside their messages, which were already translated into Morse and set out letter by letter and word by word on graph paper. He flexed his fingers.

Theresa said, 'I hope you're not going to spend the next half-hour sending tena koutou, tena koutou, tena koutou, katoa.'

'Don't be cheeky,' Bub said, and commenced.

After half an hour Bub stopped sending to massage his cramping hand. 'I keep wanting to add a dubious "He says" to that last bit.'

The message he was sending read: *Invisible, intangible monster cause of casualties. Zone is quarantine made by man who follows monster inter-dimensionally.*

Theresa said, 'What do you want to bet they'll fire thousands of questions at us—when they figure out how—and we'll have to repeat all that, as if they think we're having them on, or we're nuts, or lying?'

William said, 'In that case we can send a message saying: "We're not going to change our story no matter how many times you ask".'

Oscar said, 'That last bit will get the string theorists all hot.'

'What's a string theorist?' Theresa asked.

'A physicist with theories about multiple dimensions—stuff in addition to space and time. Most physicists think string theory is pretty bogus.'

Dan had assembled a low pallet of flattened cardboard boxes. He was lying down just beyond the outer ring of the bull's-eye. He said, 'You know, when the lights are off, I can actually see the satellites. Dozens have gone over.' Then, 'When I was a kid there were mostly only stars up there.'

Oscar asked whether he could take a turn. 'It's like texting. It's easy.'

Bub gave Oscar the switch and the next message. Oscar asked what it said.

'Kakapo all good but running low on feed.'

Oscar set to work. His dots were much sharper than Bub's.

Jacob got up and stretched. He asked if anyone wanted him to microwave them a frozen pie. Bub said yes, and a can of Coke would be nice, though not microwaved. Several other people put in their orders and Jacob edged past the bundle of cables running through the supermarket's wedged-open back door.

Bub told Oscar to stop, and turned the page. He tapped the paper. 'Send this for ten minutes. It says: *Could you signal us by bouncing light off clouds out to sea?*'

'Which shows that Bub *does* think he's more savvy than the officials,' William said.

Oscar began rattling again. Two light bulbs popped. Oscar stopped and looked at Bub. Bub got up, covered his hand with his sleeve, unscrewed the blown bulbs, and replaced them. He said, 'Good to go,' and Oscar began again.

'Whatever they send back—from wherever—other people will be able to see it,' Theresa said. 'That's why we can't expect them to answer right away. They're going to have to think about the ramifications of broadcasting our

369

conversation to all and sundry, given the inter-dimensional monsters and aliens. We might have to wait for a time while they deliberate. Meanwhile everyone can give Bub their brief personal messages.'

'That won't be happening,' said William.

Bub said, 'Don't you have anyone you want to send a message?'

'Nobody who wouldn't be acutely embarrassed. My friends and acquaintances are very private people.'

Dan, visible as a lumpy patch of shadow beyond the flickering field of light said, 'Bub—William means his friends earn more than you do.'

'Everyone earns more than me. But I'm asset rich. I have Dad's boat, and his quota, and his flat in Stoke.' Bub addressed this to Belle, who smiled. 'I rent,' she said. 'I haven't got a bean. I haven't even paid off my student loan.'

'We can sell our stories,' Warren said. 'They'll be bidding for them.'

'So—we aren't going to die?' Dan said, tentative.

'Opinions vary,' William said. Then, to Oscar, 'Be careful not to run the words together.'

The last thing they sent was a list of names. Their own, and their dead.

Kate couldn't be angry at the others for hoping for the best. She'd always been a forward-looking person herself. When her children tried to open a discussion about Enduring Power of Attorney she'd given them short shrift. They spent far too much time listening to earnest talk about such things on the radio and television. Enduring Power of Attorney, indeed. She'd put an end to the discussion by saying, 'However did people manage their arrangements before someone came up with Enduring Power of Attorney?'

It had always been in Kate's nature not to reflect upon

the past, but to have the next day in view, the next week. Manageable periods. When she was still living independently she planted bulbs in April and took her frost-sensitive pot plants indoors. She put in her broad beans in May, and her tomato seedlings in October. She bottled her peaches and her tomatoes and made a batch of breakfast yoghurt every Sunday. Each morning she checked the TV Guide and would circle any programme she might want to take a look at. She hadn't wanted a video recorder or a DVR—if she missed something then it couldn't have been that important.

Holly had thought Kate inconsistent in this. Wasn't recording a programme the same as bottling tomatoes? But of course it wasn't. The talk, the spectacle, all that only wiled away time, and arguably wasted it too. Preserves were for nourishment, and against waste.

Kate's room at Mary Whitaker was always orderly and neat. The cleaners would dust and vacuum, but they knew to respect Kate's arrangements. Kate had a place for everything, and she believed there was a time for everything too.

It was one thing to wait on the pleasure of the Almighty, and quite another to wait for a monster to get around to picking the bones of your character. This in mind, Kate had taken herself off all her heart and blood pressure medications. Now she was waiting. Waiting and hoping for a quick calamity that couldn't be alleviated by anyone whipping her off to hospital. That blessed No-Go was *her* Enduring Power of Attorney.

Kate had made her plans, but she did feel a little uncomfortable about her sons, though neither of them was under fifty, and if they couldn't take care of themselves by now then they'd never be able to. Anyway—she wouldn't be sending them any messages. She couldn't face making an explanation, about Holly, about what the others said Holly had done (while exonerating Holly from blame, since, of course, the blame lay with their monster). Let someone else

371

tell Holly's story. After all, all that Kate could think to say was that she didn't know what had come over her daughter. She didn't understand it.

Kate wouldn't send a message, or leave any letters, but she would leave something. Every evening for weeks she'd been knitting. She was making hats for her granddaughters, who were all in their teens or early twenties, and were lively, go-getting girls. The hats were smart multicoloured beanies. Kate was sure they'd suit the girls. She had three finished, with cards pinned to them—*to Kirsten, from Grandma*; *to Bridget, from Grandma*; *to Tessa, from Grandma*.

That would have to be enough.

The day after they sent their first communication, everyone but Kate was a little on edge.

Oscar complained that if people staggered their breakfasts he'd still be doing the dishes when it was time for lunch. Theresa and Bub had an overemphatic discussion about how best to rig a rope ladder down the bluff on the shoreline track so they could pick up flotsam and not have to wait for another easterly gale. (Bub had already tried to row to the cove, and hadn't counted on the outgoing tide. His dinghy had drifted towards the No-Go without his noticing. He felt faint, couldn't manage the oars, and had just enough wit left to roll out of the boat into the water, and swim to shore. The dinghy had yet to turn up again—if it ever did.)

After lunch Jacob stormed out and removed the hoe from William's hands and asked him what part of 'you have to take it easy' did he not understand? Dan articulated what they were all thinking: 'We can't expect to hear anything back until its dark.' He sounded dubious, as if he longed to be contradicted.

Oscar went to feed the cats.

Bub and Belle retired to Sam's bach to cook themselves

dinner and share a bottle of wine. They hauled Sam's pretty pink Formica table out into the front yard and sat where they could watch the sun setting behind the hills.

Night fell. After dinner Oscar cycled off and spent half an hour throwing stones at the streetlights along the seafront, managing to crack only one casing. He rode back and came in complaining to everyone that there was too much light. How were they supposed to see anything out there, anyway?

William and Theresa were in the atrium with the lights off and the doors open onto the terrace. 'We're keeping an eye out,' Theresa said.

'And?'

'The officials are still deliberating, obviously,' Theresa said. 'It'll take them time to work out how to answer. It's actually harder for them to talk to us than it is for us to talk to them.'

'Stop making excuses!' Oscar said, and crashed off upstairs.

'Go to bed,' Theresa said to William. 'You look exhausted.'

'Yes—come to bed,' said Sam.

At this William met Theresa's eyes, and cool venom seemed to shoot through her. The look was regretful, and complicit. It told Theresa that William was conscious he was being kind to Sam, kind because she deserved kindness and he felt some species of loyalty to her, and it turned out that her duplicity wasn't duplicity after all, and didn't even call for his forgiveness—but that he didn't want her any more.

A few weeks back Theresa would have shrugged and privately congratulated Sam on her escape. She might have said to Sam that William was pretty, but no prize. Now she felt terribly sorry for Sam, not so much because, when she discovered it, Sam would be wounded even by this gentle letting-down—but because William was a loss. A real loss. The realisation came thundering in on Theresa. What a man he was. How difficult, questionable, and overbearing;

and how different, distinct, honest even.

For a moment Theresa felt that her bristling scalp might actually lever the top off her head. This riot of feeling was so out of the blue, so off the scale (she began explaining herself to herself like some police spokesperson sticking to safe sound-bite language in a television interview). The feeling was inappropriate, and disproportionate. And then she thought 'What if this isn't me—this enthusiasm? What if it's the monster?' Theresa took a mental step back, to take a good hard look at her feelings, and promised herself that, in future, she'd do a better job of policing them.

Bub and Belle sat on in the dark, gazing out to sea. At 2am they finally went indoors, lit some candles, and went to bed.

Dan shuffled out onto the terrace to join Theresa and, at around three, when she checked her watch, he was asleep, his chin silvered by stubble (he had always shaved before), and his mouth bracketed by deep grooves. Theresa got a rug and draped it over him. Shortly before dawn all the tui started singing—earlier than the other birds. The Nokia ring tui came and perched in the bouquet of the jacaranda above the graves.

One grave was covered in petunias that were just coming into bloom; the others were still fresh and dark. The tui began its upbeat little song. Dan went and fetched the shotgun. 'I'm going to shut that fucking bird up for once and all,' he said.

'Oh no, don't,' Theresa said, pleading rather than firm, and that stopped him.

'We've been waiting all night,' he said, agonised.

'We have to be patient.'

His back was to the light and Theresa couldn't read his

face. He said, 'Look, it's good that you're so staunch. And I know that you, more than anyone else here, can imagine how the authorities are going to go about handling something like this. But don't you think they're being extra harsh?' He took a deep breath and went on. 'Either things don't work the way I think they do, or—well, like, in the *Wahine* disaster, they always talk about how people broke the police cordon to jump into the waves and haul the lifeboats out of the surf at Eastbourne beach. Ordinary people, with stacks of blankets, and thermoses full of soup. Everyone soaking wet and cold, and doing their best. *Wahine* wasn't that long ago. We aren't that different. *New Zealand* isn't that different. How come this disaster has been taken out of the hands of the ordinary people who just turn up to help?'

'There are the bottles.'

'That's mostly Oscar's mum and dad and some bloke who can't bear to think we don't know what bloggers are saying about us.'

'Okay, then *we're* the ordinary people.'

'But where's everyone else?'

'It's possible the guys monitoring the satellites can see things we can't, and it will take them some time to figure out what information might help us, and what might be too discouraging.'

'You think? But couldn't they just say, "Hi, we got your messages; more later"?'

'Yes,' Theresa said, passionately. 'Yes, they *should*. They should move mountains to talk to us.'

Dan fiddled with the gun, breaking it open and fingering the flat ends of the shells in its chambers. 'If they're this cold, how can I know they're looking after Fay and the kids?'

'Of course they are. And it isn't coldness, Dan. It's over-cautiousness, officiousness, paranoia. Something along those lines.'

'My family lives one week to the next. We always

375

thank God when the money comes in—my wages and the Working For Families. But lately we've even had to go to the food bank.'

'There'd be a huge scandal if your family wasn't being given all the support they need.'

'I think *people* are good,' Dan said, resolute. 'But it's the government and the army and the rest of them I'm worried about—and only because they haven't answered us.'

'They'll have their reasons.'

Dan closed the gun with a metallic snap and flung it over his shoulder. 'And I'm scared,' he said, abruptly.

Theresa pressed her lips tightly together, and nodded.

'I'm *tired* of being scared.'

Theresa didn't answer, and after another moment, Dan started off down the steps saying he'd see if he couldn't bag something fresh. He paused on the driveway and, without turning back, asked, 'So you reckon they'll look after my kids?'

'Of course,' Theresa said, rushing to reassure him—and not listening properly.

Dan returned with two fat rabbits. He was jubilant. He skinned them and had a lively consultation with Jacob about how they should be cooked.

Everyone had watched all night, or made the attempt. They were all too tired to last till dinner so the rabbit casserole was lunch.

They all thanked Dan, but after lunch was cleared away William found him sitting in the atrium, in gloom of a deep degree. But everyone was gloomy, William thought. Even Oscar was swearing at his game and slapping the controller on his leg.

Bub turned up and grumped about how he and Belle hadn't been invited to share the casserole, and Theresa said, quietly, but acidly, that Bub couldn't expect to have it both ways—to be left alone, and included.

Before dawn the following day Dan got ammunition from the manager's office. He filled his pockets with shells and then collected the shotgun from where he'd left it, clean and broken down, on a sheet of oily newspaper in the atrium. He had to pick his way through a field of towels laid on the floor. Belle was so low on feed for her birds that she was having to find things to eke it out. She'd washed the salt from all the supermarket's packets of roasted macadamias, and then spread the nuts on towels to dry.

Dan put his gun back together. Then he wrote a note and left it on the dining table. *I reckon I can get a couple more bunnies*, it read. *When Belle comes to get the nuts ask her and Bub to lunch. They missed out last time.*

Dan headed up to the arboretum. He spotted a rabbit cleaning its whiskers in the first rays of sun. He took aim, and squeezed the trigger. The rabbit jumped, then tumbled limply in the grass. Dozens of other rabbits became visible as they scattered across the field.

When Dan picked the rabbit up it was still alive, panting little puffs of steam. He quickly broke its neck, draped it over his shoulder, and stepped back into the trees. He'd wait for the other rabbits to reappear.

A few minutes later the sunlight reached him, and a breeze trailed its scarves across his face.

Behind him, deeper in the trees, something made a soft, hollow thud. He looked and, in the dark depths of the exotic forest, he saw brightness, a patch of light as blue as the sky. Dan set the gun over his other shoulder and walked into the arboretum.

★

The first gunshot woke Theresa. She immediately hauled herself out of bed, put on trackpants and a T-shirt, and ran downstairs. There she found Dan's note. Well—she thought—he'd got it half right. A note was good, but if he'd said something the night before she'd have been able to ignore the gunfire and go back to sleep. Perhaps he had said something and she'd missed it. After all, no one else got up to investigate. Theresa imagined the other survivors, either in the know or exhausted by alarms, turning over and pressing pillows to their ears.

Theresa took herself back to bed, climbing back into her own warmth. A short while later she heard the second shot and slipped into sleep thinking of a rabbit stew with plenty of rabbit in it.

Bub and Belle appeared at breakfast. Bub sat down and accepted a cup of coffee. He said he wanted Oscar or Sam to help him make a rope ladder they could lower into the cove where the bottles collected. 'It'll be a fiddly job. Sam's patient, and Oscar's a fiddler. The hard part's going to be rigging the ladder down the bank—finding something to attach it to.'

Belle poured her rinsed macadamias from the towels into a pillowcase. She shook it, and the nuts made an oily rattle. She said she was going to mix them in with the kakapo's normal feed and see if they'd go for it.

Theresa asked Warren if he'd go look for Dan. 'He should be back by now. He'll have gone up towards the reserve, or maybe on to Cotley's orchard. I'm going to check there.'

'There are rabbits on people's lawns,' Bub said. 'He could just as easily have taken a walk through town.'

'The shots I heard came from behind the spa.'

'Can I have a gun?' Warren said.

'What for? Rabbits?' Bub said.

William, who was nursing a cup of tea (he wasn't allowed coffee anymore) said, 'There's no danger out there. Or nothing you can shoot at. The thing about an invisible monster is that you can't even close your door on it. You wouldn't know whether it was outside or shut in with you'

Theresa looked around to see who was listening. Oscar was on his daily bike ride. Kate was in the kitchen and out of earshot. The vulnerable people at least were spared William's bad attitude. She said to him, 'You've got no grasp of the concept of morale, have you?'

'We've got to stay positive,' Warren said, a little mechanically. 'Or, as Jacob would say, just chill.'

William weighed this up. 'I'm pretty sure Jacob tells us to chill because he's worried about our hearts. And I'm not forgetting for a second that the Wake is working on some weapon only I can use, either against myself or you people. Some customised delusion. By all means think positively. But it won't save you.'

Theresa turned away from William in disgust and, ahead of time, thanked Warren for helping her see to it that Dan was all right.

Warren found Dan spreadeagled on the billowing silver fabric of a still partly-inflated balloon. The ground around the balloon was scuffed up as if Dan had scrabbled through the pine needles looking for something.

The balloon's payload, a plastic canister, was open and empty. The bags of pellets—kakapo feed—had been ripped out of the canister and cast around the clearing, again as if a desperate search had at some point turned to the fury of disappointment. Dan's heels were under his backside. The gun lay across his legs. Blood and brains had splattered the bole of the tree, and more blood haloed Dan's head, its surface sometimes sleek and sometimes dull as the wind stirred the balloon and made the skin forming on the blood bunch into fine wrinkles. Warren took a good long look. Then he hurried, slithering and stumbling, in the direction of the spa.

Theresa and Jacob carried a roll of masking tape and a number of plastic rubbish sacks into the arboretum. They went over the site carefully before they moved Dan. They too looked for whatever Dan had been so desperately seeking—but found nothing more than the balloon, canister, and packets of feed.

Jacob slipped a bag over Dan's head and another over his legs, then Theresa fastened the join with tape. She wound another length of tape around the wrapped body from head to foot. They rolled the bundled body off the balloon and across the turf till it was well out of the way. Then they gathered up the smeared fabric of the balloon and put it to one side, before once again searching the container and the ground all around it.

There really wasn't anything else; no packet of papers, or DVD, or flash drive—no word from the world outside.

Theresa and Jacob carried the news back, but not the body. They'd bring Dan in after they'd talked to everyone.

Before they went indoors they stood for a moment by the jacaranda tree and looked at the graves. Theresa's hand sought Jacob's. 'I don't want to see another one,' she said.

Jacob knew she meant she didn't want to bury Dan here. The group of long mounds were already an accusation—a very personal failure for both the nurse and the police officer.

'If the newest grave is here, out in the open, *they* can see it.' He meant that the people monitoring the satellites could register another death.

'They don't care.'

'There must have been other balloons,' Jacob said. But

he didn't believe it. It would have been easy to put the same message with every balloon—so why didn't they?

'Come on. It's time to tell everyone,' Theresa said. 'We'll need help with the body, and the kakapo feed.'

PART EIGHT

Sam never had much to say for herself, and Bub was often comfortably quiet, so Oscar didn't mind too much that they had been at work for over an hour without a word beyond the most practical exchanges.

Sam was holding a block of wood over the top of a metal stake, while Bub hammered it gradually into the path of the shoreline track, twenty metres above the cove where the bottles collected. Bub was using a sledgehammer, but holding it close to its head and scarcely doing more than letting it drop onto the piece of two-by-four.

Oscar didn't have a job of his own. On the day they'd buried Dan he had helped Bub make the rope ladder. He was now sitting on its coiled length, waiting. He was thinking about his grandmother, and something she'd once told him. 'As a girl I was in and out of hospital with tuberculosis of the bone,' she'd said, and had lifted her trouser leg to show Oscar the rumpled scar on her shin. 'I couldn't gad about like my classmates. But I learned to be a most patient person, and it has stood me in stead.'

Oscar wondered whether, when he got out of Kahukura, in whatever kind of life he'd contrive afterwards, he'd be 'a most patient person'.

He could feel the hammer blows through the soles of his feet. But there was another sound—a labouring engine— that filled the silence between each blow.

'Bub!' he said. 'Stop for a second.'

Bub paused. They listened to an engine shift gears and recommence roaring.

Bub pushed past Oscar and hurried to the bend from

which the town was visible. Sam and Oscar joined him.

There was a dust cloud above the clearing in front of the closely woven galvanised steel of the predator-proof fence. The digger they'd used to make the mass graves was at work, charging forward a short distance then backing off again, cab tilting as the whole machine rose on the heels of its tread. The sound of the engine ricocheted around the hills.

'Who is that?' Oscar said. 'I can't tell from here. And what are they doing?'

Bub dropped the sledgehammer and set off running.

'It will be there,' Sam said softly. Her face was dreamy.

Oscar followed Bub, but Sam hesitated. She wanted to go where she knew her wind would be—the thing they were all calling a monster. But she didn't want them to see her with it. They'd been angry at her the other day when Bub and Jacob had brought Dan's body back, wrapped in rubbish sacks. When they set Dan down under the jacaranda, the wind had come. People were crying, and it came as if it craved salt. Sam, standing among the stunned and weeping survivors, had let the wind turn her. It was like the wave pool at the aquatic centre—safe for anyone who could swim. It was airy and liquid and solid, all at once. It cupped her like a hand around a lit match on a windy night. And then Warren shouted at her.

There was a fall of stones behind Sam. Myr slithered down the bluff and fetched up against Bub's metal stakes, where he stayed, rocking like a feather caught in the tines of a fork. His force field deactivated. His feet touched the ground, and he came towards her.

Sam backed off.

Myr stooped to retrieve Bub's sledgehammer and began to do what Bub had been doing—hammering the metal stakes into the ground at the right angle of bank and path.

386

Had he been watching them work? Was he now lending a hand?

Sam returned her attention to the digger. It was motionless. She made out a figure in front of it, against the predator-proof fence, doing something to the gate of the reserve. She couldn't see clearly enough through the settling dust to determine who it was. The figure paused to check its work, then hurried back to the machine and climbed into the driver's seat.

Behind Sam the pounding continued. Myr was at work on the second stake, the one Bub had already hammered to the correct depth. He was driving it right into the ground. He'd done the same with the first—only a few centimetres of metal now protruded.

Sam asked Myr what he was doing—he was leaving nothing for them to tie the ladder to. He ignored her and kept up his assault. Sparks flew. The stake was visibly sinking. Sam saw a crack appear in the ground, growing with each blow.

Myr dropped the hammer and put his foot on one stake. He pressed it back, then leaned his weight on it. The crack widened. It snaked between one stake and the other. Myr wiggled the stake with his foot—it moved with a ripping noise. Myr lifted his foot then pulled both stakes out of the now wide crack. He used one to probe its edges, wriggled it back and forth at the corners of the gap he'd made. The gap looked like a mouth in a loose jaw, dropping open.

Sam again asked Myr what he was doing, and he continued to ignore her. He dropped the stakes, braced his hands and hips against the bank, and pressed hard on the path. The patch of ground by the crack sank, then tore loose, and came away. A whole shelf of earth tumbled down the bluff, in streamers of grass roots and a confetti of clods. The path had gone. The bluff continued to crumble quietly. Myr picked up the stakes and threw them down into the cove, then pitched the rope ladder after them.

Myr was on the far side of the gap from Sam—not that she had any desire to go near him. She wanted to know why he'd just done that. Why he wanted to make it impossible for them to collect their messages. But she knew his answer would be enormous, and something she couldn't hope to understand. So she didn't ask. She simply turned from him and ran back towards Kahukura.

Belle had spent her morning in the reserve, on the far side of the ridge, in a grove of old-growth totara and rimu. She was checking for signs of seeds on the trees, doing what she would normally do, had none of this happened. Doing her job.

Once they'd buried Dan, Bub had gone back to the clearing for the canister. He carried it to the spa and wordlessly presented it to Belle. When she saw what the canister contained she was so relieved she almost wept. Until then she hadn't understood just how anxious her solitary watch had become.

The survivors were all upset about Dan. They'd guessed that Dan had killed himself because the balloon came without an answer—without a show of interest. But Belle had been answered. She'd asked for help, and packets of food had been packed up, and the balloon had found its way in on a gentle breeze. The world had wished her charges good health.

Belle calculated that the feed would do her kakapo for another ten weeks. She'd gone to the grove to see how much fruit was forming. If there was a good crop the kakapo wouldn't just survive, but would flourish and breed. They at least would go on uninterrupted. Belle peered into the treetops and dreamed about a future—not her own.

Being in love had somehow made Belle's life lighter to

her. If she had to die, then dying was just another thing she and Bub could do together. It would be easier together. And if the trees were full of fruit, then perhaps one of next spring's little star-eyed chicks would be named Belle, and another Bub.

The grove was peaceful. Belle's happiness felt permanent.

The hill was high and its stone crest tended to reflect sound back towards the bay but, after a time, she became aware of a noise, a roaring.

For the sound to carry so far it must be loud—a heavy engine, its gears chopping and changing. The roar was accompanied by clanks, and a twanging, like breaking wires. It was the sound of a machine savaging something metal.

Belle started back up the trail to the ridge.

She got there first. She ran into the dust that hung, as if hesitant, before the bush. The door of the utility shed was open, and Belle's initial thought was that she was glad she'd made sure to close the storage bins, and wouldn't have to wipe dust off the bagged feed. Then she registered an oddity. The mesh of the predator-proof fence was too fine for much dust to blow through, and the gates were made of the same stuff—so how was it that the billows of dust were coming towards her at ground level? She could hear an engine howling in the heart of the dust, and a ringing sound, a chain flexing, link adjusting to link—then a thrum, and metallic wrenching.

A gust of wind hit Belle's back, and the dust blew away before her. She saw the fence, a broad, twisted ribbon of mesh pulled from its uprights, some of which were still firmly rooted, while some were skewed. Several had been dragged right out of the ground, concrete footing and all.

The predator-proof fence ran for half a metre below the ground—so had come out leaving a trench, like a knife mark in a wet cake. As the length of mesh came free, the chain slackened abruptly. The digger the chain was fastened to jumped backwards, tilted, then dropped with a thump. The digger had backed into Belle's quad bike and nudged it over. The bike tipped, then began to roll. Belle followed it with her eyes and only then saw Theresa—her shaggy red hair and pale, resolute face. Theresa was running towards the digger. She saw the rolling quad bike coming towards her, and dived out of its way. But the bike hit a big tussock. It bounced up and veered right into Theresa's dive. Woman and machine collided. The bike altered direction again, very slightly, but Theresa spun and tumbled, landing face down on the grass.

The digger continued to reverse, and its chain tightened again, singing. Another three metres of fence pulled free of the ground. Dust poured up the slope and forced Belle to drop her face and close her eyes. She was shouting, and her mouth filled with grit. It grated between her teeth. She opened her eyes again, shaded them with her arm, and squinted into the haze.

Warren was standing up in the cab of the digger, looking back at Theresa. He stayed there a moment, poised, balancing in the plunging machine, then jumped out and made off.

Belle's eyes were streaming. She didn't see where Warren went. She only watched the digger. It was locked in reverse, pulling steadily away. The fence resisted and the chain hauled the front of the digger down. It would rise up onto the toes of its tread, then its bucket would brace against the ground, and it would lose traction, slide forward, and fall down four-square again. Belle watched this bucking motion for a minute, then, at a point when the tread was squarely on the ground, she rushed at the machine, jumped over the grinding, juddering tread, and caught hold of the frame of the cabin. She climbed in and tried to make sense of the controls. She looked for a clutch, a brake, before noticing the swinging keys.

She grabbed the keys. And, at that moment, the chain

parted. The digger rebounded backwards. The chain recoiled and lashed, ringing, against the bucket. Belle grabbed the levers, curled up over them, and jammed her legs under the dashboard. The digger flipped right over and rolled, the chain winding around the bucket and cabin, its loose end lashing the ground. Belle was showered with chips of stone. Hanks of grass came in and thumped her, like fists in boxing gloves. She hung on grimly at the centre of the big, articulated metal missile. Then the engine stalled. The digger stopped rolling and came to rest on its roof, rocking violently. Belle's knees slammed into her jaw, her teeth closed on her tongue, and blood filled her mouth. She gasped and actually felt her teeth slide free of her own flesh. Blood bubbled out of her mouth and ran into her nostrils and her eyes. It ran in a hot wash over her forehead and into her hair. She hung on to the knobs at the end of the levers, suspended above the dented roof of the cabin, her knees over her head, partway through the kind of backflip she hadn't performed since she was seven and playing on the bars at primary school. The digger gave a final hiss and the bucket dropped—the hydraulics had lost pressure. One of Belle's shoulders gave an agonising pop and she let go and fell onto the dented metal of the cab's roof.

There was a scuffling noise. William slid in beside the digger, looked at Belle, then thrust his hands through the window, clasped her under her arms and hauled her out. He dragged her away from the teetering machine. He used his cuff to clear the blood from her face. Then he grimaced and subsided till his forehead was touching the turf.

Belle tried to say 'Theresa' and the part of her tongue she'd bitten through flapped against her lower lip. Blood poured out over her chin. She drew her wounded tongue back into her mouth and closed it, kept still, breathed through her nostrils where blood was already drying and stiffening. She couldn't lift her right arm, so pointed with her left.

William looked, exclaimed, got up, and went to Theresa.

Jacob gave Sam some tweezers, angled the treatment room's magnifier, and set her to picking grit from the graze on Theresa's face.

Theresa was unconscious. Her right hip was coming out in black bruising and there was a long bloody slot in her right buttock where her heavy belt had been pulled into her flesh. The bike had caught on the empty belt clip where, in the early days, she used to fasten her gun. The bike had struck her and pulled her with it for a moment. Her pelvis wasn't broken—as far as Jacob could tell—but he wouldn't really know what state she was in till she woke up and could tell him where it hurt, and what could and couldn't move.

Belle was sitting with Bub. He was holding a packet of frozen peas to her face. Jacob came over and asked Belle whether the Tramadol he'd given her had taken effect. She nodded. He had her open her mouth, and inspected her tongue. He warned her not to talk—she was going to have twenty-four hours on boiled water, and then be taking any nourishment though a straw. Jacob got Belle to brace against him, then he popped her shoulder back into joint. He gave Bub the sheet and some scissors and told him to make a sling.

Bub asked, 'How's William?'

'He can't run places,' Jacob said. 'I've told him.'

'I'll stay with him from now on,' Sam said.

'Well, actually, I need you to help find Warren. It's a division of labour thing.'

Belle made muffled, throat-only protests, and Jacob patted her leg. 'I can guess what you're trying to say,' he began, and had to look away from Belle because her eyes filled with tears. 'I'm going to give you a couple of sleeping pills and a good drink of water and send you to bed. You

392

have to give your tongue a chance to heal. Bub—'

Bub glowered.

'—you and Sam have to find Warren. We can't just abandon him. William can't exert himself. I shouldn't put this on Oscar, and right now I have to stay with Theresa. I can't leave her till she wakes up.'

'Okay, okay,' Bub said. 'Once Belle's asleep I'll go and look. But that fucker better pray that Sam finds him before I do.'

'Bub,' Jacob warned. 'He's still my friend.'

Belle grunted and slapped one hand on the tabletop. Bub realised what she wanted. He found a pad and pen and gave them to her. She wrote *Kakapo! Cats!* Then stabbed the pen into the paper several times and cried so hard her lips unsealed with a sticky ripping noise and a combination of saliva and blood clots dribbled out of her mouth.

Bub stared at her. His face emptied of expression. Then he said, 'It's okay, babe. I'll do whatever needs to be done.'

It was Sam who found Warren. She followed her wind to where he was. Her wind was being mild, she thought. Warren had summoned it, and it had come at speed, like a dog racing off to find a thing it has great hopes of— something to play with, or eat—something it then noses and rejects, before gambolling back to its master.

Warren was kneeling, defeated, in the disturbed leaves by the bloodstained tree where he'd found Dan and the balloon. When Sam came into the clearing the wind shifted from him and came over to her.

'Hello,' Sam said, to the wind.

Warren looked up. 'Hello.'

'Are you all right?' Sam said, this time to Warren.

'How could I possibly be?' Then, 'Don't bother answering.'

Sam said, 'My old ladies would always say "Can't complain", whenever I asked them how they were.' She then said to Warren what she'd always say to her old ladies. 'But is there anything I can do for you *right now*?'

'Well—I guess you could try listening to me for a change. Or rather you could make your pointless listening face, since you won't follow what I have to say.' Warren paused and looked suspicious. 'That is still *you*, isn't it?'

'Yes. I'm Samantha. You have to come back with me, Warren. We're all worried about you.'

'I don't believe it. There's a whole lot of other things you're more worried about. Same with *those* people.' He indicated the place where the balloon had landed.

Sam said, 'Jacob is very worried. He sent me.'

'Oh—so it's Jacob now.'

'What?' Sam was confused.

'It's Jacob who's in charge.'

'Why do you always talk about who's in charge? He's upset. I've found you, and you're all right. Come back with me, Warren. Jacob isn't angry.'

'Do you know why I did it? Pulled down the fence?'

Sam was quiet. Warren would tell her anyway. People never waited for her to say she was listening, they just told her what was on their minds.

Warren gestured around the clearing. 'Those kakapo are more important to the people out there than we are. And to Belle—the blameless Belle. When Bub brought in the feed, she looked happy. Dan was dead, and she looked happy. Imagine caring more about birds than people.'

'We just found the wrong balloon for us. One that was just for the kakapo.'

Warren started shouting at her. 'How thick can you be? There would have been messages with every balloon, if there were any at all! The people out there aren't stupid, they just don't care!'

Sam was a little alarmed by Warren—but she had been raged at by unhappy and confused rest home residents, so she did what she always did when dealing with them; she was firm, and gently scolding. 'Now now, that's quite enough of that,' she said.

The wind thought it wasn't enough. Sam could feel its attention wandering. It was passing back and forth through Warren and pushing him, like a cat bored and disgusted by a half-dead mouse. Sam was so puzzled by its behaviour that she said out loud, to Warren, 'What's wrong with your feelings?'

Then the wind suddenly gave a seismic twitch and began again with its momentous revolutions as Bub ran into the clearing.

'I'm okay,' Sam said. 'Warren is just cross.' Then, 'Bub. You shouldn't get overexcited.'

Warren retreated to the bloodstained tree. Sam saw that the blood seemed to be running upward. Then she realised it wasn't blood—the blood had long since dried. It was a thick, glistening column of ants trooping up the tree trunk, to a dense, black gathering where the crusted blood and other matter was. The ants exploded away from Warren as he backed against them, then, in their confusion, began to climb into his collar and hair.

Bub advanced on Warren, stood over him, and raised his fist. It was only a threat, but Warren began to shout. 'Yes, why not?' He was weeping with fury. 'I always knew it would come to this—you fucking bashing me!'

'What do you mean?' Bub's anger was mounting. 'Why specially me?' Bub grabbed the front of Warren's shirt and shook him, thumping him back against the tree trunk.

'That's right!' Warren shouted. 'I made your girlfriend cry. That's all it takes for you, isn't it? But when you were carrying bodies, I was too. What did Belle do? She carried a mop!'

Bub continued to shake Warren, really angry now. 'It's weeks since the burials, and all you've done since is climb in a bottle, and make Jacob miserable! And what do you mean saying "my girlfriend" as if Belle isn't someone in herself? She's gutted! She's asked me to kill all the cats, for Christ's sakes. The poor cats.' Bub began to cry too. He slammed Warren hard into the tree, and then dropped him. Warren slumped, his head lolling.

Sam lunged at Bub and seized his arm. She pleaded with him to stop, and he did step back. He was up on his toes. It was as if he couldn't set his heels down. His fists were clenched and bouncing. To Sam it looked as if Bub wanted more to show Warren that he wanted to hit him, than actually do it. She relaxed a little. She tried to think of something to say to coax Bub away. He'd calm down. He was Bub. Bub was good.

But then Bub looked at Warren and seemed to see something further to offend him. He hauled off and kicked Warren once, hard, then flicked Sam off his arm. She fell back onto the mussed ground. She was looking up at the sky, past leaves interleaved with leaf shadows, a pattern in many shades of green. She heard the rubbery impact of Bub's boot on a fleshy portion of Warren's body. She thought how upset Jacob would be. She had to stop this. She needed to be stronger.

Bub heard Sam behind him. Her voice was a croak. 'No, no, no,' she said. 'That was supposed to make a difference.'

Warren was scrambling to safety, moving around the trunk of the tree. Bub followed him and swept his legs out from under him. Warren sprawled, and this time sensibly stayed down.

Bub checked behind him. Sam was curled up, gripping her guts. She was white, and her lips were grey. Bub was positive he'd only knocked her off-balance. He wouldn't have hurt her.

Then he saw what was happening. 'Oh Jesus,' he said and, paying no further attention to the felled Warren, he scooped Sam up and sprinted off through the forest.

When Bub came running with Sam, shouting that she'd switched over and needed help, Jacob didn't pause to ask questions. Once they had Sam settled in her room, Jacob dismissed Bub and went straight to work, treating Sam with the atropine eye drops and alupent. He kept his finger on her pulse for a whole three hours, and felt it gradually pick up its pace. Then he just sat with her.

Oscar appeared with coffee and pot noodles. Jacob asked him whether there was any sign of Warren.

Oscar shook his head. 'And Bub has gone to sleep, so I can't ask. But Bub would have said if he'd found Warren, right?'

Jacob looked at Sam. 'Maybe Sam saw him.'

'How long till she wakes up?'

'I don't want to disturb her,' Jacob said. 'It can wait.'

Bub woke with a start. He dropped Belle's hand. They'd been holding hands, and he was in a chair by her bed. The curtains weren't drawn, and the window glass was black.

Belle was fast asleep, on her back. She'd been sleeping fitfully—every time she turned over a jolt of pain from her shoulder would wake her. Jacob had given her some more painkillers an hour ago, and she was finally far down, motionless, breathing deeply and peacefully.

Bub left Belle, quietly closing the bedroom door. He wanted to see whether Warren had dared to come back. He wouldn't, Bub thought. He'd be holed up in some abandoned house, working his way through its liquor cabinet and feeling aggrieved.

Bub was a little worried about Warren—and guilty that he hadn't done as Jacob had charged and brought the man back into the fold. 'It's us against *it*,' Jacob had reminded Bub. 'We can't let it divide us.'

Fine, thought Bub. Warren could be drunk all the time, dice with his health, OD, refuse to listen to any of his friends' advice and finally stuff up big time, but he, Bub, was supposed to behave with unwavering altruism.

Bub went to find Jacob, but he found William instead, sitting by Sam's bed. 'Jacob is with Theresa,' William said, 'seeing if she's got movement in all the right places. She woke up.'

Bub went and watched Jacob and Theresa. She was swivelling her feet and pressing back on Jacob's hands as he put pressure on her toes. She was saying, 'I don't think anything's broken. I have the bones of a horse.' She tried to smile at Bub, then aborted the smile when the scabs on her cheek rumpled. 'How's Belle?'

'She's fast asleep,' Bub said.

'I've got her rinsing her mouth every few hours with warm salt water. I don't know what else to do.' Jacob looked drawn with worry. He asked Bub whether Warren had turned up.

Bub shook his head.

'Was there no sign of him?'

Bub tried to keep a straight face. 'I saw him. Then Sam got into difficulties, and I had to see to her instead.'

Jacob made a list of who was fully fit. 'Just you, me, and Oscar. And I have to stay with my patients. I blinked with Curtis. I'm not going to with Belle and Theresa. I need you to go looking for Warren again tomorrow, Bub. You and Oscar have to do it. You can split up. You have to persuade him to come back and be looked after. He's not safe out there alone.'

'No one gets left behind,' Theresa growled, like someone in the movies. Then, 'Can you mend the fence?'

Bub said, 'I'll have to try patching it somehow. But Belle wants me to deal with the cats.'

Theresa was horrified. 'You mean kill them? No!'

'Belle and I used to count them when we fed them, and their numbers were never stable. We wondered if they were picking and choosing which feeding spot to come to. But then we figured some were just too freaked out by things and had gone feral. And you know we hear them fighting at night—territorial disputes from all quarters.'

'But—no,' Theresa said. 'She can't ask anyone to do that.'

'She's right, Theresa,' Bub said. 'I'd rather poke out my own eyes than kill the cats—but Belle's right. It's the sort of decision the Department of Conservation makes all the time when it clears offshore islands of pests, or culls Kaimanawa horses. You do know that absolutely everything that isn't indigenous is here on sufferance? It's just that now—here— there's no one else to do the dirty work we expect done. It's not all that different from having to bury people.'

William arrived in the doorway. 'Raised voices,' he said. 'I think we're supposed to guard against that.'

'Get William to do it, Bub,' Jacob said. Then to William, 'Belle thinks it's necessary to kill the cats. And you're not soft-hearted.'

There was a silence, then, 'Okay. That's something I can do,' William said.

'You can fix yourself later,' Jacob said, and touched his own heart.

Bub was thinking about the cats, in their daily clusters, their eager trotting, and pert tails, and tiptoe smooching.

'But what about the rats?' Theresa said. 'Don't the cats keep the rats down? Aren't the rats just as dangerous to the kakapo?'

'To eggs and chicks, not adult birds,' Bub said. 'That's my understanding. And there are no eggs or chicks at the moment.'

Theresa asked whether anyone had been watching for messages.

'Oscar's on night duty. So—actually—he'll be sleeping tomorrow. He won't be any use looking for Warren.'

'There aren't enough of us now to run our lives,' William said. 'To mend fences, watch the skies, defend the nests, and bring black sheep back into the fold—to make an archetypal list.'

Bub promised Jacob he'd spend a couple of hours looking for Warren, starting as soon as it was light. And later in the afternoon, when Oscar was up, they could try to mend the fence.

William listened as Bub organised himself and made promises to Jacob. Theresa was insisting that she could help. Surely she could do something. No one spoke to him again and he understood that he'd been handed the job of getting rid of the cats, and they didn't want to hear about it. Now they wouldn't even look at him. It wasn't that he was a pariah— more like a condemned man, or a sacrifice. He was in some kind of sacred space. But the task was a technical as well as a moral one, and William didn't have the first idea about how to kill cats. He was thinking poison, because they were numerous, and wary, and individualistic, and agile. He'd seen them being fed, and knew they didn't all crowd in at once. There was a hierarchy, and some animals waited till the others had finished. Anything fast-acting would warn them. Anything slower acting and he'd never be sure it had worked.

He went downstairs and peered into the filing cabinet in the manager's office at Jacob's collection of medications, many of which had doses dangerous to humans. But which drug, and how much would he need, and how could he disguise its taste?

William closed the drawer, turned out the light, and went to the kitchen.

The range had browned ripples of burned egg on its elements, and the counter top was clouded. As William stood there he realised he'd come as if to consult Holly's ghost. Holly had chosen oleander because for some reason she happened to know that, now and then, people accidentally poisoned themselves with that ordinary garden plant. William wondered was there anything that regularly, accidentally, poisoned cats? Since he lived in California, he knew oleanders were poisonous, but here he was, surrounded by unfamiliar plants.

William filled the electric kettle and switched it on. He listened to the clatter as water turned to steam right by the element. Then it settled to boil. He spooned camomile tea leaves into a small glass teapot. He thought about his own kitchen—the one he never cooked in. He saw himself cutting up melon for breakfast. He'd arrange it on a plate, rinse the knife and the chopping board, and that was all the use he'd make of his kitchen. He saw his espresso machine. He saw a bottle of red wine standing on his glass counter top. His house was empty, the city was humming around him. Then he was in the street hurrying to the intersection to catch the F train. He was going out to eat home cooking. He got off midtown and walked towards the bay. He pressed the buzzer to his friend's apartment. She released the lock and sent the elevator down to him. She opened her door. He kissed her and gave her the flowers he'd bought on Stockton Street. He watched her use her kitchen scissors to snip the stamen and sepals from the lilies. Saffron pollen spread softly and transparently on the film of water at the bottom of her sink. She would put the lilies up high to keep them from her

401

cats, but even then the stamens would eventually fall and then the pollen would be everywhere. 'So it's better just to cut them off,' she said.

'What does lily pollen do to cats?' he asked.

'Liver failure, I think.'

Liver failure was gradual and insidious. The cats would sicken and stay put. They'd crawl under houses, hide, die.

William had never plotted to kill anything. He'd only been fatally forgetful, leaving his cousins out in the freezing weather. How many times, in his head, had he gone back into the house to pull a rug off the couch, a quilt off the bed, to cover them? He'd do it over and over whenever he was tired or unhappy—he'd take a minute, go back, and find something to keep them warm.

The accident had happened three weeks before his ninth birthday. When that birthday came he was in a foster home. He didn't tell anyone. Several years later the attentive foster parents took note of the birthday and there was a party and presents and a cake, and William—who loved to be the centre of attention—felt ashamed to be noticed. It was wrong to measure his progress away from that day. And yet here he was, still alive. Alive, and doing it again, pulling the quilt from his cousin's bed. Or—he'd go back in the middle of the night and see that his drunken uncle had carried the barbecue indoors to keep the room cosy while they all went on drinking. He'd see it, and *do something*, and it would make a difference that he was outdoors when everyone else was indoors.

He was standing outside his uncle's house. His breath was fuming in the frozen air. Someone was calling him back in, as if they needed his heat. The mountains were on fire. The state trooper and the national guardsmen were waiting at the plastic-draped gate. 'Step in here, sir,' said the national guardsman. 'It's nice and cold in here.'

★

A slightly clammy hand dropped onto William's. He opened his eyes—they had been screwed shut—to see Sam's bony, blunt-tipped fingers. She was pressing down hard because she was using the kitchen counter to hold herself up. 'Don't,' she said.

The tea in the pot in front of William was deep yellow, stewed, and no longer steaming. William stayed still, his blood blowing in his ears. He knew that there was something else there in the kitchen with him and Sam. He couldn't feel it, but he knew she could, and that she'd got out of bed to investigate.

She was wearing only a man's T-shirt. Her feet were bare, and she was shivering. William pulled off his sweater and put it over her head, then left her to do the rest herself. He poured the tea into a cup and put it in the microwave to reheat. He said, 'Is it gone yet? The Wake?'

'It's back upstairs,' she said. 'It's leaning on someone, I'm not sure who. And I'm too tired to chase it from place to place.' Sam sat on one of the tall stools and put her feet up on another, between herself and William.

William took the cup from the microwave, warmed his hands for a moment, passed it to her, then gathered her toes between his warmed palms.

She said, 'Whatever you were feeling, you have to not feel it any more. The Wake had a real taste for it.'

The next morning Bub and Sam went out in different directions to look for Warren. It was Bub who found him.

Warren was lying where Bub had left him. He had crawled to the far side of the sullied tree and was slumped face down, his shoulder against the trunk, his knees tucked under him, and one ear pressed to the pine needles, as if he was listening for footfalls. His face was piebald with patches of dark blood. His eyes were open, and dull, their surfaces dry.

Bub stood with both hands clamped over his mouth, stifling sounds that wanted to escape him and be heard— noises of anguish. For a few minutes all he felt was a scalding shock. This was followed by a feeling that Bub knew he'd have from now on, would have all his life, in the foreground of every other feeling. It was shame. He had done this. He'd lost control of himself, and his malice had made his hands and feet so insensitive that he couldn't feel and see what he was doing, the violence he was doing. He wanted to say to Warren, 'But I didn't hit you that hard.' But he must have— because there was the blood, crusted thick on the back of Warren's head. The last time Bub knocked him down Warren must have cracked his skull. The bunched tree-roots near Warren's head were blood-smeared.

Bub was frozen with horror. He had killed Warren. Had killed his friend's friend. He had made a corpse. He had made *another corpse*. For a long period he paced, and pulled at his hair, and made futile wishes. He wanted to absent himself, but he kept being where he was, circling that poor body.

Bub was guilty, so he was wary too, and when he heard someone coming it took all his strength not to flee. He knew he couldn't do that. He wanted what he had, so he was going back, to the others, to Belle, to confess and be judged. There wasn't any way around it.

Myr came into the clearing. He stopped at a respectful distance.

Bub found himself pointing inarticulately at the hunched body. He pointed, and looked at Myr with swimming eyes. He scrubbed his face with his palms.

Myr's silence must be sympathy. It was a captivating and resilient silence, and it seemed to work on Bub, to slow his agitated stamping, to make him stop and listen.

Myr said, 'Will you want to bury him in your small graveyard?'

This remark struck Bub to his knees. He wrapped his arms around his head and wept. He sobbed and wheezed.

'I've seen this before,' Myr said, gentle. 'You begin by needing your own dead near you—then feel outnumbered by graves.'

Bub ground his knuckles into his hot eye sockets and tried to stop weeping.

'You don't want to be the one to break the bad news,' Myr said.

It was then that Bub realised that Myr had no idea he was crying because he was culpable. Myr thought Bub was simply grief-stricken, and unready to tell the others that they'd lost yet another of their number.

'Did you quarrel with him?' Myr asked. 'He was off on his own.'

Bub nodded, then lied, 'We quarrelled with him.'

There was a period of stillness disturbed only by Bub's shuddering breathing. Then Myr said, 'Perhaps it would be kinder if your friends could think that this man has only shunned them and hidden himself.'

Bub stopped sniffing and blearily regarded Myr.

'It will only work if you can dissemble,' Myr said.

Bub opened his hands to gesture at Warren's body.

'Yes. We'll have to bury him,' Myr said. Then, 'Would that help, do you think? Would that make their lives more tolerable?'

Bub bit his lip. He tried to keep his face still. Myr really seemed not to suspect him. He was offering to help Bub quietly dispose of the body, so that the others could go on imagining that Warren was still alive.

Would that be better? If Bub postponed his confession he could go on, for a time, being what the remaining survivors needed him to be—steady, reliable, strong.

'What do you say?'

Bub managed to nod.

Myr told Bub that he'd fetch what they needed. He told him to wait, and strode away through the trees.

Bub sat down and tried to collect himself. This was his first test, and it was an easy one, he told himself. He would simply do what he was told. It didn't seem to have crossed Myr's mind that he'd killed Warren. But, of course, Myr would expect Bub to be upset. Later, Bub knew, he'd have to pass harder tests. He'd be under closer scrutiny. He'd have to keep up a pretence that Warren was alive. He'd have to continue searching for Warren, and act anxious, but not too anxious, since everyone knew he was angry at Warren. And he'd have to continue to bad-mouth Warren, because to stop altogether would be suspicious.

Bub's thoughts went around in little self-consuming circles. Several times he was roused, startled by a sound— two branches knocking together, the thud of a falling pine cone. He found himself talking, telling Warren off. 'Why did you have to say you expected me to hit you?' he whispered. 'Why did you have to do that? And why didn't you have any sympathy for Belle?' His accusations got away on him, till he felt like a mountain climber trying to sprint down a slope of shale ahead of a landslide. The words would merge soon into some hoarse, senseless noise. He found himself glaring resentfully at Warren and asking why he'd had to *die*? Why did he have to go and do a thing like that?

Oscar was cycling to his house to feed Lucy. On the way he spotted William in an overgrown garden, scissors in hand. Oscar squeezed his brakes and dropped his feet onto the road. 'What are you doing?'

'Gathering a remedy. What about you?'

'I'm going to feed Lucy.'

William pulled a plastic bag out of his pocket and positioned its opening under an orange lily. 'Do you have a cat cage, Oscar?'

'Yes.'

'Bring your cat to the spa. You can keep her in your room.'

Oscar was puzzled and alarmed. To him any change in routine signalled calamity. Every day the adults were more secretive and peremptory. He said, 'Lucy's happy where she is.'

'Because the predator-proof fence is broken we have to get rid of all the cats. And Lucy is going to have to stay indoors.'

'Oh,' said Oscar.

When he was sick and Myr was seeing to him, Myr had said something about how his people wondered whether these monsters weren't—what was it he'd said?—'a provision for the end of the universe'. Oscar had been thinking about that word 'provision'. If something was a provision then someone had provided it. Like God. Oscar thought that this made Myr's people's ideas seem religious rather than scientific— and less likely to be true. He hadn't been at the meeting where the adults had talked about the monster and the man in black, but they'd been yelling, and it was impossible not to pick stuff up. But since then, Oscar had been so busy thinking about the end of the universe that he hadn't thought too hard about what he'd actually overhead—that the Wake wouldn't leave till there was nothing left for it to eat, that it would only go once they were all dead.

Now he found himself thinking about it. The kakapo had always been Belle's business. But William had said 'we have to', which meant that all of them were now the birds' custodians, and that it was their responsibility to make sure the kakapo survived the breach in the predator-proof fence until the other barrier—the No-Go—was gone.

Right up until this moment Oscar had felt safe—sort of. He'd felt he was behind a last line of defence, and all the adults had ranged themselves along it, in front of him. He'd gone on feeling that despite what Holly had tried to do, because he knew she'd meant, in her crazy way, to save him. But watching William snip pollen-furred stamens and sepals from the centre of the tiger lilies, Oscar realised the line had moved, and that there were now no people in the preserve—only endangered birds.

William fastened a twist tie around the bag and slipped it into his pocket. 'Go on, Oscar, get your cat. Or—do you need help carrying her?'

'No. She's little.'

William made shooing motions.

Oscar pushed off and rode away.

Bub discovered that the arboretum had a fairytale forest on one of its borders. He was there, in the twilight, following a line on the forest floor, the mark of something dragged, something insubstantial, for the disturbed leaf litter wasn't gouged down to rot, only scuffed, its top layer parted. The line meandered through the trees.

Was the forest thickening, or was night on its way?

Up ahead there came a sound, a light, metallic rattle. Bub caught up with the shadowy figure ploughing the shadow. It was Myr, dragging a long-handled shovel. They had been together—but Bub had forgotten it. They were looking for a place to bury the body. Bub took the shovel from Myr. Its concave side was dry and unused, the green anti-rust coating unmarked. Bub turned it over. Its convex side was wet and dark, and when Bub gave Myr a wounded look, Myr said, 'That's not going to get us anywhere.'

Bub woke up. He was lying beside Belle. The lights were low, the windows black. Belle had hold of him; his shirt front was bunched in her hand, as if she knew he'd get up before she woke. How did she know that? He hadn't yet begun to avoid speaking to her. But that was what it was going to be like. Bub knew that if he talked to Belle eventually he'd be moved to tell her that it was her fault too, and that Warren had been right, her value system was skewed. People *were* more important than kakapo. Bub hadn't cared about the kakapo, had only cared that Warren had injured her. But Warren hurt her by accident, while acting more in grief than malice, and *if only* Belle hadn't made such a meal of her responsibility.

Bub looked at Belle's sleeping face and felt cool towards her, and contaminated himself.

The kitchen. Morning. Jacob was waiting for the lemonade he'd boiled to cool. He'd put some into ice trays for later and would take the rest up to Belle, for her breakfast. In a few days her tongue might be able to handle soup, or some of that cardboard-and-vanilla flavoured instant yoghurt they were eating now.

William was at the central bench. He emptied eight big cans of chunky beef-and-gravy cat food into a container, and produced a plastic bag from his pocket.

Jacob looked away. He rattled the spoon in the pot, pushing air into the cooling liquid.

William was mixing and mashing. Jacob heard the container sealed, then the rustle and zip of William's backpack. William washed the bowl and fork, and put them on the draining board. Then he left. Jacob heard the solid sound of the Mercedes door closing, then the whisper of its engine.

Jacob decanted the lemonade into a large mug, and then took it and a wrapped straw upstairs.

Belle was out of bed and had showered. She produced

a writing pad and pen from the pocket of her robe, and wrote: *I can't manage to wash my hair yet. Should I be babying my shoulder?*

'To be on the safe side,' Jacob said. He gave her the lemonade and sat down with her on the edge of the bed. 'Where's Bub?'

Belle gestured at the bedclothes, both sides were rumpled. Then she shrugged her good shoulder.

Jacob said, 'He's looking for Warren. He spelled me for a little while when I took Warren's car and criss-crossed town calling. Warren's ignoring us. He's still angry. After Dan's funeral we had an argument. I didn't listen to him.' For a moment he brooded. 'I was *tired* of listening to him.'

Belle opened her mouth to speak, and dribbled the lemonade back into her cup. Blood feathered in the liquid and turned it pink.

'Sorry, I'll leave you to concentrate on that. I'll bring the rest up in a jug and you can just keep topping up. You must be pretty hungry.'

Belle nodded.

'Try to stay in bed. Conserve your energy. That'll help.' Jacob got up. 'I'll go see what Kate wants for breakfast. She's been a bit off-colour.'

Kate was dead. Her body was undisturbed. Her skin was cool, her cheeks sunken, her nose sharp. Her wristwatch was on the nightstand, ticking. Next to it was a book, face down, a fat novel, with perhaps seventy pages to go. Beside the book were her reading glasses.

Jacob took all this in, and got down on his knees at the bedside. He touched Kate's forehead again, this time in blessing. She had gone quietly. She was reading a book, and had taken off her glasses, turned off the bedside lamp, and gone to sleep. Nothing had touched her, or taken her.

Jacob put his head down on the bed and cried, in grief, and gratitude.

The cats came, and coalesced into a furry flood on the wave-scoured concrete of the boat ramp. They gathered at William's feet, looking up at him, and their triangular faces were like open flowers. Some were so eager they trembled. Or perhaps it was simply emotion. They'd had homes, and their own people, and meal times—for people and for cats. Now *this* was all they had, and when it arrived it was being-not-forgotten that made them tremble.

William went down past the high tide mark, shuffling, because the cats kept diving at his legs. He opened the container and tipped out a third of the mix. The cats hunched, and showed him their sharp shoulder blades and quivering tails. They jostled and settled. William moved on and poured out another pile of the saffron-tinted meat, and then another. He rinsed the container in the sea—then let it go and watched it drift away. He left the clustered animals and walked back along the shore. He sat down, and cleaned his hands with warm, dry sand.

Oscar fixed himself something to eat. It was 7pm and there wasn't any dinner. He ate in his room. Lucy purred and kneaded, and gave his plate a cursory lick, then jumped down and continued to roam. She sat on the back of the armchair and gazed out the window, then got down and sniffed the gap under the door, then went on nosing the skirting, and the wardrobe. She cried at the corners of the bathroom, and knocked things off shelves.

Finally Oscar had had enough—he left her and went to prowl about the spa himself.

Kate's room was closed and unlit—no one was keeping a

411

vigil with her body. Jacob had dug only half her grave. He'd had to stop because his hands were blistered.

Sam was standing at William's door. When Oscar went by she turned to look at him—her expression cold. She was concentrating on something, and he was irrelevant.

Belle was dozing. When Oscar looked in on her she started and raised her head from the pillow. Then she looked disappointed. She waved, 'Hi,' and her eyes slid away from his.

'Bub's not here?' Oscar said.

Belle shook her head.

Oscar went downstairs. He found Bub sitting by himself in the dark atrium, his elbows on his knees, hands clasped, head bowed.

Oscar said, 'I think Belle is expecting you.'

Bub raised his face. The twilight made his skin grey. He nodded, and got up slowly and stiffly, and trudged to the stairs.

Oscar looked out the door and saw the rectangle of the latest grave, now deep enough to fill up with shadow. The spade had been left thrust upright in the piled earth.

Oscar found Jacob and Theresa on the terrace, Theresa sitting rigid, wrapped in a rug and bolstered by cushions.

Jacob was holding a mug. It was steaming. Oscar looked at the steam and his eyes teared up. The steam seemed like a last flag, still flying. That Jacob had made himself a hot drink, and had made Theresa comfortable, that was good. *Something was still good.*

Oscar sat down with them. Theresa turned her bruised face and gave him a little smile. Then they just sat, the three of them, no one saying anything.

After a time Oscar said, 'It isn't overcast.'

'No. It isn't,' said Jacob.

'So they don't have the option of bouncing light off clouds.'

'That's right.'

'Then what are you watching for?'

'For balloons,' said Theresa. 'For lights in the town.'

'For Warren,' said Jacob.

Theresa said she should go back to bed. She was stiffening up, hurting more today than she had the day before.

Jacob said he'd give her something for nerve pain; it would make her sleep. He helped her up and they went away together.

The cup was still steaming.

Jacob had given Theresa two amitriptyline tablets, and she couldn't open her eyes. She felt flattened, a paper-thin woman floating just under the surface of a still pool. She wasn't alone. Now and then, she could hear pages turning. Her lips were stuck to her teeth. She wanted to ask for a drink but couldn't stir even to do that.

The slight, intermittent sound kept repeating—the faint fingertip rasp and flap of pages. Then Theresa heard a voice. Sam. 'Don't you ever read thrillers, or magazines?'

'Sure, for the solution. But wasn't it you who was asking for a book like a boat?'

It was William who was sitting with her. Sam had just come into the room. There was the sound of furniture being dragged, and William said, 'You don't have to sit all the way over there.'

Sam: 'That book you recommended wasn't really a boat for an atheist.' A pause. 'Why did you pray with Jacob? Bub thinks you're only hedging your bets.'

'Bub has principles and sticks to them. Praying with Jacob is something I can do for him. I'd do anything for that guy. He's a good person.' Pause. 'So is your sister.'

'I know.'

'Your sister once said to me—about you—"Sam is my

You". One of her old ladies had told her that everyone has a You.'

'I think that "You" is the same as the "Thou" in the twenty-third Psalm, "Yea though I walk through the valley of the shadow of death I shall fear no evil, for Thou art with me".'

'I think the Thou in the twenty-third Psalm is supposed to be God.'

'Yes, but,' Sam said, and then, after a long pause, 'Bub is Belle's Thou.'

Silence. Theresa's ears were straining so hard that her mouth filled with saliva and her cheeks came unstuck. She issued an involuntarily spluttering wheeze.

'Theresa?' William said.

Theresa hushed. The sine waves behind her eyelids became bolder and greener.

Sam said, 'My sister can be your You as well as mine.'

'Why do I feel like you're telling me I'm not your business?'

'You are my business, William. But you want me to say—'

'How could you possibly imagine what I want you to say?'

'You want me to say, *Take this cup from me.*' Sam's voice lifted to override his. 'That's what you want. You think that, because I have appetite, I must want to live. You think I'm like my sister, only more sophisticated. But we were never alike. My sister could tolerate the secrecy, and the discontinuity, and the fact that her life made no sense. I couldn't. But look—can't you see?—it turns out that it wasn't a life, it was a destiny.'

Theresa tried to open her mouth. She wanted to tell Sam that she *did* have a life, that she was distinct, that there were plenty of people walking around who might remember a person's birthday but who never showed anything more than a ceremonial interest in others, and therefore had nothing much going on inside them. Life wasn't a set of social functions—like being a cop, or a caregiver, or a big shot lawyer. It wasn't a CV. It wasn't influence—how many people listened to what you had to say. It wasn't even having been sometime the hapless witness to one of the big moments of history and therefore having a gosh-how-amazing biography. Life was the other stuff, like not being sad in front of someone you're grieving for; or kneeling to pray to a God you don't believe in to make a believer easier in their heart; or not giving your family the terrible truth they might think they're owed, but knitting the grandkids hats instead; it was knowing enough to say that you *wouldn't* say, 'Take this cup from me'. Because that's what Sam meant. She meant, 'This is my cup. *My cup runneth over.*' And she had said, 'You are my business, William,' because she meant to save him. She'd figured something out and was going to try somehow to save them all.

Theresa made a noise, a sticky grunt.

William took her hand. He said, 'Jacob was pretty confident about the dose, but you've been down for hours.'

Sam said. 'Some people are sensitive to amitriptyline.'

William lifted Theresa and put the rim of a glass to her lips. She sipped, and croaked out her thanks. He laid her down, and she felt herself slipping—everything flattening out once more. 'You don't have to sit with me,' she said.

'No one likes it downstairs any more,' Sam said. 'We are all upstairs. Just sitting.'

'What time is it?'

'Seven,' William said.

Theresa opened her eyes. The light bristled with rainbows.

'Christmas Eve,' Sam added.

Theresa said, 'The man in black removed the messages from the balloon.' She was certain she was right as soon as she heard herself say it. It seemed her brain had been busy

415

while she was semiconscious, and had made the necessary leap of intuition.

Sam said, 'That makes sense.' She thought for a bit. 'Myr told me that, with other survivors, he'd tried everything. He'd stayed away from them, he'd helped them, and he even killed them himself.'

'Christ!' said William. 'The sound I heard in the forest the night I chased him was the sound of a balloon coming in across the treetops. And he led me away from it!'

'He's trying to kill us by killing our hope,' Theresa said. Then she fixed her gaze sternly, if blearily, on William. 'Because he at least understands the concept of morale.'

'I've been cultivating a healthy cynicism.'

'You were cynical, but that didn't help you work out what he was up to.'

'You're the cop. You're supposed to work things out.'

Sam said, 'It's been blowing quite hard from the northwest for ages. Most of the balloons they sent would have blown right over. If more had made it we would have got to at least one before Myr did. What he's doing—it's not much of a plan.'

'If that's *all* he's doing,' William said.

'No one failed us,' Theresa said. 'That's the point. Dan shouldn't have despaired.' Then, 'Sam, can you go and talk to Myr? Persuade him to give us our messages. And—also—maybe can you tell him we have reason to hope?'

William wondered what they were thinking—the two women, looking so knowingly at each other. It was a very deep communication, and it didn't include him.

Finally, Sam said, 'Yes. I'll do what I can.'

★

The following morning Sam got up long before everyone else. She showered, and blow-dried her long wavy hair. She put on her designer blouse, boyfriend jeans, and pastel pink ballet flats. She left her room and pushed Oscar's door open. The tongue of its lock was still retracted, a lump under layers of scuffed gaffer tape. Sam crept into the room.

Oscar was curled up with the covers over his head. His cat was tucked neatly in the crook of his legs. Oscar didn't stir—he was in the deep, competent sleep of a teenager's morning. Lucy gave a little chirp when Sam picked her up, but she didn't struggle.

In the kitchen Sam found two chickens thawing in the refrigerator. Someone had remembered Christmas— probably Jacob. He'd cleaned the kitchen too. Sam noticed this, and it only hardened her resolve. She didn't really know Jacob, but here was everything she needed to know. Jacob was heart-struck, but deeply civilised. Sam thought about the smug misanthropists who like to claim that civilisation is a thin veneer. They didn't know people.

Sam sliced a leg off the smaller of the two chickens, and carefully pared the icy meat from the bone. She cut the meat up, put it on a saucer, and filled the saucer with warm water to thaw the ice. Then she drained the water off again, and put the plate down for Lucy.

Lucy gobbled her food, settling back onto her haunches only when the plate was nearly empty. She'd had personal service all these months, but still acted as though she might be in competition with another cat.

When Lucy was done, Sam carried her outside. She put the cat down, then stamped her foot. Lucy laid her ears back and streaked off under the oleanders beyond the graves. There she crouched and glowered at Sam.

The morning was a little cool, so Sam went back for the cashmere shawl she'd stolen. Then she set off in search of Myr.

It was another overcast day, and it had been blowing. The sea, in a haze of water vapour, and chilly, looked like an image on Sam's computer's default media player a second before it made its adjustments for more light—there was an even fog over the seascape, like a view through sheer blinds.

Sam made her way through the streets to the paved walkway by the beach. She watched a shag upturn itself and slip into a smooth swell. Foam was making a tattered lacework on the rocks of Matarau Point.

Sam walked along to her bach and let herself in. There were flies in the living room. Bub and Belle hadn't done the dishes after their last meal. Sam filled the sink with hot water and a splash of detergent—then only washed one knife, an oyster knife with a strong blade. She used a fresh dish towel to dry it, and then slipped it, handle up, into the back pocket of her jeans.

She stood for a time and looked around. The living room had once been their bedroom—hers and her sister's. Back then there were net curtains on the front windows. The kowhai at the window was smaller then, and its trunk wasn't wrapped in tattered bandages of lichen. Sam thought about the kowhai's age and stroked her own smooth cheek.

She left her bach and walked to the end of Matarau Point to look back at Kahukura. She checked for house lights. The house where Myr had kept her prisoner was dark, but beyond that, in a ten-year-old subdivision—a development of only four streets to the northeast of Stanislaw's Reserve—one house was lit up like a beacon.

Sam walked back the way she'd come. She wished for the sun—even the smeared and melting star that showed through the No-Go. Just ten minutes of full sunlight—as Kahukura would sometimes get even on those days when the clouds sat like a loose lid along the coast and the sun would only show for a few minutes as it came up, and for half an hour as it went down.

The pohutukawa at the base of the point were coming into bloom, glossy and rain-washed. The biggest tree was in full flower, crimson, plush, sombre, and godlike. Sam stood for a time beneath it, taking in its sour fruit perfume.

The new subdivision was a place Sam usually avoided. It was bleak and orderly. Its houses had plastered walls and glass balconies, and loomed to the boundaries of their decisively fenced sections. Homeowners' sovereignty had trumped privacy in those streets.

The garage of the lit house was open. Sam went in. There was an internal stairway. It came out facing a huge vase on a sideboard under a mirror. The vase was as big as the trunk of a small tree, and stood in a mulch of leathery, fallen petals.

Sam stumbled when she saw the vase. It was her sister who had gone through the houses, and so she wasn't used to this very particular dissolution—ruin in the province of the house-proud. The flower arrangement was dead, and mummified. The water in the vase had long since evaporated, and there was no residual dankness. The house was dry and clean—was one of those places whose occupants had been off at work when the Wake came.

In the mirror Sam saw Myr, approaching from some distance off, traversing a slot-like room. It was a large room, but with a disproportionately low ceiling and painted too uniform a colour.

Sam went to meet him, but then walked right by him. She wanted to get out onto the deck—out in the open air. Her time was shrinking, and there was still no sun.

Myr followed her. 'What do you want? Isn't it a little late now for us to finish our talk?'

'You mean to say that that ship has sailed?'

'I did expect to see you before now. The people I do tell normally have many questions. They don't believe me, and it takes a long time to satisfy them.'

'Satisfaction isn't a word I'd have used.'

419

'And your situation is unique. There is much we might have explored.'

Sam looked away. 'I know. You began to hope—and you hated that.' Then, 'This is what you do; squat in the more habitable houses.'

Myr waited, alert, to see what she'd say next.

'Or if it's winter and raining, and there's no shelter, I suppose you just kill all the survivors to hasten the Wake on to somewhere where you'll be more comfortable.'

Sam heard his sharp, indrawn breath. She wanted to look at the view, but felt uneasy about turning her back on him. Fearing for her safety rather than her sanity was a strange experience for Sam. But, then again, this was the first time she'd ever felt she really had something to live for. She said, 'We know you removed the messages from the one balloon we managed to find.'

He didn't respond.

The deck looked across Kahukura beach, past the headland of the shoreline reserve, and out to sea. The cove where the bottles collected was clearly visible, and Sam could make out a blur of yellow on the beach there, a bundle of nylon rope. Sam made a guess. 'And I know you sabotaged our rope ladder.'

'You watched me do it,' he said.

'Didn't my friends tell you that there were two of me?'

'They tried to explain something they called Dissociative Identity Disorder. There is one Sam under another, they said, neither Sam knowing what the other knows. I spoke to the other Sam when I was helping to care for your sick. The slow-witted Sam.'

So—that's what he thought was happening. *Still*. Good. She said, 'I left myself a note about the rope ladder. That's what I do.'

'Of course.' Myr hesitated, then said, with some warmth, 'With two distinct selves—two quite separate

420

consciousnesses—you might survive for a long time. You could keep shaking the Wake off.'

'And keep you company?'

'I haven't wanted company,' Myr said.

Sam looked out again, across the bay. The dull day was brightening, not because the cloud was clearing, but because the sun was higher and lighting the cloud. She widened her eyes and felt the light fall into the back of her skull. It filled her head. She said, 'You told me that we're all going to die. That there's no hope for any of us.'

'And now I'm telling you that you could last, Sam. You survived the Wake's first attack. No one does that. Your self-bewitchment must be very powerful.'

'But—as I said—we're all going to die.'

'Ah,' Myr said. 'You are thinking of the others.'

'Of course I am. But I might be thinking of you too. The Wake taxes you, Myr, even if it doesn't know you're there.'

Myr put a hand to his brow, a hand that trembled. The gesture was too habitually languid to activate his force field, but the tremors did. His fingers skittered on the nothing-visible centimetres above his skin. Sam watched this and thought how deliberate he must always have to be, and what vigilance and discipline that would require. And she thought that she couldn't know how human he was, but at least she could appreciate the demands of a life beyond the range of instinct and common sense.

Myr said, 'I'm tired. I admit it. And if I can't have your company, I want to hurry to the next place. I hope the next place is almost empty. This settlement stinks of death.'

She said, 'You've been a good soldier.'

Myr dropped his hand. He relaxed. He was giving things up.

She said, 'You know how the Wake works. It's your teacher. So—you've separated Bub from us by giving him a secret, a private sin.'

Myr was amazed. 'How do you know?'

'Warren wasn't badly hurt. I saw that much. But he hasn't come back, and Bub is slowly falling to pieces.'

'No, you're right, Warren wasn't hurt.' Myr spread his hands and looked at them. He said, 'I killed him.' Then, 'You poisoned the cats.'

'William did. It was deemed necessary. We want to protect the rare birds in the reserve. There are only one hundred and forty of them in the world.'

'So you understand necessity.'

Yes, Sam thought, it was necessary for William to feel the way he felt now. It had been necessary to let the cats go. And now she had to get Myr to come with her. She said, 'But Bub doesn't deserve to suffer like this. I want you to come with me and explain that it was you who killed Warren. He has to be made to believe it. He won't take my word for it.'

Myr watched her, wary. 'Have you tried to tell him what you've guessed?'

'Yes, of course,' Sam lied. 'I'm only here now because he won't believe me. None of them see me as very reliable. Come on, Myr, do this for us. We'll all be gone soon. At least let us go without imagined sins on our heads.'

Sam pulled the knife out of her back pocket, showed it to him, and told another lie. 'This is the knife the spa's chef used to cut off his own ears.'

Myr's gaze moved between the blade and her eyes.

'I've taken to carrying it to remind me of the extravagance of the Madness.' She stretched out her hand, twisting the little blade slowly in the air between them. She said, 'It's not as if I can hurt you with it.'

'No, you can't.'

She turned the knife so that the handle pointed his way. 'But now I want you to carry it.'

'Why?'

'In case something happens. In case you need it.'

He frowned. 'Why would I need a knife? Am I now suddenly talking to the simpler Sam? '

Sam shook her head. She returned the knife to her pocket and swivelled her hips to show him where she'd put it. 'Just remember, I have a knife in my back pocket.' Then, 'Come on. Follow me. You can't save us, but you can honour us by telling the truth.'

Belle was sitting on the terrace, sipping from a box of chocolate-flavoured UHT milk. When she saw Theresa coming she got up to rearrange the cushions on the seat opposite. Theresa was making slow progress, sliding her feet rather than lifting them. She said, droll, 'Having got myself up, I'm not going to immediately sit again, Belle.'

Bub was finishing Kate's grave. He and Jacob had been taking turns to dig. Kate's body was lying under the jacaranda on a flattened patch in the otherwise overgrown lawn, grass full of dandelions, daisies, and cow parsley. Jacob was sitting cross-legged by the body, sewing up Kate's shroud.

Belle noticed that Theresa had strapped on her gun. She gestured at it.

Theresa stuck her thumbs under her belt and hitched it up. 'I'm not going to be caught out again, like I was when Warren decided to tear down the fence.'

Belle produced her pad and pencil from her sling, and wrote, *But you wouldn't have shot him.* She tilted the pad to the light.

'No,' Theresa said. 'To shoot anyone I'd have had to decide it was absolutely necessary. And—you know—I'm not sure I have that kind of confidence anymore.'

Oscar tried to use reason. His reason told him that he should stop looking for Lucy this side of the spa. The dogs had been cooped up for days. They'd been fed and watered, but were lonely and restive. When Oscar came near their makeshift run, they erupted, barking, and threw themselves against its fence. They seemed to have forgotten who he was. They glared at the air above his head and snarled, their lips writhing over their bared teeth and black gums.

It stood to reason that, with all that barking, Lucy wouldn't be anywhere near them.

Oscar walked down to the feijoa hedge. He crouched, peered into its grey interior, and called. 'Lucy, Lucy, Lucy? Where are you?' Then, 'Come back.' His voice cracked. He fought the tears that were threatening to come and drown him.

He didn't even notice Sam walking through the gate, Myr behind her.

Sam looked very slight and pretty in her chiffon print blouse and ballet flats. Her instep showed when she lifted her feet. Myr had a graceful walk too, if odd. He never dropped his feet, but placed them carefully, with a minute hesitation before making contact with the ground—he'd learned to walk without activating his force field. Looking at him, Theresa thought, 'How could we ever have imagined he was like us?' And Sam too. She and the other Sam might be identical, though one was a little more worn, but this one had something joyful about her. She looked as if she thought she was bringing them all a splendid gift.

Theresa made her painful way to the terrace steps. Belle joined her, took her elbow and helped her down them. 'What on earth is wrong with those dogs?' Theresa said. 'Could you see to them?'

Belle nodded and set off towards the dog-run.

Sam stopped, and looked around. Her smile faded. 'Where's William?'

'I believe you have brought me here to talk to Bub,' said the man in black. 'Not William.'

'Yes. But wait a minute.'

The short walk to where Sam and Myr stood was quite difficult for Theresa. It wasn't that anything in particular hurt—only her tendons were tight, and her joints felt dry. She said, 'Sam—William won't have gone far. He's helping Oscar look for his cat. She got out.'

Sam cupped her hands around her mouth and shouted William's name.

Jacob said, 'Don't sound too urgent. Remember he's not supposed to hurry.'

Sam looked momentarily stricken, then she spotted Theresa's gun and settled into a calm—the kind of calm perhaps of someone who's been enjoying the view from the summit of a very high mountain and is beginning to think of the journey down. She said, 'Since you're wearing that, I hope you're prepared to use it.'

Theresa touched her gun. 'Use it on whom?' she said. Then, 'You were supposed to ask this guy about the messages.'

'He doesn't have them.'

'I'm afraid I destroyed them. But, yes, there were messages.' Myr said.

Bub threw his spade down and strode over.

Myr met Bub's eyes and said, 'I killed that man— Warren—it wasn't you. I killed him to further thin your ranks. And when I saw that you thought you had killed him, I let you think it.'

Bub's face filled with fury.

Jacob moaned, '*No.*' He sounded broken.

'There,' said Sam, her voice utterly calm.

In the short silence when everyone was digesting what Myr had said, and he was waiting respectfully for the anger he must expect and also know he was due, the silence of

425

Bub's long indrawn breath, a breath taken to fuel some kind of strenuous retaliatory act—in that hush Oscar could be heard, making his way along the boundary, weaving in and out of the oleanders, calling his cat. 'Come back, come back, come back.' He was in tears.

'And there,' said Sam.

Something strong, and something new: Bub's righteous fury, and the tears of a staunch and patient boy.

There. Take that.

The Wake was present already, circling Oscar like a cloud of carrion birds, and sometimes deviating to make a pass above Jacob as his needle went in and out of the seam that closed the cocoon of Kate's shroud. The Wake passed through Jacob and his blistered hands. He had washed his hands that morning before he peeled potatoes, oiled and salted them, pricked two lemons and pushed them into the cavities of the chickens, and then put the chickens in well-floured roasting bags, and into the oven. Bub had come into the kitchen while Jacob was working, and made some mordant remark about what Dan's kids might be having for their Christmas dinner.

The Wake was telling Sam all this—as if offering her reciprocal gifts. It was telling her that it loved her, because none of this would have as much savour if she hadn't helped it to understand how these people's raw feelings attached to feeling-things, to my sweetheart Belle, to Lucy, to Christmas, to how Kate had had to bury her own daughter, and the immensity of pity—for Kate, and for Warren—that Jacob could not get out of his head.

Belle returned from her futile mission to placate the dogs in time to see Bub in a rage, nose-to-nose with the man

426

in black. Myr's force field was pressing the blood out of the tip of Bub's nose, and making strange flats lozenges on his cheeks.

Jacob was standing over Kate's small shrouded form, watching Bub close on Myr. Jacob had both hands pressed to his head in the universal human gesture of distressed helplessness.

Belle saw that Sam's hands were raised too, like a saint's to bless, or a witch's to perform an incantation. Tears were pouring down her face, and she was saying something over and over, so slowly and clearly that, after a couple of repetitions, Belle was able to read her lips.

Belle suddenly understood why the dogs were howling. She pulled her pad out of her sling, extracted the pencil from the spiral binding, and wrote, *The Wake is here. Look at Sam.* She showed the pad to Theresa, who didn't look at it but only brushed Belle aside, impatiently knocking the pad out of her hands. It fell into a smoke bush by the terrace. Belle was too starkly scared to make any move to retrieve it.

The Wake was a hot whirlwind. First it smeared Sam with her own tears, then it sucked them away. It closed about her.

I will never see you again, Sam thought. *It's all right. Don't hurry. Mind your heart.*

She began to recite lines from a poem. She'd had it in her head for days, as if she'd been working herself up to say it to William. *'Come with me and be my love, and we will all the pleasures prove.'* She said it to the Wake instead. Her lonely outrage was a better offer. Better than Bub's righteous fury, or Oscar's grief. Better than anything. There was nothing like it anywhere.

Her sister's cot wasn't yet disassembled. It had air in it still. The mattress and bedding were on the floor, that bunny blanket Fa loved, on one side pink rabbits on a white field, and on the other white rabbits on pink.

This time Sam wasn't little, and standing in her own cot, watching. She was beside her uncle, colluding with him, helping him collapse Fa's cot. Together they transformed the place where her sister had slept from a container into a flat square; two layers of bars, so closely overlapping that even a toddler's fist wouldn't fit through the gaps. *Clack*—and it was closed.

I will never see you again.

I *know* never.

Fa.

Gentle Sam arrived, and found that, although she wasn't in the forest with Bub and Warren any more, Bub was still shouting. Why did her sister have to keep leaving her like this—in the middle of trouble? Bub shouted, and Sam's eardrums fluttered as if she was on a train in a tunnel and another train was passing alongside, pushing all the air out of its way.

There was something else wrong, apart from angry Bub. Sam looked around her and saw that she was standing in the long grass by the graves, and that there was another shrouded body, a small, narrow form. Jacob was standing beside it. He'd been stitching up the shroud but was now pulling the needle out of the pad of his hand.

Sam turned back to Bub in time to see him clash foreheads with the man in black. Bub lost his balance and staggered. The man in black stepped away and brought his hand up to touch the sore place. And then he slapped himself several times—each time a little more forcefully. He looked amazed. Then he turned his eyes to her. 'So, there really are two of you,' he said. Then, 'Come here.' He reached out his hands, palms up, friendly and coaxing.

One moment Bub was leaning on the solid transparency of Myr's force field, then suddenly there was nothing between him and the man, and Bub's skull thumped against Myr's.

Theresa watched this. She saw Myr discover that his force field had vanished. Her understanding followed his by only a few seconds.

The dogs stopped howling. Abruptly, as if someone had switched them off.

Theresa knew what had happened. Sam had somehow so captivated the Wake that she'd captured it, or the part of it that was in this world. Sam had then changed places with her sister. She'd gone away and taken the Wake with her. Theresa saw this much at least. She saw *a respite*.

William arrived, breathing hard, pale and anxious. He saw that Sam was in tears and hastened to her.

As William came, his arms open, Myr closed on Sam. Sam spun to face him, her expression fearful. 'You threw our ladder down the bluff,' she accused. 'I saw you do it.'

In the sharp and oddly motionless light Theresa glimpsed the knife handle poking out of Sam's back pocket. Her first thought was, 'How careless, that'll stick her if she sits down.' Then she realised that it was the knife that Myr wanted.

William had come. Sam saw that he looked worried. Then his face changed—just a little—but Sam noticed the change. She wasn't clever, but she always paid attention to other people's feelings. She saw that William was just a little bit less concerned than he had been a moment before, when he thought he was running to help her sister.

The sight was somehow too bright for Sam, or too dark for her. She put her hands over her eyes.

★

Theresa shouted, 'William! Sam has a knife!'

Then both men had their hands on it. Sam's pocket ripped. William tried to shove Sam out of the way, but Myr seized hold of her hair.

Then, because Myr had spared a hand for Sam, and because he hadn't any experience defending himself, William got the knife from him—the oyster knife with its short, sturdy blade. William's hand swept up and the knife skittered across Myr's collarbone, parting the pristine black cloth of his shirt, and making a bloody notch on the underside of his jaw. Then William's arm came around—it was all one movement—and he brought the knife in under Myr's sternum.

Despite everything she knew about him, Theresa was still surprised by the skill and decision of William's movements—and shocked as he clasped Myr to him, the knife between them. And shocked again that Bub, seeing the attack, darted in and rammed his elbow into the small of Myr's back, so that Myr's body bore down on the blade. Bub pushed, and then jumped back as if scorched—though it was perhaps only that he was propelled by disgust at what he'd done.

William and Bub acted so quickly, and in concert, that it struck Theresa that they'd been primed to do this for a very long time—to kill the man in black.

The dogs were quiet, but there was a sound of something coming from farther off—a faint pounding noise.

William was staring into Myr's face, and his fist worked between their bodies. Blood darkened the seam between each of his fingers, then spilled out, reddening his fist. Myr's knees buckled, and William let him go. Myr sagged to the ground. The bloodied knife remained in William's hand.

There was another sound, a growl and clanking as something heavy and slow tackled the sloped road on the far side of Matarau Point. They all stood frozen, listening to its progress.

Theresa made a sound herself then—a small noise of puzzled distress. She didn't understand her own unhappiness. It was as if she had been under the water and had made a long ascent and the surface was now in sight. She was going to be all right—so what was wrong?

Three helicopters were coming in across the bay, flying low and fast.

Myr was on his back, his eyes open and blinking. Blood bubbled between his lips. His mouth moved. He was inaudible above the *thump, thump* of the choppers. Theresa knelt by him and put her ear to his lips.

He whispered, 'You have to make sure.'

Theresa couldn't figure out what he meant. She met his gaze.

Myr tried again. 'You have to make sure it doesn't come back.' He coughed. Blood splashed across his cheek and the dark brilliance began to ebb from his face.

The helicopters thundered past. One came around and circled back to hang above them. The long grass of the lawn rippled, parted in many places, flashed white.

Everyone was looking up. Sam too, bewildered and astonished.

Then, all at once, Theresa understood what she had to do. She unclipped her holster, and took out her gun. She stepped back and took aim. She gave a wordless cry that still said, quite clearly, *It was always going to be like this*, and pulled the trigger.

Someone knocked her down. And when she opened her eyes, and peered out from beneath Bub's bulk, she saw William cradling Sam, holding her close to protect her ruined face.

The helicopters hovered, their rotors shaking the air.

PART NINE

The people who came and took charge said that they wanted to carry the survivors away separately. It was the principle of not putting all your eggs in one basket. Bub watched as everyone else conceded. But he refused to let go of Belle's hand. He glared stubbornly at the man trying to reason with him. The man had an American accent, regional rather than TV, and Bub could only make out about half of what was being said to him. It didn't help that he was having difficulty with facial expressions, as if he'd forgotten how to read the faces of people he didn't already know.

The soldier who strapped them into the helicopter called them 'Mr Lanagan' and 'Miz Greenbrook'. He offered them earplugs. Bub put in his own, then patted Belle's sling, where she'd been keeping her writing pad and pencil. Even if they couldn't hear, they could communicate. But Belle shook her head; she'd lost her pad.

The soldiers who had arrived in the helicopter closed its doors, and stayed on the ground themselves. The vibrations intensified, then lessened as the chopper left the ground. It went straight up, slowly swivelling. Bub saw the branches of the jacaranda lashed by wind from the rotors, scattering blossoms over the five mounded graves, and into the one empty.

The chopper's nose dipped and it flew off across the settlement, passing over the supermarket carpark and another chopper, set neatly down on their house-paint bull's-eye, rotors still lazily twirling. The aircraft they were in was American. The one on the ground belonged to the Australian Navy. The helicopter flew over the beach, and

435

the *Champion*, at her mooring, stern-on to the outgoing tide.

When they were halfway across the bay, the sun came out.

William was to be taken by road in an ambulance. Jacob insisted on briefing the paramedics. William watched Jacob scratch his head and slowly summon each thought. He talked about valve damage and pacemakers, then said apologetically, 'But I'm not a doctor.' He asked for water, and squeezed the plastic bottle to rinse William's blood-smeared hands.

'I'm not hurt at all, Jacob,' William said.

Jacob imperturbably went on rinsing, drying, and inspecting William's hands. William let him do it. Everyone else was being patient—the soldiers, the paramedics, though their heads kept swivelling this way and that, keeping an eye out for danger, for 'any changes', as William overheard an officer warning them.

A soldier placed a hand on Jacob's shoulder and coaxed him out of the back of the ambulance. And that was William's final sight of Kahukura—Jacob being led away by several people, all handling him gently.

The paramedics wanted William to lie down, so he did. One of them opened his shirt and taped sensors to him, then fiddled with a monitor. He heard a clunk as someone closed the ambulance doors.

After that he minded the curves of the road—the turn out the gate into Bypass Road, several more long curves, and then the roundabout where Bypass, Beach, and Peninsula Roads intersected. The ambulance climbed the bluff, was briefly level on its summit, and then it went on down.

In hindsight it was clear to William what had happened. And if he'd been there when she had arrived at the spa he believed he would have been able to read Sam's blunt determination. He would have guessed what she meant to do—and still he would have fought, against her wishes, and his own interests, and against the world, to keep her alive.

William imagined Sam, where she was now, swallowed by the monster, and in stasis, pinning it in place, her stopped self indigestible, and impossible to spit out.

Theresa was gathered up by her own people—the police. 'We may not be in charge,' said one, 'but we made a pretty good case for taking care of you ourselves.'

She found herself seated between two colleagues in the back seat of a big Toyota utility. 'Sorry it's scruffy,' the driver said, 'but it was the biggest vehicle we had on hand at the eastern limit of the Zone. And I guess it's pretty good for travelling incognito.'

There was a steel grille behind Theresa's head. Through it she had a glimpse of a clawed plastic pad, where a police dog usually lay.

Her colleagues knew better than to keep talking to her. But they did answer her occasional questions.

'Was there a gun trained on me there at the end?'

'That's why Bub Lanagan jumped on you. He signalled them not to shoot.'

'Has anyone explained?'

'What you were doing? There was some explanation. So far it doesn't make much sense. But don't trouble yourself. It's early days yet.'

Someone patted her hand.

'Can I ride up in front?'

They pulled over and let her out. The roadside was weirdly silent.

She said, 'Are there no birds?'

'They'll be back.'

The sergeant from her station helped Theresa with her

seatbelt and then took her place in the back. They continued on. Theresa watched the road unfold. She'd realised that she had been tired of all the old pictures. At last she could turn the page.

There was a section of road just beyond the turnoff to the old Moutere Highway that had always made her happy whenever she was travelling along it out of Stoke. The road dropped down and there was a vista: fields, a windbreak of Lombardy poplar, everything gold and green, and *composed*. When the Toyota reached that bit of road, Theresa looked in her wing mirror; she looked back, then forward. Either way that corner was a karanga—farewell, welcome, farewell.

Theresa began to pay attention again when the vehicle doubled back near the airport and crossed the railway tracks. The driver—a woman constable Theresa knew, but whose name had slipped her mind, saw her interest and began to explain. As Theresa could probably imagine there was one big base of operations. 'But the place we're taking you was set up some weeks ago to be ready for you all.'

'Did you know?' Theresa said, puzzled. How could anyone have known that they'd escape?

'I think it was more an act of faith,' said the sergeant.

They turned onto the Monaco Peninsula.

'It's sufficiently isolated. And because it's a narrow bit of land, it has a controllable perimeter,' said the driver. 'It's close to the airport, and yet out of the way—to minimise its impact on the city.'

They were speeding through a corridor made of traffic control barriers. Beyond them on the sloped lawn before the breakwater, and in the carpark of a faux-Elizabethan inn, Theresa spotted clusters of satellite dishes. There were people standing on the roofs of TV News vans. Long-barrelled cameras swivelled to follow the car.

'Has the port been closed all this time?' Theresa asked, thinking of the city.

The driver said, 'The port, the National Parks, Highway 60, fucking everything. You can't imagine—'

The driver was hushed by the sergeant.

The car turned into the entrance of the Grande Mercure. Theresa had been to the hotel complex three years before, for a friend's wedding. She remembered the immaculate enclosed greens, and tables set up under Mediterranean pepper trees, tables covered in white cloths and mounds of yellow-throated white orchids.

They glided past gabled brick buildings—semi-detached cottages with mullioned windows, climbing roses, rough-hewn wooden doors and lintels.

They slowed and entered a narrow lane between two rows of cottages. There was a checkpoint at the head of the lane, the only one on the whole journey—though Theresa had registered a mass of military vehicles immediately over the other side of Matarau Point.

Once they were through the checkpoint, Theresa saw that the faultlessly groomed green she remembered was covered in generator trucks, and a vast tent with plastic flooring. A number of vehicles had pulled up inside the tent. The police vehicle coasted in, and was directed to a particular spot.

And there they waited. Theresa's hands found each other in her lap, and gripped hard. She looked out through the windscreen at people—*too many people*. Then she had a little jolt—and the sergeant looked at her, concerned.

She had spotted Jacob. He was some distance off. The perspective of the tent was strange. The floor was made of blue matting, and its honeycomb pattern seemed to swarm whenever Theresa moved her gaze. The light filtering through the white PVC of the tent was so uniform that it confounded normal vision and made everything indistinct.

Jacob was surrounded by his family. That must be them. Parents, siblings, cousins, aunts, and uncles. They were in a kind of prayer huddle, only they hadn't 'left space for the

439

energy', as Theresa's high school soccer coach had used to say. Jacob's family were so intent on him that they'd made a spiral rather than a circle. Those with the greatest claim were pressed bodily to him, the others winding in after them. As Theresa watched, the spiral closed like a valve, and Jacob was lost to her sight.

She couldn't see Oscar—who might be hidden somewhere in any of those screened bays to one side of the long space. But Bub and Belle were visible. They'd just climbed out of a black vehicle with a wide wheelbase—Theresa didn't recognise what it was, because it looked so strange where it was. Bub and Belle's escorts were directing them to different corners—to a group of around twelve people, a mix of Maori and Pakeha, and another smaller group, consisting of Belle's mother and sister, who both looked like Belle, and a man, probably the sister's husband. Theresa watched Bub and Belle refusing once again to be parted. They exchanged a look, then turned away to call to their families, who swooped, Bub's lot jostling aside furniture and people to get to him.

But once they reached the couple, their family members hesitated. They looked shy. Bub and Belle began their introductions—so that instead of being embraced themselves, they ended up at the centre of a lovely dance of handshake and hongi, hugs and kisses.

Theresa realised that her colleagues were detaining her. They were trying to explain something. Someone said, 'Your mother and sister are here,' then added a 'but'. Theresa heard the 'but', and went deaf. She thought she was being prepared for bad news.

But then Theresa caught sight of them. Her sister was standing, fidgeting, and shifting her weight from foot to foot. Her mother was a little further off, sitting on a folding chair, holding a cup of tea, and conversing with an attentive attendant—a uniformed police officer. Her mother looked unflustered.

The sergeant said, 'Oh good. Here he is.'

Someone opened Theresa's door and helped her out. Theresa recognised the pleasant, freckled face of the head of the Police Association—her union. They had only kept her so that he could have a word.

He settled his hands on her upper arms, and held her gently. 'Theresa—can I call you Theresa?'

'You just did,' said Theresa, and her apparently pert answer caused a rush of happy laughter all around her.

He smiled, then collected himself and gazed at her with solemn tenderness. 'I want you to know that we are all very proud of you.'

Her tears were unexpected. She hadn't expected them— even if they had. Someone offered her a clean handkerchief. They wanted to console her, but their kindness felt paltry. They meant well, but she felt petted, rather than loved. She tried to say that it was Sam. Sam had saved them. Had maybe even saved worlds. She tried to say that she—Theresa— had only understood what was necessary. Like William poisoning the poor cats.

Then she broke away from her colleagues and was running, painfully, but with desperate determination.

There were too many people in the tent. Theresa barged through them. She refused to recognise faces. She rushed right past her sister. Her sister could wait. Theresa didn't know at what point she started to do it—but she found herself shouting his name. People got out of her way. They turned their bodies to make a channel she could flood through unopposed. Some of them even pointed the way for her.

Theresa finally saw the green and yellow reflective stripes of the ambulance. William was sitting on a gurney, his shirt was open and wires were strapped to his chest. Several doctors were gazing into the monitor he was attached to. Everyone around William was busy and, at the moment Theresa saw him, none of them was actually looking at him, or touching him. He was a silent island. The doctors did look when he got up from the gurney—but by that time she had reached him and he had opened his arms and gathered her to him.

The juvenile gannets that came, midsummer, to roost on Matarau Point, were back again, and utterly unperturbed. They could be seen by day in search of game, making their long sweeps and sudden plunges. The flock of gulls that huddled near the boat ramp, fruitlessly waiting for scraps and cat food, only flew so far, before circling back to the beach. But at night, when it was quiet, the kakapo had been heard booming, getting on with the business of wooing.

Highway 60 was open to through-traffic, though there were interlocking plastic barriers erected all the way along Bypass Road, and an armed checkpoint at either end of the settlement, something like the one William had gone through near Jolon when Big Sur was burning.

Almost everyone in Kahukura was in uniform, though some of the uniforms were unprepossessing, like the green shirts and shorts of the Department of Conservation. The rangers were busy up at the reserve, digging a trench for the new stretch of fence, digging by hand, because the noise levels in Kahukura were—as one of them told a reporter—'simply unacceptable'.

The mass graves had been opened in the white light of chilly, antiseptic tents. Army ambulances came and went. Somewhere the oily parcels were unwrapped. Photos were taken, and matched to those in the definitive databases of Belle Greenbrook and Warren Kreutzer.

Up at the spa one of the ambulances parked on the driveway backed into the long grass to let a police car go by, on its way out again. The two constables waved their thanks. They were looking satisfied, and one was nursing a cat cage, dandling his fingers through its wire to caress the tired, puzzled, beige Burmese, and soothe her crying.

No one had noticed the water-dimpled writing pad lying in the mauve haze of a smoke bush that grew by the spa's front steps. On the pad's exposed page were two lines, written in fading pencil.

But you wouldn't have shot him.

The Wake is here. Look at Sam.

ACKNOWLEDGEMENTS

A heartfelt thanks to all those who read and commented on this novel as it grew and mutated: Natasha Fairweather, Kelly Link, Gavin Grant, Ellen Kushner, Jonathan King and David Larsen.

Thanks also to Ursula Poole for kakapo insights, and to Tracey Sullivan of the Pharmacy Guild of New Zealand for advice on what might be in a small-town pharmacy.

Thank you to my mother, Heather Knox, whose motor neurone disease, with its enforced silence and isolation, and its long slide, motivated this novel, and whose valour and stoicism inspired it. And thank you to my sister Sara and my husband Fergus—You and You.